AVENGING ANG[illegible]S

by

Glen Davies

About the Author

Glen Davies is an Anglo-Welsh writer, born in Liverpool and brought up in North London.

Glen worked in teaching, in the theatre and as a hypnotherapist, while finding the time to write a number of novels, five of which have already been published.

Glen now lives close to the beautiful Gower peninsula and combines writing and hypnotherapy with tranquil coastal walks.

Also by Glen Davies:-

Fool's Gold

Storm Before Sunrise

To the Ends of the Earth

Elusive Liberty

In memory of the Suffragists, who struggled for so long to bring the vote to the women of Britain, and to those in other parts of the world who are still struggling today.

Thanks to my readers, Angharad, Jane and Carole, to Paul, to Sarah, and to Michael for all his technical input.

Cover: Paul Whittaker

www.whiteswanpress.com

FastPrint Publishing

www.fast-print.net/store.php

First published in 2013 by Fast Print
in association with White Swan Press

Avenging Angels

A catalogue record for this book is available from the British Library

ISBN 978-178035-630-3

An environmentally friendly book printed and bound in England by

www.printondemand-worldwide.com

Mixed Sources
Product group from well-managed forests, and other controlled sources
www.fsc.org Cert no. TT-COC-002641
© 1996 Forest Stewardship Council

This book is made entirely of chain-of-custody materials.

AVENGING ANGELS

PART I

'They've rallied magnificently,' he said. 'Driving lorries and ambulances, working on the railways, and even in the munitions factories. The nation is grateful to the women.'

'It needn't be,' she replied with spirit. 'We are the nation - half of it, at least. Even if you don't deem us worthy of a vote.'

London 1914

The little square behind Chancery Lane was thronged with people. Many had paused to put down their umbrellas as the heavy shower passed. A loud clanging reverberated around the street and some of the passers-by jumped and gasped as the pavement vibrated beneath their feet. After a moment they grinned sheepishly at one another, before going on their way into Fleet Street, past the boarded-up windows of the German baker's shop, but one young woman with a black armband on her shabby coat stayed frozen, cowering against the wall, a bundle of papers at her feet, the edges staining on the wet pavement.

'Give us all a fright, didn't it?' said the office-boy, stepping out of the stationer's doorway where he'd been sheltering from the downpour. He picked up the papers, laughing heartily. 'Did you think it was the Germans?' There was another clanging and she cringed away, eyes wide in panic as he pushed the papers at her. 'I know they shelled Yarmouth, but even their bloody great guns can't reach to London.'

'He's coming,' she whispered, rocking back and forth on sodden boots.

'Who? The Kaiser?'

'He's coming!' she said shrilly. 'Didn't you hear?' Her voice dropped to a whisper. 'They've just unlocked...!' She put her hand to her mouth and bit her thumb. 'No...no...can't give in now...mustn't give in...'

'What *do* you think you're doing?' demanded a well-bred voice. The boy turned to see a fashionable lady at his elbow, a look of anger on her face.

'Trying to help is all,' said the lad sharply, 'so don't you be making any more of it than there is. It was the brewer's drayman rolling the barrel down into the cellar...made us all jump...but her...well, it's set her all over the place. Don't think she's all there, see.' He tapped his forehead.

'It's all right,' said the newcomer, taking in the white, purple and green-striped ribbon in the lapel of the shabby coat. 'Look, thanks for your help, but best leave her to me. I'll take her to the tea shop.'

'She's well beyond a cuppa tea, she is. Large brandy – that's the ticket.'

2

The day had started badly and just gone from bad to worse.

'Miss Shaw! *Shaw!*'

Sylvia jerked herself upright, felt her head spinning. She took a firmer grip on the filing cupboard and tried to focus on the diminutive figure at her side.

'You are paid to work, not to sleep, Shaw!' snapped the supervisor.

'So sorry, Miss Canning,' said Sylvia, trying to control the slurring in her speech. 'Just - a dizzy spell...' The weather was unusually oppressive for so late in the year, she hadn't had a decent night's sleep in months, and to cap it all she'd been up half the night with her mother. If she didn't get some rest soon, she was going to crack up again.

'Then a turn in the fresh air will do you good,' said the supervisor in freezing tones. 'Take these files across to the new transport depot. In future kindly confine your late nights to the end of the week.' She offered a parting shot over her shoulder. 'I find it a melancholy reflection, Shaw, that one previously so dedicated to our cause - and honoured for it - should now be so devoted to frivolity.'

Sylvia fought back the wave of hysterical laughter which threatened to overcome her. Let the old dragon think she'd been out on the town! Even though nothing could be further from the truth. Canning had never been one of the easiest women to work with, but now that Sylvia was a paid worker instead of a lady volunteer, it was even worse.

She thought back wistfully to the camaraderie of the early days when she'd worked in the offices of the NUWSS, with suffragists, factory workers, lady volunteers and shop girls side by side. But now the Women's Suffrage offices had been turned over to government work and most of the younger women had joined the Voluntary Aid Detachments, or gone to clerk in government offices so that the men could enlist. Old biddies like Canning were left to boss the show, treating those who remained like servants.

Frivolity. She rolled the word around in her mind as she drew on her coat, hat and gloves. What a delicious, decadent sound the word had. What she wouldn't give for a little frivolity now! She tried to recall the last occasion when she had been wined and dined - it must have been when Freddie was still at Oxford. Probably an excursion into the country with one of his fast friends in their fast cars - but the where, when and who escaped her. The time was too distant and the memory too deeply buried....

She'd been concentrating so hard on staying awake that she hadn't noticed the change in the weather. As Canning came to the doorway with an armful of files carefully wrapped round in oiled paper, the threatened storm broke; rain lashed down on the corridor skylights like dried peas rattling on a drum, and the less skilled type-writers had to hunch over their machines in the half-light, peering for the right keys.

Cursing her folly in leaving her umbrella at home, Sylvia tucked the files under her arm and crossed to the desk in the outer office where the petty cash box was kept. As she opened the lid, Canning's hand came from behind her and snapped it closed again, almost catching Sylvia's fingertips with the sharp metal edge.

'The fare for the omnibus,' she protested. Any other supervisor would have provided cab-fare, but she knew Canning's meanness too well.

'A mere twenty minute walk.' The supervisor's mouth puckered as though she'd swallowed a lemon.

'I say! Won't that be a bit much for her?' said the young woman at the next desk. She looked anxiously at Sylvia, and the coat which hung so loosely on her frame. 'I don't have much on this afternoon. I'd be happy to take the boxes across for you, Miss Canning.'

'If you are short of work, Prosser, I can find plenty for you.' Prosser's shoulders slumped. She was not one of the independent lady volunteers either, and couldn't afford to cross the supervisor. With an apologetic smile for Sylvia, she returned to her work.

'You don't hold yourself too much of a lady to walk, Shaw?' Sylvia shook her head. 'Good. We mustn't forget there's a war on.' With a smile like a death's head the supervisor turned the key of the cash box. 'In future anyone who requires transport must pay for it themselves.'

Sylvia was seething so much when she emerged from the offices that it was a wonder the rain didn't turn to steam as it landed on her. Canning *knew* she couldn't afford the price of the omnibus. Making her walk was in outright defiance of the directive that all women in Sylvia's situation were to be cossetted until they had their strength back.

Out of the corner of her eye she could see the tip of the feather on her hat drooping in the driving rain. The hat would be ruined. Damn

Canning! She was so busy trying to think of ways of avenging herself on the tyrant that, as she turned out of the maze of courts clustered around the Middle Temple, she stepped straight into a puddle. She cursed again as the water found its way into the light summer boots. While their few remaining worldly possessions had been stored in an outhouse, someone had stolen her best pair of winter Burlingtons. With the pressing need to find new lodgings, she'd no hope of buying a replacement pair. She filed the thief alongside Miss Canning in her mental torture chamber.

Emerging from the alleyway onto the hustle and bustle of Fleet Street, she watched for a gap in the traffic to cross to the Law Courts. Beyond the griffin pedestal, which marked the limit of the City of London, the newsboy, hunched in a doorway to shelter from the heavy rain, was crying the latest news about 'Gallant little Belgium' – an entirely different Belgium, apparently, from the one that had been universally condemned only six years before for their horrific torture and massacres in the Belgian Congo.

After the isolation of the previous months, the boy's harsh tones assaulted her ears. Her arms ached with the effort of holding the files in their slippery wrapping and her feet were sodden, but she thought of Pip's sacrifice, and Freddie at the recruiting office, and told herself that she could do her bit. Even if it meant putting up with wet feet and sadistic supervisors. She put her shoulders back and marched grimly on towards Holborn. Until the clanging of metal on metal sent her into the deep, deep darkness that still haunted her, day and night….

3

In the lawyer's chambers on the edge of the Temple, the man turned away from contemplation of the raindrops running down the windows that looked out over Fleet Street. Thin and wiry, dressed in an overcoat that had seen better days, he perched on the edge of his seat, his gaze darting from the dog-eared paper in his hand to the man in the lawyer's frock-coat, seated behind the leather-topped desk, finishing his conversation on the telephone.

'I'll keep it brief, sir,' he said, as the lawyer set the earpiece back on its rest. 'Understanding from your clerk that you're off to France this afternoon with the Parliamentary delegation...?'

If he was expecting to learn any more, he was disappointed. The other man remained resolutely silent, only inclining his head a fraction.

'So you'll be visiting the front lines...?'

'I imagine so. Now, what have you got for me?'

'I hope I haven't overstepped my orders, Mr Bryson,' said the shabby man, 'but it's concerning that young person you asked me to find in the spring...'

Bryson sat forward in his chair and in the draught of the sudden movement a paper slid from the desk to the floor. 'You've found her?' he demanded.

'Not exactly *found*, sir,' said the detective cautiously. 'Only if you remember, the trail ran cold in May when she put her old mother in the cottage hospital, and then disappeared herself.' He paused, trying to work out why the well-heeled lawyer, with all his Society connections, should be interested in the whereabouts of a young woman last heard of in one of the less salubrious parts of the capital. 'Well, I'd slipped a few coins to one of the porters, to let me know, like, if anything more was heard.'

'Yes, yes.' Bryson's grey eyes lit up and a lock of thick black hair fell forward over his forehead. 'Get to the point, Thurrock.'

The detective almost shredded the paper in his agitation. 'This is difficult for me, Mr Bryson. 'Cos I feel I've let you down. See, I got a message from the porter last month, sayin' there was some more information. I should ha' gone straight away, but the news was already almost a week old, so I didn't feel like the trail was going to be in the least warm. My wife said as how one more day wouldn't matter. See, our son's in the army, regular soldier, and his regiment was leaving that day for France. Reinforcing the Expeditionary Force....And then you were off travelling and before you come back Sir Herbert had sent me off to Ireland on the Boyle case....' His voice trailed off miserably.

'I see.' Bryson leaned back in his chair and closed his eyes for a moment. When he turned his attention back to Thurrock his face was expressionless once more, giving no clue to his inner turmoil. 'Are we any the wiser as to what this news might have been?'

'I went straight, soon as I came back from Ireland. The porter told me the young female - which we suspects is this Miss Fletcher-Shaw, though that's not what she called herself when she brought the old 'un in - this young female had swept up to the hospital in a smart carriage with a coat of arms on the door, and took the old lady away again.'

Thurrock tapped his teeth. He'd give a guinea to know why Max Bryson was chasing a flighty bit who'd put her old ma in a workhouse - and for all that it said cottage hospital over the door, there was 'Workhouse' in large letters, carved high up on the wall in the stonework for all to see. Most likely while she went off on a spree with her fancy man. It wasn't for any current cases: Thurrock knew them all and this young female didn't fit into any of 'em. So what else? Unusually for a man of his age and standing Bryson wasn't married, but certainly up to a few years back he'd had a mistress in keeping in St John's Wood, like most of the nobs. Chasing after cheap skirt didn't seem his style at all.

'Too much to hope that the porter recognised the carriage? Or the coat of arms?'

'Afraid not, sir. More of an automobile man, he is. Now if it had been an automobile, he could have given us make, horsepower, the lot.'

'But it was a carriage.'

'Definitely.' Thurrock cleared his throat. 'I did my best with the livery and the coat of arms, but by the time I got to him, he'd been out on the spree seeing *his* son off to the war, and he couldn't remember a blessed thing about it.'

4

The destroyer left Newhaven at midnight and lights were extinguished as soon as they left the harbour. The dignitaries, who included the Lord Chief Justice, the Attorney-General and a flock of Treasury officials, had gone below to their cabins, but Lloyd George, feeling restless, invited Max Bryson to take a turn on deck before turning in.

'You won't smoke on deck, will you, sir?' the petty officer entreated the Chancellor of the Exchequer. 'Only there was a German submarine seen off Cherbourg only this morning and even the glow of a cigar can give us away.' Deprived of his late night smoke, the Chancellor gave up after a couple of turns around the deck.

Stretched on a hard, narrow bunk, Max tried to sleep, but his thoughts were in too much confusion. The request from David Lloyd George, Chancellor of the Exchequer, that he should join the tour of inspection of front line positions had come as a bolt from the blue, but he'd had no hesitation in accepting. It was an opportunity to be of service, for at thirty-five he was considered too old to fight. There was anyway a perfectly good standing army, composed of fitter and more active men than he, trained and ready to fight the war against the Kaiser as they had fought in the Crimea and in southern Africa.

His lawyer's instincts had always preferred discussion and compromise to the exercise of force and he was happy to put those talents at Lloyd George's service in melding together the disparate throng of military and diplomatic representatives running affairs in northern France. Both Lord Kitchener, Secretary of State for War, and Sir John French, commander of the British Expeditionary Force, had opposed the tour of inspection, but they were too busy feuding with each other to make more than a token protest.

Bryson's mind wandered back to the meeting that afternoon in his office. Just how close had he come to finding the lady whose whereabouts had been vexing him for the last six months? He'd told himself, and Thurrock, that his interest in Miss Fletcher-Shaw was purely professional, and that he merely wanted to reassure himself that the family, after a few very difficult years, had not gone under completely. Indeed, he'd told himself this on so many occasions that he'd almost come to believe it. But the news, brought to him by Thurrock, that she was not only well, but was apparently now moving in the best society, judging by the carriage with the coat of arms on the door, had not brought him the comfort he'd anticipated. And now, when he'd been honoured with inclusion in the parliamentary delegation, the memory of her was obtruding far too often into his thoughts.

Pacing the decks of the destroyer again the next morning - they'd had to steam out of the ordinary route and the crossing was taking far longer than the ordinary packet boat - he was vexed to find himself wondering which sprig of the nobility she was about to marry. Really, he had far more important matters to concentrate on - not least the strong possibility that a German torpedo might come at them out of the half-light and send him, the Chancellor, the Lord Chief Justice and all their assorted secretaries and aides to the bottom of the Channel!

They were met at Dieppe by a French Government delegation and drove through Beauvais and Senlis, reduced to ruins by the German bombardment. At Creil, close to the line of the German advance from

Belgium, they crossed the river on a pontoon bridge, passing through countryside almost entirely abandoned by its inhabitants.

Even Paris seemed like a deserted city when they finally reached it: the Government had fled to Bordeaux, and the usual bustle and vivacity of the city had gone with them. The few inhabitants on the streets were almost universally dressed in black, and only very old men stood guard outside the public buildings. Still, it could have been worse: not long ago, before the Battle of the Marne, it had looked as though the Germans would sweep into Paris as swiftly as they'd swept through Belgium.

After a day spent in discussions with the generals in charge of munitions for the ever-lengthening front, it was a relief to leave Paris and motor back north to Amiens, GHQ of the Northern Army of France, where they were to be addressed by the Commanders in the field. They passed through Montdidier a bare hour after German aeroplanes had bombed the town; plumes of smoke were still rising from the ruins. To the north and east they could hear the crack of shells and the rumble of artillery. Lloyd George, unlike the other government delegations, was putting his party very firmly on the front line.

Military headquarters, however, had been established at a safe distance from the major fighting, in various comfortable châteaux commandeered for the duration of hostilities. At General Balfourier's headquarters they met General Foch, who had taken part in the Battle of the Marne. Bryson made notes of the conversation, though Lloyd George had such a good memory that they'd probably be superfluous.

'Tell the British Cabinet there will be no more retreats!' said the French general grandly.

'Ah,' said Lloyd George, preparing to enter the conference room. 'But can I tell them whether there will be any more *advances?*'

Later that morning Max was gazing glassily up at the intricate gilded plasterwork on the ceiling when a French general thumped the table and brought him back to the present with a start. He brought his eyes back to the files in front of him, but he hadn't missed much. The generals - Belgian, French and British alike - repeated themselves so much that the listeners in the elegant salon could get by listening to no more than one word in three. Nevertheless, he owed it to the Chancellor to give him the clearest opinion he could, so he forced his mind back to the notes.

At last the military briefing was over and after a sumptuous banquet the delegation broke up into smaller groupings and prepared to depart to different sections of the front where forces were consolidating after the recent battle. Bryson fell into conversation with the Maharajah of Bikaner, splendidly dressed in jodhpurs, medal-hung silk tunic and elaborate turban, en route to visit Indian troops on the front line.

Lloyd George, dressed in his customary dapper style in a simple light tweed, had a last word with each of the medal-hung dignitaries, smoothing down ruffled feelings in his own inimitable manner, while Bryson and the Maharajah chatted to the major who had been delegated to take them out to the front line.

The young officer had come through the battle with no more than a graze on his forearm and was eager to get back to his men. He had little patience with the formality and wordiness of HQ, and wanted to show the delegation what matters were really like for the soldiers. Bryson assured him that this was precisely what Lloyd George wanted to see. 'Real fighting units on the front line. Nothing stage-managed for him.'

Flags fluttered above the château, outlined in the unseasonal sunshine. If it hadn't been for the distant boom of artillery they might have been guests taking their leave at the end of a pleasant weekend house party. Around them on the elegant terraces, delegates, attachés and generals were still puffing themselves off to the Chancellor, each claiming to have been the saviour of Paris - the hero whose plan had driven the Hun back across the Marne.

'Almost as many French plans as there are generals,' sighed Bikaner, whose Indian troops had suffered badly in the recent fighting. 'A great pity that not one among them anticipated an attack through Belgium!'

5

Sylvia slumped into her seat in the tea room. It had been a tremendous strain to stay on her feet until the parade had passed: young men in new uniforms, bayonets fixed, joy and pride on every face. The band had played endlessly the same half dozen tunes, but at last she'd seen Freddie, hemmed in by two bespectacled clerks, winking broadly as he passed her. He'd looked absurdly mature in his khaki coat, a state he'd signally failed to achieve either at Oxford or in his banking frock coat.

She'd tried to keep up with the parade, but she was still infuriatingly feeble. In the end she'd given up, and made her way to the teashop where she'd arranged to meet him, even though he could only snatch a few minutes to be with her. She didn't have that much time herself, for it had been quite a struggle to persuade Canning to allow her an hour to say her goodbyes, but she wasn't going to miss the chance of even ten minutes with her brother. Being much nearer to her in age than Pip, Freddie filled such a great part of her childhood memories.

Besides, Pip was gone, lost in one of the North Sea battles that had given Britain such a disastrous start to the war. The news had almost sent her back into the downward spiral of despair, but she had tried to stay strong for her mother's sake, only to find herself in the end accused of being heartless and unfeeling.

She breathed in the aromas: tea, coffee and the spicy, buttery smell of toasted teacakes. She loved the new teashops that were springing up all over London - Lyons, ABCs, Kardomahs.... They seemed to her almost a symbol of women's new-found freedoms as they took their rightful place in the world, replacing men like Freddie who were marching off to war. If only she had the money to indulge herself, she'd visit a tea-shop every single day, she decided, just to be alone - and yet not alone.

Such solitude was something few young women in her position had ever known, going from constant supervision in their parents' house to the same position in their husbands'. Until the advent of the tea shops, there had only been hotels or taverns, and no decent girl could be seen with a man in either of those. But tea-shops were different. Freddie, if he ever got here, might be her brother, fiancé, cousin or lover: no one cared. Not the office boy eating his tea in the corner; not the businessman in the corner making short work of a hearty steak and kidney pie; not the mother and daughter considering a dainty double-decker plate of cream cakes to accompany a pot of the best Orange Pekoe, and certainly not the young couple in the window, gazing shyly at each other over the rim of their tea-cups.

When the nippie came to the table she ordered for both of them. It was hard, coming to terms with the fact that the family she'd dreamed about through the last miserable months no longer existed. On their father's death, both her brothers had had to take employment with provincial branches of the bank, one in Glasgow and the other in Yorkshire. Neither had been in a position to take leave when she was sent away and could no longer care for their mother.

On the outbreak of war Pip, as a former naval cadet, had been snapped up by the Navy, and lost within months. Now Freddie had come back to the capital only to join up. Once again she would be left with no one but a mother who could hardly bear to speak to her. But at least she and her mother now had a proper roof over their heads, thanks to Gwen Jameson, the young artist who had come to her rescue in Chancery Lane.

She looked up as Freddie's slim khaki-clad figure appeared in the doorway, and was overwhelmed by love for him, and a terror that she might never see him again. She tightened her hands together to stop them shaking and prayed desperately, for the first time for many years. 'Keep him safe. Oh, God, keep him safe!'

6

The aigrette of ostrich feathers on the front of the Maharajah's turban nearly came to grief on the roof of the car, and they had to open the hood to accommodate him. The major reluctantly took his seat in front with the army driver. After the recent exhibition of injured dignity and personal empire-building at the château, he'd really wanted to hear what Lloyd George had to say.

As the elegant landaulet drew away from the château, leaving behind the preening diplomats, attachés, and advisers with almost as much gold braid as the feuding commanders, there was a collective sigh of relief.

The dapper man with the heavy moustache closed the dividing screen and looked at his companions with a twinkle in his eye. 'So what do we think of the generals, eh, boys?' asked Lloyd George, unperturbed by the fact that he was addressing two humble aides and a Maharajah in the same breath.

Incongruously Max observed that the corners of the Chancellor's eyes crinkled in just the same way that Miss Fletcher-Shaw's did, as though they could both see something infinitely ridiculous in the human condition, even when matters were at their most serious. 'It amazes me that the Germans aren't already in Paris,' he said, settling into the comfortable leather seat and blanking out the distracting image.

'If it had not been for good old Galliéni and his taxi-cabs, I do believe the enemy would be encamped in the Place de la Concorde today,' said the Maharajah. 'You didn't hear the story?' he said, seeing Max's puzzlement. 'Galliéni, you know, is military governor of Paris. As the German army swept towards them, he saw that General Kluck had left his right flank exposed. Military transport was not to be had, so good old Galliéni commandeered the Paris taxis to hurl the Paris garrison against Kluck. Saved the city.'

'Joffre was against it at the time,' said Lloyd George, 'but now he's taking all the credit for himself.'

'The French commanders spend too much time bickering amongst themselves,' said the assistant from the Treasury.

'...and with our commanders, who are themselves busy bickering with Kitchener. We can only hope that Galliéni and Joffre will bring a more positive drive to the Allied cause.'

'Joffre seems absolutely certain that the Germans won't break through his lines,' observed the Treasury man.

'But equally, it seems certain that *we* can't break through the *German* lines,' said Max. 'We may have the best cavalry in the world, but with the Germans starting to bed in in their trenches, I'm not as confident as our generals that they're about to charge through and scatter the enemy all the way back to Berlin.'

'It will be interesting to see what the men at the front think about it,' agreed Lloyd George. 'I always go for the view of the man at the sharp end of the action, rather than the one in the château, miles away from the front line.'

In a dusty little hamlet from which all inhabitants seemed to have fled, a car was waiting to take the Maharajah to where the Indian regiments were billeted. After jovial farewells, the Chancellor's landaulet turned down a muddy track. As if to echo the Chancellor's words, the whine of shells became more frequent and the booming of heavy artillery over to their left grew louder.

There was a lull in the firing as they drew up outside an old barn which was serving as battalion headquarters. To the front of them, over to the left, sappers were enlarging natural declivities in the ground to make trenches, rather like a huntsman's hide, to afford the riflemen some protection against enemy fire. At sight of the car, the orderlies and men taking a brief break in the late sunshine leapt to their feet, stubbed out their cigarettes and stood to attention for the major, only belatedly recognising the much-photographed and caricatured face of the Chancellor of the Exchequer.

The officer in charge was a fresh-faced young man with a straggly fair moustache, grown in a vain attempt to make him look mature enough to be commanding so many older men. Suppressing his surprise, he showed them round the farm shack which served as field kitchen, then the horse and mule lines, a cheerful and boyish smile on his face which did not fade even when the shelling started up again about half a mile to their front. His joviality was explained by his sergeant, who disclosed that the young officer was to set off next morning on compassionate home leave, his wife having just given birth to their first baby. The captain blushed crimson, for he had endured much chaffing from his men on the subject, but Lloyd George soon put him at his ease and with a little urging, the young officer drew out a photograph of his wife.

There was no doubt the Chancellor had the common touch. He was soon chatting to men and officers like an old friend. The captain, when induced to bring his mind back to the matter in hand, proved a thorough guide and, unlike the generals at the château, seemed willing to answer questions with a disarming frankness.

'There seem to be more shells coming from their side than from ours,' commented Lloyd George, lowering the field glasses to look sideways at the captain.

'We'd fire more if we could, sir,' said the officer, receiving the nod from the major to speak out, 'but we're not getting the supplies. Not many of the heavy guns have come up yet, and those we have are rationed to just a few rounds.'

'At last. Someone who's not toeing the official château line,' muttered the Chancellor to Bryson. 'Are you telling me there's a shortage of shells?'

'Both shells and guns, sir. When you're moving forward, you want light guns that can keep up with the advance. But once you're attacking an entrenched position, as we are now, you need heavy artillery, and we don't have enough of that. Whether we haven't *got* heavy guns or they're just not getting through to the front fast enough, I can't tell. But we're not being idle, sir.' The shells were landing a little closer, but still over to their right, and he had to shout to be heard above the noise of the barrage. 'When we were told to ration the heavy shells, some of our engineers went collecting old jam tins - ' He stepped closer to the edge of the wood, where some of the men were firing out of something that resembled no gun they had ever seen. 'They stuff the tins with nails and gun cotton and fire them out of a soldered up drainpipe. I can get one of our men to show you; he was an engineer in civvy street and - '

He half-turned at the whine of a shell overhead. The words of warning were hardly out of his mouth when the shell landed at the end of the depression, exploding in the mud with a soft *whump*, and sending shrapnel and shards of shell-casing hissing through the air.

The thought of the young widow and the fatherless babe galvanised Max into action. Grabbing the captain by his collar he hurled him towards the Chancellor, just before the shrapnel would have cut him in two. Soldier and politician executed a slow pirouette, clasped in each other's arms like loving dancing partners, then hit the earth together in a tangle of limbs.

Bright light surrounded Max like a cloud, and a split-second later came the punch that felled him face down in the dirt. In the silence that followed the explosion, he thought*, now I'll never find her*. As the bright light engulfed him, he could have sworn he heard a lark singing overhead.

7
February 1915

The heavy door swung to. Sylvia slumped against the panels, a wave of exhaustion washing over her. She had to get back to bed before she dropped in her tracks. She tried to summon up the energy to put one foot in front of the other, but it eluded her. Closing her eyes she took a deep breath, trying to imbue herself with positive thoughts: at least after that chance meeting with Gwen Jameson in Chancery Lane she now had a roof over her head and some better paid work at the transport depot. But would it be enough?

Ahead of her she saw nothing but bone-tiring days and endless lonely nights of complete exhaustion. And now, with Freddie's death, barely a month after Pip's, no prospect, even when the war was over, of anyone to share it with. She thought, not for the first time, of opening the box of Freddie's effects, loading his spare pistol and putting an end to it all.

Only the thought of her mother stopped her. She had abandoned her once; she could not do it again. She straightened her back and was struggling to force some iron into her legs when, on the far side of the studio, away from the ghostly white fog of the February night that swirled beyond the huge uncurtained windows, something - someone - moved in the shadows. The bare boards creaked and she almost dropped the candlestick. As the light spluttered and died she gave a small mew of fear, then berated herself for her folly. Sylvia and her mother had two small rooms off the studio, but they were there on sufferance. Any of the artists who paid rent could use the studio whenever they pleased.

'G-Gwen?' she stammered, peering into the shadows.

'No. It's me.' The voice was male and instantly recognisable. She felt a burst of anger at him for giving her such a fright, but bit her tongue, remembering her indebtedness.

'Mr Jameson. I didn't hear you come in.' Usually, when he'd been out drinking with his fellow artists, the entire house heard him, staggering from wall to wall, cursing and stumbling, until his sister rose to pour black coffee down his throat. Octavius Jameson did nothing in moderation.

'Returned early,' he said, crossing the room with heavy footsteps. 'Couldn't concentrate on the brandy. Concerned about you. Poor girl. Terrible loss...'

It was a great effort to keep her eyes open and she sensed, rather than saw him materialise at her side. He unclipped the small gold cigar lighter from his watch chain and relit her candle, illuminating them in a small pool of golden light.

Vexation gave way to embarrassment at the figure she must cut with her hair down round her shoulders. She drew her shawl close, trying vainly to cover the worn nightdress.

'Poor Sylvie.' He always got her name wrong. She'd almost stopped noticing. 'Another bad night?'

She nodded. 'The new medicine isn't helping as much as Nurse Payne hoped.' When had he put his arm around her? His hand stirred and she felt sparks of heat from his fingertips burning through the thin cotton of the nightdress.

'You must get in a night nurse.' His detachment from reality irritated her, and the irritation was the spur she needed to pull herself together.

'I can barely afford a day nurse.' So much better if her mother had stayed in hospital...but she had insisted, indignantly, that public wards were only for the poor.

She stepped away from him as casually as she could manage. It would be all too easy to give in, rest her head on his shoulder and let him take over.

'You could always let me help you. My offer - '

'It's very kind of you, Mr Jameson, but - '

'Octavius.' He brought his face down to hers and smiled, the corners of his full mouth curving and his blue eyes glinting in the candlelight. 'Would it be so difficult, Sylvie?'

His nearness was having an unsettling effect on her. It must be all the sleepless nights. 'Should you wish me to sit for you again, Mr Jameson, I would be only too pleased to take up the offer. Perhaps at the weekend....?' She'd hoped to spend Sunday catching up on much needed sleep, but shortage of money was so acute that she couldn't afford to turn down any opportunity.

'You know that wasn't what I meant, Sylvie,' he said, a trace of impatience in his voice. He snatched up her hand and laid it against his cheek. 'But you're far too tired for rational thought, my poor dear.' He turned her hand over and dropped a kiss on the palm.

In spite of herself she shivered at the feel of his beard against her skin. All too aware of the turmoil he so often managed to arouse in her these days, she quickly withdrew her hand and stepped back towards her own door. 'I - I must try to get some rest,' she stammered.

To her relief he took his dismissal well. 'Til morning,' he said with an unsteady half bow. 'Continue our discussion then.'

She whisked herself into her own room and wished, not for the first time, that there was a key for the lock. As she set the candle on the bedside table she swore softly: in her haste to reach her mother's room before she woke the entire house, she'd forgotten to pull the covers up on her own bed, which had now lost any warmth it had previously held. She thought of going to the kitchens to re-fill the stone hot bottle, but she was in no fit shape for further encounters with Jameson.

The clatter of bottle on glass, followed swiftly by a curse, finally decided her to stay where she was. Shivering, she slid between the cold sheets, drew the heavily embroidered quilt around her ears - one of the few items salvaged from the house sale - and tried to will herself back to sleep, to snatch a few more hours before the opiates wore off and her mother began to stir again.

Octavius Jameson's words would not stop running round her head. There was no danger he would even be awake before she left the house, let alone coherent, but when she returned tomorrow evening he would be there, larger than life, as he always was after a few hours of painting and a few bottles of wine shared with his fellow-painters, and the question could not be put off forever. Meeting Gwen Jameson in Chancery Lane, which initially had seemed such a lifesaver, was turning out to be something of a mixed blessing.

She shivered again as she recalled the pressure of Jameson's lips and the soft bristles of his beard on her hand, arousing feelings which she had thought suppressed during the years of debt and death and misery. Just one more thing she didn't want to have to deal with.

She had a sudden longing to be a little girl again, sure in the knowledge that Papa would make all well for her. But Papa, worn out by the strain of the drawn-out legal proceedings, had not lived to see the outbreak of war, though the tragic events of this last twelvemonth would certainly have killed him anyway. Thank God he had not lived to see the death of both his sons and the straits to which his widow and daughter had been reduced.

'Would it be so difficult, Sylvie?' Jameson's words echoed through her head. Difficult? Yes. *Impossible.* To accept more help from him, knowing that it could only be paid back in one way....in his studio, modelling - but this time far more than her profile. Within a few days of their arrival he'd offered what seemed to her a fortune to model *au natur*....and she knew that would end, inevitably, in his bed.

Living here the last couple of months, surrounded by artists and their models, she had seen a side of life which had initially shocked her to the core, and would have overset her strait-laced mother completely, had she had the strength to leave her room, or sufficient awareness to realise how far they had fallen. Respectable marriage would not be a consideration in Jameson's world. If she threw in her lot with him, she must be prepared to be a wife in every way but one. From what she'd heard since moving here she would be mistress, housekeeper, nurse and soother of the troubled artist - but she would wear no wedding ring. In the society of which she had once been a part, she would be an outcast, a disgraced woman.

But was she not already that?

She wriggled against the cold sheets. It would be so much easier if he didn't awaken in her those warmer feelings she had thought forgotten. But however much she absorbed herself in her work and her mother's care, however often she told herself that she was a mature and intelligent woman who was meant for better things, there were always wakeful times such as this, in the still small hours of the night, when she was forced to acknowledge that she was still the same passionate girl who had looked forward so eagerly to being a bride.

She had not been fortunate in the men who admired her. First there had been Hugh, so handsome, so correct, so very upright in his manners and morals. In her adoration she had seen the young officer as a pillar and a strength, and yet, when notoriety had begun to attach to their family because of her father's law suits against the Government, Hugh had given in to his uncle, the General, and uttered the dreadful ultimatum that they must drop the case or drop the marriage plans. With a breaking heart she'd returned his ring and within a year he'd found a more malleable wife. As a regular officer he would have been six months at the Front by now. To her shock she could hardly remember what he looked like.

Then there had been Jeremy, the family solicitor, stout and balding, still living off dusty memories of athletic prowess before the turn of the century. He had offered her his hand, manfully pretending that he didn't in the least care about the family notoriety, and telling her what she'd always known, that he'd idolised her for years. She'd been ashamed of herself then, for she and her brothers had always laughed at his worthy passion, but she could not love him and bluntly told him so. In rejecting Jeremy and domesticity in Wimbledon she'd turned her back on the last hope of a decent marriage. Her mother had never forgiven her for that, nor for the subsequent shame she had brought on their name.

And now there was Octavius Jameson. A very good artist - one day he might even be a famous one. Already there was a constant stream of society sitters wishing to have their portraits painted in the modern style, but unlike many artists he was not totally reliant on his work, being the recipient of a number of legacies from elderly spinster aunts, on which he and his sister managed to live well enough.

The rambling Chelsea house with its high uncurtained studio windows looking towards the river had at first seemed like a welcome haven, the cost - sitting occasionally for Gwen and her brother in her few leisure hours - a most agreeable change from sick nursing or clerking. But she'd sensed from the beginning that the predatory look in Octavius's eye was not for her perfect profile alone. Men had looked at her before in that way and it was hard to behave in a proper manner when part of you cried out to find out just what lay behind that look.

Some of the Suffragettes were against any alliance with men - 'Votes for Women and Chastity for Men' being one of Christabel Pankhurst's less realistic slogans - but Sylvia had never been among them. She agreed with Millicent Fawcett and the moderate Suffragists of the NUWSS that the fight for equality was not mutually exclusive with marriage and motherhood. Yet here she was dwindling into an old maid. Or rather, she corrected herself tiredly, dwindled. At the age of almost thirty, there was no doubt that the present participle no longer applied.

8

She was sure she'd only just closed her eyes when heavy footsteps on the staircase woke her up. It was too early for any of the artists, she thought drowsily. Only Nurse Payne made that much noise on the stairs, but it was far too early for her.

She rolled over and was sinking back into slumber when the adjacent door was flung open with unnecessary violence. Footsteps advanced into her mother's room and she heard Nurse Payne's customary hearty 'And how are we today?' which always made her mother wince.

Sylvia jolted upright, her heart beating erratically. She peered at the clock in the half-light, only to find to her distress that the hands had stopped shortly after four o'clock. Which explained why the alarm had failed to ring at half past six.

She flew out of bed, cursing under her breath as she stubbed her toe on the iron bedstead. Not only was she late for work, but she hadn't washed and dressed her mother either. Nurse Payne, who never tired of repeating that only the most pressing pleas had persuaded her to enter the portals of such a disorganised household, would not be at all happy.

Sylvia made her flustered apologies to the grim-faced nurse, agreed that she was asking her to exceed her normal duties, offered her an extra sixpence for her trouble, knowing she could ill afford it, and dashed back into her own room to splash her face with cold water, twist her hair up into a knot on top of her head and drag her clothes on. In her haste she tore one finger and the edge of the nail on the metal fastenings of her skirt. She swore one of Freddie's riper curses, then swore again as she saw that small scarlet drops of blood from the cut finger had marked the front of her best cotton work blouse. Wrapping a handkerchief around the finger to staunch the cut, she undid the tiny buttons down the front of her blouse, ripped it off and thrust her arms into her spare blouse, struggling to fasten the slippery pearl buttons without bleeding over that one too.

She reached out for her fob watch, remembering too late that she'd pawned it the week before to pay for the new medicines. Mother's watch had gone missing last week - probably under the bed, or buried among the quilts. That would probably have to go too – if she ever had time to find it. With a frantic look over her shoulder at the lightening window she dragged on her boots, then, button hook still in her hand, hurried in to her mother, gasped out a brief good morning and farewell in one breath to the confused soul, and rushed down the stairs, shrugging herself into her jacket as she went. She forced herself to stop by the hall mirror and took a moment to catch the strands of stray hair with a couple of combs before jamming her hat on her head. As she stabbed the hat pin through the felt cloth, she heard the echo of a voice reverberate around the empty hall.

'Another provocative hat, Miss Fletcher-Shaw?' said the shadowy face in the mirror. 'I struggle to reconcile your desire for such very feminine fripperies with your strong political convictions. But I suppose you want to have the best of both worlds....'

The blood drained from her face and she felt sure she was going to faint. She'd put Max Bryson out of her mind two years ago, parcelled up with the painful memories of the court case which had cost her father his money and probably his life. Why, after all this time, should she remember the clever, rather aloof man who had taken them through the intricacies of their fight for justice?

The old wall clock in the hall wound itself up noisily to strike the hour and she came back to the present with a start. She released her grip on the marble-topped hall stand and smoothed down the skirts of her shabby coat. Adjusting the little arrow-headed pin on the lapel, and straightening the purple, green and white ribbons, she forced Max Bryson back into the dusty recesses of her mind. Between the suave society barrister and the former occupant of Holloway Prison there yawned a vast social and moral abyss.

9

'Max, there you are.' The elderly man had a peevish expression that sat ill with rosy cheeks, white hair and whiskers. He stumped across the room, lowered himself into a broad leather chair and held trembling hands out to the coal fire while he caught his breath.

'Sir Herbert.' The man behind the desk suppressed a sigh and laid aside his pen. 'You should have sent Harris. I would have come to your chambers...'

'No, no. Couldn't put you to the trouble of all those stairs. Not in your condition. What would your mother say, eh?'

Patting his pockets in some distraction he missed the flash of anger on his partner's face. At last he drew a bundle of papers from the depths of his frock coat. 'Bills from the agency,' he explained. 'Harris can't match them to any of the cases...'

Bryson lurched unsteadily across the room and almost snatched the papers out of his partner's hands. 'Those are my bills - for private work,' he snapped. 'I specifically asked Thurrock to send them directly to me for payment.'

The older man cleared his throat. 'You must see, Max,' he said at last, 'that using the Chambers' facilities in this way...not quite the thing. Some of the partners are asking questions.'

Half-turning his back on Sir Herbert, Bryson struggled to control his anger, looking out of the window to the formal gardens below, where a mass of men in khaki were being bellowed at by a sergeant-major. 'I employed the detective agency on a private basis,' he said over his shoulder. 'That makes it no one's business but my own.'

'That's what Smedley said, when he had that reporter investigated...just before the Marconi scandal broke and he was implicated. Then there was the time - before you joined us, dear boy - when the senior partner used old Thurrock...this one's father...to have his wife followed. Very messy business that turned out to be...Actions and counter-actions for adultery and alienation of affections...'

'Nothing of that nature, I assure you,' said Max, propping his shoulders against the panelled wall and shifting his weight. He knew how rapidly scandal could fly around the chambers and then around the rest of the Inns of Court, where everyone knew everyone else. 'I give you my word there's nothing in this to embarrass the partnership. And I depend on you, sir, to put a stop to this damned gossip before it gets out of hand.'

10

But gossip once started is not easily stopped, as Max discovered when he called on his mother a few days later on the way to his club.

A rotund lady with iron grey plaits looped over her ears was nearest the door when he was announced. Casting aside her tapestry she bounced to her feet, trailing a shawl behind her and clasping her plump hands before her in an attitude of prayer. 'My dear Max!' Spinning on her toes and tangling herself in her shawl, she twittered: 'See, my dear Alice! Dear Max has come to see you!'

'Thank you, Mrs Jennings, I think I can still recognise my son's voice,' said the woman seated by the fire. As she made to rise, and Mrs Jennings hurried to help, she went on, a little more curtly: 'And I believe there is nothing amiss with my legs.'

Her assistance rebuffed, the elderly lady turned to the visitor. 'My dear Max, and how is your poor leg today? I was telling Colonel Anstey only the other day what a martyr you are to - '

The man in the doorway looked down at her with a face stripped of all expression. 'So kind of you, Mrs Jennings, to concern yourself with my well-being.' He held the door open. 'My mother will ring if she needs you.'

'Of course. Of course. Such a devoted son! I always tell my nephew there has never been such - ' The door closed on her fading words and Bryson let his breath out in an indignant sigh.

'How can you bear it, ma?'

'What choice do I have?' Lady Alice crossed the room to kiss her son. 'But let us not waste time talking of her. I fancy you're limping a little more heavily today, Max.'

His lips twitched. 'You see a great deal, ma, for someone in your situation.'

'Fiendishly annoying, my dear,' she agreed, with a smile that took years off her. 'Out of the corner of my eye I can still see the dust on the mantelpiece, or a dropped thimble, but if I mention either, everyone assumes I've had a miraculous healing.' She reached out a thin, elegant hand and ran it wistfully down the leather spines of the books tightly-packed on the shelves. 'But even the dust on the mantel begins to pall when it's the only entertainment.'

'Oh, ma, I wish there were some way - '

'Hush, my dear. Nothing to be done. Let's not talk about it.' Head on one side she felt her way back to her chair by the fireside, weaving cautiously around the clutter of small tables and what-nots with their silver-framed photographs, albums and delicate china ornaments. 'Now, what's this Herbert's telling me about you employing detectives?'

He turned from contemplation of the glowing fire. 'It's fortunate I've never had a desire to run off the rails,' he said acidly, 'for it's quite certain your spies would find out every detail and retail it to you.'

'You make me sound like your aunt Sophia, constantly cross-examining her sons as if they were still ten years old instead of five and thirty! Spies indeed! It's simply that Herbert believed you'd aggravated your injury in pursuing some woman...and while I may not be Sophia, I am not unnaturally eager to know what my son is doing, hurling himself down a flight of stairs in pursuit of an unknown woman, particularly - '

'...particularly at his age and in his state of health.'

'Quite so. But if you don't choose to tell me, I shall try to curb my curiosity.'

'No you won't.' The wicked grin took years off his face. 'You'll just ask Herbert next time he comes a-calling, and as my revered partner hasn't even half a notion what is going on, I'd really rather tell you myself.'

He shifted his weight and rested one foot on the brass rail in front of the hearth, while he searched for the words to start his tale.

'Do you remember the Fletcher-Shaw case?' he said abruptly, when his mother had all but given up hope of hearing anything more from him.

'Of course. Young school boy at the naval academy, falsely accused of stealing something or other, and given no chance to defend himself, because the academy claimed to operate on military law rather than civil.'

'Quite so. Poor little beggar, the Admiralty refused him any presumption of innocence.'

'You turned it into quite a *cause célèbre*, I recollect. Demanded an inquiry and then a trial. Maddened the PM beyond belief, and scuppered your political career, but in the end you proved the boy innocent. I seem to remember Mrs Jennings reading something or other about him out of the paper a few months ago, but you know how she mumbles. Can't make out half of what she's saying. I daren't ask her to repeat it, or we're there all day.'

'Philip Fletcher-Shaw. His sister called him Pip. Barely sixteen when he joined up, but of course last August the recruitment officers were willing to blink at that. Half the Boy Scouts and Army Cadets in the country seem to have talked their way into the Expeditionary Force. But Philip went down on the *Cressy* - you may recall, it was torpedoed last autumn.'

'By a German submarine.'

'Yes. It was standing by to take the men off the *Aboukir* before it sank. Philip was only a midshipman when he went down, but he was awarded a posthumous medal by the same War Office that tried to deny him a fair trial only a few years ago.'

'Poor boy! So young!' said Lady Alice, her unsighted eyes welling over. 'His family must be grief-stricken.' She hesitated a moment and then said, in what she hoped was a casual manner, 'I suppose you came to know them well in the course of the case?'

'What you mean is, is this where the young lady fits in?' said her undutiful son.

'I'm not yet in my dotage. I can still put two and two together.'

'And come up with the right answer,' he said wryly. 'But I'd better go back a few years to explain it all.' He lowered himself gingerly into the nearby chair, wincing as he stretched his leg out. 'Harold Fletcher-Shaw and his daughter were the prime movers in demanding a civil trial and then pursuing the case against the government. Her brothers, even the youngest whose reputation was at stake, were far more casual about the matter, especially as time went on and the costs inevitably mounted. I recall the older boy, Freddie, had to leave Oxford, but he'd never been a great scholar. Fast cars and gambling were more his line, though there was no harm in the fellow. But Miss Fletcher-Shaw was as adamant as her father that justice must be done, even though one of the first casualties was her own engagement.'

'If she was so passionate about justice, the two of you must have got along extremely well.'

'You would have thought so. But the young lady disapproved of my politics, my morals, and just about everything else about me,' he said ruefully. 'She accused me of staying with the case only to bolster my own career.' He paused a moment as the maid came in with the tea tray, and waited until she had set everything out and closed the door behind her before he went on.

'About a year ago I saw the notice of the old man's death in the papers,' he said, lifting up the teapot. 'I hadn't seen the family for some months but I wished to send my condolences. I knew they'd been forced to move soon after the case, so I contacted Jeremy Lang, the family solicitor who had brought me the case. He told me the family were in fairly desperate straits – I hadn't realised how bad things were. I had offered to finish the case *pro bono*, but the old man was too stiff-necked to accept. I wanted to call...to see if...if I could be of service, I suppose, but Lang gave me to understand that the family were not receiving callers. He told me he was going to take care of Miss Fletcher-Shaw and her mother.' He paused to sip his own tea. 'As he was an old friend of the family, it wasn't my place to interfere. Besides, I'd hardly endeared myself to her - she was an ardent fighter for the women's vote and we'd argued more than once on the subject. I thought no more about them - I beg your pardon?'

Lady Alice looked up innocently from her tea cup. 'Nothing, my dear. Pray go on.'

'I expected to see an announcement of her engagement to Lang in the papers, but it never appeared.' He set his cup down with a frown. 'Some weeks later my letter of condolence was returned to me from Lang's office. It appeared Miss Fletcher-Shaw had rejected him and the idiot had gone into a sulk - never even thought to take a forwarding address when they moved. So I employed Thurrock to find out her whereabouts. This was last April, I believe. He succeeded in tracking down the doctor who had been treating Mrs Fletcher-Shaw but by the time he got there, the two of them had vanished without a trace. Eventually he found that the mother had been put in a hospital, under what I can only assume was her maiden name, but there was nothing to be got out of her: she'd lost what little sense she ever had.'

' Max!'

'I'm sorry, ma, but the brains and common sense in that family most certainly came from the father. An obstinate old man, but I admired him.'

'And the young lady too, by the sounds of it.'

He shook his head. 'I've no reason to think she thought anything of me. Of course when I first met her she was engaged to that fool Hugh Osborne...'

'There are a great many fools and idiots in this story?'

He had the grace to look abashed.

'You do not usually become so involved with your clients.' Lady Alice turned her head in a vain attempt to make out the expression on her son's face with what little sight she had left. 'It's a great deal of trouble - just to deliver a letter of condolence.'

Max shrugged and fell silent.

'So you called the detective off the case?' she prompted.

'Pretty well. But Thurrock had kept his contact at the hospital and in late summer he was tipped off that Miss Fletcher-Shaw had turned up in a carriage with a coat of arms on the door and swept her mother away. I found out too late to follow it up, but I told myself I could stop worrying about her; she wasn't friendless after all. And then I went to France and – and came back with this.'

He rose unsteadily to his feet and crossed to the windows. 'I was in hospital when I read the news of Pip's death. The newspapers dragged up the past, of course, and there was talk of the widowed mother and a sister, and a brother missing in action, but no mention of husband or fiancé. I cursed myself for letting the trail go cold. I began to fret even more about what had happened to her, all alone, with no one to look out for her. I thought again about that coat of arms on the carriage and wondered whether I'd abandoned her to - '

'A fate worse than death?'

'She might not have seen it that way. She was an extremely modern woman.'

'A suffrage fighter, you say?'

'Not a militant, she assured me, but nevertheless of the most ardent type.'

'Then she won't expect you or anyone else to feel responsible for her.'

'That's what I tell myself. Thurrock sent in his last report in the

New Year, so it was a bit rich being hauled over the coals by Herbert so long after the event.' He turned back to his mother and said softly: 'And then yesterday I saw her.'

Lady Alice sat bolt upright. 'Are you sure it was her?'

'Yes. It was a few days after Herbert's visit. The noise from the drill sergeant in Temple Gardens was unbearable, so I was looking out of the front office onto Fleet Street, thinking about something - I can't now remember what. It had just stopped raining. She paused, just across the street from the chambers, and tilted her face up to the sky to check the clouds. Then she took down her umbrella.' His mouth softened into a smile. 'She had on the most provocative hat. Quite unsuited to work in the city.'

'Assuming that is what she was there for.'

'It's the only explanation. A young lady walking unescorted in the city....'

'Most improper.'

'Most.' He saw his mother's lips twitch. 'I know. I have outdated notions.'

'She may have been there for all sorts of reasons. Perhaps she was seeking legal advice.'

'I'll never know.' He leaned on the mantelpiece, his hand shielding his face even though there was no one to see the anguish. 'This cursed leg gave way on the stairs, and I lost her. By the time I reached the street it was full of a trainload of Belgian refugees and Sylvia was nowhere to be seen.'

11

Jemmy balanced the cloth-covered tray on one arm and turned the brass knob. For the third day running Mr Bryson was standing in the window aperture, his broad shoulders blocking much of the light as he scanned the street below. He'd always liked Mr Bryson - shortly to become Sir Max, if rumour was correct - because he spoke politely and took the trouble to explain things to him, rather than just shouting 'Here, you boy!' as so many of the other barristers did.

Kicking the door behind him with his heavy boot, the lad crossed to the desk, flicked the cloth over the leather-tooled top and set out pots of beer and plates of bread, cheese, raised pies and cold meats.

'Any change, guv'nor?' he asked, setting a plate and a pot at Mr Bryson's elbow so that he wouldn't have to stir. Like his father said, you couldn't do too much for a man who'd saved Lloyd George's life, even if he never spoke of it. Second most important man in the British war effort, was the little Welsh Wizard, according to Jemmy's father. And the way Asquith was making a mess of things, maybe even the most important.

Bryson smiled over his shoulder. 'Thank you, Jemmy. No change. All quiet.'

'All quiet along the Potomac, as me granddad used to say.'

'Didn't know you had Yankee ancestry.' Bryson shifted his stance, but without taking his eye off the lunchtime throngs emerging from Fleet Street offices and the busy courtyards and alleyways of the Temple: bowler-hatted clerks and printers hurrying to snatch a bite in the taverns and pie shops that lay beyond St Clement Dane's, silk-hatted solicitors in earnest conclave with bewigged barristers as they hurried to and from the Law Courts.

'Granddad was a balloon observer in the War between the States.' He swallowed the mouthful of pie hastily so he wasn't talking through it. 'Met Mister Lincoln too - afore he was President, that was. He'd not been out there long when the fighting started, but after, he couldn't settle to living with the people he'd been fightin'. Pa says coming back to Blighty was the worst move Granddad ever made. But that's only 'cos Pa don't want me and me brother to go off to war.'

'I can understand his feelings. In America you'd be safe. They show no sign of joining the fray.'

'Ma reckons I've grown a full inch since they turned me down in August,' said the lad, wondering why neither his father nor his employer could see what a lark it would be for a young man like him to travel across the Channel and take on the Hun. 'Besides, I heard as how Kitchener's getting' up a special regiment of men no taller'n me.'

'Don't be in too great a hurry, Jem. You're young yet.'

Jem rolled his eyes. Everyone was always saying that to him. 'But what if the excitement's all over before I get out there?' he said plaintively.

'I don't imagine you're in any danger of missing the *excitement,'* said Bryson with an edge to his voice. 'Once the New Year was upon us, even the most blinkered politician had to accept it wasn't going to be all over by Christmas.'

Jem chuckled. 'Pity you're not still in the House, guv'nor. You'd tell 'em a thing or two, having been out there yourself.'

Max didn't feel that one aborted fact-finding tour made him an expert on the conduct of the war, but Jem, turned down out of hand for being too young and too small, had settled on him as a fit subject for hero-worship, being the only man in Chambers to have been to the Front. Experience had shown that it was easier to go along with this than fight it.

He picked at the refreshments which Jem had brought in, keeping one eye firmly on the street below. Among the black-hatted City men and khaki-clad soldiers, a few women, clerks, typewriters and telephonic operators, passed in and out of office doors, brightening the streets. There would be increasing numbers of them soon, to replace the men who were going off to war, but some, like Herbert, still looked at them askance. Often the special constables on traffic duty, whose job it was to hold up traffic to allow pedestrians to cross, would affect not to see the women, who resorted to weaving between the moving cars and carriages, at imminent risk to their life and limbs, to catcalls or admiring whistles from the cab drivers.

The City and the Inns of Court were proving resistant to change, despite patriotic calls to release more men for the fighting forces. In the Temple they were accustomed to the occasional smartly dressed lady alighting from a carriage or a hackney, but young females on City streets and at omnibus halts were a different matter.

Bryson passed his hands tiredly across his eyes. Fashion had become more austere in the seven months since the outbreak of the war, and there was a singular dearth of fashionable hats on the streets this afternoon. He was resigning himself to the fact that today, like the rest of the week before it, would not produce a sighting of the elusive Miss Fletcher-Shaw, when Sir Herbert came puffing up the stairs.

'Mr Harkness has been looking for you everywhere, boy,' he said, trying to look fierce. 'Really, Max, you know we're short of messengers since William joined the colours.'

Jem was so vexed by the mention of William that he forgot the respect due to the senior partner, and said pointedly that, beggin' Sir Herbert's pardon, but it was still his dinner hour, so that technically he was at liberty to join the guv'nor in his vigil at the window.

'That's all right, Jem,' said Max, turning away from the window. Some of the clerks thought it a lark to throw William in Jem's teeth to madden him, for his fellow messenger had just scraped the height requirement and been sent to the Rifle Regiment in a smart new uniform. 'Finish your lunch, take the tray back to the landlord and then you'd better be about your business.'

Jem, muttering under his breath, cleared up the remnants of the lunch. As he was wrapping the untouched slice of game pie in his handkerchief, he paused, transfixed. 'Fancy hat down there, guv'nor,' he muttered, dropping the pie to tug Bryson to the window. 'Don't get many of them for a fiver - and certainly not in the City.'

12

The cold wind plucked at Sylvia's hat as she hurried down the street, and whipped stray strands of hair into her stinging eyes. She suppressed a yawn with difficulty: she had not yet recovered from this morning's unfortunate late start. Canning had taken particular delight in heaping more work on her desk than could possibly be dealt with in the course of a morning, but there was no point in complaining. Canning had been furious ever since Sylvia had returned from her errand in the rain, with the news that she'd landed a late shift at the Kingsway transport depot at considerably higher pay, and would in future work mornings only at the offices. That chance meeting with Gwen had solved more than one of their problems - at least for the time being. It had been worth every feather of the ruined hat!

Dodging through the traffic where it slowed and divided to pass around St Clement Dane's, and ignoring the sarcasm of an irate cab driver, she wove her way through bunches of idling clerks and messenger boys in front of the Law Courts, turned up Chancery Lane and cut up through Bell Yard, holding her handkerchief to her face as she hurried past the cast iron structure of the public urinals.

On the corner of Carey Street, Gersher's polony sausage shop had had some windows smashed just before Christmas, when the German navy had shelled Scarborough and Hartlepool, and killed so many innocent civilians, and then again a couple of months ago when the Zeppelins had attacked King's Lynn. The unfortunate family of Polish Jews had fled and the boarded windows were now plastered with Kitchener's recruiting posters.

In the present atmosphere there wasn't much chance for anyone with even vaguely Germanic names - and for the average English man or woman, that meant anyone from anywhere east of France. Belgians, French refugees from Alsace, Polish and Russian Jews were having as hard a time as German emigrés, especially in the East End.

Even Tommy Lyons, with his growing chain of teashops, had been denounced by Liptons, the tea merchants, because some of the Board of Directors had unusual Jewish names. It was disgraceful that people should be persecuted for so little reason. She would certainly have patronised Mr Lyons' teashops as a gesture of support for fair play - if only she'd had the money.

She paused outside the coffee shop on the corner of the alley and sniffed the air. Delicate odours from within mingled with appetising aromas from the adjacent pie shop where a tray of fat sausages sizzled over a grill. Her stomach rumbled, reminding her she'd eaten no breakfast. She glanced back at the clock above the gateway to Lincoln's Inn, but it had been stopped, like all London clocks, supposedly to deprive the enemy, if he landed, of vital information.

Down another alleyway, past another restaurant. More tempting, tormenting aromas. She tried to ignore the ache at the pit of her stomach. If she hurried, could she snatch five minutes in the works canteen before she started her shift? She might even be mistaken for a full-time worker and be given a meal for a penny. With any luck.

She crossed Lincoln's Inn Fields, churned up, like every available patch of open land in the capital, by the marching and counter-marching of Kitchener's trainee army. She held her skirts close to stop them trailing in the mud.

Surely that was the same boy who had been behind her when she'd paused at the coffee shop? For a brief moment panic threatened to swamp her, but she resisted the temptation to run. With the additional pay and the pawnshop she'd finally paid off the last of the family debts and no one any longer had reason to follow her. She was a working woman now - with two jobs at that! Last week at the depot she'd made enough to be paid in Lloyd George's crisp new paper Treasury notes and although it was still a struggle to meet the high price of mother's medicines, for the moment she owed no one.

When she reached the depot there was no sign of the boy and she told herself that tiredness was playing tricks with her mind. With a smile for the one-legged watchman she passed under the arched entrance and through a side door, unpinning her hat as she went. The noise in the depot was deafening. Unlike the office she'd just come from, where all the typewriting clerks had separate booths, there were no partitions here. Clerks shouted, messengers sped, and female typewriters clattered out requisitions in long vaulted rooms where the noise rose to the ceiling and washed back down again to assault the ears.

Posters on the walls behind the female clerks asked 'Is your best boy wearing khaki? Does he think enough of you to fight for his country?' She couldn't see the connection, but no doubt the best brains at the War Office had worked long and hard on this piece of emotional blackmail.

Her head was throbbing with the noise and the lack of food. She ought to take an aspirin - or a *helicon*, as they must now learn to call them, aspirin being apparently a German name - but she'd used her last one a few days ago when her internal workings had finally and painfully returned to normal and, to use the female clerks' coy phraseology, given her the first visit of the Red Cardinal in the months since she'd left Holloway.

She hurried between the serried rows of desks towards the back of the building. Here lanky youths in woollen caps scurried back and forth pulling boxes and packages off shelves and stuffing them into packing cases, which the men carried out to the yard for loading.

She ducked into the locker room and changed into her uniform. Glancing in the mirror above the washbasins, she wrinkled her nose at the picture she presented. Her honey brown curls had sprung up the moment she unpinned the fashionable hat, and she knew from experience that nothing she could do would flatten them. Her eyes matched the uniform a treat, she told herself mockingly: greeny-brown sludge colour. She'd used the last of her La Rola Rose Bloom yesterday, when she'd been as white as a ghost. Today there wasn't even a scraping left in the little pot, so she pinched her cheeks to give them a little colour, then bit her lips, grimacing anew at the curving scar at the corner of her mouth. She was stuck with that for life, though at least Lady Harriet's surgeon had been able to take the ragged edge off it. With time, she'd been promised, it would look like one more dimple. Shrugging herself into the three-quarter Burberry and cramming her cap back down over her rebellious curls, she emerged from the locker room, still a little self-conscious in the divided skirts and boots, and made haste to the canteen.

Amazing how the smell of boiled cabbage penetrated even over the stench of carbolic and bleach, not to mention the peculiar odour of those rubberised wader stockings they were presently sending out to the Front. Now that was a smell that took hours to get out of your lungs. Lined with wool, and complete with a bicycle repair kit to patch any rents, the waders were supposed to make trench life bearable for 'our gallant troops' until spring sunshine dried the Flanders mud and the cavalry could advance once more.

Our gallant troops - such an abstract phrase. But bring the microscope up and look a little more closely and that amorphous khaki mass shook out like a kaleidoscope until it separated into individuals, young men just like her brother, laughing and gambling and joking on the surface but, underneath, the same brittle bones and vulnerable flesh and blood as Freddie, who now lay rotting in the Flanders mud beneath their feet.

The familiar blackness threatened to sweep over her and she had to give herself a mental shake. It doesn't do to think too deeply on it, she scolded. Load the boxes and carry them from depot to railway station, that's all you have to do. Don't think about what's in them, or whether the men who were given wader stockings in the first delivery had lived to see the next - that way lies despair. Because then you'll think about Freddie. He didn't make it, and nor did Pip. Not a grave between them for Mother to mourn over. There never will be. Just as there will never be anyone else to share the burden.

Take a deep breath, don't go off into a funk. It's all down to you now, Sylvia, my girl, so get a grip on your feelings *and damn well get on with it!*

She followed her nose to the subterranean room where the second shift was queuing round the canteen for a ladle of cabbage and potato stew and a lump of bread. Some of the men in front of her were making disparaging remarks about the food, and she grew increasingly impatient as she listened to them. If only the queue would shift a little faster! She ought to be out in the yard by now, carrying out her checks, but an empty stomach on top of the lack of sleep might do for her altogether. She couldn't risk a faint: it had taken long enough for her to be accepted by the predominantly male drivers who felt that the only place for a woman was in the office with the clerks, and even then only under sufferance.

She looked up with a start as stew was slopped onto her plate and recognised the face behind the cauldron as an erstwhile fellow campaigner for the vote. Stella, she thought, and smiled weakly across the counter. There was a title somewhere, but she couldn't think what it was. Perhaps an Honourable. There was no acknowledgement of her tentative greeting, and when one of the men behind her muttered something about sucking up to the staff for double rations, she moved on. No doubt she'd changed dramatically in the last few years. In the drab khaki tunic and culottes there was little left of the once elegant Miss Fletcher-Shaw.

Those female clerks who were still in the canteen had crowded together and the only seats free were close to the male drivers and yard workers. She sat down at one end of the table, conscious from the grins on their faces and the ribald laughter that they were watching her and talking about her behind their hands.

'Close the door, Mr Nash. Turn the key...'

She bit deep into her lip until she tasted blood. She couldn't fall apart now, in front of all these people.

When she had herself under control once more, she picked up the slice of hard, dry bread and reached for the shiny lump of butter substitute in the centre of the table, but Tom Barlow, slack of mouth and slack of belly, reached out a hand and skidded it down to the other end of the table, out of her reach.

She bit back the words that sprang to her lips. She couldn't afford to alienate the men, however childishly they behaved. She had to work with them and they could make life even more uncomfortable for her than they did for the female clerks. When she'd first started working here, there had been all the usual tricks played on apprentices, like sending them to ask the supervisor for a long stand, or to the mechanics for a round nut, but for her there had also been remarks full of innuendo, spoken in tones just loud enough to be heard, but soft enough that, should she be foolish enough to protest, the men could claim she was eavesdropping on a private conversation.

With a forced smile she asked the nearest man to pass the margarine.

'She wants the Maggy-Ann, Tom!' He used the slang term for the oily lump.

'So I've heard.' Barlow leered down the table at Sylvia. 'Don't have natural urges, these Suffragettes. Reckon they can do without men. Maggy-Ann, Sarah or Jane - all the same to them.'

As ill-luck would have it, a group of clerks, among them Maggie Mitchell, a shy youngster in her first post, passed close to the table as they left the canteen.

'Strange stuff, this Maggy-Ann,' said Barlow, fixing the young typist with his gaze as he poked his finger into the margarine. 'Nice and firm your Maggy is, but soft and giving when you shove in your - '

His last words were drowned in a shriek from the scarlet-faced Maggie, who fled back to her desk, tears of humiliation streaming down her cheeks.

At any other time Sylvia might have given into the urge to throw her stew in the bully's face, but today she was too exhausted to take on the defence of half the human race. Besides, she had tried it before and where had it got her? Three months of pain and humiliation. Her hand slipped to the corner of her mouth and she felt the pain of the metal against her teeth, tearing at her flesh, rough hands on her body, pinning her against the boards, sliding under the coarse fabric of her prison uniform, fingers brutal on soft flesh ...

'Close the door, Mr Nash. Turn the key...'

Perhaps it was time to throw in the towel here and look for a full-time job. Not as a typewriter - she wasn't fast enough - but as a shop assistant or a bank clerk - she was, after all, her father's daughter. At least the hours would be regular and she might be able to get a little more sleep. And she wouldn't have to deal with Barlow and his ilk. But that would hardly be doing her bit for the war effort - and if Pip and Freddie had done it, so could she.

Arthur Bradshaw, the consumptive young man who was her supervisor, chimed in on her thoughts. 'Leave her alone, Tom Barlow. And the rest of them. The women are doing their bit for the war effort, same as us.'

She shot Arthur a grateful smile and dunked her bread in the stew to soften it. Her mother would have been horrified, but she would rather die than use the margarine now.

She would have liked to sit a moment longer after she'd finished the last mouthful, to let her food go down and show the obnoxious Barlow that she was not going to be driven away by his loutish behaviour, but the clock on the wall was ticking away and she still had all her checks to do before she could start loading.

'Not fit to be out in the world, these women,' said Barlow, picking his teeth as she passed down the table. 'Too much of a strain for 'em, see, the struggle to be our equals.'

Sylvia barely checked her stride. 'In your case, Barlow, we'd have to go a long way *back* to be your equal. Because there hasn't been anyone like you since the missing link swung down from the jungle trees.'

There was a burst of loud laughter from Tom's companions, and she left the canteen to a scattering of applause from the clerks.

13

It was late afternoon when Max descended from the taxi at the underground station on the corner of Kingsway and High Holborn, and the sky was heavily overcast. Leaning only occasionally on his stick, swinging his injured leg to walk as normally as possible, he found the building Jem had described. It was one of the new edifices which had been erected along Kingsway a few years before, at the same time as Hammerstein's doomed opera house, when all the tumbledown Tudor houses had been cleared, from Lincoln's Inn to Clare's Market and Drury Lane.

It seemed to be entirely occupied by offices. He remembered Miss Fletcher-Shaw had worked occasionally in an office as an unpaid volunteer, addressing envelopes for the Suffrage cause, before the family had fallen on hard times. Adjacent to the office building was an expanse of cleared land, still awaiting redevelopment at the onset of the war. Beyond the fencing the area was covered with serried rows of parked lorries, some marked with a Red Cross.

Jem's brother Jack - shorter, skinnier and even less potential soldier material than Jem - was standing in the porch of the new church on the opposite side of the road, out of the worst of the cold wind. Slipping the lad half a crown Max took his place and resigned himself to a long, cold wait.

He hadn't been there long when dusk fell and the lamps were lit. The level of illumination on the streets rose only slightly, for since the Zeppelin attack on King's Lynn had come dangerously close to the royal family at Sandringham, only a fraction of the street lamps were lit at one time and even those had been blue-painted on top to prevent the light-spill guiding the Zepps in. The lamps at the mouth of the tram tunnel had also been painted over so that they didn't spill light out onto the road and the special constables on guard at the entrance stood in deep gloom. They were taking a close interest in him, lurking so long in the church porch: he hoped they wouldn't think he was a spy. Inside the offices a positive army of clerks, almost all women, were briefly silhouetted against the windows as they hurried to draw the blinds.

Max's back grew stiff as he shifted his weight from one leg to the other, wondering how long he could stand this. Then, at a quarter past six, the windows darkened once more and a small group of men drifted up to the entrance, exchanging the odd quip with the night watchman, clad in an ancient scarlet uniform from the days before khaki. With a groan, swiftly bitten off, Bryson straightened up, crossed the road and hovered close to the entrance.

As a nearby clock struck the half hour, young women began to pour out of the doorways, coats and shawls drawn up around their ears against the cold east wind. Most of them wore jackets over shirtwaists and skirts in severe colour and cut, and there was little sign of extravagance in hats. Some were met by lovers or brothers waiting on the pavement outside; others made their way in twos and threes, arms linked, towards the tram stop. Max, standing at the back of the little knot of waiting men, watched closely as the women passed under the gas lamps. None of them was Miss Fletcher-Shaw.

The flood of women turned to a trickle and then dried up all together. The night watchman was looking at him curiously.

'Are there any more still to come?' He made sure the light from the watchman's lantern fell on the florin in his hand. 'I seem to have missed ...'

'That'll be it for the transport clerks, sir,' said the watchman, stumping across the archway, his wooden leg striking hollowly against the cobbles. 'They all leaves together, see? Only be the duty drivers now, and they leaves the back way.'

Max leaned against the wall, easing the shooting pain in his hip, and cursed under his breath.

'A cold night to be standing about, sir. Like me to get you a cab? Only I couldn't help noticing...Boer War done this for me. Where d'you get yours?'

'In France.'

'Blimey, Guv! You're old enough to have more sense! Not like the rest of them young fools who went rushing off to the Front. Leave it to us Reg'lar soldiers, you should. No place for all you volunteers.'

Max's lips twitched. He must look older than he thought. 'I wasn't a volunteer. Government observation team.' He closed his eyes and saw once again the bright light, heard the deafening explosion, felt the sudden loss of feeling.

'Government, eh?' said the watchman doubtfully. 'I wouldn't want to get anyone into trouble.'

'This isn't official. I'm not here to inspect the - '

'Transport depot. Oh, that's right an' tight then. So who was it you wanted to see? There's only the lorry drivers and dispatch riders left now. Most of them'll be on the road till late. There's a train bringing back wounded from the front, so there's them to be distributed round the London hospitals and the supplies to be loaded on before it goes back.'

'It doesn't matter.' His shoulders slumped. 'I'll try another day.'

14

Sylvia made her way along the Embankment more by habit than intent. Mind and body had detached from one another some time in the late afternoon and since then she'd functioned like an automaton. The cancellation of the last transports owing to the non-appearance of the hospital train had meant an earlier finish. Now she could look forward to a few hours of unexpected leisure.

She prayed that her mother would not be too restless this evening, and allow her at least to nap. Just thinking of the overstuffed feather cushions of the commodious armchair in the corner of her mother's bedroom made her limbs heavy. Her mind was beginning to drift away, but she was brought back with a start when a tug making its way upriver hooted mournfully as it passed under the Albert Bridge.

She was still in the same detached state as she crossed the road, and was fortunate not to be run down by a passing cab. It was her habit to enter by the side door and pass up the back stairs to their rooms, so she was not best pleased to come face to face with Octavius Jameson at the bottom of the front steps. With the wide differences in their waking hours she had, until today, successfully avoided him since their candlelit meeting in the studio.

'Sylvie, my dear!' He tipped the brim of his wide felt hat and ushered her up the front steps, his arm not quite touching her shoulder, but preventing her from slipping away. 'I've been anxious about you.' Dropping his cloak and hat carelessly on the hallstand, he urged her up the stairs ahead of him.

Her heart was thudding against her ribs at the nearness of him. She'd been too long apart from the company of men to be confident in her ability to cope with him. Would he repeat his offer? Would she know how to deal with it? Did she *want* to deal with it?

In her exhausted state she seemed to have no will of her own. Almost before she knew what was happening, she found herself in another of the rooms off the main studio, relieved of her coat and perched on a little gilt chair in front of a welcoming fire.

'You must have a glass of wine,' said Octavius, brushing her cheek with his hand as he passed. 'Put some colour back into those cheeks.'

Well, why not? she thought, and wondered for a moment whether she had spoken out loud. How long was it since she'd drunk a glass of decent wine? Watching Octavius, she was mesmerised by the flow of ruby wine into the crystal glasses. On this gloomy, gas-lit day she could almost see the Mediterranean sunshine emanating from the glowing liquid.

The fire was warm and she slipped the buttons on her jacket. As she reached out to take the glass he caught her fingers in his and bent to brush her hand with his lips. Her stomach lurched as though she'd already drunk half a bottle.

She must pull herself together: this was no way to deal with the problem. Freeing her fingers she raised the glass to her lips. In her nervousness she drank too deeply and the warmth of it washed through her veins. She felt it flowing through her body to her toes and her fingertips - and every point between.

'Sylvie, my dear...' When had he gone down on his knees? 'Never go back to that wretched transport depot. I must have you here, to paint you every day.' He cupped her face with his long, strong fingers and she wanted to lay her head on his shoulder and weep. 'You will be my inspiration,' he breathed, as his busy fingers slid down to her throat, then her shoulders, turning back her jacket and trapping her arms in the sleeves, so that she was unable to stir even when his fingers began to slide the little pearl buttons on her blouse out of their loops. He lowered his mouth to hers and kissed her gently, smothering the gasp that escaped her as his hands found and stroked the rising swell of her breasts at the top of her chemise. 'I must paint you in every way.'

She ought to protest, but the feel of his hands as they slipped inside her chemise bewitched her, lighting little fires on her skin and robbing her of the powers of speech.

Again his lips found hers. She closed her eyes and gave herself, uncaring, to the moment. He could do with her as he wished: she no longer had the power to gainsay him. This was what she'd been waiting for, all these long, lonely days - and nights. His lips moved to her throat and then to nuzzle the soft skin below her earlobe. 'You are my inspiration, my love,' he murmured. 'No longer Sylvie, now you are the muse. You are Laura to my Dante, Lizzie to my Rossetti.'

It was too absurd, and the absurdity broke the spell. 'Lizzie to your Rossetti?' Amusement bubbled under her voice. 'He exhumed her coffin, didn't he? To get his poems back? Thank you, but if I die I'd much rather be left in peace.'

'You're not as cool as you think,' he said hoarsely. 'I've seen that pulse beating at the base of your throat. You are a warm and lustful woman and I can show you - '

The break in mood brought her roughly to her senses. Her colour high, she rose abruptly from the chair, leaving him off-balance and looking rather foolish. She turned her back to him while she buttoned her blouse back up. 'I daresay I may be warm and - and lustful, Mr Jameson,' she said, with a composure she did not feel, 'but I am not warm and lustful for you. It would kill my mother if I entered into such a relationship - for you were not proposing marriage, were you?'

Still on his knees he looked at her, bewildered, trying to work out where he had taken a wrong turning. He'd been so sure that he held her in the palm of his hand, debating whether to sweep her off to the day bed he kept handy for such occasions in the adjacent room, or simply take her on the floor, in front of the fire.

'No, I thought not.'

He rose hurriedly, desperate to redeem the situation. 'Marriage? Hah! Mere convention, my love. We soar above such petty considerations!' He caught her hand again and squeezed it, confident of his ability to reignite the smouldering flame. When she didn't snatch it away he reached out, emboldened, and ran his free hand slowly down the side of her face. 'Your skin cries out to be painted. The suffering in your face...the shadowing of your hollow cheeks...' He dropped his hand from her face and brushed the side of her breast. 'Contrasting with the lushness of your figure, it's quite...'

The touch, and the memory of the madness it had brought out in her, was sufficient to bring her back to earth. She removed his hand. 'It's the first time I've thought of prison pallor as an enhancement,' she said, with an attempt at lightness. 'Though in truth I think my paleness owes little to prison. After all, it's eight months since...'

Eight months since they strapped me to the plank bed and held me down, hands moving all over me, squeezing, humiliating...

'Close the door, Mr Nash. Turn the key...'

Her breathing grew ragged and the red wine began to return, burning the back of her throat. She was going to be sick.

Hand to her mouth she forced herself to start breathing again, but slowly. She wanted nothing more than to escape this room, this heat, this disturbing presence, but it was vital they part on good terms. She did not think him vindictive, but where else would they go if he threw them out on the street? 'I'm always willing for you or Gwen to paint me...'

'Another head and shoulders!' he said savagely.

Her sense of the ridiculous came to her rescue again. 'But with the prison pallor....' She chuckled as she crossed to the door. 'How could you resist?'

Octavius did not share his sister's sense of humour. 'You know how I want to paint you...' he said, interposing himself between her and the door.

'In the nude? I think not,' she said curtly. 'There is younger, firmer flesh than mine. I cannot see the attraction of protruding ribs...'

His eyes lit up. 'But just imagine the *chiaroscuro...*'

'The what?' For a moment she seemed to be looking in on the scene from outside. How absurd that she was still here, bandying words with the man who'd tried to seduce her.

'Light and shadow,' he explained. 'I can see it already...'

'No, you can't!' There was a burning light in his eyes and her cheeks went scarlet as she realised he was mentally undressing her. She clenched her fists. 'Please let me pass,' she said, struggling to keep the tremor out of her voice. 'Nurse Payne...'

He loomed over her and for a moment it seemed that he was going to use his superior strength to force her to stay, but to her relief there was a footfall on the landing. The door opened to reveal Gwen in her dusty painter's smock.

'When will I see you again?' said Jameson in an urgent undertone. 'You know how much it means to me.'

Sylvia could only shake her head. Gwen didn't seem to see anything odd in Sylvia's presence in her brother's private rooms and after a few words of greeting launched into a discussion of her current *oeuvre* with her brother. Sylvia slipped out and hurried across the upper landing to the backstairs.

Her arrival without warning and from the wrong direction immediately brought her another problem, for she came face to face with Nurse Payne, gossiping with one of the Jameson's servants. She had no objection to the nurse chatting when her mother was asleep - she knew herself what mind-numbing boredom there was in time spent with the invalid - but what she couldn't blink was the sight of her mother's mother-of-pearl fob-watch pinned on Nurse Payne's uniform, hastily covered up, and the two women gorging on the claret jelly Gwen had given her the day before to tempt the invalid's appetite. In icy tones she demanded an explanation.

Nurse Payne, sure of her indispensable importance to the household, answered with insolence. But she'd chosen the wrong day to bandy words with Sylvia. Before she knew what was happening, she found herself on the wrong side of the door, with half a week's wages, threatening law suits to the door knocker.

15

For once Eithne Shaw slept the night through and Sylvia, lying wakeful and fretting in her own bed, had ample time to regret her action. If she'd not been all on end after the scene with Jameson, she might have thought a little more deeply on the implications of sending Nurse Payne packing. Not many would work for the money she could afford, and nurses of any kind were harder to find now than they had been in August. So many had gone to the military hospitals, at home and abroad.

The day had not been a complete washout, however. Contrary to the doom-laden prophecies of the knife-happy doctor to whom she'd been sent soon after her release from Holloway, she'd survived three difficult situations today - two of them with men! - and neither Barlow nor Jameson had reduced her to a gibbering mess. She'd survived being kissed and handled by Jameson. Even, she confessed, reacted to it, however briefly. There might be hope for her yet.

In the early hours of the morning she fell asleep at last, to dream vividly about Hugh. It was in the blissful months before the court case and she and Hugh had already been engaged for some time. If it hadn't been for the unfortunate death of the general's sister, Hugh's aunt, they might have been married already. After a punting party on the river with his married sister and her friends, she and Hugh had contrived to slip away to the boat house together. It was a rare moment alone, and her every sense seemed to be heightened in his presence: the distant voices and the sweet sound of the birdsong had an abnormal clarity, as if reflected off crystal; the perfume from the herbaceous border that filled her lungs and permeated almost to her fingertips was almost too sweet to be borne, and the sun on her skin made every nerve in her body cry out to be caressed.

The shriek of the rusty hinges as Hugh pushed open the boathouse door almost made her jump out of her skin and with a throaty laugh he swept her into his arms and kissed her fiercely. Her raw nerves felt every part of his body that touched hers and the bundle of emotions that her body had become knew that something momentous was going to happen, here in the boatshed. The still small voice of reason and propriety that had stepped between them on previous occasions had long since drowned in a sea of need and want and urgency.

Lying on the boat cushions with Hugh's arms around her, there no longer seemed to be a *him* and a *her*. She was at one with him, with the plash-plash of the water against the punt, with the reflections of the sunlit water on the roof beams. She sighed drowsily as her fiancé's hands roamed over her sun-warmed body; she made no protest as he rolled his body over hers. In sleep she felt again the ardour of his desire as he pressed against her, their bodies separated only by the thin muslin of her summer skirts and the cotton of his boating trousers, felt again the warmth of his strong fingers as they began to wrestle with the hooks on the bodice of her dress, felt her own body urging him on, her own hands running daringly over his waist and cupping the firm strong curve of his hips.

But in her dreams he did not start cursing angrily when he couldn't find his way in through the high necked, boned bodice; in her dreams she did not spoil his attempted seduction by falling into helpless giggles at his rage; in her dreams his passion did not die, and she woke with a start, every nerve end in her body on fire and a blush covering her from head to toe. But though in her dreams she had known every inch of Hugh's body and explored it hungrily, when she woke up she still could not recall his face.

She'd permitted herself an extra half-hour in bed, knowing the morning would be dedicated to a search for a new nurse, but she woke from her dreams of passion as heavy-eyed as if she had been awake all night. As she buttoned up her silk blouse, she recalled the disagreement she'd had while dressing for the boating picnic. In the end she'd worn the close-fitting boned bodice as a sop to her mother: if she'd worn her own choice, a more modern loose silk top with a wide sailor collar, the outcome of the picnic - of her entire life, perhaps - would have been quite different.

She was in the kitchen preparing her mother's breakfast when Gwen came into the kitchen, yawning and still in a dressing robe.

Tossing her hair back the artist lit another ring on the gas burner and began to brew her customary strong coffee; while she waited she carved a hunk of bread and sank her strong white teeth into it. 'I say, you certainly had a day of it yesterday,' she said between bites. 'Molly's just told me you gave the Payne her marching orders. And as for Octavius...! Whatever did you say to him? He stormed out of the house last night in the most almighty rage and his bed hasn't been slept in.'

Sylvia had had ample time to consider, in the cold light of day, just how badly the scene with Jameson could have gone, and what a fortunate escape she'd had. Now she groped for the most appropriate phrases for discussing an attempted seduction with the seducer's sister, but found there were none. 'He - ah - he made me an offer which I was unable to accept,' she said at last.

Gwen's lips twitched. 'You mean he asked you to be his muse?'

'Quite. He said he wanted to paint me in the - er - '

'Naked?'

Sylvia nodded. 'Apparently my skinny ribs have excellent *caro...*something.'

'*Chiaroscuro*?' Gwen fell into peals of laughter. '*Light and shade?* Did he really say that? Oh Lord, what a seduction line!'

The laughter was infectious. Sylvia's sense of humour got the better of her and she joined in. 'Standard working conditions, I suppose? For a muse?'

'Minimum terms, one might say. Bed and board is normally the first clause mentioned in the contract.'

'Ah.'

Gwen's face grew serious again. 'It's a different world, Sylvia....but I really don't think it's for you.' She paused with the bread knife in one hand and the heel of the loaf in the other. 'Pity. He's ready for a new muse and I like you much more than his usual type.'

Sylvia was prepared to be indignant, but Gwen had meant it as a compliment.

'He'll be *so* disappointed,' said Gwen, through another mouthful of bread.

'But only for a while. There are many models far more beautiful than I.'

'But none who has ever said no to him. This will make him the devil to live with.'

'Not getting our own way is something that happens to us all,' said Sylvia with a shrug. 'He must get used to it - like the rest of us.' She poured the warmed milk on her mother's gruel and began to stir it. 'It won't take us long to pack.'

'Don't be ridiculous!'

'We can hardly stay now.'

'He'll calm down in a day or two,' said Gwen. 'He's not really the selfish monster he might sometimes seem. He wouldn't want to drive you away.'

'Under the circumstances I don't see how I can possibly stay.'

'It may be awkward but - can you afford that much pride?'

Sylvia flushed and bit her lip.

'At least promise me that you won't leave without having somewhere else to go.'

From the street below came the sound of a car drawing up outside the house. Gwen dropped the knife and crossed to the window to look out. 'Drat!' she exclaimed. 'That'll be the Countess of Ardingley - she wants to have her grandson's portrait painted.' She grabbed a paint-stained overall from behind the door and began to haul it on over her nightclothes. 'Oc said something the other day about an appointment, but you know what he's like. He'll be so caught up in his sulk he'll have forgotten all about her. But if he loses this commission he'll be even more furious.'

Sylvia looked down at the long low cream and bronze convertible, with its hood up against the cool spring breezes. The driver had just handed a rotund lady down and she was talking animatedly over her shoulder to someone still in the vehicle.

'Great patron of the arts, the Countess.' Gwen calmly finished plaiting her hair and coiled it up on top of her head as if it was an everyday occurrence for her to receive countesses in her nightdress. 'Knows all the politicians too. Oc has been trying to persuade Lloyd George to sit for him for months now.'

Sylvia pulled a face.

'No, not your favourite person or mine,' agreed Gwen, 'but it can't be disputed that he's the man of the moment. And a portrait like that would guarantee Oc a hanging at the Academy. Then they'd be more likely to take his other work, the more modern stuff.' She pulled down the sleeves of her artist's smock as she heard footsteps on the stairs. 'Ah well, to me falls the salvation of the honour of the Jamesons,' she laughed. 'Again.'

'I'll be finished in the kitchen shortly. Then I'll stay in mother's room, out of the way.'

'There's really no need. This is not the usual stuffy aristocratic female.'

By the time she had her mother's tray assembled, the visitors had arrived in the studio and Sylvia heard Gwen switch effortlessly from Bohemian artist to gracious hostess, seemingly unperturbed by the fact that her brother was probably slumped over - or possibly under - a table in some low drinking club, and that she was receiving his clients practically in her nightclothes.

She hovered behind the kitchen door, wishing that they would hurry and go. There was quite enough to do this morning: it had been a mistake to take the extra time in bed.

'Now, what can I tell you about this picture,' came a rambling voice from the studio. 'It's a portrait of a young lady...how...well...quite handsome, I suppose. Though the colouring is a little...well, not quite what one might have expected. And...I have to say...one can see the mark of the brush, which I wouldn't have thought was quite...So sorry, my dear, to be critical of your husband's canvas, but...'

'My brother.'

'But I must be honest...you know, dear Alice, I always promised...well, I can only say as I see...while you do not, sadly...such a tragedy.'

Intrigued, Sylvia peered around the door and saw one short, solid figure clutching at the arm of another, more slender woman. The latter, almost as tall as Gwen, with silver gilt hair drawn up in an elegant chignon, was half-turned away from the easel, her fists clenching and unclenching as her companion twittered endlessly on.

At last she turned back to Gwen. 'Perhaps *you* could tell us about your brother's work, Miss Jameson,' she said, overriding her companion. 'I understand you are also an artist. Perhaps we might hear about your work too.'

Sylvia took the opportunity to slip out of the kitchen with the tray, intending to pass unseen to her mother's room, but as she opened the door with one hand, concentrating on keeping the tray level with the other, her mother called out in a peevish voice, demanding to know why her breakfast was so late and where in the world was Nurse Payne?

Distracted, Sylvia relaxed her grip. The tray tilted, the teapot slid on the polished wood, and scalding tea slopped out of the spout and over her hand. She bit off a curse just a second too late and three heads turned as one in her direction.

With an apologetic smile she whisked herself into her mother's bedroom.

16

Bryson stopped the cab at the foot of the Duke of York's steps. A little exercise in the spring sunshine would clear his head. As the sun caught his face he recalled the unexpected vision of Miss Fletcher-Shaw beneath his office window. There had been something child-like about the way she had turned her face to the sun like a flower, revelling in the warmth as though she had long dwelled in darkness.

He ought to have tracked her down by now, but so much else had got in the way. If Sylvia Fletcher-Shaw *was* a clerical worker at the depot, it would be easier to go directly to the offices than to loiter around the area hoping to observe her arrival or her departure. The special constables by the tram tunnel would be sure to take him for a spy if he returned. The specials were mostly old men brought out of retirement to replace the police who had joined up in great numbers; a few days ago one of them had shot a deaf man near a railway bridge, because he'd failed to respond when challenged.

Safer by far, he decided, to present himself at the offices, where his credentials as a member of Lloyd George's advisory committees would carry him past any resistance. Of course Miss Fletcher-Shaw might yet refuse to see him, but that was a chance he'd have to take. At least he'd be able to put his mind at rest.

Ludicrous that he should be driven to such lengths to find her, when he'd started out merely wanting to deliver a letter of condolence, but now that both her brothers were dead, she could be in dire straits indeed. Despite his best efforts, and the fact that he had halved his usual fees – even offering to continue the case *pro bono*, although Harold had been too proud to accept that – the court case had taken too much of the old man's money.

He'd planned to go to the depot today, but had been summoned instead to the Treasury, where the Chancellor was meeting the trades unions to discuss how best to increase the numbers of munitions workers and get the urgently needed shells out to the troops with the minimum of delay. And in wartime, duty must come first.

He'd reminded Lloyd George that he was no longer a politician, and his inclusion on the Chancellor's team might cause offence.

'Hang the politicians, boy!' the Chancellor had exclaimed. 'Successful men of push and go, that's what we need now. And whether that means a good lawyer like you, or someone running a railway or the miners' union, I want them on my team. It's the only way we're going to win this damned war, take my word for it.' From having initially opposed the war, LG had thrown himself into the war effort at full pelt. While Asquith's Cabinet still met only once a week, the Munitions team were meeting, in one form or another, pretty much every day.

Max breathed in great lungfuls of the warm crisp air. The unexpectedly warm March sun had brought people out in their droves and he steered a careful path between them, leaning on his stick. Khaki-clad soldiers on furlough walked across the crocus-studded grass with wives or sweethearts; nursemaids wheeled perambulators along the paths; children in pinafores or sailor suits bowled hoops past convalescent soldiers sitting on the benches, or stood on the ornate bridge bemoaning the loss of the ducks - just one more aspect of life which had been sacrificed to the war. It was felt that the water, so close to Buckingham Palace, would on bright nights act as a beacon to the Zeppelins which had already tried to bomb Sandringham, and so the lake had been completely drained.

He'd been an invalid for too long, going everywhere in cabs and relying on others to run about in his place. Lloyd George had kept his place for him, no doubt feeling some responsibility for his situation, but he couldn't rely on the Chancellor's good nature for ever. He must earn his place, as he always had done. If this was how the rest of his life was going to be - and the doctors and specialists held out little hope of change - then he must come to terms with it, and build up the rest of his body to take the strain. He wasn't ready for his Bath chair yet.

His better spirits lasted only until he approached the Treasury: he wasn't looking forward to another confrontation with the Secretary of State for War. Lord Kitchener was still insisting on War Office control over munitions supply, even though the Shells Committee set up in the autumn of '14 had folded because Kitchener was too busy to attend the meetings. Meanwhile the artillery was limited to seven rounds per gun each day, when they needed at least thirty to make any impact on the entrenched enemy. Yet any suggestion that 'Lord K' should delegate authority beyond his tiny circle of sycophantic young officers was fiercely resisted.

Max's own research, to which he'd been set by Lloyd George, revealed that Kitchener's massive recruiting campaign early in the war had too often taken skilled workers from essential industries, such as heavy metalworking, engineering, and the dangerous and highly skilled task of manufacturing high explosive shells. Many thought it past time for the man to go, for muddle and equivocation was no recipe for success, either on the Home Front or the Western Front. Unfortunately, Kitchener's face on the earlier recruiting posters, together with Asquith's endlessly repeated policy of 'wait and see', had allowed Kitchener to portray himself as the focus of all patriotism, and it would not be easy to persuade the public to accept a replacement.

As Max made his halting way to the board room, gritting his teeth against the pain, one of Haig's subordinates overtook him, holding forth to the civil servant at his side. 'Absolute nonsense holding talks with these damned munitions workers,' he was saying. 'If the Chancellor's not careful, he'll give them an inflated idea of their own importance. As Haig says, they're too fond of their drink. Take two or three of the drunkards out and shoot them, and then we'll see how shell production will go up!'

'Quite right, m'dear fellow,' said the civil servant. 'And when they've done that they can show a little support to Kitchener and do something about the Commander of the BEF p.d.q!' Rounding a corner the pair came face to face with Arthur Balfour, who had clearly heard every word.

As the two civil servants scurried off, flushed with embarrassment, Balfour fell in step with Max. 'How are we ever to win this war with the Kitchenerites and the Frenchites at each other's throat?' demanded the former Prime Minister, slowing his pace to walk with Max.

'It doesn't fill you with confidence, does it?' responded Max. 'After all, if you and Lloyd George can work together for the war effort, a Conservative and a Liberal, then why not the Secretary for War and his commander in the field?'

'Matters have gone too far for that,' said Balfour with a long face. 'The feud grows worse by the day. Only the other day Kitchener complained to me that French had asked for five thousand shells and then used ten thousand! Far too extravagant! Then I commiserated with Kitchener about the terrible casualties and he said: "It isn't the men I mind. I can replace the men at once. But I can't replace the shells so easily." '

At the far end of the Treasury board room stood Queen Anne's throne, unused since the time of George I when - since the king spoke no English and his ministers no German - meetings about the royal budget had been abandoned by mutual consent. Max took his place at Lloyd George's elbow as the Trades Union members crowded in to the room. Those unable to find a chair settled on the steps to the throne.

Halfway through the morning, as the trade union representatives put their points about the need to curb the profits of the owners of the munitions factories, and support the rights of the workers, Max looked up from his notes and across at Balfour, who had been unusually silent throughout. Although Balfour, in his long political career, must have addressed many assemblies composed largely of workmen, this was the first time the former Prime Minister had found himself on the receiving end, being talked to by *them*, and there was a look of total bemusement on his face. Lloyd George, however, was in his element, chatting affably with trade union men and ministers alike. Max's eye moved on to where one of the trade union men sitting on the steps had propped his elbow on the throne. His lips twitched. If Queen Anne could look down now...!

17

Sylvia emerged from the agency in low spirits. Not all of her efforts had succeeded in engaging a nurse to start before next Monday, and even then she was not wholly persuaded of her suitability. At a time when every nurse available was being drawn into the military hospitals, and the authorities were having to supplement them with young and untrained VADs, only the elderly and incompetent were still left on the books. Even they were in such short supply that they could pretty much name their own price. Soon it would be a choice between paying a nurse and buying food. If only her mother had been willing to stay in the hospital...

She stopped to buy an apple from a costermonger in one of the back lane markets. Her head was throbbing again and she couldn't face the men in the canteen today.

On the edge of Lincoln's Inn Fields she was held up by crowds of women and old men, applauding enthusiastically as the volunteer regiment marched back to barracks from training, the brass and pipes of the military band filling the still air with *Tipperary* and the *Marseillaise*.

Didn't they know any other tunes? She clutched at her head, trying to block out the melody. On every street these days there was a band playing, but the bright patriotic tunes were dirges for those whose men would never come home again.

Stumbling into the square she slumped on a bench which some local worthy had erected at the time of the late Queen's Jubilee. As the sun made rainbows in her falling tears, the ghosts of the Third London Territorials marched past her, the band playing the same tunes it had played when Freddie had marched away. Once more Freddie winked broadly as he passed her, hemmed in by the two bespectacled clerks. Did they hem him in still, side by side beneath the cold Flanders mud, with the other clerks and managers who had exchanged ledgers for rifles, and debits and credits for the whine of bullets?

Freddie had been one of the first to fall when his company was rushed up to the front, dead before their gear had even caught up with them. Hastily buried where he fell, the line had advanced and retreated over his grave so many times in the following days that his resting place had been lost.

Society prescribed a longer period of mourning for a parent than a brother, but it would be a long time before she came to terms with the loss of Freddie. Closest to her in age, she could hardly remember a time when he wasn't there. Besides, her father had been ill for so long, and it was in the nature of things for the parent to die before the child.

The clock over the deserted tea room in the centre of the Square was silent, its hands permanently stopped at ten to two, but she knew it was time she took herself off to the depot; at least there the work was so demanding that there was no time to feel sorry for herself. She turned her wet face to the spring sunshine and tried to collect herself.

As she returned her handkerchief to her pocket and buttoned her collar she realised that the ghostly sound of marching feet had not completely faded. A procession of men, women and children was passing along the street. Some of the Belgian refugees carried babes in arms, others their pitifully few belongings, wrapped up in an old blanket. The children were bewildered by the upheaval, but the adult faces were wracked with despair and desolation. They'd lost their homes, their country, and in many cases their loved ones as well. These were the people Freddie had been fighting for. Suddenly his sacrifice didn't seem quite so pointless.

A small child, trotting hard to keep up with her mother, was crying bitterly, the words tumbling out pathetically weak. The language wasn't French, but words were superfluous anyway: the pinched face and over-large eyes told their own story. On impulse Sylvia walked across and handed her the apple.

18

By the time the meeting at the Treasury broke up, it was too late to go to the depot. Max decided to call in on his mother on the way home.

'Pour yourself a brandy,' she said, as Mrs Jennings reluctantly departed, trailing shawls. 'And you can pour me one too.' She felt her way to her chair and sat down with a sigh. 'Talk to me, Max, dear. Tell me what's going on in the world. If I have to discuss the abominations of the latest fashions, or the folly of youth with Henrietta Jennings much longer, I shall go mad!'

'You have to replace her, ma.'

'I intend to. I have a number of feelers out already. But don't let's talk about her - we do that all day as it is. Tell me, how was the mad Welshman?'

'Excellent.' Bryson splashed brandy into two glasses and pressed one into his mother's hand. He gave her a summary of the day's events, explaining how the Chancellor had managed to persuade the men that their interests would not be harmed by working with him to improve the output of munitions. 'Just as well he managed to talk them round,' he went on, 'for Balfour was no help at all - reduced to silence for the first time in his life.'

'I confess I never thought Lloyd George much of a statesman. He has always had the reputation of a rabble-rouser....'

'Unfairly so. He's certainly the man to get things done in a crisis.'

'And that's what's needed now. I am sadly disappointed in Mr Asquith. I had hoped for better things from him.'

'Mother, how could you? After all, anyone who could marry Margot Tennant....!'

'True,' she said with a peal of laughter. 'An execrable error of taste and judgement.'

'I thought you might be at her dinner this evening.'

'I couldn't face it. At least, not with Henrietta in tow. I think I'd rather meet your David Lloyd George... In the beginning he was so against war that I thought he'd snatch at the first overture from the Germans, but he's turned out to be quite a terrier.'

'Fortunately for our men at the front. He's almost the Minister for War now - second only to Kitchener.'

'Lord K of Khaos?'

'You've heard that too?' He refilled his glass and sat down opposite her, rubbing his hand along his thigh to ease the stiff muscles. He ought to take another of his doctor's little pills, but alcohol numbed the pain just as well, and more pleasurably. 'The trouble with men like Kitchener - and Haig - is that they only see the military side of the war,' he went on. 'There's the political and the economic side too. If we don't produce the shells here, then the army can't fire them over there. Lloyd George favours commandeering the munitions factories for the duration - it's the only way to get production up to steam. But it's a bold step to take - for government, for the owners and certainly for the workmen. They fought hard for their rights, and he's the only man who could ask them to give them up for the duration.'

'One wonders why they don't put him in complete charge of munitions.'

'First we have to wrest the reins from Kitchener. I think it's only a matter of time.'

'Haldane might have some influence with Kitchener,' she suggested, sipping at her brandy. 'He did such splendid work reorganising the army.'

'Not a hope. You haven't seen the papers. Not satisfied with whipping up a rage against German aliens, Bottomley's wretched *John Bull* has turned on Haldane. Ridiculous charges. He studied at Göttingen as well as Edinburgh - years ago, of course, he must be sixty if he's a day - and he makes no secret of his admiration of German culture. That, with the fact that he called his dog Kaiser...'

'Not an uncommon name before the war. Remember Mrs Jennings's hideous little pug? He was called Kaiser too. The ghastly beast bit you, I seem to recall.'

'Not me.' His voice thickened. 'That was Esmond.' He limped across to the window, unable to bear his mother's expression. 'But it's gone beyond Haldane's dog, ma. *John Bull* has even printed a story that Haldane's the Kaiser's illegitimate son!'

'Such a dreadful rag. Surely no one believes such nonsense?'

'Many people do. They feel if it's written in the papers then it must be the truth. That wretch Bottomley has a great deal to answer for.' He crossed back to his mother's side. 'Now, that's enough of politics - '

'I never thought I'd hear you say that.'

'I surprise myself sometimes. But what I really want to know is, how is your search for the new Mrs Jennings progressing?'

19

The following afternoon Lloyd George was driven down to his new house in Walton Heath - fire-bombed by the Suffragettes just before the war - and Max Bryson at last had time to himself.

As the cab drew up outside the transport depot he reflected how much freer his life was since he'd given up his parliamentary seat. He was surprised at how little it had grieved him. Once he'd had a vision of a career in politics, and even lusted after high office, but he was achieving so much more working with Lloyd George's committees outside Parliament than he could ever have hoped to achieve within it. Besides, there was no place for party politics in the middle of war.

How Miss Fletcher-Shaw would have laughed to hear him confess to that.

It was just before three when he entered the depot and the noise hit him like a blast. When the man at the front desk asked him his business he could hardly make out his words above the shouting of the messengers and the clattering of so many typewriting machines.

'If Miss Fletcher-Shaw could be told that she has a visitor,' shouted Max, handing over his card. 'I understand she's in employment here.'

The man drew out a register and ran an ink-stained finger down the columns of names. 'No one here of that name, sir. Sure you have the right depot?'

'She was certainly working here last week.'

'There's lady volunteers, besides the regular clerks, but they're not so reliable with attendance. Check with the clerical supervisor; she might give you better information.'

He handed Max over to a messenger boy, with an instruction to take him to Miss Jameson. Max saw a tall young woman, dressed in a loose pinafore gown over a simple blouse with a Vandyke collar. She was sorting papers brought in by runners through a door from the yard, and seemed as oblivious to the noise of the offices as she was to the metallic banging and clattering emanating from the other side of the door.

Her keen brown eyes were at odds with her bohemian style of dress. She looked down at the card and then back at Max. 'Miss Fletcher-Shaw?' she repeated, rather frostily. 'Are you a relation of the young lady?'

Men were used to being cross-examined by any guardian of young ladies as a matter of course, but in his present state he hardly posed a threat to anyone's virtue. 'An old family acquaintance,' he said, unwilling to expose his interest to those piercing eyes. 'I knew her brothers well.' It was stretching a point, but instinct told him his search was nearly at an end.

'No one of that name here,' said Gwen briskly. She saw his shoulders sag and had to harden her heart. The last thing Sylvia needed was more ghosts from the past. Even now Sylvia wasn't sure that she had paid all her father's creditors. As Bryson turned away, a bell rang in the depths of the warehouse. 'Sorry I couldn't be of help,' she said curtly as she turned on her heel and left the desk.

As Bryson put out his hand to pick up his card a bulky man slid out from behind the counter. 'Won't get a straight answer out of her,' he said, turning the square of pasteboard towards him and squinting down at it. 'Their sort sticks together, if you know what I mean. I might be able to help you. Barlow's the name.' He beckoned Max through a nearby doorway. 'This bit you're lookin' for - tall and thin, is she?'

'Quite tall.' Hardly thin, though, as he remembered. The sight of her curvaceous body could be quite distracting when he was supposed to be concentrating on her brother's lawsuit.

'Right argumentative bit,' sneered Barlow.

Beauty and brains. Max remembered the delicious verbal jousting which he had so enjoyed, and their last disagreement, when only her father's entrance had stopped him ending the argument with a kiss. If Esmond had not died, would he have said to her what he'd vowed never to say to another woman?

'Sort o' curly hair? Light?'

He'd stood behind Sylvia once, listening to Jeremy Lang's monotonous voice and imagining how her hair would look unpinned and tumbling down her back.

His fantasies were interrupted by Barlow's harsh tones. 'Temple?' he said. You a lawyer then? Gaarn, I allus knew she was runnin' from summat.' He winked broadly. 'You goin' to give the uppity bitch her come-uppance?'

Max itched to put this despicable lump of humanity in his place, but he was the only source of information he'd turned up. He drew out a coin and held it above Barlow's hand.

Barlow gestured at the back door. 'Down the yard towards the gates. Ask the duty man. He'll tell you whether she's in. Shaw, she calls herself - Miss Sylvia Shaw.'

Emerging into the cobbled yard Max wondered whether the man had sent him on a wild goose chase. In one corner young men in long waterproofs and huge leather gauntlets were polishing motorcycles and sidecars while they waited for dispatches; in another, mechanics changed wheels or dived under bonnets with wrenches and oilcans. To his right, canvas-sided lorries lined up to be loaded with sealed drums and tea chests. From the far side of the yard, on the derelict land where lorries with red crosses on the side were being sluiced, inside and out, by men in leather aprons and knee-high boots, came a nauseous stench of disinfectant.

His eye was caught by a messenger boy emerging from a half-timbered building, so out of place it might have escaped, not just the slum clearances, but possibly the Great Fire itself. Perhaps Miss Fletcher-Shaw - Miss *Shaw* - was working in there, checking dispatch notes from the lorries. It didn't seem at all suitable.

He picked his way down the cobbled yard, around piles of crates and parked lorries, leaning on his stick. 'Watch your step, sir.' The duty man put his head out of the sentry box by the gate. 'You've missed the main offices. Just go back up the yard...'

Max shifted his weight, no simple matter on the slippery cobbles. 'I'm looking for - '

A klaxon blared behind him as a lorry with a heavy canvas lumbered towards the gateway. With a curse he stepped back, came up sharply against the sentry box, and staggered as pain lanced through him.

The window folded back and the driver's face appeared in the opening. 'I say, didn't mean to startle you,' came a familiar voice from under the peaked cap. 'Only you're supposed to keep this exit clear.'

His jaw fell open and for once in his life he was struck dumb. As he pulled himself together he saw the driver's eyes widen. Her face turned dead white. Then she stepped on the throttle and roared away.

20

The shock of coming face to face with Bryson had shaken Sylvia more than she realised, and she crashed the gears abominably as she slowed to join the queue of traffic across Waterloo Bridge. Freddie would have been appalled....no...mustn't think about Freddie. Nor about Bryson, with the inevitable memories of Pip. Poor Pip, gone before he'd truly had a chance to grow up...

Damn Bryson! What right had he to intrude in her life and bring back all the memories she had tried so hard to suppress?

Anger, and the need to keep her attention on the road, the steering wheel and the gears, stopped her from being totally overset by the encounter. Her legs and arms aching from the constant declutching and gear changing, she wrestled the lorry through the London traffic towards the Old Kent Road, fiercely blinking back the tears when they threatened to fall.

Why was it that as soon as you told yourself you must not think about someone, then your mind immediately filled with memories of them? When her attention was needed on the road ahead, all she could think about was Pip, the unexpected baby of her parents' middle years, spoilt darling of the family, lying in the metal coffin of the sunken warship, in the cold, cold waters of the North Sea.

A picture came into her mind, a bright summer's day shortly before the court case, before Bryson came into their lives, when the worst that faced the family was the propriety of Sylvia spending two mornings a week at the offices of the NUWSS addressing envelopes for the cause of Votes for Women. It had been one of those rare days when the air seemed to sparkle, when the sun picked out every leaf, every blade of grass with an almost unnatural clarity, when every word spoken and every note of birdsong vibrated beyond hearing and into the soul.

Freddie, home for the vacations from Oxford, had challenged her to a set of rough tennis on the lawn; Pip was scoring for them, lounging on the grass in his flannels, in spite of mother's remonstrances about grass stains. On the terrace father was making acerbic remarks about the discomfort of garden chairs while mother sat at the wrought iron table, pouring tea. Now that image had been shattered just as surely as if the Kaiser had walked in through the garden gate and lobbed a bomb into their midst.

The memory was more than she could bear. When the traffic began to thin, just where the slums of the Old Kent Road began to give way to open fields, she swerved across the road and onto the grass verge. As she switched off the motor she began to sob, her shoulders heaving uncontrollably. She had so prided herself on not giving way to her emotions, on holding them back in order to be a strong support to her mother, yet here she was howling like a child, a little girl again, only now quite bereft of all those who had loved her. Her father dead, and now Pip and Freddie gone too, and her mother quite lost in her own world, no comfort at all.

At last the memories faded, leaving only Max Bryson to fill her mind. What had he been doing at the depot? It must have been pure mischance. He wouldn't have been looking for her - unless there were even more bills that father had been unable to pay... In her agitation she twisted her handkerchief, and told herself she wished it could be the wretched man's neck. But that was hardly fair. Without Mr Bryson's help, Pip would have been stuck with an unjustly tarnished name for the rest of his short life.

Anger proved harder to sustain than sorrow. She caught her breath with a shudder and gradually came back to her surroundings. Traffic was still moving past her, but vehicles were less frequent than in London. Ahead of her a milk cart was drawing away from the verge, and the local women paused with their slopping milk jugs to look at her curiously.

She looked at her mother's pretty fob watch. It would have to be sold before long to pay for the new nurse and then she would have to force herself to wear Freddie's wrist-watch, found at the bottom of his kit-bag of spares all those months ago, together with the spare gun and holster, all sent out to the French depot only to be sent straight back again. Almost twenty minutes had passed since she'd pulled in and she berated herself for her self-indulgence. There were crates to be delivered to the hospital, goods or passengers waiting for the return journey. She had a job to do and she jolly well ought to get on with it!

The milk cart drove past her, the old horse's hooves clip-clopping and the milk cans rattling. She opened the window and took a few deep breaths, then she mopped her eyes, blew her nose fiercely, and turned the engine over. At least she didn't have to get out and crank start it - one of the few privileges which her stay in prison had gained her was to be first in line for the self-starters, she being considered still too feeble to turn the handle. She reached across to close the window, for the bout of weeping had left her cold and shivery; under a hedge whose twiggy growth was veiled with the pale green of swollen leaf buds, she saw an untimely primrose struggling through last year's matted grass.

She felt a quiver beneath her ribs and tears started to her eyes again, but this time with a different emotion. With a sniff she set off again, and whenever her mind threatened to drift back to Bryson and the memories he had awoken, she concentrated instead on the primrose, the pale yellow blooms a symbol of new life among the debris of the old.

She almost missed the turning to the hospital, for the typed instructions were not clear, and all signposts had been taken down in case of invasion. To deal with the unexpectedly high number of maimed and wounded men, hospitals had been hastily set up in schools, factories and country houses and over the past few months she'd visited many of them. This one was new to her, but at last she turned in at the stone gates, steering her lorry down an avenue of ancient trees and alongside bowling green lawns towards the beautiful Georgian mansion.

Beds had been set up on the elegant terrace so that the patients - amputees by the look of the tented bedclothes - could take advantage of the weak spring sunshine. At the back of the house a team of VADs - all looking far younger than the statutory nineteen years of age - unloaded the cases of Scrubb's Ammonia, the flasks and bottles of anaesthetics, and the wound dressings.

Tea was being served in the main ward, and she was made very welcome. The convalescents in their hospital blues took advantage of a new face to flirt outrageously with her. For their sake she made the effort to laugh as they cracked jokes, and to pass on the little she knew of the latest news in London. It was a quiet time, said the volunteer nurse with the shiny brown bobbed hair, showing her through the nurses' sitting room to the bathroom beyond. They'd had no amputations for four days.

'It won't last,' she said with a distinct tremor in her voice. 'Eight of our convalescents are going back with you: that means they'll be sending us more, fresh from the front. The gramophone will get a hammering.'

'The gramophone?'

'We keep it going all day in the ward when we're operating. Drowns out the screaming, you see.' This from a girl who before the war would have had nothing more challenging than a game of croquet to fill her days. She was eager to unburden herself, continuing to talk to Sylvia through the locked board door of the closet. 'The ones who've just been operated on, they scream so terribly with the pain, then half of them start all over again when they discover what we've had to do. We had one in here with both legs gone and...and everything...all his m-male b-bits...ripped off in the explosion, you see. Never stopped screaming for two days. He had a fiancée too: she managed to get down here and sister had to tell her that he hadn't...that he could never...' Her voice tailed off, half-drowned in barely suppressed tears.

When Sylvia emerged the young VAD was examining her reflection and tidying her hair. In the small mirror over the sink her reddened eyes met Sylvia's. 'I - I sometimes wonder how much longer I can stand it.'

'Why did you volunteer?'

'Boredom, I suppose, after my brothers enlisted. And mother was so proud, you see. She boasts about me to all her friends on the Red Cross Committee. It would kill her if I chucked it all in now.'

Looking at the chalk-white face and dark-circled eyes, Sylvia couldn't help thinking it might just as easily kill the daughter if she *didn't* chuck it in. 'There are lots of other ways you can do your bit, you know,' she said as she dragged the comb through the tangle of curls before cramming the cap down on top of them. 'You could try driving, like me. Or the depots - they're always crying out for more clerks.' She patted the girl's arm. 'We're not all cut out to be Florence Nightingale. I'm certainly not.'

Back in the wards eight soldiers were waiting for her, in various states of disrepair, some with bandaged faces, others with only light dressings, two with half an arm missing and one with only one leg. Discharged from hospital to return to the bosom of their families. She saw from her roster that three others beside the amputees had Blighty wounds, and would never have to return to the hell of the Western Front. You could tell them easily, even before you'd seen the wounds and the dressings; the difference was in their eyes. Those who knew that a summons from the War Office would soon cut short their reunions had a blank, almost dead look in their eyes; the others, in spite of their injuries, had relief in theirs.

The sitter in the cab with her was a gruff sergeant with a nicotine-stained walrus moustache and one arm still in a sling. As soon as he found she had no cigarettes in the lorry to share around, he decided she wasn't worth talking to, and whistled *Tipperary* through his teeth throughout the journey. On the outskirts of London, when she'd turned off her headlights and had to rely instead on the indifferent illumination from the painted street lamps, he insisted on stopping at a tobacconist's and spent the rest of the journey making roll-ups. All the way up the Old Kent Road she had the added vexation of his cigarette smoke to deal with.

She hadn't smoked since going into Holloway - there simply hadn't been the money. She'd thought she was over the craving, but the smell of it started up the desire again. When he unexpectedly offered her one, she was sorely tempted, but she knew that smoking one cigarette would lead to a heightened desire for another, and there was no more spare money now than there had been six months before. In spite of the sergeant's protests she drove the rest of the way with her window wide open.

They dropped the last of the men off at Paddington, with their travel warrants. This time she'd be spared the usual problem of the sitter pleading with her to spend her off-duty hours brightening his home leave. The surly sergeant had made it quite clear that he detested women, severally and individually. When he crossed the Barracks yard without a word of thanks or a backward glance, he was still whistling *Tipperary* through his teeth.

Back at the depot she drove cautiously into the yard, though there was no one around but the night watchman in his sentry box. Avoiding the main doors into the building she slipped in through the small cut-out in the great double gates, startling the night-duty mechanic who was brewing up his cocoa over a spirit stove.

When she'd changed back into her skirt and blouse, she slipped out the same way. She half-dozed through the bus journey to Chelsea, and made her way along the Embankment by the light of the searchlights quartering the sky overhead. All she needed now was another encounter with Jameson to put the tin lid on a terrible day.

21

Halfway through Saturday night, soon after Sylvia had dropped into the deep sleep of exhaustion, there came a clatter of footsteps on the stairs and a great many voices laughing and calling out to each other. She groaned and put her head under the covers, hoping that the crowd of drinkers - no doubt from the *Eiffel Tower*, Octavius Jameson's home from home - would settle down for a deep and meaningful artistic discussion. But no such luck. Someone had brought a wind-up gramophone into the studio and after a deal of good-natured argument a record was selected and put on the turntable.

Abandoning all thoughts of sleep she lay in her bed listening to the strains of the familiar music. She'd played it many times, teaching Freddie the turkey trot, the latest dance craze. She remembered how her father had complained about the noise they were making. Now she could hear the shuffle and tap as the visitors danced up and down the uncarpeted floor: this was going to be a long evening.

Halfway through the second record her mother began to call for her. Sylvia's room had no direct access to the backstairs and the only way to her mother's room was through the studio. Remembering that Gwen was away visiting friends that weekend, Sylvia dragged her skirt and shawl over her nightdress before venturing out.

She slipped out, nostrils twitching at the smell of cigarette smoke. Everyone appeared to be engrossed in the pile of records, deciding what to play next.

She pressed herself against the wall, hoping to pass unobserved in the shadows, but Octavius caught sight of her. 'Sylvie, my love! Allow me t'innoduce you to Rosie,' he said, shrouding her in brandy fumes as he dragged forward a plump woman with a generous bosom in some danger of spilling out of its confines. Rosie, at a guess, was the barmaid from whatever hostelry he had last visited. She certainly stood out from the women who were generally to be seen around the studio: art students in floating robes or society ladies in elegantly draped dresses. 'Iss Rosie's birthday. We're cereb- cereb - cerebratin' darlin' Rosie's birthday.' He snatched at Sylvia's hand and enunciated more carefully: 'She would be honoured if you would join us.'

With a withering look Sylvia repossessed her hand, turned on her heel and went into her mother's room, shutting the door in Jameson's face.

'Too much noise, Sylvia.' Her mother drew her rose pink bed-jacket closer about her shoulders. 'Tell Freddie to take the needle off. Papa doesn't care for such music.'

'No, mother.' She'd learned from bitter experience that there was no point in correcting her. Unable to cope with the pain of loss, her mother had retreated into the past and pulled up the drawbridge.

'You may tell cook that dinner this evening was *not* up to standard. Not at all. She will have to pull her socks up, as you young people say, if she is to stay with us.'

'Mother, I do the best I can, but - '

'And tell the butcher that with the money we pay, I require only the best.'

Sylvia suppressed a snort of laughter as she imagined what response she would get from the local pie shop if she passed on *that* message.

'And there was a strange taste to the butter. If cook has allowed it to turn...'

The only strange thing about the butter was that it was margarine, all they could afford these days. But she couldn't tell her that: margarine, like Board Schools and public hospital wards, was for the poor, not for the widow of a bank manager.

'Go to sleep, mother...I must get back to bed. It's very late.'

'Fetch me Nurse Payne.' She started to shift nervously around the bed.

Wearily Sylvia explained, for perhaps the twentieth time, that the new nurse would not arrive until Monday morning. She saw to her mother's needs with as much patience as she could muster, reflecting as she slipped across the landing and down the backstairs to the closet that she was not of the heroic mould from which nurses were made.

She made her mother as comfortable as she could, poured her medicine and was about to return to her own room when there was a burst of raucous laughter from the studio. 'Told you she wasn't wearing any drawers!' a man bellowed.

Her hand fell from the doorknob and she pushed the chair under the handle. Nothing would persuade her to cross through the studio again tonight.

The celebrations went on far into the night and Sylvia dozed uneasily in the armchair, jammed against the curtained door to the landing. Just before dawn the drunken carousers began to leave, one announcing at the top of his voice only inches from her ear that he'd promised to look in on Henry's party. Every time a pair of feminine feet tip-tapped their way down the first few steps, Jameson hurried out to stop them on the landing. 'When shall I see you again?' he whispered to each woman in turn. 'You know how much it means to me.'

The same meaningless words. If she hadn't been so tired she might have laughed.

In the early light of dawn the studio at last fell silent. Sylvia slept until eight, when her mother awoke and querulously demanded her breakfast. After listening carefully at the door Sylvia crept out. The studio was littered with the detritus of celebration and the morning light fell cruelly through uncurtained windows onto the dissipated faces of the sleeping guests. Octavius sprawled across a sofa with his hand thrust down the barmaid's bosom; Rosie lay on her back, skirt up to her garters and her mouth wide open, revealing a number of gold teeth.

Recoiling from the rank scent of drink and debauchery, Sylvia tiptoed to the kitchen and picked her way through the wine bottles. She wrinkled her nose again at the musty smell emanating from the sink and was relieved when she picked up the kettle and found it was already full. She lit the gas, set out a tray and willed the water to boil before any of the guests awoke.

She almost made it, but as she emerged with a tray of tea one of the male guests staggered past her into the kitchen. As she crossed to her mother's room, she heard him being copiously sick in the kitchen sink.

22

Sylvia spent the rest of the day closeted in her room, trying to update her old straw hat with a bottle of black dye, a long quill feather and a few jet beads stripped ruthlessly from the bodice of one of her mother's old dresses. Later, if she was feeling daring, she might even take a few inches off the hem of her working skirt, woefully out of date now that hems no longer swept the floor, and badly worn into the bargain.

Perhaps she could scrape a few pennies for cheap braid from the street market tomorrow. A row or two of the latest Belgian blue along the bottom would update the skirt no end. She still took an interest in the fashions, even if she couldn't afford to buy the navy and the black of the latest modes, and she wouldn't go about looking any dowdier than she needed. There might even be enough dye for her summer boots, which were looking decidedly shabby. Nothing made you look poorer than shabby footwear and just because she *was* poor, she didn't see any need to look it. She smiled wryly. Perhaps she was more her mother's daughter than she cared to admit!

There was no hope of indulging her usual Sunday pleasures: without Gwen to listen for her mother, her customary walk along the Embankment was out of the question, and there was far too much noise to sleep. Before Octavius had retired to his room and drawn the shades, he'd summoned the cleaning woman from the next street, with her daughter, to clean up the house. No day of rest for any of them.

Sylvia had directed the charwoman to start in the kitchen and as misfortune would have it she was there, washing the black dye off her hands, when a visitor came calling. She had just flung open the sash window to air the room when she saw a sleek car disappear round the corner, leaving a lone female standing on the doorstep below, pulling impatiently on the broken bell pull.

The visitor looked up at the sound of the opening sash, leaving Sylvia no option but to hurry down and open the door.

The woman looked vaguely familiar, but her deep fur collar was drawn up against the cool wind blowing off the river, concealing her features.

'I'm afraid Mr Jameson is - not at home.'

'No matter,' said the visitor. 'It's not Mr Jameson I have come to see. I am Lady Alice - '

'The Countess of Ardingley.' Now Sylvia recognised her. 'You came to the studio.'

'Indeed. Pray call me Lady Alice. I do not often use my title.'

'I'm afraid Miss Jameson is also not at home. She is at present in the country.'

'No matter. My business is not with them, but with you.' As Sylvia blinked at her in surprise she said impatiently: 'I have sent my driver on an errand. Do you propose to keep me standing on the doorstep until he returns?'

Such forthrightness left Sylvia no choice but to invite her in, but she had the presence of mind to lead her to Gwen's sitting room, which had escaped the worst depredations of the night's carousing. The visitor made her way with great care down the hall and into the room, but Sylvia had to shoot out a hand and steady her when she almost came to grief over Gwen's cat. To her surprise she felt a tremor run through the woman and realised that she was older than her upright stance and deportment had led her to believe. Keeping a firm grip on her elbow she saw her safely to a comfortable chair.

'I can't imagine what business you could have with me. But please, do sit down.'

Lady Alice settled her skirts around her and looked over Sylvia's shoulder in a most disconcerting manner.

'Some people find it very off-putting, this being *almost* looked at,' she said abruptly. 'But it's the only way I can gain an impression of you. I have very little sight, as Miss Jameson may have told you.'

'I'm sorry. I had not realised...'

Lady Alice waved her words aside. 'Enough of that. The last thing in the world I wish to dwell on. Tell me - are you pretty?'

Sylvia choked. 'N-not really, ma'am. Passable, but certainly far from beautiful.'

'I have an impression of your hair. But what colour are your eyes?'

'A sort of greeny-brown. I was told recently that they match my khaki burberry coat very well.'

'Not much of a compliment.'

Sylvia's lips twitched. 'I don't think it was intended as such.' She decided she'd had enough of this cross examination. 'You say you have some business to discuss with me?'

'A matter to our mutual benefit. I understand you have no fixed employment at the moment?'

'I hold two positions, but either - or indeed both - could be terminated at any time.'

'Then my offer might be of interest to you.' Again that piercing over the shoulder gaze. 'I am seeking to employ an intelligent young lady as a personal assistant. Miss Jameson thought you might wish to be considered for the post, but I had another person to interview, recommended to me by my friend Lady Harriet Castleton.' She sensed, rather than saw, the young lady shudder. Intrigued, she pressed on. 'Imagine my surprise when this morning after church Lady Harriet gave me this address! Could you be the young lady she had told me about? Could Miss Shaw and Miss Fletcher-Shaw be one and the same?'

'Indeed they could,' said Sylvia, struggling to control herself. The mention of Lady Harriet's name brought back memories of the day when she'd emerged from the darkness of Holloway into the too-bright summer light, and been swept into an embrace of violets and lilies, then laid back tenderly against the cushioned seats of an elegant horse-drawn carriage, her injuries fretted over, her bravery praised. If it hadn't been for her mother, they could have had her protection still. It was good to know that her kindly care had not been totally withdrawn.

She was not aware of her hand slipping to the side of her mouth, as if trying to hide the scar. Time stood still and she could still feel the pain of the shattered tooth, the scarred mouth and the shock of discovering that her country was at war.

'Lady Harriet recommended you most highly - as did Miss Jameson when I mentioned the matter to her in passing. In my situation I need someone with initiative, but who can also take her place in society, as I dine out a great deal - sometimes in political circles. It is not a permanent position, only until my daughter-in-law returns from abroad. But almost certainly six months. Lady Harriet was adamant that you would fit the bill.'

'Lady Harriet is too kind,' said Sylvia, 'but she must have forgotten to mention that I'm not free to take up any position which means living in.' *And I'll warrant she also failed to mention my criminal record!*

There was a burst of raucous laughter from the studio and a crash, followed by the tinkle of breaking glass. One of the bodies, perhaps stirred into life by the doorbell, had tried to negotiate the stairs without realising the level of general intoxication. There was a shrill volley of abuse from the charwoman, who had probably only just finished cleaning the stairs, and then the sound she had been dreading, her mother's cry of distress.

With a flurry of stammered apologies, Sylvia abandoned her visitor. She took the stairs as fast as her clinging skirts would allow, ignoring the charwoman and the half-recognised poet sitting midway down the stairs, head in his hands, groaning.

Her mother had been awoken by the sudden crash, but she was still bleary with the medicine and it took only a few moments to settle her again. Sylvia drew the covers over her shoulders and turned away from the bed, only to find her visitor, who she thought she had left safely downstairs, standing in the doorway.

She gave a helpless shrug. 'As you will gather, Lady Alice, I am rather tied to my present situation.' She took her visitor by the elbow and steered her back out onto the landing. 'So I shall have to decline your kind offer of - '

Lady Alice turned her head slowly. 'You think your mother would rather stay here than be nursed in comfort in Ardingley House?'

'But - nursing my mother takes up a great deal of my time. I'm not sure there would be enough left to serve your ladyship.'

'Tut, girl, I'm not proposing that *you* nurse her. Ardingley House is regrettably full of people determined to find someone to fuss over. And I would much rather it was not me. I may have lost my sight, but there is nothing else the matter with me.'

'I believe you, ma'am. I thought I'd left you safely downstairs!'

'Oh, I can still manage stairs. Carefully. My greatest loss is that I can no longer drive myself. I did so enjoy that freedom.' As if to echo her words, there was a discreet toot on the horn from the street below.

'I understand that you drive?' said Lady Alice as she allowed herself to be led downstairs again.

'I do. My brother taught me.'

'Even better - my own driver wishes to enlist.'

Sylvia crossed to the window and watched the sleek machine draw up at the kerbside. 'You mean - I could drive you about in that?' she gasped.

'I imagine it will make quite a change to the lorries - Miss Jameson told me about your work at the war supplies depot. Now I wouldn't wish to stop you doing your bit for the country. I don't go out every day.'

This was the strangest employment Sylvia had ever been offered. 'But if you don't want me every day, then what duties and - and - '

'And remuneration?'

'Something I'm afraid I have to consider.'

'Of course. As an independent young lady...' Lady Alice went on to name what seemed to Sylvia to be a fortune, considering that keep would have to be found not just for one but for two.

'For that you would require a great deal!'

'The main requirement is adaptability. I don't need a full-time secretary, and I can't bear the thought of a full-time companion. You have a pleasant voice and when we both find ourselves at leisure you might read to me. I do miss my books. But I don't want you fussing around me every waking minute. Mrs Jennings - my present companion - equates loss of sight with loss of brain. What else? Oh, yes. On occasional afternoons I need to be driven to meetings of my committees, though how much longer....' Her voice trailed off and Sylvia saw from the pain on her face that she was not as philosophical about her encroaching blindness as she might wish the world to believe.

Lady Alice cleared her throat and carried on. 'Several evenings a week I dine out. You would drive me there, sit with me at table and assist as needed. I don't appreciate attention being drawn to my condition and above all - *I don't want nurse-maiding.'*

'That much is perfectly clear, ma'am.'

'Good. We will rub along all the better for that.' Lady Alice put her head on one side, looking for a moment like a bird - a soft dove, perhaps - tucking its head under its feathers. 'I understand that you have suffered sad losses in the present conflict.'

Sylvia swallowed and nodded. It wasn't easy to talk about her brothers to people who had not known them.

'I'll assume that was an affirmative,' said Lady Alice briskly.

'Y-yes.'

'Do remember that I can't hear you nod. As to your losses...you'll be of no use to me if you insist on shutting yourself away from the world. I need someone who is prepared to be out and about. In wartime there are many who go into society in black gloves.'

'I prefer to do my mourning in my heart, ma'am, rather than on my sleeve.'

'I commend you for it. Now - will you come and work for me?'

'You really would not mind me finishing off at the depot? At least until they can replace me?'

'We must all make our sacrifices. Yes, I'm sure we could find the time for you to continue with a few shifts a week - if you have the energy for it. To be frank you sound as though you could sleep for a week.'

'A month,' said Sylvia ruefully.

After that matters seemed to run away with her. 'No time like the present,' said Lady Alice briskly. In the late afternoon the car returned and their few belongings, swiftly packed into boxes and Gladstone bags, were loaded into the capacious luggage locker. While the driver, a strong young man with a broad grin that reminded her heartbreakingly of Pip, carried her mother down the stairs, wrapped warmly in a nest of quilts, Sylvia left a note with Molly explaining what had happened, thanking Gwen for her kindness and begging her to call at Ardingley House as soon after her return as was convenient.

As the driver started up the engine Sylvia took a last look at the house that had given them refuge in their hour of need and then hurried down to the hall to put on her hat and coat. Catching sight of the arrow-head badge she swiftly unpinned it from the lapel and placed it in her bag. Part of her was ashamed at her action, but her overriding concern was for her mother and how much better the new situation would be for her. She'd placed her own principles ahead of her mother's welfare once before: she wouldn't do it again.

23

The journey to Ardingley House passed in a daze, from which Sylvia took some time to emerge. On their arrival at the imposing town house Lady Alice took charge, issuing orders and sending servants scurrying. Before Sylvia could gather her wits, her mother was whisked away in the strong arms of the young chauffeur and settled in a small modern wing of the town mansion, with a white-haired nurse watching over her.

'Now you can stop fretting about her,' said Lady Alice, shooing Sylvia out of the sick room. 'Nanny Armstrong has been with the family all her life. Don't be deceived by her age: she's as competent as she is kind.'

'But - '

'The maid should have finished opening up the rooms by now, and I suggest you take the time to settle in,' said Lady Alice, sweeping Sylvia up flights of elegant balustraded stairs, along portrait-hung corridors and across lofty landings panelled in highly polished wood. 'You must have a few undisturbed nights: you'll be no use to me if you fall asleep at the wheel, or in the middle of the Asquiths' dinner.'

'But - '

'But me no buts, my dear Miss Shaw. Tomorrow will be time enough to show you around the house. Much of it is closed up anyway, or turned over to the Belgian refugees. Three families, the last I heard. We can discuss your duties then. Lizzie will bring a dinner tray to your rooms - '

'But I'm not an invalid.'

'And with care you won't become one.' They stopped outside a panelled door halfway along a corridor hung with oriental paintings. Lady Alice patted her arm. 'Rest is probably all you need: I suggest you treat yourself as gently for the next few days as you have clearly been treating your mother.'

She turned to go, her silken petticoats swishing. As she put out a hand to guide herself round a table cluttered with china buddhas and laquered mementoes of the east, and rather unfortunately placed near the head of the stairs, Sylvia was reminded of her duties.

'Shall I see you safely downstairs?' she asked, hurrying after her employer.

She was rewarded for her pains with a scathing look. 'I came to this house as a bride thirty years ago. I know every turn on the stairs, every step in every flight. I think I may be trusted to find my way around it more easily than someone who has only been here five minutes.'

'I beg your pardon,' said Sylvia. She'd regretted the words as soon as they were uttered. Lady Alice had, after all, led her unaided through the maze of corridors, and Sylvia herself had not the remotest idea how to return to the main house. 'I had not intended - '

'No, I beg yours,' interrupted Lady Alice, and the anger faded as swiftly as it had come. 'There was no call for me to be so snappy, for this is all new to you. But do remember that I don't want nurse-maiding, won't you? Then we shall go along very well together.' She turned back to the stairs. 'I shall leave you to settle in. If there is anything you require, you need only ring.'

Sylvia turned the brass handle and stepped in to her bedroom, barely suppressing a gasp as she took in her surroundings. The room was modest compared with what she had so far seen of Ardingley House, but considerably larger than the room she'd occupied in Chelsea, and furnished with a luxurious simplicity that far outstripped any room she'd ever seen. The walls were painted in pale grey-green, with plaster mouldings and cornices picked out in a darker shade, and opposite the door were two high windows draped in curtains of the palest eau de nil which had been drawn against the encroaching darkness. To her right stood a bed with delicate matching drapes descending from a corona on the ceiling, and a coverlet of darker green embroidered in peach and terracotta in the oriental style. On a graceful bamboo table glowed an electric lamp with a peach tasselled shade.

The entire wall facing the bed had doors in it, painted to match the walls and at first sight almost disguised by the elegant mouldings. In front of them, on a sculpted oriental rug, stood her two scuffed Gladstone bags, looking rather out of place in the midst of such elegance. Her hairbrush, pins and meagre toilet articles, including the empty pot of La Rola, stood forlornly on one corner of the bamboo dressing table: thankfully the maid had taken away the ragged cardboard box in which they had travelled. In some trepidation Sylvia crossed and opened the first door: there in solitary splendour hung her spare skirt, a couple of blouses and the one formal dress which had not been stolen from their boxed possessions while she was in prison.

Poor Freddie. Faced with a sick mother, a sister in prison, and the pressing need to return to his employment in Scotland, he'd done his best. But she wished he'd found somewhere safer to store their belongings. She'd had no need of evening dresses in the last six months, but now she was very underdressed for her surroundings: no wonder the Countess had suggested she dine in her room.

As if on cue a knock fell on the door, followed by a maid with a large tray.

'Goodness, miss, thought you'd be in bed by now!' she said.

Sylvia glanced at her mother's watch and realised she had been standing in the middle of the room for some time. That had been happening to her a great deal too often in the last few days, since the shock of seeing Bryson.

'Still,' the maid went on, 'seeing as you're still up and about, you might as well have this at the table in your sitting room.'

'My - ?'

'Sitting room.' She nodded at the far corner of the bedroom. 'If you'd open the door for me, miss?'

The third door, which Sylvia had thought part of the wardrobe, opened into an elegant peach-walled sitting room furnished with a small lady's bureau, several comfortable armchairs, three oriental cabinets and a small oval table on which the maid commenced to set out a selection of dishes from the tray.

'I could light the fire for you, miss, if you was cold,' said the maid.

'No need, thank you, er - '

'Lizzie, miss.'

'Thank you, Lizzie. But I'm quite warm enough.'

'Lovely and warm these rooms always are,' said the maid, taking the opportunity to assess the newcomer, knowing full well that she would be interrogated on her return to the kitchens. 'They get the sun nearly all the day through. That's why the Countess chose them. Being one as always feels the cold.'

'But these aren't Lady Alice's rooms, surely?'

'No. The *young* Countess, I was talking about. That's Lady Alice's daughter-in-law.' She stood back and looked at the table with satisfaction. 'There. You tuck into that, miss. Pick you up proper, that will. And Lady Alice says you're to be sure and drink that glass of wine.' She turned in the doorway. 'I'll turn down the bed and set your things out in your bathroom. You just ring if you want anything, otherwise I'll leave you in peace.'

'Th-thank you Lizzie.' She managed to suppress her astonishment at the mention of 'your bathroom'. Presumably another hidden door to be investigated.

'Lady Alice says not to get up in the morning until you're well-rested, because she has no appointments. Ring when you're ready for breakfast and I'll bring it up.'

As the connecting door closed behind the maid, Sylvia sipped at her wine and looked around her in amazement, wondering whether she should pinch herself. In the space of twenty-four hours her life had turned around completely. She could only hope that in another twenty-four hours it wouldn't turn back again: after all, it had happened before.

But to dwell on that now would be churlish in the extreme. She turned back to the table and a shiver of delight shook her as she uncovered the heated dishes one by one. Helping herself to generous portions of everything she discovered that it all tasted every bit as good as it looked. Lady Alice had the services of an excellent cook.

She couldn't finish the half of it, for her stomach had grown unaccustomed to large meals, but she drained her glass and felt the warmth run through her veins. When she could eat no more she returned to the bedroom. The maid had turned down the bed and laid Sylvia's old nightdress across the soft sheets, where it looked even more worn and faded than it had in Chelsea. In the far corner another disguised door stood ajar and beyond it she found a bathroom; on one wall hung a long mirror with electric lights above and to the side of it, and on a heated bar beneath was a selection of thick fluffy towels. A pull on the cord lit up all the mirror lights, cruelly spotlighting the dark circles under her eyes and the pale, drawn look on her face. Hastily she pulled the cord again: perhaps there was something to be said for poor lighting.

The bath was an elegant porcelain structure on legs, which looked almost large enough to swim in. On a ledge at the end of the tub was a row of crystal bottles. She uncorked the nearest and inhaled: June Roses, one of her favourites in the days when such things had still mattered. She turned on the taps and hot water began to cascade into the basin, but she turned them off almost immediately. The thought of a bath was tempting, but she wasn't sure she could stay awake that long. The morning would be time enough.

She was already in her nightdress when she went searching in her bag for her comb and found the arrow-headed badge. She sat for a long moment turning it over and over in her hand, then she rose and crossed to the bell-pull.

24

Lady Alice was sitting at her dressing table brushing out her hair when the knock came on the door. Annie, the personal maid who had been with her ever since she had come to Ardingley House, set aside the petticoats she had been shaking out and crossed to the door where she entered into low-voiced conversation with someone in the corridor.

'What is it, Annie?' Lady Alice put down the hairbrush and turned towards the door. 'Is Mrs Shaw unwell?'

'No, madam. It's Lizzie. Seems that young woman wants a word with you. I'm just telling Lizzie I'm sure it can wait till morning.'

'If it could have waited, Annie, then the young *lady* would hardly have disturbed me now.' It was a gentle reproof, but it was enough to stiffen the maid's back and send her grumbling back to the dressing room. Lady Alice turned to the door. 'Be so good as to show Miss Shaw the way, Lizzie,' she said.

Within a few minutes Lizzie announced the visitor, then withdrew. 'Come in, Miss Shaw, and sit down,' said Lady Alice, indicating the small chair by the little writing table in the corner. 'Thank you, Annie. That will be all.' She felt her way to the armchair nearby. 'Unless Miss Shaw would like some hot chocolate? A brandy? Bengers in hot milk?'

'No thank you.' Sylvia ignored the chair and stood in the middle of the floor fiddling with the fringing on her shawl until the door closed with a snap behind the maid. 'Much as I'm tempted by the brandy...'

'In need of Dutch courage? I do hope you're not about to tell me this has all been a dreadful mistake and you're running off to join the VADs?'

The undertone of laughter gave Sylvia the courage she needed. 'I have been somewhat less than open with you, ma'am,' she began, swallowing hard.

'You, Miss Shaw? Surely not.' More gently, she said: 'I am aware that Shaw is not your original family name. I knew that from Lady

Harriet - did I not tell you?' Now would be the moment to explain about her other source of information, but she did not. 'I can perfectly understand why you have simplified it. I used to read the papers. If that is all, I can assure you there's no need for your concern.'

'But it isn't all. When we left the Chelsea house this afternoon, I took this off my coat.' She opened her palm and passed the little brooch to Lady Alice. 'When you have seen that, ma'am, you may not be so eager to take me into your employment.....'

25

After breakfast Lady Alice settled herself into a chair in the window, leaning back to enjoy the feel of the warm sun on her face. She might take a walk in the garden later that morning, she decided. Find out how the spring bulbs were coming on. Old habits died hard, and besides, the old gardener appreciated a little encouragement.

'And so we are to wait to meet your overnight guest?' said Mrs Jennings, curiosity overcoming her at last. 'One would have expected a polite guest to be punctual to breakfast, but I understand from the servants that it's a young person, and they are not always as punctilious as their elders and betters might wish. Why, I remember when - '

'Do you have the newspapers, Henrietta?' demanded Lady Alice, cutting ruthlessly into her companion's interminable stories. 'Any further news of the landings in the Dardanelles?'

Easily distracted, Henrietta Jennings opened the papers and began to read snippets out in her customary disjointed fashion. 'My goodness!' she exclaimed after a few minutes. 'You'll never guess what that dreadful Lloyd George has said to Mr Asquith...'

'I wouldn't guess in a month of Sundays. Because quite frankly, Henrietta, I wouldn't be in the least interested. Unless he's buried him face-down in Parliament Square. Preferably with dear Margot alongside him...'

'Alice, really!' trilled Henrietta. 'To make mock of the Prime Minister! What a bizarre sense of humour you are developing, dear. Almost as strange as dear Max's.'

'One would expect us to have something in common other than the colour of our eyes,' said Lady Alice tersely.

'Speaking of the dear boy - '

'You take the words out of my mouth, Henrietta. Speaking of the dear boy, would you be so kind as to write a note inviting him to call at his earliest convenience.' A smile curved her lips and if Mrs Jennings had had any attention to spare, she would have seen that Lady Alice's eyes positively sparkled. She was looking forward to this morning.

She began to dictate the note, trying to ignore Mrs Jennings's stream of interjections which, as usual, had no bearing at all on the matter in hand.

'Have you heard from your niece recently?' she asked, a propos of nothing in particular. She'd better be careful: Henrietta's scattiness might be catching.

'I had a letter only yesterday. The dear baby is thriving, my niece tells me. I am so longing to see him again. Indeed, his mama and papa are talking of bringing him to town.'

'Much better not,' said Lady Alice hastily. 'Cities are no good for small babies. You should go to see them.'

'If only it were possible. But I have promised, Alice, that I will not leave your side while I can be of service to you...'

'I have been far too selfish in detaining you, Henrietta, and I cannot have it on my conscience any longer.' Usually she closed her eyes and let her companion's inexhaustible flow of words stream past her, but today she would have to be just as inexhaustible to make any impression. 'Just think how happy the dear little baby will be to see his great-aunt. No, I really must not keep you from your family...'

'There can be no question of me leaving you, my dear Alice. I know how much you have come to rely on me.'

'And very selfish I have been in taking advantage of your good nature when you were longing to return to the bosom of your family. No!' She held up her hand as Henrietta took a breath to begin her protest again. 'My mind is made up, Henrietta. I have been most dilatory in finding a replacement companion.'

'You must find a new driver first - in time of war that has to be your priority. Especially as Mitchell is eager to enlist. We must all do our bit for - '

'Quite.' If she got Henrietta onto the subject of patriotism they would never be done. 'Yesterday I finally succeeded in replacing Mitchell. I have a new driver to take me around. So you see, Henrietta, I really won't need to detain you any longer.'

'A man?' Mrs Jennings was scandalised. 'A man - and an employed man at that - cannot do all for you that I have done! It would not be proper. No, I must put my care for you before family, before everything.'

'You need have no qualms, Henrietta.' Lady Alice tilted her head and wished she could make out her companion's expression. 'The new driver is a woman.'

Robbed of her last argument, all Henrietta Jennings could do was open and close her mouth like a stranded fish. Lady Alice couldn't see it, but she could imagine it, and a slow smile curved the corners of her mouth.

26

Spring sunshine was filtering through the curtains when Sylvia at last opened her eyes. Beyond the windows she could hear the occasional motorcar and the clop-clop of horses' hooves. She was groping for the clock when the maid knocked lightly on the door.

By the time she'd sipped her tea, luxuriated in the warm, scented bath which Lizzie had drawn, and dressed herself in her best blouse and skirt, it was quite late. As soon as she'd seen her mother, she must present herself downstairs, ready for duty.

Nanny Armitage welcomed her to the sickroom with a beaming smile, pausing in her bustling and tidying to assure her that Mrs Shaw had had a restful night. 'Look in on your ma by all means,' she said, opening the door wide. 'She's been dozing this past hour.'

Behind the screen which shielded the patient from the light her mother was lying on the pillows, her eyes half-open.

'Sylvia!' she exclaimed, struggling to raise herself onto her elbow as her daughter came into view. 'Whatever are you doing here? You stupid girl, you will be late again! Whatever possessed you - ' She paused in her diatribe to catch her breath.

'Don't fret, mother. Everything's well.' She eased her back into the pillows and wondered how much to tell her - she didn't want to confuse her even further.

But her mother flew onto another topic in the butterfly habit which had only been exacerbated by her illness. 'That new nurse you hired is very good,' she said with a yawn. 'Much more pleasant than that terrible Nurse Payne. Perhaps you are not entirely useless.'

'There. You settle down now.' Nanny Armitage bustled up to the bed, rearranging the pillows. 'Miss Sylvia will come in and see you again later in the day.'

'She needn't bother. She only comes in to wake me up. A wilful girl, quite useless if I am not behind her every moment.' She shook her head. 'Oh, Sylvia! You will break your father's heart...'

'There now, you'll tire yourself out with talking.' As her mother's eyes closed, they tiptoed out of the sickroom, Nanny Armitage waving away Sylvia's embarrassed apologies. 'If your mother thinks I'm a hired nurse, she'll maybe think she's still in the same place. That way, she's less likely to be confused by the move. Lady Alice has asked her own doctor to call by,' she said comfortably. 'Not that he can do anything - well, I'm sure you know that, dearie, no point in deceiving ourselves, is there? - but he can tell us if there's anything else we can do to make things easier for her.'

'You're very kind,' said Sylvia with a lump in her throat.

'It's good to feel useful again.' She took up her knitting and lowered herself into her rocking-chair with a contented sigh. 'I haven't had anyone to look after since poor Master Esmond.'

'I'll bring Miss Shaw back this evening then, if that's all right?' said Lizzie, before Sylvia could indulge her curiosity.

Nanny Armitage nodded. 'I'll let you know if there's any change.'

'Lady Alice wants to show you around the house,' said Lizzie when they arrived back at Sylvia's own room, 'but she's waiting on a visitor. I'll fetch you when she's ready.' She crossed to the sitting-room door. 'I've set the newspapers out for you. Her ladyship always likes to be up to date - specially with the war.'

'Has she relatives at the front?' asked Sylvia.

'Her ladyship will tell you what you need to know about the family.' Lizzie turned her attention to fluffing up the cushions on the armchair and Sylvia had the distinct impression that she had been dismissed.

27

Lady Alice was in her dressing room, changing from her gardening dress, when her son was announced. Annie left, closing the door behind her as she went.

'No Mrs Jennings to swamp me in syrup and sympathy?' observed Max, crossing to greet his mother. 'Have you murdered her? Ought we to be working on your defence?'

'Henrietta is not talking to me.' Her lips twitched. 'Removing herself from my presence is supposed to show me how grievously I have erred.'

'I saw Mitchell in the mews. I hear you've found a new driver.'

Her head came up sharply. 'He told you - ?'

'He was quite mysterious about the fellow. But Mrs Jennings knew Mitchell was eager to enlist, so I can't see how replacing him should upset her.'

'But I have replaced Henrietta too. She will be leaving in the next few days.'

'Thank God,' he said in heartfelt tones. 'She's imposed on your good will for too long.'

'It will be a joy to see the back of her before she shatters my wits completely.' Lady Alice felt her way through the clutter of bottles on the dressing table, knocking over several as she went. At last she found the flask of perfume and dabbed a little on each wrist. 'But there is a certain amount of guilt at the same time.'

'I can't see why. You've put up with her longer than anyone else would have.'

'It can't be a pleasant prospect, moving from one relative to another, never having your own home. You know how that feels.'

'What if we were to offer her a cottage on the estate? I'd be happy to pay her a small pension just to see the back of her.'

'That would be very kind, Max.'

'Hardly. I make the offer for all the wrong reasons.' The stopper had come loose in one of the bottles his mother had knocked over and as she turned away from the dressing table he straightened it, pushing the lotions and scents away from the front edge of the dressing table to the back, where she'd be less likely to knock them onto the floor. 'Just try not to pick up any more waifs and strays, won't you? Or we shall run out of funds!'

'As a matter of fact, Max - '

'Don't tell me,' he said over his shoulder, 'the driver has an aged parent.'

'A sick mother.' She crossed to the door and opened it.

'And I suppose the companion has three indigent aunts - ' He ceased his tidying abruptly, his brow contracted in a frown. 'Mother, what's this doing here?'

'What is it, dear?' his mother called from the corridor. 'Do come along. We shall be late for luncheon.'

He caught up with her halfway down the stairs. 'An arrow-headed brooch - with purple, white and green ribbons.'

She paused for the briefest moment. 'Haven't you seen one before? It's a badge of honour for suffragettes who've been in pris- '

'I *know* what it *is*. But where did it come from?'

'Belongs to my new companion,' she said as she swept down the stairs. 'She's waiting for us in the drawing room. You'll find her a great improvement on Henrietta.'

'A prisoner?' He dropped his voice to an angry whisper. 'But I thought she came on the highest recommendation? Lady Harriet - '

'Knew exactly what I wanted.' She opened the door. 'So clever of her.'

Lady Alice had been looking forward to this moment. She would dearly have loved to see the expression on their faces, but the stiffening of Max's arm in hers and the gasp of shock from Miss Shaw as she half-rose from her chair painted the picture clearly enough.

'Miss Shaw, my son Max. Max, Miss - '

'Miss Shaw - Miss *Fletcher*-Shaw - and I have already met.' He spoke in a dry, strangled voice with no trace of his customary fluency.

'But - I don't understand,' said Sylvia, clutching the arm of the chair for support. 'He can't be your son. You're the Countess of Ardingley!'

'Dowager Countess. Nevertheless, I assure you, Max is my son,' said Lady Alice, peering from one to the other. 'I was married twice, d'you see.'

'I - you - you must excuse me.' Sylvia rose abruptly to her feet and her skirts caught the ornamental table, sending photograph frames and figurines skidding to the edge. Fumbling with the delicate items, her face white and drained, she descended even further into confusion. 'I shall leave you to - that is - you must have a great deal to - if you will excuse me, I must...'

'Nonsense. Max and I have nothing particular to say to each other. And I believe luncheon is about to be served. Is that Maisie?'

'Yes ma'am,' said the maid who had just appeared in the doorway. 'Shall I call Mrs Jennings?'

'No!' said Lady Alice and her son, emphatically and in chorus.

'Mrs Jennings is packing,' said Lady Alice, and the maid's face broadened into a smile. 'She is leaving us shortly to visit her niece. I'm sure she would appreciate a tray in her room.'

They moved to the morning room, smaller than the formal dining room but, with its highly polished yew furniture and round table, just as elegant as the rest of the house. Sylvia, trailing uncomfortably behind Lady Alice and her son, saw that Max Bryson was limping. An automobile accident, perhaps? They were becoming increasingly common as more and more people abandoned the horse for four wheels. Only a few eccentrics like Lady Harriet Castleton still drove about in their carriages, although that might change again as more vehicles were commandeered for the war.

Her butler and her son both hurried to help Lady Alice into her seat, although Sylvia felt she could have managed perfectly well without either. As the butler continued to fuss around his mistress, Bryson remembered his other duties, but Sylvia had whisked herself into her place before he could reach her side.

She would not meet his eyes, unable to face the condemnation she knew she would see there. Lady Alice might be prepared to overlook her past, but Max Bryson was another kettle of fish all together. He was straightforward and a stickler for the truth, qualities she had always admired in him, even when they had clashed over Votes for Women.

'We'll look after ourselves, thank you, Jarvis,' said Lady Alice when the dishes were on the table. 'I'll ring when we need you.'

Sylvia could hardly bring herself to look up from her plate, let alone speak, but Lady Alice kept up a flow of small talk, asking after acquaintances and demanding the latest news from the War Committee.

The conversations about Asquith, Kitchener and munitions passed over Sylvia's head. She picked at the food in front of her, her mind teeming with thoughts and fears, her heart hammering at the shock of finding herself face to face with her past. She looked up only once when Lady Alice addressed her directly and instantly dropped her gaze when she found Max Bryson's eyes on her.

What the devil was the matter with her? He would think her a complete booby, she told herself savagely. And so too would his mother, and that was far more important. Lady Alice would hardly want a tongue-tied fool to take with her into society!

But she was deluding herself. There could be no return to society for her now. Lady Alice's son was a lawyer, a brilliant lawyer, as she knew only too well from his work on Pip's behalf. How long would it be before he found out every detail of her shame, every word of her court case, every step of her humiliating stay in Holloway Prison? Although she'd given a false name on her arrest, it was a matter of record that she had been discharged into the care of Lady Harriet, and Lady Harriet knew her real name. The details of her criminal record were there for anyone who knew where to look. Nothing got past Max Bryson. And with his unemotional dedication to the rule of law he could never contemplate such a woman in his mother's employ.

'Your turn, Miss Fletcher-Shaw,' said Bryson, as though he'd read her mind. 'I have remarked on the food, my mother has passed a comment on the government. Your turn to say something. Preferably something not too provocative - the weather, perhaps?'

'Max, dear, don't be impolite.'

'I'm sure you have no interest in my views on the weather, sir,' said Sylvia, goaded into speech. 'I *could* remark on my astonishment that you are serving in Mr Asquith's government - ye gods, *Asquith*, of all people! - but you asked me not to be provocative. Which leaves me at something of a loss.'

Bryson, who was already regretting his sarcastic words, turned towards her across the table. 'Miss Fletcher-Shaw - or, no - I understand you prefer to be called - ' But he had twisted his body too sharply and pain contorted his face.

Sylvia saw new lines in his face that had not been there before. 'I - is there something I can do?' She half-rose, then sank back, wishing that she had held her tongue.

'No!' He waved her back into her seat angrily. 'It's nothing. It passes.' He drew a deep breath and tried to force the polite smile back onto his lips.

'I didn't know you'd suffered an accident.'

'Don't waste your sympathy on me,' he snapped. 'It's not something I care to talk about. Besides, you've problems enough of your own. Your mother...' As the pain subsided he forced himself to speak more gently. 'I should have asked after her before now. I was sorry to hear she's in poor health...'

'She is dying,' said Sylvia baldly. 'She never recovered from my father's death.'

'Strange. I never thought them that close.'

'Max, really!' Listening to the awkward exchanges Lady Alice wished for the hundredth time that she could read their faces. Hearing the strain in Sylvia's voice, she almost regretted her own deviousness.

'Forgive me, Miss Shaw,' said Bryson. 'I intended no offence.'

She shrugged. 'As you observed, they had very little in common. But for over thirty years mother's life was entirely focussed on my father's comfort and well-being. Without that, she has no purpose.'

'I sent a letter of condolence, but it was returned.'

She wet her lips, which had become suddenly very dry. 'Since father's death we have...moved about a great deal.'

He pressed on. 'I was so very sorry to hear about your brothers...'

Tears welled up in her eyes and she wished more than anything that she could run away from this table, from this house, from the inevitable humiliation.

'It must have been a terrible blow for your mother,' he continued. 'She must depend on you greatly.'

'Me?' She looked up with an almost hysterical laugh. 'Hardly, Mr Bryson. I'm the black sheep of the family. Never to be mentioned, and certainly not in the same breath as my brothers.' She slipped into a cruel parody of her mother's best society tones. ' "One does not know people who have been to prison." '

Oh, Heavens! Why had she come out with that now? But she couldn't take the words back. In for a penny, in for a pound, she thought. And Bryson would have found out soon enough. 'For her my disgrace was the final blow.'

An uncomfortable silence descended on the table. 'Shall we take our coffee in the drawing room?' Lady Alice reached for the bell. If only Max would say something....

Sylvia pushed her chair back. 'If you will excuse me, I really must - '

'Of course.' Lady Alice pressed her hand. 'You must be very tired still.'

'It's not that - but - ' She heard Max push his chair back but she couldn't bring herself to look at him. 'Excuse me. You must have a great deal to discuss.' Her voice sounded artificial even to her own ears.

The echo of the closing door fell into a stunned silence. Max, still standing, looked down at his mother. 'Now, mother, will you tell me what the devil's going on?'

28

Sylvia woke heavy-eyed after a night filled with fearful dreams of death and desolation. She lay on the pillows, twisting her handkerchief through her fingers and cursing the fate that had brought her under the same roof as Max Bryson. She'd been right to think that such good fortune could not last: it was only a matter of time before he drove her from the house bag and baggage.

It could have been so different. If only her nerve had held.

She was staring blankly into space when Lizzie came in with her tea. Lady Alice, she said, would be out for the day. 'Going the rounds with Mrs Jennings, to say her farewells,' said Lizzie, disappearing into the bathroom to turn on the taps.

Sylvia didn't linger in the bathroom. She didn't believe the tale of Mrs Jennings and her leave-takings: it was just a convenient excuse to be out of the way while her son delivered Sylvia's dismissal.

What a fool she'd been to blurt out to Max Bryson that she'd been in prison! If she'd remained silent.... Perhaps Lady Alice had not even told him? Did not intend to tell him? But she'd been foolish enough, in her overwrought state, to bring it out into the open, where it was impossible to ignore.

However tolerant Lady Alice might have been, her son was not. He was a lawyer; what was more, he was now working for the government, and would therefore be doubly eager to remain clear of scandal. Her foolish revelation had sounded a death knell to her hopes of a peaceful haven. Warm scented water and fluffy towels didn't have quite the same appeal when homelessness beckoned.

A visit to the sick-room left her even more guilt-laden. She used the telephone in the hall to say that she wouldn't be in to the office. Miss Prosser assumed her continuing absence was due to her mother's condition, and Sylvia didn't disillusion her. There was little point now in handing in her notice at Clement's Court when she could expect at any moment to receive her own from Max Bryson. She just wished he would get on with it: waiting for the axe to fall was shredding her nerves.

She prowled about the house all morning, quite unable to appreciate the comforts of Ardingley House, knowing that any moment the bell would ring and she would be sent for.

But when midday came and Bryson had still not appeared, she decided she'd had enough. At the depot no one cared that she'd been in prison; they only knew that, with the constant flow of new recruits for France, they were desperately short of drivers. Boldly she rang the bell and told the parlourmaid she would not be in to lunch. Since Lady Alice did not require her services, she was going to the depot and didn't know what time she would be back.

She was too on edge to face the canteen and the likes of Barlow. She would have gone straight out to her lorry, but Gwen, about to go off duty, caught her in the locker room.

'You're looking better already. A companion! Just the thing for you, my girl. Why didn't I think of it before? Much better than working for that crabby old bitch Canning.'

'Actually I'm still - '

'Octavius was furious when he found you'd gone, but he has a new distraction. Cynthia Asquith turned up with some friends last night. Very striking - positively witch-like features. He's desperate to paint her.' She grabbed her hat and prepared to dash off. 'She's married to one of the Prime Minister's sons. Oc generally prefers them married - so much less demanding. Before long he'll have forgotten you were ever there.'

When Sylvia thought how close she'd come to disgracing herself with a man who could so swiftly forget her, she could only look at herself with renewed disgust.

An afternoon on the road, delivering supplies to Guy's Hospital, Bart's and some of the smaller nursing stations, cleared her head, but she hadn't the heart for the usual banter with the VADs who unloaded her lorry. Nerves began to assail her once more as she drove back in the dusk to the depot, and she was relieved to be caught for an evening duty, even though she was only postponing the inevitable.

She collected her quota of walking wounded from the Dover train, grateful that this vehicle was not equipped for stretchers: tonight she hadn't the strength to listen to their sufferings without giving way herself. However carefully you drove, stretcher cases, mangled and mutilated in the shelling and already badly shaken about as they were handed down from the trains, would scream and howl at the slightest bump or gradient, and it took a stiff resolve to drive them through the streets of London without breaking down yourself. Regular drivers got hardened, but part-timers like herself never became inured to it. Tonight it was all she could do not to burst into tears at the sight of her own batch of sitting cases, the halt, the lame and the blind, among them a boy no more than seventeen with a heavily bandaged stump halfway up his right arm. What hope would he have of a decent job back in civvy street with only one hand?

Pull yourself together, girl! If she started weeping tonight, who knew if she would ever stop? Briskly she began to direct the soldiers into the lorry, cramming them in on old boxes and temporary seats. As she cleared the steps to make way for a man leaning heavily on sticks, she felt an arm round her shoulders and bit off a curse. This was one of those nights when she was going to have trouble with the sitter.

A voice spoke in her ear, the northern accent so thick she had trouble making it out. 'C'mon, love. Take pity on a poor wounded hero. Gi' us a kiss.' It was the young boy who had lost half his arm.

'Aw, don't get mad with me, now, gel,' he said with a wicked grin in his dark eyes. 'Only they're all tellin' me no woman'll look at me wi' this. An' I just want to prove me native charms are still workin'!'

'I ought to box your ears!' she said, but his grin was infectious, and in spite of herself she found herself smiling back, even allowing him to land a peck on the cheek before she chivvied him up the steps.

'See, it's like I've always said,' said the young lad to his mates inside the lorry. 'It's not what you've got, it's what you do with it that counts!'

As she lifted the steps in and prepared to close the door, the young lad begged to be allowed to sit up front with her, but an older man, propped on crutches, told him not to stretch his luck. It was one of the jolliest lorry loads she'd ever driven, singing and cracking jokes the whole time in spite of their wounds. Probably one of the Pals Battalions that had gone out at the beginning of the war. The idea was that volunteer soldiers would fight better with their friends and neighbours around them, and they did, but if the Battalion was engaged in a heavy action, whole districts could be plunged into mourning in one day.

'Glad to be goin' home, we are, missus, I can tell you,' said the sitter, over the sound of a raucous song she hadn't heard before. 'They're all mad out there. All them young death or glory officers with no more'n five minutes experience atween them, barrin' the Officer Trainin' Corps at their posh schools. Wonder they didn't kill more of us than they have. An' them Frenchies! D'you know, we were posted to a little village not far from Plugstreet Wood - well, that weren't its real name, but it were the best we could make - and there was this train stuck in the station, last one out from Armentières before the fighting. Hell of a mess it was in, mud, rust and bullet holes, and we'd had all the sleepers off the track for our dugouts, so it weren't goin' anywhere...But listen to this, missus. Every mornin', sharp on seven, this Frenchie railwayman climbs through the debris and sits 'imself in the signal box! Hasn't been a train for months, but there he stays till six at night, rain or shine, even when there's fightin' all around.' He shifted in his seat, easing his injured leg. 'Eeh, they're a rum lot, these Frenchies. By 'eck, missus, I'm that glad to be back in Blighty again!'

When the first batch were dropped off in Whitechapel, he stuck his head out of the window and shouted out: 'Don't forget now, pals. Meet up again this day month, down at the Pier Head!'

29

It was late by the time she returned to Ardingley House. Lady Alice had already retired to bed. In an odd way Sylvia was disappointed that the whole day had gone by and nothing had been resolved. Now it was all to wait for over again.

Too restless to sleep, she decided to borrow a book from the amply stocked shelves in the drawing room. She was choosing between two volumes when Lizzie brought in a tray with a light supper on it. 'Lady Alice's orders, miss, and you're to eat it all. You didn't eat any lunch and I don't suppose they feed you at that transport place. The butler's locked up, so just turn the lights out after you. G'night.'

At the sight of the delicate sandwiches and the hot milky drink, Sylvia's stomach rumbled. She realised she hadn't eaten since breakfast. Curled up in the capacious velvet armchair, her feet tucked up under her in a way that would have brought her mother's censure down on her head, she sipped at the glass of warm Bengers and idly turned the pages. She'd just set aside Wilkie Collins' *Woman in White*, deciding that she was too much on edge to deal with ghostly figures materialising out of the darkness, when a soft footfall outside the room brought her head up with a jerk. The hairs stood up on the back of her neck: someone was turning the door-handle.

Relief at the sight of Max Bryson in the doorway made her rush into speech. 'Goodness, you startled me!' she gasped. 'I thought everyone was in bed. And I didn't hear the doorbell ring - oh, but of course, you wouldn't...'

Bryson tossed the door-key into the air, caught it deftly and pocketed it. 'I have my own key. I occasionally stay overnight if my mother's entertaining.'

Relief was replaced by consternation. For all her earlier desire for a swift resolution, she was now tired and fretful after her long duty. Really, the last person she wanted to see was Max Bryson. She'd almost rather the ghost.

'Lady Alice has retired, I'm afraid.' She scurried past him to the door, clutching at the brass handle as if it were the last lifebelt on a sinking ship.

'No matter.' He walked across to the fire. 'It was in the hope of seeing you, not my mother, that I called in.'

'Oh.' She tried to brace herself for the blow that was about to come, but her knees were almost giving way beneath her.

'For God's sake stop dithering in the doorway like a frightened virgin!' he snapped. 'Come in and close the door.'

'Close the door, Mr Nash. Turn the key...'

Max was appalled to see the blood drain from her face. 'My apologies. That was uncalled for.' He dragged his gaze away from her, focussing on the glowing coals in the hearth. It had been a long day and a gloomy one, with bleak news of the Dardanelles landings. Everyone was in a black mood, but it wasn't fair to vent his ill-temper on her. 'Come on, Sylvia. Sit down before you drop.'

Sylvia fought back the sickness that pressed at the back of her throat. She took a deep breath and pulled herself together: they were in his mother's house and she was not a fluttering debutante but a woman of nigh on thirty. And justice forced her to add that he had never treated her in any but the most gentlemanly fashion. 'Very well.' Head up she crossed to the fireside. 'But only if you sit down too.'

He arched his eyebrows. 'Perhaps I prefer to stand.'

'As I'm forbidden to ask if your injury is troubling you, I'll assume you said that only to be obstinate,' she said, with a brief return of spirit. 'Actually, I'd like you to sit down because you're giving me a crick in the neck.'

Bryson's lips twitched, but he did sit down.

The rush of energy deserted Sylvia as swiftly as it had come. She looked up from contemplation of her hands to find his eyes fixed on her. Normally they were grey and rather cool, but tonight they reflected something of the glow of the dying coals. When he showed no sign of speaking, she drew the last shreds of her dignity about her.

'I - I know why you've come here this evening. As we appear to have run out of the usual civilities, I'd rather you came straight out and dismissed me.'

'What?' He stared at her, his brow furrowed. 'Hiring and firing are not in my realm here. My mother employs her own staff; nothing to do with me.' Absent-mindedly, he helped himself to a sandwich from the tray.

'I'm sure she listens to your advice. And I know you wish me gone.'

He choked on the sandwich. 'Why the devil would I wish you gone?'

'Because I've been in prison,' she said in a low voice. 'My only consolation is that I told your mother the truth before you could.'

'I knew nothing of your unorthodox activities until yesterday, when I found your badge of defiance on my mother's dressing table. Here, you'd better have it back.' He fished in his waistcoat pocket and placed the arrow-headed badge with the purple, green and white ribbons on the table in front of her. *'Prison.'* He almost spat out the word. 'How could you do something so stupid?'

Her hand crept to the side of her mouth. 'I don't want to talk about it,' she said in a small voice.

'Don't go all girlish on me, Miss Shaw. It doesn't suit you. Answer my question.'

She pressed her hands to her temples. 'Let me understand you, Mr Bryson,' she said carefully. 'I may not ask questions of you, but you may demand answers of me, even though I have already explained the - the matter - to Lady Alice's satisfaction.'

'Don't play games with me.'

'I wouldn't dream of it. With all your years of court experience...in comparison I am a mere amateur.'

'I want to hear the truth.'

'Part of my contract of employment?' Some obstinacy drove her not to give in without a fight.

He crossed to the sideboard and poured himself a large brandy. 'I have already explained that I am not your employer. But I am naturally concerned about - '

' - about my suitability for the post? I'm a very careful driver. If you would care to go for a spin with me...?'

'Damn your driving! Miss Shaw, I ask you again: how did you come to be in prison? You belonged to the moderate Suffragists - you always insisted you weren't militant.'

'I've always opposed violence! But sometimes the innocent get swept up too. The judicial system is not always willing to differentiate. And that's what happened to me.' She stiffened at the cynical look on his face. 'I daresay that's a tale you hear too often in court.'

'You dropped from sight in May of '14, as I remember.' His voice grew harsher. 'Last May. Surely you weren't fool enough to get involved in the march on Buckingham Palace?'

'The march *to* Buckingham Palace - don't abuse the language. We were hardly armed with pitchforks and flaming torches! We were a crocodile of defenceless women armed only with a petition.'

'The march had been banned.'

'Well, it damned well shouldn't have been! We had every right to petition the King to stop forcible feeding. It's in Magna Carta!' She could feel the warm sunshine on her face, hear the howling of the crowd, the drumming of heavy police boots. 'It was a *peaceful* march,' she said brokenly. 'All we wanted was to hand in our petition at the Palace gates, make a few speeches in Hyde Park, and go home...'

'But they only arrested those who showed violence...'

'*No one* showed violence until the police blocked our way. They said Mrs Pankhurst had been arrested and carried off. I didn't know till then that she was even there. The marchers refused to disperse...we were at the back and we couldn't see what was happening. Suddenly the bystanders were milling around among us, trying to break up the procession...' She had a brief, vivid memory of the burly shopkeeper who'd shouldered his way into the procession and smacked her across the face, of the two younger men who followed him in and grabbed her around the waist, dragging her back towards the park, groping at her breasts, leering in her face...In ten months she hadn't faced that moment, blocking it out with the greater horror which had come later. 'They manhandled us. Mauled us about...' She shuddered. 'It was horrible ...horrible... More than a thousand police and they didn't lift a finger to protect us. So some of us protected ourselves.'

'Including you?'

'I bit one man who was mauling me about, but it tasted so horrible, I knew I couldn't do it again. So I doubled up my fist, like Freddie had showed me, and just struck out.' She demonstrated to him, the thumb tucked firmly inside her fingers. 'I think it was father's ring that did it: I never intended to break the shopkeeper's nose.'

'You broke a man's *nose*?'

She turned the gold signet ring on her right hand. 'I was entitled to defend myself,' she said hotly. 'He shouldn't have molested me.'

'I'm sure he'll think twice about it another time.'

'Don't make mock of me.' Her voice shook and she blinked hard in a vain attempt to drive away the images that had been conjured up. If she dwelled too much on them she would fall apart again. 'It was perfectly terrifying. Imagine how you would have felt if it had been your wife or your daughter.'

'Thank God I have neither,' he said harshly. He crossed to the sideboard and poured out another brandy. 'Here. This will do you more good than that milky muck,' he said, wrapping her trembling hands around the glass. For a moment he held his hands cupped over hers, reacquainting himself with the springy curls on the top of her head and the way her downcast eyelashes lay against her pale cheek. He wished he could turn the clock back to the time in Wimbledon when he'd first come to know her. If it hadn't been for Esmond's death he might have told her...

Her hands were beginning to flutter beneath his like a captive bird and she lifted her eyes, wide and haunted. The room suddenly seemed unbearably warm. He dropped his hands and crossed to open the door. 'Go to bed, Miss Shaw,' he said softly. 'You're exhausted. We'll talk again another time.'

30

'I propose a little light shopping this morning,' said Lady Alice as they rose from the breakfast table. 'Lizzie tells me your wardrobe is somewhat reduced, and we have a busy few weeks ahead. There are several dinners next week, and a charity dinner for one of my funds at the end of the month. Oh, and a Saturday to Monday at Taplow Court. You must look your best for that. Ettie Desborough's guests are always in the highest style. Of course there's not the changing and parading there used to be ten years ago, when you needed four or five changes of dress in a day, but you will need a couple of evening gowns and for daytime something a little more fashionable - forgive me - than you are wearing at the moment.'

'But I am in no position to - '

'To buy new clothes? I don't expect you to. Naturally we shall put them all to my account.'

'But I couldn't allow you to - '

Lady Alice waved aside her objections. 'My dear Sylvia - I may call you that, may I not? - if you are to be my companion, and go into society, then you will need smart clothes. It is, if you like, the required uniform.'

'As I am to replace Mitchell, a peaked cap, leather boots and britches might be more appropriate,' said Sylvia, with the faintest tremor of laughter in her voice.

'I've no doubt you'd wear them too, just to shock everyone!' She patted Sylvia's hand. 'My dear, it *is* good to hear you laugh. I think it's been a long time since you did.'

In spite of Sylvia's protests the day passed in a whirl of measurings and fittings, as the chauffeur drove them from department store to ladies' boutique: Oxford Street for underwear, summer tweeds from Harrods, Selfridge's for everyday shoes and hats. There was even a sum of money advanced against her wages and she spent some on a tiny flask of perfume and another pot of La Rola.

They lunched at Selfridge's and Sylvia, remembering the fuss the butler and Max had made the previous day, made sure that any help she offered was unobtrusive. She read the menu in a low voice, making sure it carried to Lady Alice without drawing the attention of those at adjoining tables. She almost made the mistake of shaking out Lady Alice's napkin for her, but desisted in time, allowing the waitress to do it for them both - the usual German and Austrian waiters having long departed. As discreetly as she could she cut the meat from the bone, gave Lady Alice some indication as to where it was on the plate, placed her glass where she would be less likely to knock it over, then left her to it.

After lunch they purchased more shoes and hats and a handsome evening gown from tiny elegant boutiques in Bond Street. Each outfit had to be described to Lady Alice, who took a close interest in the designs, insisting that Sylvia could carry off the new, shorter style providing she had the proper hat and shoes for each outfit - 'though, I don't think, my dear, that black is quite your colour, whatever fashion may decree. I have the impression that your skin is far too pale and creamy. Navy, perhaps, or that exquisite dark coffee, would be much better. And a copy made up in a plainer material for daytime. Don't you think, Estelle?'

The modiste agreed, with no trace of condescension in her voice. 'Always had a good eye,' confided Estelle as she unpinned Sylvia in the dressing room. She tapped her forehead. 'And that's something you don't lose. Still there in her mind's eye, you see.'

'We'll have Rossiter's copy the coffee lace dress in a plainer material,' said Lady Alice as they returned to the house at the end of the day with a car full of hat-boxes, dress-boxes with ready-mades for everyday wear, and patterns and bolts of material. 'Thérèse will make the day dresses. We must arrange for her to come as soon as possible,' she went on, brushing aside Sylvia's stammered thanks. 'Perhaps you could telephone before you go on duty tonight. Annie will give you the number. Oh, and you'd better ask Annie for my diary: you can keep it for me in future and arrange your work at the depot around it. Then we'll know where we are.'

Annie hadn't shown the same enthusiasm for Sylvia's arrival as her mistress. Sylvia had greeted her that morning, but received only a curt nod of the head in return. The dresser would be none too pleased at having something as important as Lady Alice's diary taken out of her control: Sylvia decided to broach it another day, when she was feeling stronger.

With mixed feelings she surveyed the gowns Lizzie had spread out on the bed. It hardly seemed decent to care about fashion and country house weekends when men were dying in their thousands in the mud of Flanders. She went through to her sitting room and picked up a photograph of herself with Pip and Freddie, taken a few summers before. They'd been playing lawn tennis, and she was wearing a calf-length skirt and a V-necked 'pneumonia' blouse, as denounced from the pulpit. How her mother had hated that outfit!

Shopping expeditions with her mother had always started out in perfect amity, for they had a mutual delight in well-made, well-cut clothes, pleasing on the eye. They almost invariably ended in a furious row, usually over some silly detail. Sylvia's desire for an active life, however limited, always came up against her mother's insistence on the extremities of fashion: the tightest lacing, the droopiest of sleeves, the most restrictive of shoulders - whatever would reduce females to ornaments rather than living beings.

Their greatest conflict had been over hobble skirts. As women gained a little freedom, so it seemed that fashion and men colluded to imprison them. Just as young women freed themselves of tight lacing, and were enjoying the freedoms of lawn tennis, croquet - even bicycling! - fashion wanted to force them into hobbled skirts, restricting them to a pace of inches only. Well, not for Sylvia!

The arrival of Lizzie with a batch of hangers for the new purchases brought her back to the present. 'Be late for your evening duty if you don't get a shift on, Miss,' she said, popping her head around the door.

Sylvia looked up from the photograph and blinked. 'You're right. I had better get a shift on. Not to mention my boots and my trousers.'

'Culottes, miss.' Lizzie corrected her. 'And handsome you look in them too.'

Culottes, divided skirts, unmentionables, knickerbockers - so long as you never called them trousers. A pathetic conspiracy to pretend that young women weren't really wearing men's clothes, or that they weren't really doing what had always been men's work. Sylvia set the photo frame back on the cabinet, snatched up her khaki uniform and whirled into the bathroom.

31

Gwen Jameson looked up from her ledgers as the shadow fell across the pages.

'You again?' She looked up with the artist's appraising eye at the broad-shouldered man on the other side of her desk. 'Still looking for Miss Shaw? Shall I send one of the men for you to bribe? Or do you prefer to choose your own?'

Max's lips twitched. 'Unnecessary. I know her duty hours. She is currently staying with my mother.'

Gwen gulped. 'You're the Countess's son? Lord Ardingley?'

'Yes to the first. No to the next. Lord Ardingley is a golden-haired cherub of seven - no, eight years old.' He pushed his card across the table. 'Max Bryson, at your service, Miss Jameson. I wanted to thank you for having Miss Fletch- ' he stopped abruptly and cleared his throat ' - for having Miss Shaw as a house guest.'

'She was my house guest, was she?' Gwen was amused. 'I thought she and her mother were renting Fawley's rooms while he was in Scotland.'

'In a bachelor household? Oh no. Much better if she was your house guest.'

'Thus observing the conventions? How tedious.' She snapped the ledger closed. 'Sylvia Shaw is an honourable woman. There was nothing to cover up.' She put aside the memory of the day she'd found her friend in Octavius's sitting room, looking decidedly flushed, with her blouse mis-buttoned. And then all that talk of muses... 'In my world a woman's honour is assumed safe until otherwise informed. But in your circles....'

'I don't think our circles are so different.'

'But there's always gossip if you have Bohemian friends?'

'Quite so. And I prefer to deal with problems before they arise.'

'Problems for you or for Sylvia?'

'One and the same now she's working for my mother.'

Gwen set the ledger back on the shelf behind the desk. 'I hope you're not planning to take her away. She's one of our best drivers.'

'Is she?'

Gwen detected a note of cynicism, but decided to ignore it. 'Oh yes. Very popular with the wounded heroes.'

'Terms of employment are between her and the Countess - nothing to do with me.' He raised his hat. 'Good afternoon to you, Miss Jameson.'

'Good afternoon, Mr Bryson. My regards to your mother.' The bell rang deep in the warehouse, and Gwen excused herself. As soon as she was out of sight, Bryson turned and walked out into the yard.

32

Sylvia hummed softly as she stepped out onto the cobbles. The sun was shining; she'd just redeemed her watch and the string of pearls her father had given her for her twenty-first birthday; she'd sent her notice in to Miss Canning and the world was looking a great deal rosier than it had for months.

'Your usual bus this afternoon,' said the chief mechanic, sticking his head out of the workshop as she punched her card. 'Tommy Simmons gave it a good run this morning, but take a spare can. Radiator needs topping up now and now.' He wiped his hands on an oily rag hanging from his back pocket. 'We'll have it in next week and take a good look at it.'

'Okey-dokey. And what joys do you have for me today?'

He ran a blackened finger down the duty roster hanging on a rusty hook. 'You're in luck - no convoys booked in. Albert had two cases of spotted fever last night. They're beginning to slip through the net over the Channel.'

'Rotten luck.' Cases of spotted fever and brain fever were sweeping through the new recruits out at the front almost as fast as the German hail of steel. They'd been told to look out for swollen eyelids among the sitting cases, but what man with a Blighty wound wouldn't have swollen eyelids? If they didn't weep from the pain, they wept from the relief of not having to go back to the front again.

'We've been disinfecting like fury. With luck you'll just get deliveries today. You're half-loaded up for Victoria. Pick up the rest from St Thomas's.' He handed her the paperwork. 'There's a run on to get supplies to the stations.' He disappeared briefly into the bowels of the workshop, then popped his head back out. 'By the way, you've got a passenger today.'

'Inspection?'

He grinned. 'Something like.'

'Drat!' she muttered. Well, whoever he was, he needn't think she was going to duplicate all her checks if the mechanics had already done it.

There was no sign of anyone when she reached her lorry. That didn't mean she wasn't under observation. Apart from the cleaners in heavy rubber overalls and the dispatch riders in leather gauntlets, there were half a dozen men standing around the yard. It wouldn't do any harm to cast a quick eye over the radiator.

She'd just screwed the cap back on when she heard footsteps behind her. She carried on whistling the latest music hall tune as she folded the bonnet down and latched it.

'Good day to you, Miss Shaw.'

She whirled around. 'What the devil are you doing here?'

'And good afternoon to you too, Miss Shaw,' said Max Bryson. 'I am waiting to drive with you.'

'You mean - you're here to examine me?' she demanded indignantly. 'What right have you - if Lady Alice is happy?'

He raised his eyebrow. 'But she hasn't seen you drive yet.'

'And you're worried that I could wreck your expensive car?'

'It's not my car. I'm merely concerned about my mother's safety. After all, the last time I saw you, you almost ran me down.'

'That was *entirely* your fault! Popping up out of nowhere like the Demon King at the pantomime...!'

'We can stand here for another half hour arguing the matter if you like.' She followed his amused glance. Drawn by the raised voices, the men had stopped their scrubbing and polishing and were listening in hope of more fireworks.

She bit her tongue on a sarcastic response and climbed into the driving seat. She averted her eyes while Bryson made his laborious way up into the lorry, wincing as he collapsed on the passenger seat. Somehow it seemed indecent to see a strong man forced to display his weakness.

'Does your mother's car have a starting handle?' she asked. Although she was growing stronger by the day, turning an engine over manually was still beyond her.

'Self starter. Nothing but the best. Ma drove herself as long as she could. In fact she taught Mitchell to drive - he was the groom, but our old coachman hated automobiles. She taught Imogen to drive too.'

'Your fiancée?'

Settling back and straightening his leg out, he shot her a sideways glance. 'Now, why should you think that?'

'You said you had neither wife nor daughter.'

'Imogen is my sister-in-law.' He rolled his eyes. 'A terrible driver. Ma always said it took a week to recover from a drive with Imogen. I want to be sure you don't drive like her.'

'She doesn't live in London?' asked Sylvia, releasing the brake.

'Concentrate on your driving. Where are we going today?'

'Victoria.' She squinted down at the papers. 'Collecting field dressings from St Thomas's on the way.'

She manoeuvred the lorry out onto the road without crashing the gears, but she was not best pleased to see that the traffic was heavy; the unavoidable delays would give her companion too much time to cross-examine her.

Sure enough, when they were forced to a halt, after a few innocuous comments about the weather and the traffic, he began. First he asked her about her work at the depot and then, undeterred by her curt answers, he moved on to the personal. 'Nurse Armitage is keeping me up to date with your mother's progress. She tells me she's been taking out her megrims on you.'

'I can cope. Like most women I've had a great deal of practice in biting my tongue.'

'You shouldn't have to.'

She shrugged. 'People often get odd obsessions as they get ill. And I've always been a disappointment to her.'

'Surely not.'

'I failed to fit her role of obedient daughter. The nearest I came was when I was engaged to Hugh. And I even fouled that up.'

'The breaking off was not of your doing. And now that she only has you - '

' - we'll grow closer? Hasn't worked out that way.' She moved the lorry out into the traffic on the Embankment. 'Her memories grow more golden each day that passes.' She grimaced. 'Sometimes I wonder who these strange and perfect boys were. Since they died, Freddie and Pip have become paragons of virtue I can scarcely recognise, while I am the repository of all vices, primarily ingratitude.'

'You know it's not true.'

'It's still hard to ignore. She's convinced herself that if I'd married Hugh, Freddie could have stayed at Oxford. Then he wouldn't have been so eager to go off to war.'

'Possibly even more eager, as I remember Freddie! Anyway, for you to marry Hugh, your family would have had to drop Pip's case. His uncle insisted on it.'

'Mother felt - still feels - that I should have persuaded father to drop it.'

'If anyone could have done it you could have.'

She recalled how her father had grilled her and drilled her each evening on his return from the bank, revelling in her quick mind and encouraging her learning. Freddie had loved life too much to fulfil the academic goals father had set for him, but she'd been happy to please him, and grateful too, particularly when friends had been removed from school and sent to Young Ladies' Academies to be 'finished'. Now, since his death, she could see how he had relied on her, with the boys away at school, to provide the intellectual companionship he didn't get from his wife.

'You were always his favourite,' said Max.

'Was I?'

'It seemed so to me. He loved you very much.'

'Not enough to let me go. He sent Freddie to university, who didn't care tuppence for studying, but he wouldn't let *me* go.' To her annoyance she felt the tears well up, even after so long. Angrily she brushed them away. Out of the corner of her eye she saw his hand move. 'I warn you now,' she snapped, 'touch this steering wheel and you get out and walk!'

'Wouldn't dream of it,' he said imperturbably. 'I thought you might need this.'

Flicking her eyes to the left she took the proffered handkerchief. 'Sorry.' She mopped her eyes one at a time, keeping a firm grip on the wheel and her eyes sharp. Unsure whether to offer it back - especially as the powder with which she darkened her eyelashes had run - she dropped it on the seat.

At last the traffic began to move again. As they approached the bridge she stamped on the clutch and changed down the gears, skilfully steering around a policeman, two angry draymen and a large horse-drawn dray, part of whose load had slipped onto the pavement.

'Don't you find that difficult?'

'What? Double declutching?' She straightened up the wheel. 'At first, of course, when Freddie was teaching me, but no more than anyone else. After all, men aren't born with double-declutching ankles, are they?'

'Pax, Miss Shaw! Pax! I wasn't implying any superiority.'

She was overreacting. Why did he always have this effect on her?

'You should see the number of sitters who automatically brake every time they see an obstacle ahead. They wouldn't do that with a male driver.'

When they arrived at St Thomas's, the watchman directed them to the stores, where she reversed the lorry neatly up to the doors. They waited a few moments, but no one came to help her with the loading.

Max looked on in helpless frustration as she struggled with the unwieldy boxes. 'Surely you're not expected to do this all by yourself?'

'I can usually find a couple of VAD girls to help me, but they must be short today.'

A group of medical students lounged out of a nearby building for a quiet smoke. Before they could light up, Bryson limped around the lorry and called them over to assist.

'It's not necessary,' Sylvia protested.

'Of course it's necessary,' he said. The students, impressed by his air of authority, put away their cigarette cases and hurried to her aid. 'They'll have far heavier work than this to do when they go to the Front. Isn't that so, gentlemen?'

He propped his shoulders against the door, watching as they loaded the packs of field dressings. Briefly, Sylvia was caught between them in the back of the lorry as she organised the remaining space. One of them made an innocuous remark to her and to Bryson's astonishment she went perfectly white and almost cringed away from him. Had he not been within earshot, he might easily have leaped to the wrong conclusion.

'Why were you so unwilling to accept their assistance?' he asked, as she drove out of the hospital yard and turned the lorry towards Victoria.

She had her voice back under control, but only just. 'I manage perfectly well with the VADs,' she said huskily. 'Medical students are so arrogant - in training to play God and they know it.'

Intrigued, he waited to see whether she would say any more, but she fell silent, only the slightest trembling of her hands on the steering wheel betraying her.

'If you would drop me off at the bottom of Whitehall?' She resisted the temptation to ask whether she'd reached the required standard. 'At the moment I spend more time working for Government than in my chambers,'

'Which do you enjoy most?' she asked, intrigued.

'Oh, the government work, without a doubt.'

'Don't you miss the intellectual challenge of your cases?'

'Working with Lloyd George brings more challenges each day than most people can cope with,' he said, as he opened the door and reached for his stick.

'You'll stay with him then?'

'For as long as he requires my services. Although working for the government is not quite as lucrative as my legal work.'

She was faintly shocked. After all, he didn't exactly live in poor circumstances. Before she could pass comment, he tipped his hat and slammed the door. With a puzzled frown she signalled and turned the lorry back into the traffic.

33

She must have met Max Bryson's exacting standards, for the following morning Mitchell took her out for a spin in Lady Alice's wonderfully elegant motorcar, pointing out its little idiosyncracies, and watching with critical approval as she took a turn behind the wheel. Then he handed Sylvia the keys and left for Gloucestershire, to take leave of his family before heading for training camp. From now on Sylvia would take over the car, with assistance when necessary from the mechanic in the adjacent mews.

She quickly fell into the rhythm of her dual life, one day taking tea in an elegant drawing-room with Margot Asquith, the Prime Minister's wife, or Lady Astor, the American heiress, the next driving her lorry from depot to railway station or around the back streets of London.

She loved the variety: at least she was never bored. Lady Alice treated her like a slightly wayward niece, and when it was seen that she knew how to hold her cup and keep up the conversation, she was accepted in polite society. After all, she overheard someone say, Alice has always had the oddest notions.

Cabbage stew or delicate pastries; khaki uniform or fashionable dresses; Sylvia thrived on it all and some of the colour returned to her cheeks. She hoped that Imogen, the daughter-in-law never mentioned by Lady Alice, would not hurry back too swiftly from wherever she had gone.

34

Sylvia enjoyed the Lanchester for a very short period. She drove it for the third and last time to take Lady Alice to one of her committee meetings. The spring sunshine was bright as they drove through the drab streets of east London, so much quieter now than in the spring of 1914, when Sylvia and her mother had briefly lodged nearby. Women from the tenements were working in the nearby munitions factories - much better paid than charring - and so many dockers had enlisted in the early months of the war that all but the most broken-down men could get some work now.

Mitchell's directions were easy to follow. She stopped the shining motorcar between a run-down vicarage and an ugly red brick church. Two scruffy urchins who ought to have been in school emerged from the alleyway and stood open-mouthed at the sight of such splendour. Sylvia was about to offer them a few pennies to keep an eye on the motor when a spindle-legged clergyman in rusty black opened the gates, bidding Sylvia drive in immediately, for fear 'those nasty slum children' might put their dirty hands on her Ladyship's vehicle.

Sylvia did as she was bid. The elegant car, shortly to be commandeered for a staff car in Belgium, would be a rare sight in this neighbourhood. She took an instant dislike to the clergyman, mentally dubbing him Uriah Heep as he bowed and scraped before Lady Alice. Heaven help any charity cases who were reliant on him for succour: the more someone fawned over a title, the less sympathy they were likely to have, in her experience, for those in real need.

A second clergyman hurried to greet them in the hall. Reverend Harding was as short and stout as his fellow was tall and skinny; the pair reminded her irresistibly of a musical hall comedy turn she and Freddie had once seen at the Alhambra.

They were ushered along a gloomy corridor, into a large room decorated with flock wallpaper which might once have been red, but which a generation of London soot had now turned almost black. The windows were draped in dark crimson velvet which had also seen better days. Even the trees outside seemed to droop, on a day when the rest of London was bright and breezy.

The other occupants of the room, however, more than compensated, four of the chairs being taken by ladies in competition for the wearer of the most tasteless hat. The winner was undoubtedly the stoutest of the four. She had a dead fox with bright glass eyes slung around her neck, and her improbably black curls were topped with a bright green hat as big as a dinner-plate, from which descended every kind of artificial fruit and flower known to the milliner's art. The picture was completed by an enthusiastic application of pink face powder, topped by two bruises of purplish rouge to match the tiny cupid's bow drawn in above a tier of wobbling chins.

Lady Alice introduced Sylvia to the committee, smoothing down those who expressed concern lest Sylvia use a vote to which she was not entitled. It would, asserted a small woman shrilly, unbalance the entire structure of the committee.

Sylvia prudently withdrew her chair out of the main circle and sat in a corner, pen poised over her notebook, while she waited for the committee to come to order. This was familiar territory to her: her mother's only activity for as long as she could remember had been to host the monthly bridge club committee. Not that mother had ever had much to say at the meetings - her high spot had been to provide the best teas, although compliments in that quarter should by rights have gone to Cook. Then Sylvia herself had spent some years on one of the NUWSS committees, helping to preserve its reputation for moderation, sound arguments and no violence - until her own reputation had been reduced to tatters with the assault charges.

The last two members, a young man on a bicycle and the harassed chairman, hung about with mayoral chains of office, finally arrived and the committee was declared in session. It took an age to get through the minutes of the previous meeting. Decisions already taken were considered to be open to further discussion, with several of the women and the scraggy clergyman insisting on having their say over again - and at some length. There was a spirited attempt to have names taken off the charity list on the grounds that someone had heard that the women in question had been seen in company with sailors, or in a public house. The chairman, whose air of mayoral *gravitas* was deceptive, was quite unable to keep the meeting in order and discussion raged on all sides, often without any reference to the chair.

Lady Alice, when she spoke, was both compassionate and to the point. So was the young man, though his opinions seemed to count for less with the others. He was at the meeting in his capacity as a Poor Law Guardian, but in his lapel he wore the badge of the No-

Conscription Fellowship, which made him something of a moral leper in time of war.

Matters became even more longwinded once the main agenda was reached. The two clergymen had an intimate acquaintance with every last dot and comma of Poor Law and Army Council regulations, and quoted them at length, leaving the bewhiskered chairman floundering. Sylvia, sitting in the corner struggling to take notes, began to despair of ever getting to her evening duty.

At four o'clock the meeting at last showed signs of running out of steam - until someone mentioned the young women employed at the local munitions factory, whose behaviour proved a rich source of lament.

'Don't tell me all their show and fancy feathers are paid for by factory wages!' said one woman darkly. 'It's what they're doing away from the factory that lines their pockets and puts fur coats on their backs.'

'I've yet to see a munitions girl in a fur coat!' protested the young man. 'And if they *are* decently paid, it's because they do unpleasant work in dangerous surroundings.'

'Frequenting taverns and dance halls,' muttered Uriah Heep, wringing his hands.

When the woman with the dead fox started talking about 'bedizened hussies' and 'painted harlots', Sylvia could hardly keep a straight face. Catching the glint in the young man's eye, she almost disgraced herself. Averting her eyes swiftly, she turned a scornful laugh into a cough. Mrs Dead Fox eyed her askance for the rest of the afternoon.

When the clock struck the half hour, an undersized skivvy struggled up the stairs with the tea tray. Sylvia handed round teacups and plates, and while the more loquacious members were distracted, the chairman quickly wound up the meeting

The young man came to the sideboard to help, but only succeeding in getting under Sylvia's feet until she gave him a cup and plate and sent him to look after Lady Alice.

A few minutes later, while Lady Alice was in deep conversation with the chairman, he came for his own tea. 'Mark Doncaster,' he said with a smile. 'I believe we've already met.'

She looked at him, eyes narrowed. He did look vaguely familiar.

'May '14. At Marble Arch.' He dropped his voice. 'Only then you answered to the name of Charlotte Corday.'

35

The discovery that the police had a small station and charge room within the Marble Arch itself had been only one of the surprises of that awful day last May. Marched in handcuffs from Constitution Hill, she'd been charged with assault. Only the intervention of the young man, insisting she had acted in self defence, had saved her from worse charges.

Now he turned as pink as she was pale. 'I beg pardon. I shouldn't have mentioned it in company.'

'I'm glad you did. I never had a chance to thank you.'

'I don't know that I did much good,' he said gloomily, keeping his voice low. 'I wanted to testify on your behalf, but I didn't twig about the name at the station. Only found out later that every woman arrested that day had given the name of Charlotte Corday.'

It had seemed such a good idea while they were waiting to be charged. If she'd known then what was in store for her, would she have followed the older suffragettes' suggestions so blithely?

At last the committee broke up, and the harassed maid scurried round with furs, wraps and walking sticks. Mr Doncaster held Sylvia's hand a little longer than was proper and said how much he looked forward to meeting her again. The Chairman, bowing to Lady Alice, made a ponderous speech about Miss Shaw's delightful presence enabling the Committee to retain the services of their best worker. From the vicinity of the dead fox came an audible sniff.

They were driving out of the gates, with the Mayor and Uriah Heep still bowing and scraping, when a woman with a shawl around her head stepped out in front of the car. Sylvia slammed on the brakes and shot an arm out to stop Lady Alice hitting the windscreen, swearing under her breath as the car stalled.

'I'm sorry, missus. Didn't mean t'startle you.' The shawl fell away to reveal a young woman with a haggard face, pale at her own temerity, but determined to stand her ground. 'I just wanted to ask you - beg you - to put me on the list. See, I got a baby to feed and I can't get a separation allowance...'

'Certainly not!' Uriah Heep bustled round the long bonnet of the car to confront the woman. 'You're not married.'

'We would ha' been if it hadn't been for the war! He didn't leave me like this on purpose! He's a good man, Jacob is. If he'd known about the baby before he enlisted...'

'That's hardly the point.' He tried to stop Lady Alice getting out of the car, but she put him aside with one gloved hand. With a few brisk questions - and a sharp 'If you please, sir!' when the clergyman tried to interrupt - she soon had the woman's story from her.

It was a familiar tale. The woman was from Bedfordshire, walking out with a young man who'd been among the first to rush to the colours on the outbreak of war, unaware that she was pregnant. 'I dunno know what to do, missus. I lost me work, so I come down here to me brother's house. Now Jake don't know where I am, and I don't know where he is. Me brother was a sailor, enlisted. He made me an allocation of his wages, but his ship went down off Malta.' She wrung her hands. 'Truly, missus, I dunno where to turn.'

'An unmarried mother!' said Harding. 'How dare you expect - '

'Nonsense!' said Lady Alice coolly. 'If she lived in Scotland she'd be considered a wife by usage and custom, with all the rights that entails. I fail to see the difference.'

'Don't be deceived, ma'am,' he said in sepulchral tones. 'She only wants money to spend on beer and porter!' He turned on the woman. 'I saw you coming out of the King's Arms!'

'Once I been in there. And that was months ago,' said the woman tiredly. 'Landlord gave me some cleanin' work when his missus was took poorly. My neighbour, Mabel, she looked after the baby for me while I done the cleanin', but Mabel, she's in munitions now. Beer and porter? Hah!' Her voice grew shriller. 'I don't even have tea to offer me neighbour a cup. As much as I can do to manage milk for the baby!'

'Give Miss Shaw your directions, and I promise to see what I can do,' said Lady Alice. She turned to tell Sylvia to slip the woman some money to be going on with.

But Sylvia already had her purse in her hand.

36

Taplow Court, where they travelled on the following Saturday, could not have been a greater contrast. 'It will be much quieter than usual,' said Lady Alice as the chauffeur drove them and their trunks from Taplow station to the Gothic Tudor redbrick pile of Taplow Court, after a train journey expedited by female ticket collectors, guards and even women railway porters, who swung the cases and trunks on to the train with surprising ease, as if they'd been doing it all their lives. 'Ettie used to give the most lavish of entertainments, but no one wants to be seen to be ostentatious now that there's a war on.'

If this was modest, Sylvia could only wonder what it must have been like before. Lady Alice had closed up half of Ardingley House and hadn't replaced those servants who had left for the front or the factories, but here there seemed to be no shortage. A stately butler and numerous footmen lined the steps and when they stepped into the mediaeval-style hall a good half dozen maids could be seen scurrying across the open upper corridors.

Lady Desborough floated towards them on a cloud of white tulle and heavy lace. 'Alice, my dearest!' she said, enveloping her guest in a hearty embrace. 'It's been so-o long. Fa-ar too long.' She had a mannered mode of speech, drawing out each syllable to about twice its customary length.

She turned to Sylvia and took her hand. 'Wwwelcome to Ttttaplow,' she said, dwelling on the first consonant as if she had a stammer. She had an annoying habit of sweeping her eyelashes down as she spoke, which made it difficult to gauge how genuine was her welcome.

The housekeeper conducted them to a suite of rooms where their leather-bound Saratoga trunks - irreverently known as Noah's Arks to servants and railway porters alike - were being unpacked and the contents shaken out and pressed. Lizzie, who had accompanied them in place of Annie, who was in bed with a heavy cold, flitted from trunk to wardrobe, taking every opportunity to drop 'the Countess' into her conversation with the Taplow maid who was helping her. Sylvia settled Lady Alice into her room, trying as far as possible to mirror the arrangement at Ardingley House, to avoid confusion. Back in her own room she looked around her in some bemusement: she still found it hard to believe that she had sufficient clothes to fill even a small suitcase.

The room she'd been given was light and airy, somewhat smaller, naturally, than Lady Alice's, with windows that looked down from the back of the house across a flower garden and a handsome walk of trees to the silvered waters of the Thames. On the far bank were a few cottages and to her extreme right she could just see the edge of a larger building, something like a mill. While she changed out of her travelling clothes into her new navy-trimmed tunic dress with the sashed dropped waist, she tried to recall the little she had been told about her hosts.

The Grenfells - Lord and Lady Desborough - shared their time between Taplow Court, an even more splendid house, Panshanger, in Hertfordshire, and their London house.

'Ettie's one of the great hostesses,' Lady Alice had said. 'She's an heiress several times over, the last of a number of old family lines. She and Margot Asquith and the other Tennant sisters, Balfour, the former Prime Minister, and Curzon, the former Viceroy of India, were leaders of society at the end of the last century. Called themselves the Souls - you'll soon see why. Ettie was very fond of Ardingley - rather took him under her wing when his first wife died - and so I've visited occasionally ever since. Ettie and Willie have five children - a girl and a boy still in the schoolroom. Monica's gone for a VAD nurse. There are two older boys.' It was more than Lady Alice had had to say since Sylvia had arrived, but by the way she folded her lips, Sylvia felt she rather disapproved of the boys. 'Julian's at the front and Billy's hoping to go out soon.'

'And Lord Desborough?'

'Oh, we won't see much of Willie. Prefers sporting men to society gossip. He's quite shy, really, which must be hard, being married to someone like Ettie. Ardingley used to play tennis with him on a special indoor court he had built here. Sphairistik, or some such name. It was a combination of real tennis and lawn tennis - all the rage twenty years ago. Charlotte, my step-daughter, started to play to please her father, and she was an absolute whiz at it.'

At lunch Sylvia was introduced to a confusing collection of people: elderly statesmen whose names had shone some twenty years before; young men on leave from the front; their unenlisted friends, busily, sometimes enviously, quizzing them about their experiences, and a trio of handsome young women surprised to find a companion of unknown family in their midst.

The conversation was a perfect mish-mash; one moment someone was talking about the latest style in hats and teasing Lady Cynthia over her friendship with 'that scruffy little writer Lawrence', the next Ettie was eulogising the nobility of those who had died in the war and the necessity of those at home doing their patriotic duty by going on as though nothing had happened. Listening to them hold forth on the glory of sacrifice, Sylvia doubted whether any of them had suffered the loss of anyone close. She bit her tongue and confined her attentions to Lady Alice.

The afternoon was spent down by the river, in enforced company with the younger members, Lady Desborough having taken Lady Alice off to her boudoir for a cosy chat, leaving Sylvia feeling rather as though she had lost her anchor. Her hostess, who liked to organise every minute of everyone's day, would not hear of Sylvia retiring, even sending a maid for a wrap, to make sure Sylvia didn't slip upstairs unnoticed.

Thrown in among the various Grenfells, Asquiths and Manners, Sylvia felt totally out of place. Although they ranged from late teens to early thirties, they'd all known each other since the nursery, growing up with the easy knowledge that they were the sons and daughters of titles and great estates. She'd mixed easily in society when she'd been engaged to Hugh, but too much had happened to her since then; she was no longer that bright-eyed and optimistic young bride-to-be, and such ease seemed hard to recapture.

'Do your family live in London?' was the first question, not surprisingly from Cynthia Asquith, the Prime Minister's daughter-in-law. Underlying the words, Sylvia knew, was the question: Who *are* your family?

She gave a casual answer: quiet family...lived in retirement...invalid mother. No, she wasn't related to Lady Cynthia's dear friend Patrick Stewart-Shaw.

'Then you must be related to Lady Alice....' said Venetia Stanley, daughter of Baron Sheffield.

'No.' Sylvia reverted to the half-truth that she and her employer had settled on to avoid becoming a seven days' wonder with the inquisitive. 'My father knew her son, Mr Bryson - ' Well, that much was certainly true! 'Hearing of my father's death, Lady Alice invited me to live with her.'

'So you know Max?' cooed Lady Cynthia. 'Isn't he an absolute darling?' With difficulty Sylvia stopped her eyebrows raising. *Darling* was one of the last words she would have applied to Max Bryson! 'Do tell!' went on her inquisitor. 'Will he be joining us this weekend? I do so long to see him again...'

Someone suggested Cynthia was looking forward to a 'dentist' with Max Bryson and there were chuckles all round. They often fell into a private language which shut out newcomers, chatting incessantly of *floaters* and *dentists* and *dewdrops*. Sylvia had no idea what they were talking about, and she was damned if she was going to ask.

The two young men lounging at Lady Cynthia's feet lost interest in Sylvia and started to flirt outrageously with Cynthia - even though she was a married woman with a husband gone off to war. It was an education to watch Lady Cynthia play her admirers off, one against the other, even if such blatant flirtation had never attracted Sylvia. If you loved someone, what was the point in making them jealous, or trying to hurt them? She liked to think Hugh would have been a fortunate man if he'd married her - but perhaps he would have grown bored with her and thought her loyalty old-fashioned and bourgeois.

As she watched the others flirting, or fooling around on the riverbank, splashing water over each other, she felt much like a governess, so bored was she by their childish behaviour. Would she have felt that way last year? she wondered. Probably not. But so much that was of greater significance had happened to her since then.

She'd brought Jane Austen's *Persuasion* with her, but spring was coming reluctantly this year and the sunshine was intermittent. It was really too cool to sit and read. Her attention wavered and at last she closed the book and made a pretence of watching the ducks and moorhens on the river. When Billy began to bully his young sister, threatening to throw her in the water, so noisily that he scared the wildfowl away, she had to suppress a desire to tell him to behave himself.

Instead she set out to walk along the riverbank. She hadn't gone far when a young man from the Foreign Office, with a soft little moustache and softer face, caught up with her. He'd arrived midway through the afternoon and had instantly thrown himself at the feet of Diana Manners. As he knew his way around the grounds Sylvia was content to have his company, to admire the views from the rise on which the house was built, across the silver snake of the Thames to the soft green hills beyond, and to listen to his stories about the ancient burial mound of Tapp's Tump, situated so inconveniently outside the dining room window. She chatted and smiled, but was careful not to give too much away: she was sure he'd been commissioned by the ladies to find out more about her.

Later that afternoon, reading the newspapers in a corner of the library, she was amused to overhear Cynthia Asquith cross-examining Mr Cooper, her erstwhile companion, as to what he'd found out. The open window overlooked a little arbour with a rustic seat and as the various members of the party returned from their excursions, she was the reluctant auditor of several flirtatious and teasing conversations as couples - married and unmarried - detached themselves from the group and disappeared into nooks and corners.

She gave up all hope of concentration and abandoned the newspapers. She was crossing the hall to dress for dinner when she met her host. There was no doubt it was Lord Desborough, for there were few men of six and a half feet, and his powerful frame, even as he approached sixty, revealed him as the renowned athlete who in his youth had rowed the Channel and twice swum Niagara Falls. He'd been described to her as an unsocial man, who kept well out of the way and only appeared at dinner, but he sat on a sofa with her, a warm smile on his face as they exchanged the usual courtesies.

'Understand you're off to see the children tomorrow afternoon,' he said gruffly. She looked puzzled. 'The children at Whitefields, don't you know. Give them these, would you?' He handed over a large paper bag of bullseyes and toffees. 'I know Alice don't like them to have too many sweets, but they're only children after all.' He patted her shoulder. 'Tell them Uncle Willie sends his love.' The big man shook his head and went away muttering *Poor Esmond* under his breath, leaving Sylvia perfectly bewildered.

37

Lizzie flitted from Sylvia to Lady Alice, drawing baths, laying out clothes and helping them to dress their hair, all the time bubbling over with excitement and nervousness at the thought of her own dinner later that evening in the servants' hall. As lady's maid to the Countess, she would be in the place of honour next to the butler.

Sylvia fastened the redeemed pearls around her throat and looked at herself critically in the long glass. Lizzie had swept her hair up in a new style which gave her a spurious elegance, but she still looked tired and there were tiny new lines at the corners of her eyes. Still, she had a splendid new evening dress to wear, with silky soft undergarments below. She ran her hands over the heavy coffee lace and shivered with the pleasure of wearing something so splendid after so long in shabby working clothes.

There would be more guests for dinner, driving over from a neighbouring house. Mr Balfour, the former Prime Minister, would be there, so Lizzie informed them in a thrilled whisper. Almost thirty people would sit to dinner in the splendour of Ettie's dining room.

Ushered into the salon, Sylvia found herself at a loss among so many strangers, unable to tell Lady Alice who was approaching because she didn't know most of them. Lord Desborough appeared, dwarfing most of those present; with a conspiratorial wink at Sylvia, he swept Lady Alice off on his arm 'to catch up with all the old friends who have been asking after you'.

She watched their progress for a moment and decided that she liked him better than his wife. For all his shyness and simplicity he had an instinctive awareness of when to help Lady Alice out and when not to, whispering names in her ear as a guest approached, and making sure she spoke to old friends and acquaintances.

A young man, handsome in his regimentals, exchanged a few words and then, as they moved on, turned to his sandy-haired companion. 'If Lady Alice is here, can Max be far behind?' he said. 'At least I'll get a good game of tennis.'

'You've been away too long, old fellow,' said his friend. 'So no one's told you?'

'Told me what?' He took a second glass from the passing footman.

'Max can't give you a game of tennis, now or ever again. He was blown up on a trip to the front. Shell landed almost on top of them.'

Sylvia almost tripped over her own feet. She contrived to eavesdrop under pretext of admiring a portrait.

'Dead?'

'Crippled. And all to save that ghastly little Welshman, Lloyd George.'

'Good God! Poor fellow. When he lived for his tennis and his motorcar-racing.' *Motor racing? Max Bryson?* She almost choked on her sherry.

Dinner was a formal affair, and the table glowed in the candlelight as course after course was brought in. Sylvia was painfully aware that she was unbalancing the table, not least because her hostess informed her at least three times, in front of different groups of guests, that she didn't *at all* mind putting the table awry to fit her in: there was *nothing* she would not do for dear Alice in her time of affliction. Consequently Sylvia was relieved to find that Lady Alice had been seated, not at her host's side, as might have been expected, but halfway down the table, where an extra seat had been slipped in. It meant they were less noticeable, and for that she was grateful, both on her own behalf and on her employer's. This, according to Lizzie, was the first time since the onset of her blindness that Lady Alice had attended a formal dinner and Sylvia would do her utmost to make everything go smoothly.

The soup course presented no problem and for the second course a footman served Lady Alice, as Sylvia had requested, with an already filleted fish, and contrived to do so without any fuss. Sylvia chatted easily to Mr Cooper on her left, while Lady Alice made polite conversation with a young man, newly commissioned and soon to depart for Gallipoli.

Much of the conversation to their left was about the war, but what the young men from the Foreign Office had to say, whether about the Dardanelles or the recent battle at Neuve Chapelle, bore little resemblance to what they read daily in the newspapers. To their right there was a spirited argument about the rival merits of Swinburne and Keats, and across the table another young man in army uniform was holding forth about the folly of current naval strategy. Further down the table an elderly general was explaining that it was imperative not to make the British trenches comfortable: how otherwise would men be persuaded to leave when orders came to advance?

While Sylvia was cutting up the entrée for Lady Alice, the talk turned to the question of women in munitions factories: some saw it as the beginning of the end of civilisation, while others saw it as the only solution. 'In Germany everyone serves in the reserves, so the whole nation is mobilised,' said a professor of English. 'They will undoubtedly be using female labour in the munitions industry: we can do no less.'

'There's such a fascination in manual labour,' said Lady Cynthia. 'I simply loved it.'

All eyes turned on her. 'I spent some time in a factory,' she simpered, when she was satisfied that she had everyone's attention. 'I was operating a machine, cutting up little bits of rubber.' She overrode the loud expressions of disbelief. 'I did. I promise you. Oh, it was such *fun* being a factory girl! And such a thrill to be doing piecework for money.'

It was Mr Cooper, at Sylvia's side, who inadvertently pricked the bubble. 'How long were you there?' he asked, wide-eyed and prepared to be impressed.

'Two *hours*.' She clutched her soft white hands to her bosom. 'My dear, I was *exhausted.*'

The wretched woman meant it perfectly seriously, and no one else appeared to see how ludicrous it was. Sylvia struggled to keep her face neutral: she'd like to see Lady Cynthia's elegant hands after she'd spent hours scrubbing a sickroom floor.

The party broke up after dinner, the older members clustering round the fire and reminiscing about better and happier times, when they had been at the forefront of the fashionable world. The younger guests formed into groups and started to play the kind of games that Sylvia had once played with her school-friends: for a while they played Clumps, although the answer to the twenty questions always seemed to be something obscure, like 'the last straw' or 'the eleventh hour'. Then they moved on to Character Sketches, in which the person - or victim - was described by the vegetable, building, colour, flower or even dish of which he or she might remind you. Sylvia hastily bowed out of the game on the grounds that she didn't know any of them well enough. When she looked up from *Persuasion* to hear someone being described variously as a toad or a dish of macaroni and cauliflower, she knew she'd made the right decision.

She might have been persuaded to join in a game of Riddles - for Lady Alice was on the far side of the room with Lord Desborough and Mr Balfour, all three deep in conversation - but no one asked her. Just as well: she was safer with Jane Austen.

She looked up after a chapter or two as the door opened. The guests were still huddled in groups, trying to guess the answer to the current riddle. Assuming that Lady Alice and Lord Desborough had returned Sylvia marked her page.

'We give up,' said one of the men. 'Why *is* Mrs Pankhurst like a she-bear?'

'Because one's a womanly bear - and the other's barely a woman.'

As the group dissolved in guffaws of laughter Sylvia closed her book with a snap. As she opened her mouth to speak, a hand fell on her shoulder.

'Not worth the effort,' said Max Bryson's voice in her ear. 'The foe is not worthy of your guns.'

She stiffened at the touch of his hand and her words were lost in a flurry of greetings. Just as well! Hard to imagine that she'd been about to leap to the defence of the power-hungry and egotistical Emmeline, who'd done so much damage to the cause.

Ettie sprang to her feet and with much gushing about 'Ettie's wounded hero', drew Max and his companion to join her on the sofa while the game took up again. For a moment Sylvia waited for a sarcastic comment from Bryson about neglecting Lady Alice, but none came. After a brief glance at Max's companion, a handsome man in his early forties, elegantly dressed, she buried herself once more in her book.

After the tea tray was brought in, cards were called for. Lady Alice was happily occupied at the far end of the room and Max was nowhere to be seen, and before she knew it Sylvia had been coerced into taking her place at a table. Unknown to her mother, Freddie had taught her to play poker and she was able to acquit herself with some credit. It was only after the first hand that she realised they were playing for real money.

She had to back out quickly. Lady Ardingley's absent daughter-in-law might return at any moment and put her out of a job. With her mother still to care for, it would be just as difficult to find paid work as it had been before. She had to save every penny she could from her generous wages and couldn't risk losing even a shilling at cards. As she threw in her hand she saw Lady Cynthia, who had been out of the room when the tables were formed, with a look of frustration on her hard face. Swiftly Sylvia offered up her place and Lady Cynthia took it as if by right.

'Always happy to play against Duff,' she drawled, patting the young man absently on the head as if he were a deserving puppy. 'It's a guaranteed way of supplementing my income.'

'You'll need it,' said another young man. 'There's no great future for you in industry, my darling.'

Lady Alice was still chatting with Mr Balfour and Lord Desborough - 'Never known Willie stay so long in company!' exclaimed one of the card players - so Sylvia picked up her book and was heading back to the sofa when Max and his friend joined her.

'Miss Shaw, I'd like you to meet a friend of mine,' said Max. 'Eddie Seymour. Another of Lloyd George's minions.'

'Delighted to make your acquaintance, Miss Shaw,' said Seymour. 'And I'll be even more delighted if Max is right for once...He seems to think you may be able to give me a game of billiards. He being of course too ancient and decrepit...'

A game of billiards appealed more than another hour in the drawing room. Sylvia said she could indeed give Mr Seymour a game. With jokes and smiles they adjourned to the billiards room, leaving instructions with the footman in case Lady Alice needed her.

'Close the door, Seymour,' said Max as he took the cues down from the wall.

'Close the door, Mr Nash. Turn the key...'

Her hand went to her mouth and she took an involuntary step away, heart pounding at the sound of the closing door. She saw Max Bryson looking at her through narrowed eyes and tried to steady her breathing, but when she took the cue her hands were shaking.

Bryson drew Seymour away to admire a painting. By the time they returned to the table she had herself in hand once more. After a swift covert glance at her, Max settled himself down on a leather bench against the wall. Stretching his leg out before him with a half-smothered groan he prepared to score.

It was an uneven game, for Sylvia hadn't played for a few years. Fortunately Seymour didn't take it at all seriously, allowing plenty of time for conversation. She found him very easy to talk to.

'I hope you'll forgive me for dragging you away from your friends,' he said, lining up a shot.

'Hardly that. I never met one of them before today, and shall be surprised if I meet any of them again.' And not in the least disappointed, she added silently.

Eddie Seymour left her with a difficult shot and she had to reach across the table to play it. As she balanced herself, one foot rose a little way off the floor and Max was mesmerised by the sight of her silk-clad ankle and a little more.

'Good shot, Miss Shaw!' said Seymour as the ball sped into the pocket. Max dragged his eyes from the unexpected vision and added her score to the marker-board.

'They are more likely to complain that we've taken you away from them,' said Sylvia, lining up the next shot. 'Lady Cynthia kept asking me whether *darling Max* planned to join his mother. Clearly a frequent and much-loved guest.'

She missed her second shot by a hair's breadth. 'Oh, bad luck!' said Seymour.

'Never more than once a year,' said Max, rising to chalk her cue. 'Just enough for the entertainment value. Any more frequently and I'd go mad and murder someone.'

'Surely they're right up your street. All so clever with words. Everything I say they leap upon it and twist it. They make people like me look - and feel - like fools.'

'Never confuse wit with intelligence,' said Seymour.

'Took the words out of my mouth,' Max agreed. 'Why, you've more brain than six of them put together.'

She raised her eyebrows. 'A blue stocking as well as a bourgeoise?'

'Fishing for compliments, Miss Shaw?' he said dryly. She coloured and fell silent. 'Don't be misled by their patrician air, either.' He handed her back her cue.

'Well,' said Seymour, 'Curzon and Balfour, of course...'

'Curzon rose to the heights as Viceroy of India,' agreed Bryson, 'but it was his American wife's fortune that restored his estates and grand houses. And Balfour *was* rich, though he's lost much of it with his absurd Patent Battery Company. The Asquiths have as much blue blood as me - which is to say, none at all - for all the airs they give themselves.'

'You're trying to put me at my ease, and it's kind of you both. But they might as well be speaking another language. Half the time I don't understand a word they're saying. I'm just not used to mixing with the daughters of Earls and Dukes.'

'Assuming they are,' said Seymour. 'Cynthia's probably Balfour's daughter, and no one believes either Diana or Letty Manners was fathered by the Duke of Rutland.'

She straightened up from the table. 'Heavens!'

Eddie Seymour grinned at her shocked expression. 'When the Souls weren't being soulful, they were busy seducing one another's wives. Asquith's still at it - '

'You can't mean the Prime Minister?'

'Indeed I do.' Seymour made a pretence of lining up a perfectly simple shot from different angles, passing behind her and whispering in her ear: 'The War Lord seduced Venetia, so they say. Sits in Cabinet writing her *billets-doux*.'

'But she's half his age!'

'And his daughter's best friend,' said Max.

'Miss Shaw obviously hasn't met Margot yet!' said Seymour, potting his shot with ease. 'You and your mother are not taking your responsibilities seriously, Bryson. You really must keep Miss Shaw *au fait* with the latest gossip.'

'Doesn't interest me as much as it seems to interest you, dear boy.'

'How can you not be interested?' demanded Seymour, chalking Sylvia's cue before Max could get up. 'In one generation, the Souls have achieved what previously it took the Norman conquest to achieve: redistributed titles and wealth. Brought rude new vigour to the etiolated bloodlines of many of the premier earldoms and dukedoms...' He looked appreciatively on as Sylvia leaned over the table, the material of her dress taut over her hips. 'Oh, excellent, Miss Shaw!' He caught a frosty glance from Max. 'Excellent shot,' he amended. 'What were we saying? Oh, yes. And the children of the Souls - the Corrupt Coterie, as I believe they call themselves - look like continuing that service to the nation...We applaud them. After all, one must have an occupation.'

'The Corrupt Coterie?' said Max. 'More like the Pretentious Posse!'

'Dear Max! Ever the cynic.'

From Max's expression, he seemed a most unlikely candidate for what Lady Cynthia called her male 'conks'. Not that Sylvia cared one way or the other, she reminded herself.

They'd just finished the game, with Seymour beating her by a small margin, due to inexplicably poor play on his part in the last few minutes of the game, when the card players erupted into the billiards room.

'Dearest Max,' drawled Diana Manners. 'We wondered where you'd gone.'

'So long since we had a chance to talk,' said Venetia Stanley.

'Cynthia's been longing for a really good dentist with you!' chimed in one of the young men.

'Dearest Max. Darling Eddie. You're both working far too hard,' pouted Cynthia. 'It's too bad of you to abandon your friends.'

They fluttered around the table like a flock of exotic birds, while the young men set up the balls, chalked the cues and established the bets.

'So you're working for the War Lord now?' Cooper settled himself next to Max.

'Not exactly *for* Mr Asquith. I'm helping to set up the munitions team.'

'Tell us all about your time in France,' said another of the young men as Max, limping slightly, turned to clear the marker-board. 'Must have been absolutely thrilling to be so near the front line.'

'Thrilling?' Max raised one eyebrow. 'No. I really don't think *thrilling* is the word that springs to mind. Dirty, noisy and terrifying would be much more appropriate.'

'Not terrifying for you,' said Lady Cynthia, laying her hand on Max's arm. 'You were so terribly brave.'

'What a pity it had to be Lloyd George, though,' said a dark-haired young man with a sneer beneath his carefully trimmed moustache. 'No one would have cared if he went...' There was a sharp intake of breath and an uncomfortable silence fell upon the room. Aware that he had gone too far, even in such a conservative household, he appealed to Lady Cynthia. 'What I mean is, well, it - it would have made a lot less trouble for the Government. Your father-in-law is always saying...'

The anger disappeared from Max Bryson's grey eyes as swiftly as it had come. His soft voice cut into the man's embarrassed ramblings. 'You must remember there's a war on, Reynolds. Why, if you were contributing a fraction as much to the war effort as Lloyd George is - I might even try to save *you*.'

38

It was said in the most benign manner, but few could miss the savagery behind the words. Suddenly no one was interested in billiards any more. In twos and threes the Coterie followed Reynolds out of the room, joking and quipping to cover their discomfiture.

'No one is supposed to know that Lloyd George was even out at the Front,' snapped Max.

'Reynolds is a loose-mouthed fool,' said Seymour. 'I'll make sure his ear is twisted when we get back to the office. And I'm sure we can rely on Miss Shaw's discretion.'

'Absolutely,' said Sylvia, biting back the questions that crowded to her lips.

'Another game, Miss Shaw?' asked Eddie Seymour, offering her the cue. 'A chance to avenge yourself upon me?'

Sylvia shook her head. The elegant wall clock showed that the hour was late and she left, muttering something about finding Lady Alice.

'A delightful young lady, Max,' said Seymour as the door closed behind her.

'Strictly speaking, not that young.'

'Don't quibble. What I mean is, there's a youthfulness of spirit, with an impressive maturity of mind. Attractive too.'

'I suppose she is.' Max stared into space, fiddling with the chalk and wishing Seymour would change the subject.

'It's a combination one comes across too rarely.'

'Careful, Eddie,' chided his friend. 'You'll be talking about her soul next.'

'Catching, isn't it? Half an hour in Ettie's company....' Seymour lit up a cigarette and blew a few experimental rings towards the ceiling. 'I'd like you to tell me the field's clear,' he said with a curious glance at his companion, 'but that isn't the case, is it?'

Max tipped his head back, eyes closed, and for a moment Eddie thought he wouldn't get an answer. At last Max spoke. 'A year ago, no. But you know what the situation is now.'

Seymour bit his lip. 'Did you love her?'

'I don't have the right to love anyone.'

'That wasn't what I asked. Did you?'

'I might have - if the fates had not been against us.' Max took a deep breath and Seymour was relieved to see the anguish fade from his face. 'I first met her when I represented her late father in court. An excellent man: that's where she gets her brains from. At the time she was betrothed - to a pleasant enough young fellow, though I suspected even then that there was not a great deal of backbone to him. Miss Shaw and I disagreed almost every time we met, on just about everything.' His lips twisted in a wry smile. 'Most stimulating. I began to look forward to seeing her, merely in the hope of a verbal sparring match. Almost before I knew it, it had turned to something more. Although I don't think she ever realised...' He fell silent as he looked back down the years.

'You said nothing?'

'How could I? She was betrothed. And then, when the young man faded from the scene - well, it was neither time nor place for a declaration. I needed all my wits about me. I could not allow my heart to rule my head: it was a devilishly difficult case to win.'

'Against the government too.' Seymour smiled. 'I've just remembered where I've seen her before.'

'I trust you'll do us both a favour by forgetting it as swiftly?'

'Need you ask?'

Max shook his head. 'After the case was all tied up I had every intention of finding a way to strike up the acquaintance once more, on a more social footing. But it never happened. Esmond had his accident and I lost touch with Miss Shaw.' He chose his words carefully. 'Both her brothers were killed in the first months of the war, you know. But even before that, she was having a very hard time.'

'Poor girl.'

'I only recently found out just how hard. I had thought she was safe in Wimbledon. I should have looked for her straight away, when her father died, but with mother's problems, and Esmond, and bloody Imogen bolting to India...'

'...and the fight to keep the children....'

'That's the excuse I like to use. But while I'd put Sylvia to one side, she and her mother were left friendless and penniless.' His shoulders slumped. 'And in the end we lost the children anyway.'

'Only because the case was heard while you were laid up. Brace up, old fellow. You'll get them back once the appeal is heard.'

Max shook his head wearily.

'At least you can console yourself that Miss Shaw is safe and well.'

'No thanks to me. I can hardly believe the chance that brought her and my mother together. But I should have been there for her in her hour of need. And I wasn't.'

A footman came into the room and approached Max with a telegram on a salver.

'What odds do you offer on a swift summons back to London?' asked Eddie, setting his cue back into the rack

'I hope not. I'm due at Whitefields tomorrow. We haven't seen the children in a month.' Bryson read the telegram with a darkening face. 'Bets are off,' he said, passing the telegram to his companion. 'As is our journey to Whitefields.'

"Cannot condone travel on Sabbath STOP Children not available Sunday STOP Please write new arrangements STOP Will pray for you STOP Grayson" Seymour glanced at his friend from under lowering brows. 'But - damn it all, Max, if they'd sent this earlier, you could have taken Lady Alice over this evening.'

'Which is precisely why they left it so late.' He screwed the telegram up and hurled it into the fire. 'Damn them to Hell!' he swore. After a moment he turned back to Seymour, his face a mask. 'What odds do you give now of us ever getting the children back?'

39

Neither Lady Alice nor Max appeared at breakfast. Sylvia assumed that the strains of the previous evening's socialising had been too much for Lady Alice, and that she was tired. It was Eddie Seymour who pointed out that having a tray in your room was an acceptable way to signal to your hostess that you did not wish to join the party in church.

'So by coming down to breakfast...'

'You've committed yourself to trail behind the Desboroughs into the Parish Church. I was caught on my way out for a brisk walk. But I hear Ettie keeps a strict watch on the length of sermons: can't have the chef's best efforts spoiled.'

She appreciated Seymour's company in the carriage there and on the walk back. He was as sensible as she remembered, but with a redeeming sense of humour. When she was with him the time passed very pleasantly.

The Ardingley House party left Taplow Court that afternoon, and were deposited, with their trunks, at the station. The entertainment of watching Lady Cynthia and her attendant swains had palled and Sylvia was happy to leave behind a group of people with whom she had not the least thing in common and who, by the end of a second day, she'd begun to find pretty uncongenial.

Not until they reached the station did anyone think to tell Sylvia that they were not, after all, going to Whitefields, though nobody told her why. As Lady Alice and Mr Bryson both declined to go into the waiting room and spent the next twenty minutes out in a brisk breeze on the platform, Max Bryson limping up and down and his mother sitting on a bench staring fixedly ahead, Sylvia was no longer so certain that leaving Taplow Court constituted an improvement.

The journey was undertaken virtually in silence, with Lady Alice leaning back in her seat with her eyes closed and Max Bryson busily making notes in a pocketbook. Having been snapped at for a perfectly innocuous remark, Sylvia was reduced to gazing out of the window watching the fields and the terraces of workers' cottages as the train sped through the western suburbs of London. By the time they reached Paddington, dusk had fallen and they had some difficulty finding a cab to take them back to Ardingley House.

Max, who'd barely said a word since they had left Taplow Court, waited only long enough to see the trunks carried in, before taking the cab on to his club.

'I shan't need you again this evening,' said Lady Alice, belatedly remembering her companion's presence. 'Please cancel tomorrow's engagements. I don't feel particularly sociable.'

On her way to visit her mother Sylvia heard loud music - one of Tschaikovsky's more blustering compositions - booming out of Lady Alice's room. If she'd thought this position a sinecure, she suspected she was about to find that it was no such thing.

40

Lady Alice stayed in her room for three days, playing her music so loudly that it almost hurt the ears, and having her meals sent up on trays. Sylvia was in a quandary. Should she remind Lady Alice of the week's appointments, or should she leave her alone? In the end she decided to brave Annie, though the dresser had barely spoken a word to her since Sylvia had taken over Lady Alice's diary.

'Yes?' she said, when Sylvia knocked on the dressing room door.

'I - I was concerned about Lady Alice. I wondered if there's anything I can do?'

'If there was,' said Annie, 'don't you think I'd be doing it?'

She was abashed by her own idiocy. Annie had been with Lady Alice for many years; she had only been here a matter of weeks. 'I'm sorry. I only wanted to help...'

She was halfway down the stairs when Annie caught up with her.

'It's the children, see,' she said, putting her hand on Sylvia's arm and her mouth close to her ear, to be heard above the music. 'She was like this for a good month when they took them away. As bad as when she first lost Master Esmond. She'll come out of it in her own time and there's nothing you nor me can do about it.' She dashed away again, leaving Sylvia no less confused, but feeling that some sort of truce had been declared.

Each day Sylvia sent excuses to the hostesses whose invitations were stuck in the frame of the huge gilt mirror above the fireplace, stating, perfectly truthfully, that Lady Alice was indisposed. Once she'd visited her mother and informed the chef how many would be in to each meal, she quitted Ardingley House for her stint at the depot.

The work was a welcome relief. Her mother showed no signs of improvement and, listening to the loud music from the phonogram, she had the fearful thought that she might now have two invalids to look after. Max Bryson neither called nor wrote.

One thing she could do for Lady Alice was to visit the young woman, Lily Parker, who had stopped their car outside the vicarage. It had never been Lady Alice's intention to accompany them; she'd said she trusted Sylvia and Mr Doncaster to see what was what.

The Doncasters lived in a modest double-fronted house in a pretty square just east of the city. Mark Doncaster was standing in the front garden with a young woman who could only be his sister, looking at the few spring bulbs which had braved the cold weather. He was expecting to see the Lanchester, and didn't look up as she climbed out of a different car. Watching the two of them joking and smiling, Sylvia knew again a pang of loss: that should have been her and Freddie.

He was a good-looking man, particularly when he smiled, as he did when he saw her at the garden gate. He was dressed in tweed knickerbockers and a Norfolk jacket and his sister wore an almost identical costume, except that hers had a calf-length golfing skirt with a suffragette pin in the jacket lapel.

As her brother made the introductions, Nina Doncaster grasped Sylvia's hand and shook it heartily. 'Mark told me what you did in Hyde Park last year. I'm full of admiration. Frankly, it's just as well that I was never put to the test: I'm not at all sure I could have held out for my principles...'

Sylvia disclaimed any thought of heroism. 'If I'd realised what was involved, I doubt if I'd have gone through with it. My admiration is for those who knew what prison was like and yet still went back a second time. I know I couldn't have done so.'

'I'm surprised you're not wearing *your* badge,' said Miss Doncaster, closing the gate behind them.

Her brother stepped in swiftly. 'Perhaps Miss Shaw feels that it would not be appropriate today when she's representing Lady Alice and the committee.'

'That hasn't stopped you wearing yours.' Sylvia glanced up and saw the No-Conscription badge pinned to his lapel.

Doncaster ushered his outspoken sister into the front of the little green car. 'Is your usual vehicle out of commission?' he asked, squeezing himself into the back.

'Permanently. It's been commandeered for some general or other. Actually this is far more sensible. The other car positively guzzled petrol. Took it in like a sponge. Soon we'll have a shortage of fuel - so much is being sent to the troops.' She handed Miss Doncaster the basket full of bits and pieces that she'd spent the morning gathering. 'Keep your hand on the milk can, otherwise it slops everywhere, and you can never get the smell out.' Her mother was forever spilling milk over herself and the bedclothes until Sylvia had found an invalid's covered cup at the second-hand stall in Leather Lane Market.

Mr Doncaster had brought a street directory; without it they'd never have found Hope Court. About half a mile from the vicarage, not far from the river, they turned into a road with a board school at one end and a huge brewery at the other. The blank end wall of the brewery blocked off both light and access, and huge drays laden with barrels rumbled constantly up and down the street. Halfway down the road a narrow alleyway opened out into a courtyard. They had to leave the car in the alley and walk through the yard, ducking under lines of flapping washing.

A stooped and wizened old woman opened the door to them, shouting for Lily with a bellow that belied the appearance of decrepitude. Following her directions they proceeded up a flight of elaborately carved stairs which still bore the handsome wainscoting from the years when this had been a prosperous merchant's house.

Lily Parker met them on the first landing, baby propped on one hip and a look of astonishment on her face. In accordance with the charity's usual way of working she'd had no warning of the impending visit. Nevertheless she welcomed them cordially enough, leading them down a dark and gloomy side passage, across a landing with an old stone sink and tap, and then up a narrow half stair to the two rooms she occupied.

The furnishings were modest, but what there was, was clean, and there was a rag mat on the well-scrubbed floor in front of the hearth. The walls, however, had proved beyond help. Stained and dank, they were suggestive of a leaky roof. Sweeping a bucket into a corner and throwing a cloth over it, Lily nervously apologised that she'd not had time to clear away as the baby had just woken and needed changing.

Sylvia, ushered in and urged to 'take a seat, please, missus,' was horribly embarrassed. What on earth was she doing here, poking her nose into another person's business? What gave her the notion that she had any right or qualification to say whether or not Lily Parker was a deserving case? She was hardly Lady Bountiful. The brief whiff of the soaking bucket as Lily whisked it away had brought back with terrible clarity the memory of the few weeks she and her mother had spent in similar rooms, above a pawnshop not far from here, after her release from prison, when her mother had refused to stay in the hospital and then fallen out so dramatically with Lady Harriet and the other suffragettes.

Her mother had been too ill and Sylvia too frail to bring any sort of order to their lives. She'd nearly killed herself dragging water upstairs to soak the sheets in the old tin bath, bruised her thin hands trying to wring them out, and when it rained had almost given them both pneumonia trying to dry the sheets indoors. In the end she'd swallowed her pride and borrowed from the fund for former prisoners so she could pay a local washerwoman. The fund had helped her find a nurse for her mother but then she'd gone back to work far too early, determined to pay the money back.

She remembered endless discussions, in polite middle class parlours, on how to combat the apathy of working class women in the fight for the vote, but those weeks in the slums had provided the answer. When every day was a struggle to feed the family and keep the place clean - when to relax efforts for a moment meant tragedy could strike, and snatch away a child, or incapacitate the wage earner -

survival had to take priority. There was neither time nor energy for anything else.

On Lily's table was a pile of freshly ironed cot sheets and small, much-mended flannel nightgowns. A basket of ragged edged bindings, neatly folded ready for use, stood by the door into the second room. There was an overall smell of freshness about the place that suggested an idyllic cottage in the country rather than a slum terrace, but the little fire in the hearth which had been lit to heat the flatirons was flickering feebly and Lily and the baby were both wrapped in heavy shawls. Lily Parker was doing her best under very difficult circumstances, far better than Sylvia herself had ever managed.

Nina unloaded the basket onto the table, and the look on Lily's face as the crusty loaf, the can of milk, the bag of oats, tea, apples and cheese appeared from the shadowy depths, was its own reward for the time Sylvia had spent putting the supplies together.

'Bless you, missus,' she said, laying a hand on Sylvia's arm. 'You said you'd help, and you've kept your word.' She looked as if she was about to burst into tears. With a sniff she pressed the baby into Sylvia's hands. 'You hold the kiddie,' she said briskly, picking up the kettle from the hearth, 'an' I'll brew us all a nice cup of tea.'

Sylvia stood for a moment with a stunned expression on her face at finding herself with an armful of milky infant. 'You'd better sit down,' said Nina, pulling one of the two wooden chairs out from the table. Sylvia looked with trepidation at the baby, beginning to wriggle in her unskilled grasp.

'Say something,' urged Mark, as the child opened its mouth and began to grumble.

'I don't know what to say to it.'

'Him. It's a boy.'

'Sing him a song,' said Nina. 'Go on. Before he notices you're not his mother.'

'You take him, then.' She held the infant out to Nina.

'Not me,' said Nina with a teasing laugh. 'It wouldn't do for Lily to think you'd rejected her baby!'

'And anyway, Nina's meeting her young man later this afternoon.' Doncaster leaned over the back of Sylvia's chair to tickle the baby's cheek with a gentle finger. 'She doesn't want to go along smelling of - '

' - of anything stronger than lily-of-the-valley!' said his sister hastily.

Before Sylvia could palm the baby off on him, Doncaster turned away to the grate, rescuing the feeble fire with a few more sticks and a lump of coal. It seemed to Sylvia, gently rocking the baby and crooning half-forgotten nursery rhymes, that Lily was an awfully long time filling the kettle. When she came back, with a couple of borrowed cups, she had suspiciously reddened eyes. From outside the shouting of boys kicking an old ball round the court echoed up the stairs, indicating that the board school was out for the day.

Tears filled Lily's eyes again as Doncaster wrote her a chit for the coalman. 'Jake wouldn't never have wanted me to come to this,' said Lily, patting the baby's back as he dozed on her shoulder. 'Don't think I'm ungrateful, sir, but it's charity and I never thought I'd end up on the parish.'

Doncaster tried to reassure her that it wasn't that kind of charity, but she couldn't stop the tears once she'd started. 'If only someone could find 'im...then I could have his separation allowance. We'd manage then. See, I'm good at making ends meet. I know you wouldn't think it...'

Fortunately the kettle began to whistle and Lily, recalled to her duties, wiped her eyes and began to bustle about.

As she stood the teapot on the hearth to draw, and set four mismatched cups and saucers on the table, the sound of the ball ceased. 'Hey, canary! Sing us a song!' came the shout from the yard. Lily froze, then whisked the baby into the next room.

There was a rapid footfall on the stairs and a middle-aged woman stuck her head round the door. She was wearing a heavy tunic and baggy under-trousers. Her face was bright yellow and the front of her hair a lurid orange, and there was an almost palpable cloud around her head.

'Everythin' alright, Lil?' she demanded in the nasal tones of the born and bred Londoner. 'On'y I saw the car and thought it must be the doctor. It's not Alfie?'

'Stop worryin', Mabel. Alfie's fine. Just goin' off to sleep.' Lily turned to her visitors. 'This is my neighbour, Mabel Atkins. She was right good to me when I first came down. She's working in munitions.'

Introductions were made and Mabel urged to stay for a cup of tea. As they shook hands, Sylvia was hard pressed not to wrinkle her nose. The sulphurous stink, overlaying the usual sweat of honest labour, gave

Mabel the air of one who'd been consorting with the denizens of the lower regions.

Mabel was shaking hands with Mr Doncaster when she caught sight of his No-Conscription badge. She dropped his hand as if she'd been scalded, and opened her mouth to say something scathing.

Nina Doncaster leaped into the breach. 'It must be hard, working in the munitions.'

'Better now we got our numbers up,' said Mabel, turning pointedly away from Doncaster. 'We was doing terrible long shifts up to last month.'

Lily set the pot on the table and poured a little milk from the can into a cracked jug she'd reached down from the shelf. 'Good day today, then, Mabel?' she asked, desperate lest her neighbour say something rude and drive away her generous visitors.

'Always a good day when nothin' nor no one don't blow up!' said Mabel with a squawk of laughter. She registered the shock on their faces. 'Look, I won't stay. Gotta see if that good for nothin' son of mine's back from school. I'll pop round later, Lil, when your company's gone.'

'I want to do some work, missus, for sure,' said Lily to Sylvia as the door slammed behind the neighbour and her footsteps retreated down the stairs. 'I don't want charity for a moment longer than I need, but I'll be honest - part of me's glad I can't be working in the munitions, for all the money's so good. I mean, look at her now, all yellow like that. Canaries, the local lads call 'em. It can't be good for you, breathin' in all that muck and havin' it stick to your hair an' all. I wouldn't want to be bringin' all that back home to baby.'

They congratulated themselves that they'd left Lily looking less strained and worn, and much of the journey back was devoted to a discussion of what could best be done for her in the future. Doncaster had contacts in one of the new Housing Associations that were building smart new tenements not far away, and he promised to put her name forward.

Nina turned the talk back to the Suffragettes. 'Come along to our local branch,' she urged. 'They'd welcome you with open arms, as a martyr for the cause. Mrs Pankhurst herself is to address the next meeting, if she's back from her lecture tour in America. I can't go, now she's so pro-war, but you'd have a place of honour on the platform - '

'Don't let my time in prison mislead you,' said Sylvia crisply. 'I'm not a militant, never was. I wouldn't share a platform with Mrs Pankhurst if I had to crawl over broken glass to escape.' Nina's eyes widened. 'Sorry if she's a hero of yours,' Sylvia went on, 'but as far as I'm concerned, she and that wretch Christabel have done more damage to the cause than...'

Fortunately they drew up just then at the Doncasters' house, where a smart young man was waiting, and she decided, belatedly, that discretion was the better part of valour.

Nina had been stunned by Sylvia's unexpected outburst, but made a rapid recovery. 'Never mind the formal meetings then,' she said, under cover of their goodbyes. 'The parish is holding a May Fair in Jubilee Park and we're running a stall to raise money for the Belgian refugee school at Earl's Court.' She squeezed her hand. 'You're sure to know some of our members. Oh, do say you'll come.'

Sylvia promised to think about it. She wasn't against all the Suffragettes, although she was convinced that their bombing and arson campaigns had served only to set back the cause. She'd not kept in touch with those who had helped her when she first came out of prison: life had spiralled out of control so swiftly, with her mother's deterioration, the struggle for survival, the juggling of jobs to keep their heads above water. Perhaps, if she could speak to other women who had suffered in prison, she could find out how they coped with the terrible memories - and the nightmares. Too many women, like poor Emily Davison, had been driven out of their minds by what they'd been through in prison, and she wasn't going to let that happen to her.

She was in her room, changing for driving duty, when she found the little arrow-headed badge at the bottom of her bag. She looked at it long and hard, took a deep breath and pinned it back on her jacket.

41

'Oh, you'll appreciate this!' said Sylvia, folding back the newspaper and turning on from the war news. 'It's an advertisement. There's a picture of a young woman packing a parcel of comforts for her husband at the front. She's writing him a letter....' She put on her breathiest voice and read on:

Dearest, you would like to hear that I am keeping well and cheerful and that I am still using Palmolive...

She was rewarded by a chuckle from Lady Alice, the first since she had emerged from her room, with only the briefest apology to Sylvia, and no explanation. But then, as Sylvia reminded herself, she was no more entitled than any other servant to an explanation of her employer's megrims.

'Is there more?' Lady Alice was prepared to be amused.

'It goes on to say: *this woman knows HE* - in capital letters! - *will be pleased to hear that she is still using the soap which kept her so beautiful, and when HE comes back her skin will still have that velvet softness and freshness HE admired so much.*'

'As if that was all HE had to think about!' snorted Lady Alice.

'It shows what the advertisers think of women's brains,' said Sylvia with a sigh. 'They're sure *we've* got nothing better to think about! It finishes by saying that *Palmolive has a quaint yet fascinating Eastern Fragrance...* We'd better hope HE's not been serving in the Dardanelles!'

'Anything more interesting in your Suffrage newspapers?' asked Lady Alice, when their laughter died away.

'I don't subscribe anymore,' said Sylvia flatly. 'Mrs Pankhurst has started to emulate the *Daily Mail*...finding traitors everywhere – anyone who ever visited Germany or listened to Beethoven or Brahms...Even attacking fellow Suffragettes with the misfortune to have German relatives. And Christabel writes regularly from the United States, telling everyone in Britain how they should behave. I've had enough of them.'

A few moments later Lady Alice said: 'I'm going down to Whitefields this weekend. Max will accompany me, so you may wish to take a couple of days off duty.'

The vision of Max Bryson limping along the train platform trying to look after his blind mother was not encouraging. 'But you'll be much more comfortable driving, shan't you?' said Sylvia. The postponement of the visit to Whitefields had intrigued her: besides, she had Lord Desborough's errand and message to deliver.

She waited in vain to hear anything more about the children, but Lady Alice sipped quietly at her after-dinner brandy before retiring early. Sylvia, selecting a book downstairs, was relieved not to hear the blare of the gramophone.

The following morning Lady Alice took her on a tour of the garden with the old gardener. There was not a great deal to see, for the long cold spring had held back all but the hardiest plants. But Lady Alice's enthusiasm was infectious and from the brisk discussions with the gardener, and the respect with which he treated her suggestions, Sylvia could tell that gardening had been her pride and joy before her eyesight failed her.

'Do you have an interest in gardening, Sylvia?' she said hopefully, while the gardener fetched a pot of hot-house lilies he wanted to show her.

'I enjoy a beautiful garden, of course, but I know little about how it gets that way.'

'It was too much to hope for, I suppose,' sighed Lady Alice. 'And you're still young. Most women only discover gardening when they're older.' She shrugged. 'It's usually God or gardening.'

Sylvia left her in the gardener's hands while she went off to change into her uniform. She was belting up her jacket when Lizzie brought her an envelope. Inside was a brief note from Max Bryson, asking her to meet him at the end of her afternoon duty in a teashop on the Strand.

It was fortunate that she only had deliveries that afternoon, for no more than half her mind was on her driving. The other half was wondering why on earth Max Bryson wanted to see her - and why he hadn't come to Ardingley House.

42

It was still light when Sylvia emerged from the depot: a short duty, but they'd make up for it later in the week. Whenever it went quiet like this, it always turned out to be the lull before the storm.

She looked forward to the meeting with Max Bryson with mixed feelings. There was something daring in meeting a man in a tea shop, even if it was only her employer's son, but there was also the fear that he might be about to tell her that Imogen was coming back and she was no longer needed.

The suppressed tension found an unexpected outlet. At the bottom of Chancery Lane her attention was caught by a man and a woman down an alleyway, shouting at each other. The young woman was waving her hands in agitation. Without a second thought, Sylvia changed course to see if she needed assistance. But she'd misread the situation entirely. It was the young man who was in difficulties; he was backing away from a bevy of women, his face perfectly white. Two of them followed him closely, haranguing him all the while. Intrigued by this reversal of roles, Sylvia continued towards the little group.

'I tried, I tell you! They turned me down!' protested the young man. 'They say I've got a heart murmur - do you think that was a jolly thing to hear? When I've only just got married?'

One of the younger women grabbed hold of his lapel and Sylvia's lips tightened as she saw the white feathers in her hand. This must be one of the white feather brigades that some old fool of an Admiral had started up, to shame men into enlisting.

'Leave him alone!' She stepped between them, grasping the woman's wrist.

'He's a shirker!' cried the young woman, two spots of high colour on her cheekbones. 'If all the cowards like him went to the Front, like my young man's done, the Army would be in Berlin by now.'

'Hear, hear!' chanted her companions. 'Shirker! Shirker! Shirker!'

Sylvia's temper, which had been on a short string anyway, bolted free as she saw that another of the women was wearing a Suffragette pin in her lapel. 'How dare you behave like this with the movement's insignia on your breast?' she demanded, snatching the feathers from the woman's hand and grinding them in the mud with her booted heel. 'Do you think we fought so long for *our* freedom in order to deny it to others?'

'You've no right to do that!' bellowed one of the older women.

'This gives me the right!' hissed Sylvia, turning back her burberry to show the arrow-headed badge. 'What's more, this uniform gives me the right!' She whirled on the well-dressed ringleader, surveying her from her elegant hat to her highly polished shoes. 'You're so eager to tell others what they should do - but what are *you* doing for the war effort?'

'That's different.'

'No, it *isn't.* We fought for our rights - and our responsibilities. You're fit and healthy. If you want to help the war effort, join the VADs. They need nurses and clerks and drivers....better to put your energies into that than into this kind of despicable bullying!'

The young man was effusive in his thanks, and walked with her to the tea-shop, telling her in great detail about his interview and medical examination. She didn't feel the need for his escort, and the way he carefully saw her across the road would, under normal circumstances, have annoyed her, but she suppressed her own feelings. He had been publicly humiliated, and she sensed his pressing need to reclaim his threatened masculinity. How did Mark Doncaster deal with this sort of thing, as he must do, day in and day out?

She took her leave of the young man outside the tea shop. He held the door open for her, tipping his hat, and she was vexed to see that Bryson was already seated in the window, calmly observing them.

'Have you been waiting long?' she asked as she hurried up to the table.

'A friend of yours?' His words overlapped hers as he helped her off with her burberry.

'No. I just met him.' Drawing off her gloves, she didn't see his raised eyebrows.

'I've taken the liberty of ordering tea,' he said. 'I thought you might be pressed for time. I can order coffee if you'd prefer it, and some sandwiches if you have to go back on duty...'

'I'm off duty on both fronts tonight, so I shall eat at home. I mean, at Ardingley House,' she said hastily, not wanting him to think her presumptuous. 'Tea will be very welcome, though. It's turning quite cold.'

While the nippie set down pots of tea and toasted tea-cakes that gave off a delicious aroma of cinnamon and hot butter, they discussed the latest theory that atmospheric disruption caused by the bombardments across the Channel had caused spring to be so late.

'But you didn't summon me here to talk about the weather, did you?' asked Sylvia as the shop door tinkled and the waitress moved on to the next customer.

Max smiled. 'I wasn't aware that I'd summoned you at all.'

Sylvia didn't pick up the cue. 'I suppose your sister-in-law is coming back and - '

'Oh Lord, are you at that again?' He sipped at his tea. 'Look here - strictly between the two of us - it could be years before we see Imogen again, whatever my mother would like to think. In a few weeks Imogen will have seen out her mourning, but there's nothing to tempt her back here. An attractive and titled widow, her children conveniently on the other side of the world, will have a far jollier time out in India than she would in London under the present circumstances. But it is Imogen's children I want to talk to you about.'

'Why are they living in Hertfordshire? I haven't the first idea. And what am I to say if I'm asked a question or - '

'Quite. Mother won't speak of it...*can't* speak of it. She gets too upset.' He couldn't tell her why. Even now he couldn't speak of his own childhood without exposing his emotions. He set his cup back on the saucer and began to tell her about the children.

The Ardingley marriage had been a second marriage for both partners, he explained. He had acquired a step-sister, Charlotte. A few years later, a half-brother Esmond had arrived, to great rejoicing, being heir to the title. 'We all rather spoiled Esmond, much in the way you spoiled Pip. He was a delightful child. Not an ounce of malice in him. We all went along very happily together. Charlotte married Spencer Tremain, a diplomat. We were visiting them in India when Esmond met Imogen. He married her, against his father's wishes. Against everyone's wishes, actually. No one had a very high opinion of Imogen. Except Imogen herself. But Ardingley could never deny Esmond anything, and in the end he gave them his blessing.'

He paused to press another tea-cake on Sylvia, who took it hastily, even though she didn't particularly want it. It was unlike Max Bryson to be so open, and she was reluctant to interrupt the flow. 'It didn't work out?'

He shook his head. 'Esmond wanted to live in the country, at Whitefields. Like his father, he was happiest with his horses and his dogs. But Imogen wanted society, and town life. And admirers. Even after the children were born. She had little interest in the poor little devils, but Esmond adored them. Once Imogen had her title, and with the children to tie them together, I suppose they might have settled down into some semblance of a marriage, no worse than many.....but shortly after Ardingley died and Esmond came into the title, he was kicked in the head by a horse.' He gazed blankly out of the window and she sat quietly until he was ready to speak again.

'The situation brought out the worst in Imogen,' he said at last. 'Once it was clear that any recovery would be a prolonged one, she went on an extended visit to her family in India, leaving the children with their grandmother.'

'Lady Alice.'

'Yes. I was one of Esmond's trustees. The others - the Graysons - were distant relatives of Imogen's. She hardly knew them. I don't think they'd ever seen the children.' He set his cup down with a rattle and clenched his hands together. 'I should have applied for guardianship when Esmond died. There were many who advised me to do so. But she was still their mother, whatever I might think of her.'

'Then Lady Alice lost her sight.'

'Yes. Then the war. And last autumn, while I was in hospital with this cursed leg, and poor mother didn't know whether she was about to lose me too, Imogen's relatives applied to the courts to remove them from our care.'

'I see.'

'There'll be an appeal, of course. But meanwhile the Graysons are doing their utmost to estrange us from the children. And I'm not prepared to see that happen. It would break my mother's heart again.'

He looked so wretched that Sylvia reached out her hand to him across the table. He held it tightly in his until the teashop door tinkled again. Then he dropped her hand and asked if she would like more tea.

It was as if the shutters had come down once more, and now he spoke only of practicalities. The children, he explained, were still cared for by Mrs Harmitage, who had been engaged by Lady Alice when her sight had begun to fail. They lived at Whitefields, the Ardingley family estate, which was now being run - and from the tone of his voice, not too well - by the younger of the two Grayson uncles and his wife.

'You'll meet them tomorrow - I hear you've kindly offered to drive us down.'

Given his past as a racing driver, he must find it frustrating to be driven everywhere – and especially by a woman. It could be an uncomfortable ride. 'I look forward to it,' she lied.

They left the teashop in friendly accord, a culmination of the better terms gradually building between them. In the distance came the tramp of marching feet and a Scottish regiment paraded down the road, kilts swirling, to the skirl of half a dozen bagpipes.

Max came to an abrupt halt and she almost fell over her feet trying not to bump into him. 'What is it?'

'I spent part of my early childhood in Scotland,' he murmured, 'and the sound of the pipes still moves me almost to tears.'

It was on the tip of her tongue to make a flippant remark about the sound of bagpipes moving anyone to tears, but then she saw his face in the light spilling from the glass panels of the tea-shop door, and fell silent. She squeezed his arm and he looked down at her in surprise, as if he'd forgotten she was there.

43

The morning air was crisp and cold when they stopped in Charles Street the next morning.

'It's a large house for one man,' observed Sylvia as they drew up. Then she bit her lip: it was hardly her place to comment on her employer's son's way of life.

'Bought on his engagement,' said Lady Alice. 'Sadly the marriage never happened.'

Not a fortunate family when it came to marriages. Perhaps that was why she'd fitted in so well. 'Did he never think of moving back to Ardingley House when....?'

'When I lost my sight? Indeed he did. But after three days of Max and Henrietta under the same roof, I sent him back again. Open warfare on a daily basis does not make for a peaceful life.'

Bryson's arrival necessitated some rearrangement as his mother insisted that he should sit in the front, to give directions. Sylvia resigned herself to being given detailed instructions and warned about every passing dog, cab or sharp corner. She was pleasantly surprised when Bryson settled back in his seat, giving every impression of a man planning to enjoy the drive.

On the far side of Regent's Park, Sylvia pulled up outside a corner shop. 'I shan't be a moment,' she said, setting the handbrake. 'There's something I have to buy...'

A few minutes later Bryson followed her into the shop.

'I'd forgotten that you smoked, Miss Shaw,' he said. 'I must insist that you don't smoke in my mother's presence...'

Oh, *curse* it! she thought. Every time she hoped they were building some kind of rapport, he always went and wrecked it. 'It's you who has the problem with women smoking,' she said curtly. 'I can't believe your mother is so old-fashioned...'

'My feelings have nothing to do with it.' His voice was cold. 'One of her specialists holds tobacco to be a prime cause of this type of blindness. She was never a smoker herself, but her uncle had a tobacco warehouse in Bristol where she played as a child. Now she avoids tobacco and smokers for fear of losing what little sight she has left.'

'I'm sorry. I assumed....'

'That I was being my customary intolerant self? On this occasion, no.'

'I haven't smoked since Holloway. Though I won't deny I still have odd cravings now and again.'

'Then why have we stopped at a tobacconist's shop?'

She gestured to the large glass jars on the shelf behind the counter, with their striped and multi-coloured contents. 'Bullseyes and toffee for the children.' The shopman emptied the scales pan expertly into a large paper bag and handed it to her. 'The original sweets were becoming sticky, so I gave them to the Belgian children in the basement.'

'Willie Desborough, at a guess.' She nodded as she pocketed her change. 'He was Esmond's godfather. The Graysons don't let him visit.'

'Might the Graysons object to me giving the children sweets?'

'Probably. And it is rather a large bag.' He thought a moment. 'I suggest you give them to Mrs Harmitage and leave her to dish them out.'

As they followed the Great North Road out through Barnet and Potter's Bar, Lady Alice demanded from her son the latest news of the war. 'One can't believe a word one reads in the papers,' she said acerbically. 'Northcliffe can't see beyond German bakers building Zeppelins in their backyards. The man's obsessed.'

'Well, the Russians are fighting back again - '

'About time too!'

'But the Dardanelles campaign is not the success that Churchill prophesied. He may live to regret claiming all the glory at the start, when it seemed to be going well. We didn't hit the Turks with the surprise we planned and now they're digging in, just like the Germans, and we simply can't get past them. Lloyd George believes the Gallipoli campaign may even lengthen the war rather than shorten it.'

'He was always opposed to the plan.'

'With some justification. He favoured an attack through Salonika, to bring Greece, Roumania and Italy in on our side. Instead of which they're now holding back till they see how badly we're damaged in Gallipoli. Unless we pour more troops in, we can't hold our position.'

'And what does Mr Asquith have to say?'

'Wait and see?' offered Sylvia. She'd been listening intently to Bryson, while keeping her eyes fixed on the road ahead.

'Precisely.'

'That might have been acceptable in the first months of the war...'

'When he was convinced the war would be over in three weeks,' said Lady Alice. 'He told me so himself.'

'But how can he still believe it ten months later?'

'He can't,' said Bryson. 'And while he dithers, McKenna is trying to make mischief between him and the Chancellor. Really, it's the last time to be sowing strife in the Cabinet. Britain depends on a united government at this time and if we're stuck with Asquith, we're going to have to make the best of it.'

About ten miles beyond Potter's Bar, they turned down a winding country lane and immediately began to skirt a high-walled estate. They drove in through wrought-iron gates and down an avenue of stately trees to the stableyard. No sooner were they out of the car than they heard: 'Uncle Max! Uncle Max!'

'Grandmama!' The boy came to an abrupt halt, skidding on the gravel. The little girl threw herself at Max, almost bowling him over.

Sylvia stood aside while the children greeted their erstwhile guardians with energetic hugs. 'It's me, Harry, grandmama,' said the boy, catching at Lady Alice's hand. 'Emily's on your left.' There was no doubting the difference between Harry's serious voice and little Emily's piping whisper, but it was touching that he should think of a way to help, at his tender age. Sylvia thought him grave beyond his years, an impression confirmed when the introductions were made. He gave her a firm handshake and welcomed her to Whitefields.

'How is your leg, sir?' he asked as they made their way towards the house.

'Better every day,' said Bryson, smiling at Sylvia over the boy's head, begging her complicity in the lie. 'And I much prefer to be called Uncle Max.'

'It's not allowed.'

'I see,' said Bryson.

'It's easier to go along with it,' said the boy with a shrug. 'Mrs Harmitage only gets into trouble if I fight them.'

'Very wise,' said Bryson, struggling to contain his anger. 'Only take on battles you can win.'

'That's what Mrs Harmitage says. Discretion is the better part of valour and all that stuff. I say, are you really going to stay overnight? No one *ever* stays here overnight!'

'We certainly are!' said their grandmother. 'I expect my rooms still to be open.'

They came out at the front of the house, almost as grand as Taplow Court, though more classical in style. 'Good day to ye, Lady Alice,' said a voice in sepulchral tones, and a grey wraith slid out of the shadows by the long rows of steps which led up to the grand portico. He bowed over Lady Alice's hand.

A second grey wraith emerged on Lady Alice's other hand. 'Do let Grayson give you his arm up the steps, Countess,' it said.

'You forget, Mrs Grayson, I have known Whitefields for many years,' said Lady Alice.

'And could live here still. Never let it be said that Grayson and I ....' The voice tailed off as Lady Alice turned on the speaker with a withering look.

Foiled of her prey the second wraith turned on the children. 'I told you to wait quietly and properly!' she said harshly. Two spots of high colour lit up her pasty grey face as she chivvied them up the stairs. 'Instead of which Mr Grayson finds you rushing about like a pair of ruffians!'

By this time they had mounted the long rows of steps and entered a large, echoing hall where a woman in her late fifties was waiting for them, hands demurely folded. Her pepper and salt hair was gathered into a bun and she was quietly dressed in a dove grey robe that had seen better times. 'Why, bless you, Mrs Grayson. *I* said they might go down to meet them.' Her blue eyes twinkled. 'I knew you wouldn't begrudge Lady Alice a grandmother's hearty welcome.'

Under cover of another round of greetings Sylvia studied Mrs Harmitage. Either the woman was naïve, or a consummate actress. She had a way of putting matters which made it very difficult - if not impossible in front of an audience - to disagree with her.

In the absence of a housekeeper - who had quit service the previous week - Mrs Harmitage showed them to their rooms. To Lady Alice's indignation, Sylvia had been put on a truckle bed in the dressing room. 'Too mean to open up an extra room!' she fumed, to the delight of the maid who had been sent to wait on them. 'With all the income this place generates, and all the rooms there are...!' She sniffed the air.

'Damp, mould and unaired rooms. No wonder the housekeeper wouldn't stay!'

What should have been elegant and spacious rooms were cold, damp and draughty. Lady Alice sent the maid for a bucket of coal to light a fire in her bedroom and in the drawing room. Within a few minutes, both Graysons presented themselves outside her door.

'We only have fires in winter,' said Grayson in sepulchral tones, wringing his hands together. 'Fires are no' needed after March.' He glared angrily at Sylvia. 'There's gae too much molly-coddling in this generation. That's why they have such very strange ideas. Very strange ideas,' he repeated, rolling the words on his tongue. 'No, indeed, there'll be no more fires lit in this house till the end of October.'

'Unfortunately I have not your excellent constitution,' said Lady Alice, barely suppressing her anger. 'If I were to take a chill, then we would be forced to require your hospitality for much longer than a weekend.'

The threat was sufficient: the outdoor man was sent for to lay the fires.

Lunch was a miserable affair, taken in the echoing and unheated dining room, with the children being constantly nagged to sit up straight, to stop talking and not to interrupt. In the Graysons' opinion, eating and socialising did not go together. Sylvia found it hard to decide which she found most unbearable: their oily manner with Lady Alice or their brusqueness with the children.

Across the table, Max Bryson was finding it almost impossible to keep his temper. It went to his heart to hear little Emily lisping 'Yes, sir' and 'I'm sorry, ma'am,' to her tormentors, and know that at present there was nothing he could do about it. His mother had been reduced to silence and only Sylvia Shaw and Mrs Harmitage kept up any semblance of polite conversation. Fortunately there were only two courses, with thin soup followed by under-hung meat and overcooked vegetables which could better have been drunk through a straw than eaten on a knife and fork.

A short sharp shower after lunch put an end to the planned walk to the lake. Mrs Grayson slithered out of the room to take her customary afternoon nap, and Grayson, peering over his half-glasses, said that Emily too should go to her room for a rest and Henry to his for a period of quiet reflection.

‘Oh, they had an excellent night’s sleep, sir, both of them,’ said Mrs Harmitage, who on Lady Alice’s insistence had joined them for lunch.

‘In spite of all that excitement earlier?’ said Grayson.

‘When they heard their grandmother and uncle were coming to see them? Oh that was soon mastered, sir, once you had spoken to them.’ Mrs Harmitage beamed on them all. ‘They saw the wisdom of your words and soon settled down. I was so impressed by their behaviour in taking your words to heart that I promised them they should spend the whole day with Grandmother, and you wouldn’t want me to break faith, I know. They do so look to you for a moral example, Mr Grayson.’

‘We’ll go into the drawing room,’ said Lady Alice decisively. ‘Harry and Emily can show me how they are progressing with their studies. Harry, dear, will you go up to the schoolroom for a reader for Emily? Then, if the rain holds off, we may take a stroll later this afternoon.’

It took only five minutes of Emily reading from her schoolbook to drive Grayson from the room, muttering something about estate affairs. Max Bryson drew a miniature chess set out of his pocket and sat in the window in the weak spring light, reminding Harry from time to time to look to his queen, or recall which ways the knight could move.

By mid-afternoon the sun had dried up the worst of the rain, and Sylvia and Max took the children to the lake, where they passed a happy hour throwing bread to the swans and stopping Emily from falling in after it. Max identified all the leaves that Harry brought to him, taught him to imitate the blackbird’s song, told them a story about fishing with their father in the nearby river, and generally proved himself to be a perfect uncle. She was seeing an unexpected side to Max Bryson, and she liked it.

‘I wonder what my mother has been discussing with Mrs Harmitage?’ he said as she swung Emily up the steps. ‘I’ll wager a certain person wouldn’t have been so happy to leave, if he’d known they were going to spend so long together.’

Mrs Harmitage rang for tea while Sylvia took Emily to change her damp shoes.

‘Grandmama?’ said Harry, rather hesitantly, as Mrs Harmitage handed round the cups.

‘Yes, Harry dear?’

'Have you...' He dropped his eyes to the plate of biscuits and appeared to be studying it hard. 'Have you heard from Mother? We haven't had a letter for three and a half months.'

Sylvia, walking into the room with Emily, saw Bryson's lips thin, but he said nothing.

'Not directly,' said Lady Alice, 'but I heard from a friend that she is well.' She reached out and put her hand on Harry's shoulder. 'The post is so difficult from India, especially now there is a war on.'

'Will she be stuck out there for ever and ever, grandmama?' said Emily with a quivering lip.

'No, darling.'

'But when will she come back?'

Lady Alice fell silent.

'We don't know, my dear,' said Max. 'No one does.'

'I didn't mind so much when we lived with you, grandmama,' said Emily.

Harry looked nervously over his shoulder, but there was no sign of either Grayson. He put his arm round his sister and hugged her. 'It's all right, Em,' he said sturdily. 'I'll look after you. We'll do all right, whatever....'

'But then you'll grow up and go to war and I'll be left here all by my own....'

'Good Lord, the war won't go on that long,' said Harry with such an adult air that they all laughed.

'Take me to the piano, Emily,' said Lady Alice after a moment. 'You can show me how you're progressing.'

'Poor mite,' said Mrs Harmitage to Max. 'She does miss her mother so.'

'I'm sorry,' said Harry glumly. 'I wouldn't have mentioned mother... but I thought grandmama might have heard.....and...and...Emily was out of the room.'

'It isn't your fault, old man,' said Max. 'Another game of chess?'

Harry shook his head, but went to sit beside his uncle, leaning his head against his shoulder and looking for once very much younger than his years.

Across the room Lady Alice took Emily up onto her lap and listened with her head on one side while Emily picked out her latest lesson. 'Do you remember our duet, Emily?' she said, settling the little girl on the piano stool beside her, and playing a rather jolly little piece with her.

Then it was Harry's turn, and they played a military march and a barcarolle together, stopping occasionally for Lady Alice to correct his fingering.

'You make it much more fun than our tutor,' said Harry. 'He - '

Just then Grayson came into the room, the customary scowl corrugating his face. Sitting in the window seat Max cleared his throat.

'I'm very fortunate,' said Lady Alice. 'I come here now and again and I do all the fancy pieces. Your tutor has to come here twice a week and do all the hard work. A little like a master baker and a cook.'

'How so?' Harry looked puzzled.

'Do you remember the cake we had once for your mother's birthday?'

'With all the sugared swans on the top....'

'And the pink roses and the silver leaves,' chimed in Emily.

'Well, that was the skill of the master baker. But his skill wouldn't have looked very impressive if the cook hadn't baked the cake first, would it? Now, I'm like the person who makes the sugar swans, d'you see? But without the work that your piano tutor does with you, and without all the practising of scales and so on, you wouldn't be able to do the amusing parts with me.'

'Did you have to do scales, grandmama?'

'Of course. I had years and years of work before I was allowed to do all the amusing parts.' Her hands moved lightly up and down the scales to demonstrate. 'It helps enormously to know where to put your fingers. Once you have mastered the fingering, you'll be ready to go on to much more entertaining pieces. But you have to walk before you can run, d'you see?'

Next day, after church, the children were allowed to join the adults in the orangery, warmed by the feeble spring sun. Emily was sitting on Sylvia's lap putting together a jigsaw puzzle of Noah's Ark while Max helped Harry to write out his Bible passage for the day, which was the tale of the Good Samaritan. Harry started to tell his uncle about Emily mis-reading it as the Tale of the Good Smartman, and Max chuckled as the two children joked and teased each other. The little girl had a most infectious giggle and before long Sylvia was laughing too. Max thought how delightful and relaxed she looked with the little girl on her lap, eyes sparkling, their fair curls mingling. Sylvia caught his eye and smiled back at him. For once no one looked away.

Mrs Harmitage, arm in arm with Lady Alice, stopped in the doorway. 'My, what a picture,' she said simply. 'Such a pretty domestic scene. If only you could see, my dear Lady Alice. If only you could see....'

44

Emily cried when they left and it was a very subdued journey back to London. When Sylvia came in from the mews, she found Max Bryson waiting for her in the drawing room.

'Mother's gone to bed. She wished me to thank you for taking us to Whitefields.'

'I was pleased to do it. And to meet the children.' She took the glass of wine he offered. 'Is she very upset?'

'Shot upstairs as soon as Mason opened the door,' he said. 'She'll cry for an hour or two. Best leave her to it. Tomorrow will be the worst.' He stood with his back to the fire, easing his weight from one leg to the other. 'She'll be devising all sorts of ways to get the children back. I beg you not to encourage her.'

'The Graysons are soulless brutes,' she said, subsiding into the cushioned sofa. 'Quite unsuited to bringing up children.'

'Agreed. But we have to work within the law. It's slow, but it's the only sure way.'

But why is it so slow?' she demanded with a frown. 'You work for the Chancellor - can't he use his influence?'

'He's the wrong sort of lawyer.' He held up a hand to stop her protest. 'No, I know that wasn't what you meant. But, important though the children are to us, he has rather more on his plate.'

'I know. A minor matter of winning the war.'

He took his leave soon after. 'I'm glad you're here with her,' he said. 'Though this hasn't been the most comfortable weekend for you.'

'I've been in worse places. Better company at Whitefields than in Holloway.' He saw her hand creep towards the corner of her mouth and reached out to intercept it.

He looked at it a long moment, as if unsure what to do with it. At last he pressed it gently and let it fall. 'As I say, I'm glad you're here with her.'

'Oh, she doesn't need me,' she said, not sorry to turn the conversation back to Lady Alice. 'She doesn't need anyone. You've all convinced her that she can't function without a carer, but she did perfectly well at Whitefields.'

'That's different. She knows it well.'

'She knows it here. Far better than me.'

'But when she goes into society....'

'We shall see, shan't we?' She wasn't quite ready to discuss the plan that was hatching in her mind, but there was one way he could help. She gestured to the gilt-edged invitations on the mantelpiece. 'Which of these hostesses would you say was most amenable to Lady Alice and her problems?'

Bemused, he took an invitation down from the frame and handed it to her, awaiting an explanation.

'Thank you. Now, if you'll excuse me...I have my own mother to see to.'

45

When Max returned to Charles Street, his curiosity about Miss Shaw and her plans was swiftly put aside as he settled down to catch up on the many dispatches, notes and telephone messages waiting for him. It wasn't until he turned out the light and tried to settle comfortably that his treacherous mind began to think about her again. He couldn't put out of his mind the image of her with the little girl on her knee. That might have been one of his children - if only....

Two wasted lives, he thought tiredly. He remembered a personal advertisement he'd seen in the Times a few days before: *lady, fiancé killed at Ypres, will take on any wounded officer...*

Would she do that for him? He screwed up his fists and struggled to control his wayward thoughts...because he knew that was the one thing he could never ask her.

46

The East End Mission Hall was a hive of activity. 'This is where we wind the bandages,' said Nina Doncaster, opening the first in a long line of doors. Women sat at hand-turned machines, spooling up lengths of ghostly white material, like swathes of ectoplasm in the spiritualist photographs so popular before the war. Some were in drab black with shawls around their shoulders, others in fur wraps. Between them flitted half a dozen Girl Guides, collecting the reeled bandages and packing them carefully into flat boxes. 'When we've finished this batch, we're moving on to gas masks. Though butter muslin and cotton waste seem little enough protection against chlorine gas.'

She opened the second door. 'In here we make splints - papier mâché from old sugar bags. Just imagine, there were men out at the front who had to be splinted with their own rifles - and you know how short we are of arms.' She clapped her hand over her mouth. 'Better not tell Mark I said that!'

'There can be no objection to working on first aid,' said Sylvia.

'Oh yes. It's still part of the war effort. And if you object to the war *entirely*, as Mark does...It's not easy to explain, but if you feel as strongly as he does that all war is evil, then the medical services are just patching men up so they can go out and kill again.'

'Some of the Quakers are going out as stretcher bearers.'

'Mark says that's helping the war effort by releasing another man to fight.'

'You can appreciate your brother's views without necessarily sharing them.'

'The trouble is I do share them. In theory, at any rate. But now we're at war, how can I stand by and not help, just because I know war is wrong?'

'Is that why you come down here to help?'

'It's a compromise. The best I can manage. I don't actually do anything in here. I'm working with Miss Pankhurst - our other Sylvia! - setting up mother and baby clinics and crèches.' She dropped her voice. 'You know Sylvia Pankhurst was thrown out of the WSPU by her own mother?'

'Another daughter Adela was exiled to Australia! But that's Mrs Pankhurst for you. Campaigning for women's votes and running her movement like a dictatorship.'

'You really dislike her, don't you?'

'There were Suffragists campaigning peacefully for the vote long before Mrs Pankhurst took over, you know. I can't agree with arson and bombing and burning down theatres, however just the cause.

Whether it's Irish bombers killing policemen, Russian anarchists lobbing one at the Czar, the Serbs killing Franz Ferdinand or Mrs Pankhurst sending women to bomb Lloyd George's home...'

Nina swiftly changed the subject. 'Well, Sylvia Pankhurst is against the war. She's started a toy factory in an empty public house across the road with some of the mothers. Now the German can't flood the market any more, it's an ideal gap for us to fill.'

'If there's a crèche, then perhaps Lily...?'

'I'm ahead of you there,' said Nina with an impish grin. 'She starts at the end of the month. Now, we'd better see how those urns are doing. They'll all be wanting their tea. Awfully good of you to help me out - I know how jolly busy you are.'

Extremely busy, reflected Sylvia, darting about the kitchen setting out cups and saucers. There'd been a tremendous rush at the depot, as hospital tents were sent out to the front, and trainloads of wounded and dying men were shipped back, to be sent on to London hospitals and provincial casualty stations. Not just those wounded by shell and bullet: since the Germans had begun to use poison gas she sometimes found herself driving blinded and asphyxiated men who gasped for every breath, wheezing like bellows. Not many of them, however; most gas cases didn't make it back across the Channel.

Lady Alice was still content to fit in around Sylvia's duties at the depot. As soon as she'd finished here, they were driving down to Oxfordshire, to spend a Saturday to Monday with no less a figure than the Prime Minister himself.

She could have done with a free morning, but Nina had persuaded her to step in when her original helper had gone down with a heavy cold. Nina was very persuasive. Only the other evening she'd coaxed her into selling programmes at the Albert Hall concert in aid of the Belgian Refugee School.

It had been amusing to see some of the other helpers dithering over their sales, trying to calculate change. Most of them had probably never handled money before: first their fathers and then their husbands would have done it for them. Still, if that was the biggest challenge they ever met, they would have got off lightly. Newspapers and magazines were full of advertisements for Lady Cooks and Lady Housekeepers. Servants were flocking to the munitions factories for the better pay, and the middle classes could only hope to find a redundant governess or a soldier's widow to fill their shoes.

The queue for tea started as the first urn came to the boil, and for half an hour she was rushed off her feet filling and refilling teapots, handing out cups, refilling milk jugs and sugar basins. 'Be grateful you're not here at lunchtime,' said Nina. 'Then we have sandwiches and pies to deal with too.'

As the rush died down the Girl Guides began to gather up the crockery and wash it up. 'I say,' said a voice behind her as she picked up the drying cloth. 'It's Sylvia, isn't it? Sylvia Fletcher-Shaw?'

'Drusilla?' The two of them had addressed envelopes together in the offices of the NUWSS - the moderate suffragists - when they'd both been young ladies of leisure. 'My dear, it must be - '

'Years.'

'Where have you been?'

'Travelling the world,' said Drusilla. 'Well, France at least. I went with one of the hospital units to Boulogne.'

'How exciting!'

'Horrible at times, but yes, exciting too. I felt I was really doing something.'

'But I thought your parents were dead set against you nursing?'

'That was before the war,' said Drusilla with a pout. 'Then, it was a case of me setting myself up against my father, and thinking I knew better. Now he boasts at his club that his little girl's 'doing her bit' and mother drags me along to her recruitment meetings in my uniform. Amazing how it's all turned around in just a year. After all the years we struggled and fought and got nowhere...'

'Are you home on leave?' asked Nina.

'Long-term leave,' said Drusilla ruefully, linking her hands across her swollen stomach. '*I* shan't be going back at any rate. Which is vexing, because I was due to go out to Serbia with Dr Inglis. But then I married.' She looked down. 'A doctor. You'd think he'd have known better, wouldn't you? But I fell for the baby almost immediately.'

Sylvia wondered how accidental that had been, and decided she was becoming unpleasantly cynical. 'I heard Elsie Inglis talk at one of our meetings before the war,' she said. 'Very impressive. She's taking the Scottish Women's Hospital Units, isn't she?'

'About time too. Do you know what those fools at the Foreign Office said when she first offered her help? *Go home, dear lady, and sit quietly.* Can you imagine her fury? She's a qualified and experienced doctor, but she's had to wait till now for permission to go. Well, must dash. Wonderful to see you again. How's that brother of yours? Still as wicked as ever?'

'Freddie's dead.' With time it became a little easier to say, and the pain was not as sharp.

'Oh, gosh, I'm sorry.' Drusilla was unsure what to say, or whether to say anything.

Nina stepped into the breach, pushing forward a trolley with a freshly filled pot of tea. 'Here.' She took the drying cloth out of Sylvia's hands. 'This is for the committee rooms - end of the corridor, second door on the right. It's not easy for them to break in the middle of consultations, so we take it to them. You'll need about a dozen cups.'

Drusilla walked her to the door. 'You'll never guess where Gertie is,' she said.

'Gertie with the red hair? Couldn't type an address without half a dozen mistakes?'

'That's her. Clerk for an Army Supply Depot near Dover. Goes between sites on a motor-cycle. Just imagine: little Gertie riding a motorbike! Doesn't seem possible, does it?'

A long queue of people lined the corridor as Sylvia pushed the trolley through. A man in a shabby coat held the door open for her and she crossed to the first of four tables, at which sat an elderly man, two clerks and a woman with a baby on her lap. She dispensed tea, trying not to interrupt the flow of discussion, then on to the next table, where two hefty men were manoeuvring a one-legged man in a bath chair away from the table.

'Don't forget, now,' said the lawyer. 'Not a word until I have the papers together. Then I'll have the bailiffs serve him the summons at his home. Far more impact than at the factory.' He limped round the table and shook hands with the three men. As they manoeuvred their way across the hall, he turned to his clerk. 'The factory owner's hoping for a knighthood. His wife is particularly looking forward to it - and he'd very much like to be the Honourable Member for a leafy part of the shires. Bad court publicity wouldn't help him at all. So we'll put on pressure to compensate without going to court.' His eye moved on past his clerk. 'Good Lord, Miss Shaw!'

'Tea, Mr Bryson?' said Sylvia.

'You do turn up in the most interesting places,' he said with a twitch of his lips. 'But why don't you leave us till last? There's something I want to discuss with you.'

It was not Lady Alice, but Lily Parker, that he wanted to talk to her about. Lily had been in that morning to sign a declaration. 'Which means my clerk can do a search of the army lists. If we can find Jake Harrison - '

The clerk raised his head. 'And if he still wants to make an honest woman of her - '

' - then we'll bring him back on a compassionate leave.' Max frowned at the clerk. 'Why don't you talk to the next client, Mr Bowles? Take your tea with you. Then Miss Shaw can snatch five minutes and have her tea in peace.'

She'd been on her feet all morning and it was a welcome relief to sit down, if only for a few moments. She looked around her wide-eyed. 'But these people can't afford lawyers.'

'It's all voluntary.' He rubbed his eyes and she saw how tired he looked. 'Different lawyers each week, on rota, though we lost some of our most enthusiastic men at the beginning of the war.' He grinned. 'As my mother's son, I could have told them that volunteering becomes a habit.'

'This must fill a great need. I know how expensive the law can be.'

'If we get compensation we add the costs and run from those.' He shrugged. 'The clerks need paying and not all lawyers can do that from their own pockets.'

She recalled her anger that day when she'd dropped him off in Whitehall, and he'd regretted that the government didn't pay so well as the law...thank goodness she hadn't voiced her scorn out loud.

'Can you help them all?' she asked.

'No. Some come in - just like their richer counterparts - talking of their rights. A colleague of mine says when a client comes in shouting about rights and principles he always mentally rents his summer villa in Biarritz. But we can't afford that indulgence.' He leafed through the stack of papers. 'One of this morning's cases is a breach of promise. I shall do my utmost to talk her out of it.'

She rose to collect the cups. 'I should be finished here in about an hour,' he said. 'Could you drive me home to collect my bags?'

'You're coming with us to Oxfordshire?'

'For my sins.' Was it his imagination, or did she look pleased at the prospect of his company? 'Not an ideal time for one of Lloyd George's men to be visiting Asquith, with all the rumours about LG being offered the premiership, but my mother has imposed a three-line whip.'

He still had a client with him when Sylvia slipped quietly back into the committee room. She sat at the back, not wishing to disturb him. She'd seen him in court before - in the highest court in the land - during her father's lawsuit against the government, but she was interested to see how he dealt with less dramatic cases.

The young woman's face was red and puffy from crying. 'I'll make him pay for it!' she hissed. 'If he marries that Beattie, then I'll sue him, for sure.'

He sat back in his chair, easing his leg. 'You can demand that someone keep his promise to marry you, but you can't make someone love you,' he said, shaking his head. 'And what of the child?'

'Why should I care about Beattie's bastard? I'm the aggrieved party.'

'At the moment, perhaps,' he acknowledged. 'But not if you force the issue. Even if he agrees to marry you, you'll be standing between him and the mother of his child and I'm very much afraid you'll be seen as the villain of the piece. For the rest of that child's life.'

'But I'll still have him.'

'Will you? His heart will be with his child and he'll hold it against you for the rest of your life together. The man intends anyway to pay for the child's support - he's acknowledged it as his. He may also feel obliged to see that the child's mother is looked after. Not much left after all that, even from good wages.'

'But what am I to do?' she wailed. 'No one else will marry me.'

'A handsome woman like you...?' Bryson offered his handkerchief which she took, blowing her nose energetically. 'Handle this the right way and you'll be the heroine of the piece - doing the noble thing for the sake of the unborn child. Give it time and more honourable and loyal men will be popping up all over the place.'

'That was well done,' said Sylvia as the clerk showed the woman out.

He swivelled in his chair. He hadn't realised she was there.

'Praise from you is praise indeed, Miss Shaw,' he said, raising one eyebrow quizzically. He picked up the next summary. 'There's a limit to what we can do and we can't waste our limited funds salving hurt feelings.'

47

She drove him to Charles Street and he invited her to come in and wait while he changed for the journey. 'I'm assuming that a liberated woman such as yourself will have no difficulty with entering a bachelor's apartments?'

She followed him up the steps. She had no intention of missing the opportunity to see how Max Bryson lived. Quite what she expected to see she wasn't sure, but his public rooms hid no terrible secrets, bearing the hallmarks of a man of quiet tastes and sufficient funds to indulge them. Decorated in a more modern style than Ardingley House, with an occasional lamp or drape in the Oriental style of Bakst to lift it from the neutral, there was none of the ornamental clutter that had filled Ardingley House when she first arrived, the whatnots and ornamental tables that were constant hazards for Lady Alice. This room was lined with bookshelves, but with fewer dry law tomes than she'd anticipated.

She was reading the morning paper, with the terrible news of the sinking of the *Lusitania,* when his man appeared with offers of refreshment. She declined, then lowered the paper to ask whether he had been with Mr Bryson long.

'Fifteen years now, miss.' For all his modest demeanour she had the distinct impression that he was observing her closely. Perhaps Bryson didn't usually bring women back to his rooms. 'Barring the few days when the house was put on the market. Will that be all, miss?'

'Yes, thank you.' She put aside the paper and walked to the window. Bryson must be a good man to work for. No one stayed with a poor master for fifteen years. Perhaps she'd misjudged him. After all, someone who gave up his Saturdays to help the people at the Mission Hall...

There was something about the room, with its leather bound books and the large kneehole desk in the window that reminded her of her father's study. Tears pricked the back of her eyes as she remembered the irascible man she had loved so dearly.

'Ready, Miss Shaw?' said Max Bryson from the doorway. 'We don't want to keep my mother waiting.'

On the way to Ardingley House they stopped to buy the late edition of the paper, still full of rage over the loss of the *Lusitania*.

Inevitably there was a fresh campaign to intern all those of German descent for the duration of the war.

'Pretty rough on those who are naturalised subjects,' said Sylvia, as Max read out the headlines to her. 'And what if the Americans *do* eventually come in on our side? Thousands of their fighting men will be of German stock, surely?'

He grunted an assent. 'The editorial says *the most dangerous Germans are not the bakers and the waiters. It is those in high places from whom the greatest danger is to be apprehended*. The editor thinks they ought to apply the peerage rule.'

'Forgive the ignorance of a middle-class banker's daughter, but what's the peerage rule?'

'No one's eligible for a peerage unless he's of the third generation of British citizenship.'

'So they want to intern sons and grandsons of naturalised Germans? Even though they've been brought up and educated in this country?'

'That's about the size of it.'

'Well, that's scuppered the Royal Family,' she said with an irrepressible chuckle. 'The Queen's parents are German, and so was the King's grandfather, Prince Albert - and his grandmother, Queen Victoria, was all but. We'll have to become a republic by default!'

One of the Belgian refugees was at hand at Ardingley House to help load the cases onto the roof of the car and within a few minutes they were heading west out of London.

'Remind me why we're going, ma,' said Max, lowering himself into the front seat with a grimace. 'I can't think the Asquiths will be thrilled to see one of Lloyd George's men. There's quite a groundswell for LG to replace the PM.'

'Margot insisted you came with us - though that was before the present challenges, to be sure. She's been showing interest in our Flower Girls' Mission. Mr Groom is raising funds for a new workshop. Now imports from the continent have ceased there's a gap in the silk flower market.'

'And your girls want to fill it, I suppose.'

'To have the patronage of the Prime Minister's wife would be of great assistance to Mr Groom.'

'Margot Asquith taking an interest in blind flower-makers seems highly unlikely to me,' said Max, settling himself as well as he could in his seat. 'Ah well, it's been a long day...' Whereupon he fell asleep. The sound of his steady breathing was very soothing. Sylvia tried to give him as gentle a journey as she could manage, but she had to waken him for directions when they approached Sutton Courtney.

The Wharf was soon found and Sylvia had a chance to admire its design while the trunks and cases were carried in. Asquith, the first self-made man to take office, had commissioned its building, in the absence of inherited property. A prime minister had to entertain. It helped that the redoubtable Margot, his second wife, was the daughter of a rich man.

Their hostess was waiting to greet them in the hall, though her enthusiasm rapidly drained away when she saw Sylvia. 'I can't imagine why you thought you would need Miss Shaw, Alice,' she said fretfully, her long face drawn and discontented. 'There are enough of your friends here to look after you. Heaven only knows where we're going to put the girl. The house is full to the seams.' Once more Sylvia had to accept a truckle bed in the dressing room, as if she were the maid. It didn't bother her, but Lady Alice was furious. When Sylvia went downstairs to make the usual dinner arrangements, she was not too surprised to find herself heartily rebuffed.

Lady Alice was appalled when she was told that they were to be separated. 'I can't do it,' she said, panic not far from her voice. 'I'm supposed to be impressing all the guests, and encouraging them to make donations. And the thought of making a show of myself in front of Margot, of all people...I shall go down and speak to her.'

'She was quite determined. She won't upset her table for anyone. She said it was bad enough that she had to have the Asquith boys sitting around the table like a row of tailor's dummies.' To her relief she heard her employer chuckle. 'I can't wait to see these stepsons of hers.'

'Who is she sending you in with?'

'Bonham Carter.'

'Her husband's secretary. Maurice is a pleasant young man. You'll have no problems with him.'

'And you've nothing to worry about either. You already have it down to a fine art. Remember: meat or fish at six o'clock, potatoes at twelve, vegetables at nine and three. I've spoken to the butler - there'll be a footman behind your chair.'

'But if I have food around my mouth....'

'Well, actually, none of us can see if we have food on our lips,' said Sylvia, thinking evil thoughts about Henrietta Jennings. Busy making herself indispensable, she had only succeeded in totally sapping Lady Alice's confidence. 'Just use your table napkin a little more often. The fish will be boned, the meat will be cut up. You're to go in with Mr Balfour, and Mr Seymour will be on your other side. Eddie will look after you.'

Lady Alice took her mind off the forthcoming trial by supervising Sylvia's *toilette*, insisting that she wear the new short-skirted evening dress they had bought. It was a daring tunic style that ended well above the ankle, and under other circumstances Sylvia would have enjoyed making a stir with a new fashion. But for now all her energy had to go into encouraging Lady Alice. That was, after all, what she was here for.

She was still experiencing a certain amount of trepidation when they went down with Max. The three of them barely made one sound person between them, she thought tiredly: one blind, one lame, one with a mind still liable to be overthrown by the slightest word out of place. She fixed her company smile on her face and went in.

Henry Herbert Asquith was a portly, florid-faced man of about sixty, who greeted each of his female guests, especially the younger ones, with a squeeze of the hand and an arm around their waist. He didn't seem at all like a man under attack in Parliament and the popular papers over the shell shortage; he seemed far more interested in flirtation, gathering a harem of young women around him, chief of whom was Venetia Stanley, whom they'd met at Taplow. Margot Asquith, rouged and shrill, bore down on them. 'An interesting tunic, Miss Shaw,' she said, scanning Sylvia from top to toe. 'But haven't you forgotten to put on the skirt?'

Sylvia bit her tongue on an acid answer. Margot's next triumph was to introduce Venetia's admirer, Edwin Montague, into the group. The more wounded Asquith looked, the more Miss Stanley flirted with Montague, and the more Margot gloated.

Just before they went into dinner Max drew Sylvia away from Duff Cooper, who was regaling her with an item of gossip about someone she'd never met. 'There must be some mistake,' he hissed. 'You and mother aren't together. I'll tell Margot to change...'

'Don't you dare!' snapped Sylvia. 'Honestly, you're almost as bad as Henrietta Jennings. The way you all fuss around her, it's a wonder she has any confidence left at all.'

He looked at her, enlightenment slowly dawning. 'This is what you were planning to do anyway, isn't it? A quiet revolution, just like the way you've been clearing the rooms at Ardingley House...the absence of all those tables and ornaments is a great improvement, by the way.'

'Just clearing her path.' She was relieved that he didn't see it as interference. 'Now it's so much easier for her to move around. As for this dinner – yes, it was what I was planning. It's only the venue that has changed. But don't you see? The only way for her to come to terms with her blindness is to bolster her confidence in everything else. Or she might as well give up and go into a convent!'

Max spent much of his dinner craning his neck to see how his mother was managing, leaving Lady Cynthia sulking on his left, but Lady Alice managed her dinner perfectly well, with only the smallest assistance from the footman behind her chair - and a watching brief from Eddie Seymour, alerted earlier by Sylvia.

Sylvia, while keeping a weather eye across the table, found pleasure in her release from responsibility. She chatted happily to Maurice Bonham Carter, Asquith's secretary, having despaired of getting any response at all from Margot's stepson on her other side.

After dinner, Margot Asquith sought Sylvia out. 'So you are one of these agitating women who have caused my husband so much trouble,' she said, her long, bony face thrust close. Sylvia wondered what she would say if she knew her husband's government had sent her to prison? Only the anxious look on Lady Alice's face made her resist the temptation to say it.

'I have campaigned for votes for women and the right to stand for Parliament,' she agreed. 'I believe women should have the same rights as men.'

'And the same obligations?'

'Of course.'

'You'll be wanting to serve on the front line next!' scoffed Mrs Asquith.

'There are many ways of serving one's country without firing a rifle, ma'am,' said Sylvia, refusing to be drawn.

'Women with rifles! What a terrible thought! All wanting to wreak vengeance on my husband!'

Seymour came to sit by Sylvia. 'It seems to me, Margot, that their kind of vengeance comes in a pretty angelic form: there are women working as nurses, drivers, canteen workers - '

'Miss Shaw herself is a driver at a War Supplies Depot,' said Max, joining them. 'She's certainly doing her bit for the war effort.'

Sylvia smiled her thanks at the two men for their support. 'You see, Mrs Asquith, we can be loyal to our country and still think we deserve equal worth, equal dignity and equal rights when it comes to choosing those who govern us.' Eddie Seymour, returning Sylvia's smile, resolved not to leave it too long before he declared his interest.

'In other words, Miss Shaw,' said Margot, determined to have the last word, 'you demand the vote - like that dreadful Mrs Pankhurst - with stone-throwing and arson.'

'Not at all. I am a Suffragist, and my protest has always been peaceful.' She caught the glint in Max's eye and looked away hastily.

'The Government simply cannot be seen to give into violence,' said Margot. 'Imagine my husband telling Mrs Pankhurst he would give women the vote!'

'Then invite Mrs Fawcett and the non-violent Suffragists to Parliament and announce it to *them*. They are far more numerous than the militants, and they've campaigned peacefully for over half a century.'

'Can't put Mrs P's nose out of joint,' said one of Asquith's young men. 'She's become such a rallying point for you women and the war effort.'

'From America? Hardly. Besides, we didn't need her - or anyone else - to tell us our duty. British women are as patriotic as British men. It will be a tragedy - and a travesty - if, in years to come, only the violent ones are remembered, like Mrs Pankhurst and poor sick Emily Davison, instead of Mrs Fawcett's legions of peaceful Suffragists.'

By now the rest of the men had come in and Margot hurried across the room to organise them. Lady Cynthia called Max over to listen to her husband's war poetry, which she was about to read to Countess Benckendorff, wife of the Russian ambassador.

'How long has Lady Cynthia's husband been at the front?' whispered Sylvia.

'All of three weeks.' There was a pained look on Max's face. 'But he's been writing this slushy nonsense for years. He only needs to give it a suitable war title, and with the Asquith name the publishers will fall over themselves to buy it.'

Away from Asquith's immediate entourage, the talk inevitably turned back to the rumours that Admiral Fisher, in conflict with his minister, Winston Churchill, was about to resign, and whether this would play into the hands of those demanding the Prime Minister's resignation. Asquith was well out of earshot of this discussion, being more intent on detaching Venetia Stanley from the conversation she was having with Mr Montague. Sylvia wondered how Margot could bear to see her husband behave so in front of his guests.

Someone accused Lloyd George of fomenting discontent and whipping up the shells shortage for his own personal advancement. Max felt impelled to defend his absent master, and the discussion grew quite warm.

'You see, Miss Shaw, this is why my husband and I decided not to give you the vote. The rough and tumble of parliamentary business would be too gross for a proper and modest lady to bear.' Margot Asquith contrived to say it in such a way as to suggest that she doubted Miss Shaw had had any modesty to start with. 'It would inevitably destroy the caring nature of young wives and make us unsuited for the gentler task of bringing up the next generation.'

'I'm sorry to think that any decent man should be forced to go daily to such an improper place,' said Sylvia gravely. Someone behind her gave a choked laugh. 'Surely the answer is to civilise the place, not shut out the civilising influences.'

'Women in Parliament might civilise the atmosphere,' agreed Eddie Seymour who, with others, had dropped the argument over Lloyd George and was listening eagerly to the exchange, hoping that Margot might at last have met her match. 'There are plenty of men who'd prefer to work without all that uproar and unpleasantness.'

Margot was not going to be robbed of her prey. 'But the night sittings...'

'...which only a fraction of the current members attend...'

'And the long hours....'

'Any shop girl could give you the answer to that,' said Sylvia, struggling to keep the scorn out of her voice. 'Start at ten in the morning and have shorter vacations. Fit in the business of the House on a standard working day.' She darted a glance at Max. 'Not so convenient for all the lawyers and businessmen, but it might give us a parliament more representative of the people who elected them, rather than one where the Members combine two jobs - and give the lion's part of their time to the one that pays best.'

'We must allow for your enthusiasms, Miss Shaw,' said Margot, with a trill of false laughter, 'but you are very far removed from the realities of the situation.'

Sylvia couldn't say more without offence. Margot sprang up and dragooned a reluctant guest to entertain them at the piano. Eddie Seymour hung on to his seat next to Sylvia, and whispered in her ear, under cover of the piano, that Mrs Pankhurst and Margot might actually have a great deal in common.

'Emmeline Pankhurst was always a Kensington and Chelsea sort of suffragette,' she agreed. 'And, like Margot, only interested in anything as long as she can run it!'

48

Neither Bryson nor Seymour were at hand the next day when Sylvia came out of the drawing room, where she'd left Lady Alice discussing her Flower Girls' Mission with Margot Asquith. She was heading for the library when a door opened and Venetia Stanley came hurrying out, her face pale and distracted.

She brushed past Sylvia and hurried away.

'Ah, my dear young lady,' said a voice behind her. 'You haven't seen the park yet, have you? The motor is already waiting.' Asquith took Sylvia's hand before she could protest, and showed no inclination to let it go. There was no one else around. How was she to refuse no less a person than the Prime Minister?

'I - it's most kind of you, but - '

'Delighted to have your company.'

Sylvia began to panic. 'I'm not suitably dressed...'

'James will fetch you a motoring coat,' he said, summoning a servant. 'And there are plenty of rugs in the motor.' He helped her into the heavy coat, and she steeled herself to ignore his hot breath on the back of her neck and the strong smell of spirits.

A sleek dark car, long, low and powerful, sat outside the front door - no one would think of requisitioning the Asquiths' car! At the sight of the chauffeur sitting in the front, her unease subsided.

As they drove around the countryside, Asquith pointed out to her places of interest, waxing lyrical about the nearby city of Oxford, which he clearly loved with a passion. She began to wonder whether she'd done him an injustice, and forced herself to sit back, admire the scenery and hold up her end of the conversation. The man would surely behave himself in front of his servants.

But Asquith wasn't in front of his servant. He was behind him, and separated from him by a glass partition. She could hardly believe it when he slipped an arm round her waist. Before she could protest, he conveyed her hand to his lips and pressed a kiss on her fingers. She tried to pull away, but he proved very tenacious.

'Close the door, Mr Nash...'

She felt the familiar waves of panic beginning to wash over her and forced herself to breathe slowly and force them back. She could hardly make a scene in front of the chauffeur. Besides, this was no sadistic bully, but the Prime Minister of England!

'Please, Mr Asquith,' she said, with as much firmness as she could muster. 'I really must protest!'

'Dear Miss Shaw,' he muttered dreamily, and began to suck her fingers.

She was going to be sick, she was sure of it. What little strength she had was sapping away.'Please, Mr Asquith!' She said it again, more loudly, but the chauffeur continued to look rigidly to his front. He must be inured to his master's behaviour, probably saw it every day. Asquith sucked more strongly at her fingers and her disgust turned suddenly to fury. This was her *host!* What right had he to treat her in such a disgusting way? With a sudden access of strength she snatched her hand away and buried it beneath the car rug over her knees. Brazenly she leaned forward and rapped the glass with her free hand.

'Please return me to the house,' she said to the chauffeur as he pushed aside the screen. 'I am feeling rather unwell.' She turned pointedly aside from her fellow passenger and gazed rigidly out of the side window.

Max Bryson was pacing up and down in front of the door waiting for her. 'Oh, thank goodness!' she exclaimed, almost falling out of the door in her eagerness to get away from Asquith. 'I'm so glad - '

He interrupted her before she could pour out her tale. 'My mother is waiting for you to take her down to tea,' he said repressively. 'Let me escort you to your room to tidy yourself.'

Recalled to her senses she allowed herself to be drawn into the hall. Indignant though she was, it wouldn't do to make a public scene. There was Lady Alice's fundraising to think of. Besides, Max worked for the Government.

The footman informed them that tea was being served in the drawing room. 'Excellent!' said Asquith, rubbing his hands. 'Just what we need to warm us up, eh, Miss Shaw?' With a beatific smile he disappeared into the drawing room.

'I can't believe you were so foolish as to go out alone in a car with him!' hissed Bryson as he hurried her down the corridor. 'There's a reason they call him 'Squiffy', and now he's about to lose Venetia he's bound to be looking for a replacement - '

'It's a little late to tell me that now,' she protested, high spots of colour on her cheeks. 'Where were you when you were needed?' Before he could answer, she opened the dressing room door, shot inside and closed it very firmly in his face.

With shaking hands she washed herself as thoroughly as she could, but it would take a long soak in a hot bath to wash away the contamination she felt.

It took some effort to pretend to Lady Alice that all was well, and to brace herself for a return to the drawing room. Max had been cornered by Lady Cynthia, who was gazing up at him with her narrow cat's eyes. Sylvia went to the tea table to take two cups from Margot Asquith. As she passed the Prime Minister, he looked up from his conversation and beamed at her as though nothing had happened.

A slender young man folded up the newspaper he was reading. 'Rheims Cathedral and Rupert Brooke - two such sad losses,' he said to Sylvia. Before she could agree with him, he sighed heavily and said: 'The destruction of cathedrals and poets - the only things which matter in this war.' She whisked herself away to the window before she said something she shouldn't.

Eddie Seymour promptly detached himself from the man he was talking to and crossed to her side. His calm good sense came as a welcome relief. Nevertheless, she could hardly wait to leave and when she drove the car out onto the London road at the end of the visit, she felt as though a weight had been lifted from her shoulders.

49

A week touring munitions factories with Lloyd George left Max enthusiastic but exhausted. On his return he ordered the cab to take him on to Ardingley House. His mother, he told himself, would be eager for the latest news.

He found Eddie Seymour comfortably ensconced at the window table, looking through an illustrated catalogue with Sylvia.

'Mr Seymour is a frequent visitor,' said Lady Alice airily. 'He took us out to dinner the other evening, and he and Sylvia have just returned from the exhibition at the Tate.'

'You didn't go with them?'

'My dear Max, Miss Shaw is past the age of needing a chaperone. And of what interest would it be to me to go to an art gallery?'

He gritted his teeth and told himself not to be a dog in the manger, but every time he called, it seemed that one man or another was there, paying his respects. If it wasn't Eddie Seymour, it was Mark Doncaster, in earnest discussion about charity work.

'Another one who seems to be here every other day,' he complained as Doncaster took his leave. 'It does me no good to have conscientious objectors visiting the house.'

'I can't see how it can affect you in the slightest, my dear,' said his mother acerbically. 'After all, it isn't your house.'

Acknowledging the truth of that didn't make it any easier for Max: he enjoyed Sylvia's company and he was finding it increasingly difficult to share her with other men, men who were still whole and could offer her what he could not.

There was no respite at work either. Lloyd George was being pressed to stand up to Asquith over the shells shortage, but he was in a difficult position. He was boosting production wherever he could, and cracking down on the excessive profits of the armament manufacturers, but every move he made was blocked by Kitchener at the War Office. There was more urgency in confronting this problem, he felt, than in who led the Parliamentary government: that, said Lloyd George, was no more than a game of musical chairs. Much more important, he told his team, to find those men of *push and go* – which Max took to mean men with drive and determination, who could take over the production of war materials and get things moving: they owed that much to the men at the front.

'It's amazing how many odd people have popped out of the woodwork since LG made that appeal,' Max said to Eddie Seymour. 'But there are some good fellows among them. I'm seeing some tomorrow while you're in Newcastle.'

'Should be an interesting trip,' said Seymour, taking his turn on tour. 'Kitchener only wants us to see those munitions factories that are working well, but LG insists on seeing them all.'

'It'll be a long day then. I'd back LG against Kitchener any time.'

50

Max was pleased to find Sylvia alone when he called the next evening. She was still in uniform, the green of her tie picking up the green in her flashing eyes. The crumpled newspaper was proof, however, that she was in no mood for small talk.

'Have you seen this?' she demanded, almost before Max was through the door. She slapped the paper down on the table, with its report of the march of the Stock Exchange members on Parliament prominently displayed. 'What happened to the law that no procession may pass within a mile of Parliament?'

'Feelings are running high,' he said mildly. 'Nearly twelve hundred civilians on the *Lusitania* killed by a German submarine...'

'*Damn* their feelings,' she snapped, pacing up and down in her agitation.

'Miss Shaw!'

'Remember Black Friday? November 1910. *Women* were arrested just for *trying* to present a petition to Parliament. The *Morning Post* even said they should all be transported to the prison colonies in Australia! But the top-hatted gentlemen of the City are allowed to march right up to the gates. Welcomed into Central Hall - they even had Members come to talk to them. A breach of Parliamentary privilege if ever there was one!'

'Strange things happen when there's a war on.'

'I might have guessed you'd use the war as an excuse,' she jeered. 'Why can't you just admit it? There's one law for men and one for women and no amount of pretty talking will change that!'

51

She'd calmed down a little by the time Eddie Seymour next came to visit, which was just as well, for she was no cook and she'd left it to the last minute to make her promised contribution for the Suffrage Stall at the May Fair.

'I told him Lady Alice isn't at home,' said Maisie, when she finally tracked Sylvia down in the kitchen. She pursed her lips in disapproval as Miss Shaw went on rolling out the dough. 'He insists on seeing you.'

'I can't leave this now,' said Sylvia, brushing her hair out of her eyes with the back of her hand and leaving a smudge of flour on her face. 'You'd better show him down here.'

The maid was scandalised, but she did as she was bid, and Eddie Seymour was treated to the sight of Miss Shaw taking the second batch of biscuits out of the oven, her skirt tightening across her hips as she bent down to the oven.

'He-llo!' he said, with an appreciative smile on his face. 'Sacked the cook?'

She turned her flushed face to him. 'Mr van den Hoep has gone to see his nephew off to the front. And I must have these wretched things ready for the May Fair on Saturday.' She glanced up at the rain-streaked windows. 'Providing the fête isn't a complete wash-out.'

'Strange - I never thought of you as a domestic soul. Here - you've got flour on your nose.'

She caught her breath as he reached out and ran his finger over her skin. After a long moment he let his hand fall.

'I won't shake hands,' she said with a nervous laugh. 'It wouldn't do for you to turn up in the Chancellor's office with flour smudges.'

He bent his head down to her. 'I'll settle for a kiss,' he murmured.

She turned her face away and went on transferring the biscuits from the baking tray to the cooling rack as if he hadn't spoken. 'I think these will do,' she said shakily. 'The first batch came out like bullets. I'd feed them to the birds, but it would break their beaks.'

He laughed, not at all put out by her rejection. When he reached out to pick up one of the latest batch, she rapped his knuckles with a wooden spoon. 'They're in aid of the Belgian refugees, you know,' she said with mock severity. 'You'll have to come to the May Fair and buy one.'

'Nothing would give me greater pleasure, but sadly I shall be back in the north again, inspecting shell factories. Assuming Asquith's still in office and I'm still in employment.'

'Is there any doubt?' She turned her attention to the next batch of dough, cutting out circles with a turn of her wrist and placing them on the empty tray. 'Max is away again, so we're not getting the up-to-date news.'

'It's coming to a crisis, right enough. The attack on Aubers Ridge had to be called off because our gunners ran out of heavy shells. Shrapnel has little effect on the trenches, so when our men went forward they were caught on the wire and the German machine guns simply mowed them down. Terrible loss of life. It will be in all the papers tomorrow. This time the commanders went direct to the newspapers - and who can blame them?'

'And Fisher?'

'The rumours are true. He's resigned the Fleet - says Churchill is constantly overruling him. He'll be a great loss - and at the worst possible time, just as LG thought he'd brought Italy in on our side.'

'Do you think Asquith will resign?'

'Depends how hard he's pushed,' said Seymour. 'We can only hope...'

When he was gone, she took a plate of the little biscuits up to her mother's room.

'No change, dearie.' Nanny Armstrong bustled about to make tea in the little kitchen adjoining the invalid's room. 'Won't be long now, I shouldn't think.'

'Perhaps I'd better not go to the May Fair.'

'Nonsense. What can you do that I can't?' Unspoken between them was the knowledge that Sylvia's presence, far from pleasing her mother, only served to irritate her.

Sylvia fixed a smile on her face and picked up the tray. 'Tea up!' she said. 'Look. I've baked you some biscuits.'

'You?' Although she grew weaker by the day, Eithne Shaw's voice had lost none of its bite. 'If it's as good as your knitting, or your embroidery, you might as well send for the undertaker now!'

Sylvia poured milky tea into her mother's invalid cup, trying to ignore the hurtful words.

'A little late to be learning housewifely duties now,' her mother grumbled on. 'Too late now you're on the shelf. Drove Hugh away with your stubbornness. Thought yourself too good for Jeremy Lang.' She shook off her daughter's helping hand and called for Nurse Armstrong. For a moment she lay back against her pillows, her face grey. When she'd caught her breath again she said: 'Why did God have to take my *sons* away?'

Sylvia held back the tears until she was outside the door. 'She's in a great deal of pain,' said Nanny Armstrong, patting her arm. 'She didn't mean any of it, I'm sure. Why, you couldn't have done more for her.'

'I don't know why I let it upset me. It's nothing she hasn't said before.'

'I'll give her some more of the doctor's bottle. It will ease her.'

Ease her out of her pain and into the next world, thought Sylvia. But that was all anyone could do for her now.

52

The drenching, sweeping rain of the previous few days had disappeared overnight and on Saturday she alighted from the omnibus outside Jubilee Park in bright sunshine. It seemed like months since she'd been out in the warm sun, with no one to think of but herself - for a whole day! The boxes of biscuits and the knots of Belgian blue ribbon had been delivered the previous day, and she'd left the car for Piet, one of the Belgians, to drive Lady Alice out in the afternoon.

She shook out her crushed skirts and made her way along the path indicated by the young man on the gate, to where the booths and stalls were being set up. She'd deliberated long and hard on what to wear and had finally settled on an elegant light wool costume with a broad band of Belgian blue around the raised hem of the skirt, and a darker sash around the tunic to match. High buttoned navy boots were daringly revealed by the calf-length skirt, and the attractive navy hat, worn at a jaunty angle, was trimmed with knots of matching ribbon.

The persistent cold winds of the last few months had delayed the spring flowers, but today in the park spring and summer seemed to have come at once. Daffodils and tulips were in belated bloom while the rhododendrons were already flaunting their bright and blowsy flowers; the pink and cream of magnolia petals glowed against the misty green background of the opening leaf buds of birch, larch and willow, and in the damp earth beneath the trees, bluebells and windflowers bloomed side by side. The sight of so much beauty stopped her in her tracks and brought a smile to her face.

A well-dressed man stopped on the path beside her and raised his hat. 'A splendid sight after such a long winter,' he said with a smile. Before she could respond, he swooped down, picked some of the spring blooms and presented them to her with a flourish. 'To wear in your hat,' he said.

'It's very kind,' said Sylvia, rather taken aback, 'but I'm sure you ought not. The gardener...'

'...is employed by the corporation. Paid for by our rates and taxes. Therefore in our employ. Planting bulbs and seeds paid for by us. Think no more of it.'

Rather self-consciously she set the flower stalks in her buttonhole, just above the arrow-headed brooch. 'I see we're going the same way,' he said, falling into step with her. 'Indeed,' he nodded at her brooch, 'we are also coming from the same direction.'

She looked at him with renewed interest: a male supporter of female suffrage was a rare enough bird, and one to be cherished.

Her heart sank into her boots when she came in sight of the Suffrage booth. Manned by the usual mixture of ladies draped in fur and lace, working women in plain tweeds, and younger women dressed in khaki, the booth was swathed in a large banner which read: 'Women for the War Effort'. That was guaranteed to offend those Suffragettes, like Sylvia Pankhurst, who were against the war. And the positioning of the booth was guaranteed to offend most of the rest, as it was attached to the No-Conscription stall, to which her escort, after a brief bow, made his way.

From the little knot of well-dressed women behind her, tending the spirit stove and setting out tea cups, she could hear plenty of barbed comments about their situation. The WSPU members were all behind Emmeline and Christabel Pankhurst in their whole-hearted support of the war, even conscription if necessary.

'Oh, don't listen to them,' said Nina sunnily. 'They've been looking for a fight for ages, trying to divide up the sisterhood.'

Easy for her to say, thought Sylvia, when her allegiance was clearly to her brother and his fellows in the No-Conscription movement. Maybe she should have listened to Max when he cautioned her against the Fair, saying that she didn't know who she would be associating with. She'd given him a short answer for attempting to interfere - a pity, since they'd recently been getting on so well. Now she thought he might have had a point.

The two booths had prime position, directly on the path from the entrance gates and in the lee of the old house at the centre of the park. Built as a hunting lodge for a Stuart king's mistress, it had by the end of the nineteenth century become so encroached upon by the streets of east London that it was as impossible to live in as it was to sell. The family had struck upon the bright idea of gifting the house and park to the borough in Victoria's jubilee year, which at least meant that they gained a title out of their white elephant.

In the adjoining booth, the man who had given her the flowers had taken charge and sent the others scurrying around, setting out petitions and pens while he tested the megaphone.

'See Bertie Russell is here,' said one of the older women.

'Stirring everyone up as usual,' said Florrie, one of a pair of stocky cousins from Whitechapel who had taken over the family business cleaning office windows when the men of the family had enlisted. 'Ah well, there's no show without Punch.'

'What did he say to you?' asked Nina, who was setting out some remarkably ugly embroidered pen holders on one corner of the stall while Florrie and Winnie hung Suffrage colours of purple, white and green from the angles of the booth.

'Who?'

'Bertie Russell. The man who walked you here,' said Nina's friend Agnes. Her tunic skirt was even shorter than Sylvia's and drew all eyes as she reached up to pin the bunting around the booth. 'He stood for Parliament on the Women's Vote once, you know. Lost, of course. He's a No-Conscription man now. Did he give you those flowers?'

Sylvia nodded slowly. Looking up from the photographs of the Earl's Court Refugee School waiting to be pinned up on the boards, she saw Russell smiling at her across the half-partition. Without his hat he was shorter and older than she'd realised.

'I heard he's on the look-out for a wife,' said Agnes, *sotto voce*.

Nina frowned. 'I thought he was having an affair with that actress - what's her name? Connie something?'

'He is. And with Ottoline Morell. That tall horse-faced woman with the red hair. That's her husband next to her.' Agnes nodded at the adjacent booth. 'But he has to marry and have an heir. Countess

Russell, eh?' She giggled. 'I wouldn't let a few mistresses stand between me and a decent title.'

With a wry smile Sylvia turned back to the trays of biscuits. After all the years of fighting for equal rights, very little had changed.

By the time the gates opened, the booth looked very smart, with all the bunting, the knitted purses and mittens, handmade goods and bric-a-brac, photographs of the Refugee School and Canteen, biscuits and cakes and the box for the Serbian Smoke Fund, with three cigarettes artistically arranged next to a trench lighter.

The cigarettes proved to be something of a trial for Sylvia: every time she leaned forward to hand tea, take money or wrap purchases, her nostrils filled with the smell of tobacco and she had to resist the temptation to reach out and take one. 'I am no longer a smoker,' she told herself sternly.

As the public began to circulate around the stalls, the No-Conscription Fellowship inevitably came in for some abuse, but most patriotic citizens were distracted by the women in the adjacent booth, and persuaded to buy a cup of tea and a Belgian biscuit, all proceeds to go to the Refugee School. Only one group of inebriated young men gave them any real trouble, name-calling, and trying to drown out the megaphone. Outnumbered by the men manning the booth, they moved on at last, leaving only the stink of drink behind them.

Sylvia wrinkled her nose. 'They must have been drinking solidly all morning!'

'There's been drunken gangs goin' round the East End for days now, ever since the *Lusitania* was sunk,' said Winnie. 'Beatin' up everyone with a German name that they can get their hands on, an' drivin' them out in the middle of the night.'

'They've not got the brains of a flea between 'em,' said Florrie scornfully. 'They smashed up the pub on our corner last night. Owner's a Scotchman, but they said Machin looked German enough for them.'

By half past two they'd sold almost all the biscuits and a great many of the hand-crafted items, steadily replenished from boxes at the back of the booth. It amazed her that anyone should buy the ugly knitted purses and mis-shapen mittens 'to send to your own special soldier'. People must be more patriotic than she'd given them credit for.

She wondered what elegant hands had made such a mess of the knitting: Lady Eleanor's, she guessed. She'd only stayed an hour, standing at the back all the time, unwilling to soil her hands by dealing with the general public. Sylvia wondered why she'd bothered to come.

'Better have some more of Winnie's mittens out,' said Agnes cheerily. 'When she and Florrie come back you'd best take a break, Sylvia.' She looked over at the No Conscription booth. 'Oh, what a pity. Bertie Russell's already gone.'

'Went off about half an hour ago with the Morells,' said Nina. 'But I'm sure Mark would be happy to go around the fair with you.'

'Thank you all for your kind endeavours,' said Sylvia with a mock curtsey, 'but I am *not* in need of an escort!'

Her ears pricked up at the mention of a name she recognised from her time in Holloway, one of the three who, like her, had been taken to the punishment cells away from the others. 'No point in looking out for her,' said the woman. 'She's one of Lady Harriet's now.' She turned her finger around at her temple. 'Completely mad, poor soul,' she murmured. 'If Lady Harriet hadn't taken her in, it would have been the asylum for her.'

Lady Harriet was one of the number of titled ladies, comfortably well-off, who had supported the cause, although mostly with funds, rather than at what Freddie would have called 'the sharp end'. One or two, like Constance Lytton, daughter of an earlier Viceroy of India, had put themselves through arrest and force-feeding, but most ladies had contented themselves with arranging to bring the sick and exhausted ex-prisoners off to the country, or spirit them *out* of the country in those cases where they were released under the Cat-and-Mouse Act, and in danger of being taken back to prison once their health had improved.

Lady Harriet, she learned, was still caring for sick suffragettes in her grand London house, where Sylvia had spent time on her release and only left - far too soon - because her mother had proceeded to fall out with everyone at the house, accusing all and sundry of having led her 'poor deluded daughter' astray.

She remembered the kindly woman doctor who had come up to Lady Harriet's grand mansion to tut-tut over the cobbled stitching of her torn mouth carried out in Holloway Prison, before carefully cutting it back open and re-stitching it, wearing a pair of enormous round magnifying spectacles that made her look like a curious frog. 'There. No laughing for a month and it should end up looking like a dimple. Only don't let Harriet take you to her nerve specialist,' she'd said severely as she packed up her medical bag. 'He claims a high rate of success, but ask him how many are still alive after two months...'

Eavesdropping openly now, she learned that Lady Harriet's equally grand country home had been turned into a convalescent home for those who had developed heart conditions from their rough treatment in prison, and would be invalids for the rest of their lives. Some had even died. Constance Lytton was reputed to have carved a V for votes into her chest with a sharpened hairpin; she was now a complete invalid, confined to her bed. Others had suffered total mental collapse. Inevitably Emily Davison's name came up, with the old debate about whether she really had intended to kill herself under the King's horse. 'Force-fed forty-nine times,' said Agnes in an awed whisper. 'That's enough to drive anyone out of their mind.'

'You know, I heard that some of the prisoners in the north were force-fed other ways...even worse ways...' said another. She whispered in her companion's ear.

'No! I don't see how that can even be possible...!' protested Agnes. 'Oh, I feel quite faint...!'

Sylvia shivered and moved away. So much for her hopes of discovering how other women had coped with their ordeal...the simple answer was that they hadn't.

It had been a mistake to come. The walls of the booth started to crowd in on her and the megaphone announcements sounded curiously distorted. She forced herself to take a deep breath, digging her toes into the ground, reminding herself angrily that she wasn't ready to be *one of Lady Harriet's* just yet.

She was slipping out of the back of the booth when Nina tugged on her sleeve. 'I say, isn't that Lady Alice's son?' The crowd was thinning out around the booths, most of them heading for the bandstand where the Mayor was giving his speech, exhorting citizens to spend and spend for the splendid war effort, but although Sylvia craned her neck, she couldn't see Max.

'I must have been mistaken,' said Nina.

Sylvia was about to come back with a witty remark when the Suffrage booth began to sway. The front counter fell off the trestles with a crash, narrowly missing Nina's feet. Nina shot out onto the grass, almost colliding with one of the attackers.

The drunken louts had moved on from hurling insults and abuse and were rocking the uprights of the No Conscription booth in an attempt to overturn it. If one booth went, so would the other.

As the back awning of the Suffrage booth flapped in, the kettle slid off the spirit stove and splashed its contents liberally across the ground. Someone screamed as hot water caught her shoe, and women rushed towards the swaying door in a panic.

'Stop that!' cried Mark Doncaster, interposing himself between the gang and the booth. 'You'll injure the women!' One of the attackers whirled him round and jabbed a fist in his face while the rest of the gang, intent on total wreckage, rocked at the supports and tore at the canopy.

Nina leaped on her brother's assailant, grabbing the back of his collar and trying to haul him off. With a curse, the man flung her aside. Nina went one way and her elegant mercury-winged hat went the other, to be trampled into the mud. As Sylvia hurried to her friend's aid, one of the gang barred her way.

'You a Hun-coddler too, darling?' he jeered, jabbing his stiff arm into her bosom. Sylvia reeled back with a cry of pain, her arms shielding her chest from further assault. Out of the corner of her watering eyes she saw the gang laying into Mark Doncaster and his companions. Florrie, arriving back from her break, shot past her, sleeves rolled up, and began to even the odds.

The last of the women had barely escaped the collapsing booths when the overturned spirit stove ignited the bunting. Blue flames crept up the frame, licking at the edge of the awning. Trapped between the booths and the house by the fighting, they watched with terror in their eyes. A few of them, hardly more than schoolgirls, began to cry. Winnie, seeing Florrie in the thick of the fight, leaped onto the back of Doncaster's attacker, belabouring him with work-hardened fists. 'Get this one off me, Greg!' he bellowed, trying in vain to dislodge her. 'Load o' bleedin' Hun-lovers! Should lock 'em all up and throw away the key!'

'Close the door Mr Nash. And turn the key....'

A bearded thug grabbed one of the young girls, grunting filthy words at her. The girl screamed, wide-eyed with fear, and Sylvia lashed out without thought. The man reeled back, blood pouring from his nose. She froze to the spot, appalled by her own actions. He came at her once more, fists flailing, and though she ducked, his fist caught her on the temple. As she fell, a stick flashed by her face and struck her attacker on the shoulder. 'Keep your hands off her,' growled a familiar voice.

She shook the blackness from her head and tried to struggle to her feet. 'Max, no! Look out!'

'Max? Ho, we got ourselves a Hun, boys!' Another thug drew his foot back and Bryson was kicked and jostled to the floor.

'No!' she screamed.

'Told you they was all Hun-lovers!'

Max went down fighting, with Winnie and Florrie in full support, but it was only the sound of the police whistles that brought the uneven conflict to an end.

A large rough hand dragged Sylvia to her feet. 'I thought our troubles with you lot were over,' said the burly sergeant.

'It wasn't us.' She wriggled out of his grip and hurled herself down in the mud where Max lay white and still. 'Oh God, Max!' she whispered. 'What have they done to you?'

Doncaster turned on the policeman. 'Don't just stand there,' he said, wiping the blood out of his eyes. 'Get him an ambulance.'

'The Conshies give orders now, do they?' sneered the constable.

'Do it, you fool,' said Sylvia savagely. 'He's badly hurt.' And when the policeman still didn't move, she screamed at him. 'This is Lloyd George's right-hand man! Do you want to explain to *him* why you left him lying in a pool of blood?'

53

Sylvia closed the door, shutting out the clatter and chatter of the ward, until the only sounds were the unnaturally loud ticking of the clock on the wall opposite the bed and the gentle, doomed fluttering of a moth as it battered its wings against the window pane.

She set down the basket, cupped the insect in her hand and reached out of the hinged upper pane to release it. When she drew her hand back in, she fancied she could still feel it fluttering against her palm.

The wave of emotion that swept over her at the sight of Max lying in the hospital bed, eyes closed and face as white as the starched counterpane, took her by surprise. Without her realising it, he had once more crept in under her guard.

She turned away, unable to look at him lying there so helpless. If only she hadn't defied him and gone to the May Fair! He might have gone on for years coping with the earlier injury, but now, by her folly and stubbornness she had brought him to this. Tears prickled at the back of her eyes and she groped for a handkerchief.

'Come in, Miss Shaw. Forgive me if I don't get up.'

She jumped at the sound of the voice. When she turned back to the bed he was regarding her with that level, steady gaze.

'I didn't mean to disturb you. The nurse said you were sleeping, but that I might just look in.' Nurses treated you differently if you were in uniform - doing your bit, like them. Bit of a fraud really, to be wearing the uniform at all, as she hadn't reported for duty for several days, but in a city increasingly full of khaki and wounded heroes, it made her feel a little more comfortable. And today it had served its purpose.

'I wasn't sleeping.' He shifted restlessly. 'I've hardly slept since I came into this accursed place. I keep my eyes closed to avoid inane conversation with Nurse Jackson. While she's around the ghost of Henrietta Jennings will never cease to haunt me!'

'I'm happy to see you're still in good spirits.'

'In my customary bad temper, you mean.' He smiled up at her as she put the hothouse grapes on the bedside locker. 'Good of you to visit.'

'I would have come before, but they wouldn't let me in. Family only for the last few days. I've had to wait outside.' She swallowed hard. 'They say the shrapnel has shifted. You're to be operated on...'

'Yes.'

'I feel responsible for what happened. I'm so sorry - '

He held up his hand. 'Miss Shaw, I was there. I know exactly who was responsible and it was not you.'

'Nevertheless...'

'Let's hear no more of it.' His mouth tightened as he saw the strip of plaster along the hairline beneath her cap. 'How is your head?'

She tilted her uniform cap forward to cover it 'Oh, this is nothing. Only a flesh wound, really.' It was more than that, having been inflicted where there was very little flesh. She'd spent an unpleasant half hour having it stitched and whatever they'd swabbed it with had long since worn off: her head had been throbbing dully for days.

'And the others? Doncaster looked to be in a bad way, but I have so far failed to find news of him here.'

'A broken shoulder and several cracked ribs. Florrie and Winnie have black eyes, but they said it was worth it. Everyone else is fine...battered and bruised, but nothing more serious. Nina has taken Mark to relatives in Lincolnshire to recover.'

He frowned. 'Was my mother here earlier?'

'Yes. But they hustled her out when the specialist came to see you.' Lady Alice had been too upset to come when Max was first admitted to hospital, and Sylvia was cross that they'd turned her out on her first visit. 'You looked pretty much out for the count by the time he'd finished. Piet has driven her home.'

'You didn't go with them?'

'Stayed to have my stitches checked. I'm not really supposed to be in here, but I wanted to bring you these.'

'I've been hoping you'd get past the dragon at the gate.'

'Sister Eames? She doesn't know I'm in here. Five minutes only, the nurse said. And I'm not to agitate you.'

'Far from it. I'm delighted to see you. You see, Miss Shaw, there are two things I need you to do for me.'

'You have only to say...'

His lips twitched. 'Better hear what they are before you rush in.' He shut his eyes tightly as a wave of pain swept over him and instinctively she reached out and held his hand. When at last he opened his eyes again he tried to smile up at her, but it went awry. 'First of all I would ask you to take care of my mother - while I am in here and - if I don't - '

She dropped his hand as swiftly as if it had burnt her. 'That goes without saying. She's been so good to me.' Her voice grew sharp. 'How could you think it necessary even to mention it?'

'Forgive me. A bed of pain is not the best place for clarity of thought,' he said, aware that he'd caused offence and playing shamelessly on her sympathy to excuse him. 'It's only natural I should worry what will happen to her if all of this - ' he swallowed hard '- if I don't make it through.'

'You will make it through,' she said fiercely. 'You *will*.'

'I have every intention of doing so. But I'm also a realist. The surgery is - not precisely straightforward. That's why I want you to marry me.'

Her hand flailed against the basket of fruit, sending the hothouse grapes rolling across the table. Her mouth opened and closed several times but no sound came out.

'Anyone would think I've asked you to commit murder,' he said mildly.

'*Marry* you?' she said at last. 'Are you mad?'

'Is your objection to the state of marriage, or to the suggested partner?'

'Neither.' She coloured hotly. 'I - I mean - both.' She turned away to the window.

'Perhaps you already have an understanding with someone? Eddie Seymour? Mark Doncaster? Or that painter fellow?'

'Octavius? Good Heavens, no! I have no thoughts of marriage. Not with anyone!'

'You must know I'd need good reason to ask it of you. Will you sit down and hear those reasons out?' he asked softly. 'Preferably without wrecking the rest of my room?'

She flushed and muttered something under her breath, then, when she sat down, she busied herself picking up the grapes and replacing them in the basket.

'Would you sit where I can see you?' He patted the counterpane. 'Perch on the bed. Please?' It was important to him that he could see her face - and that she could see his. 'I find it tiring to turn my head always to the side.'

She leaned one hip against the side of the bed, taking care not to jostle him.

'Look at me? Please?' She took a deep breath and looked him in the face.

'There isn't the time to talk this through in a leisurely manner,' he said quietly, 'nor to hedge my words about in case I cause offence. Naturally I want to make sure that you and my mother are taken care of in the event that I don't survive....' She opened her mouth to protest again, but he held up his hand. 'Please. No platitudes.' He took a deep breath against the pain; it was a struggle to marshal his arguments when his brain felt like sawdust. 'If I don't make it through, then Esmond's children will be left to the mercy of the Graysons. You've met them...I don't need to tell you.... Before I'm even cold in my grave they'll have my mother out of Ardingley House. They'll dismiss Mrs Harmitage and take the children off to Scotland. God knows what kind of an upbringing they'll have. Without supervision Grayson will run through the money in no time. Harry will be left with nothing but the title - and who knows what will happen to poor little Emily?'

'But surely your mother - '

'What chance would she have to keep track of what was happening in Scotland? And she couldn't pursue the application for custody - her blindness would always count against her. You, on the other hand, as my widow...'

'Don't!'

'... would have both status and right.'

The door opened and Sister Eames came in, tutting loudly as she saw Sylvia leaning on the bed.

'I shall have to ask you to leave, miss,' she said, bustling to the bed and smoothing down the counterpane. 'We're expecting Mr Harbury-Morton again this afternoon, and we must have our rest, Mr Bryson, mustn't we?'

Max bit back an acid retort. 'A few minutes more, if you please, sister,' he said at last.

'Come, come, Mr Bryson. We know how important our rest is, don't we? Mr Harbury-Morton will expect us to be at our best for the investigation, you know. It will take a great deal out of us.'

Max's lips went white. 'Mr Harbury-Morton can go to the - '

Sylvia hurried into the breach. 'We won't delay you much longer, sister. But it's vital Mr Bryson should relieve his mind of any worries before he undergoes surgery.'

'I think you may leave it to the medical staff to decide what's vital for the patient, miss.' Sister Eames gave the counterpane one last tug into line and stalked to the door. 'I shall return to prepare you for Mr Harbury-Morton in exactly five minutes, Mr Bryson.'

The door snapped closed. Sylvia moved back into Max's line of sight. 'You'd better say the rest of it quickly, before she comes back,' she said with the ghost of a smile. 'I'll bite my tongue and hear you out.'

'I'm sorry if you feel I'm putting pressure on you.'

'Pressure?' She gave a slightly hysterical laugh. 'Whatever gave you that idea?' She dropped her eyes. 'Sorry. I said I wouldn't interrupt.'

'If I could think of some other way to do this, I would. But there is no other way. So. If you marry me, you will inherit my estate, such as it is. There's the house in Charles Street, and another in the country.'

'I couldn't marry you for your money!'

He waved an impatient hand. 'There's enough to care for my mother - and yours - and keep you in some comfort for the rest of your life. And as my widow, you would be trustee in my place for the children.'

'And keep them safe from the Graysons?'

He nodded. 'The court case comes up soon. I wouldn't like to think I've wasted all that effort.' He shifted and winced. 'Whatever you may feel about it, what I propose ensures that those I care about - and that does include you - will be looked after if the worst happens.'

Her head jerked up. Slow colour crept into her cheeks as she took in what he'd said.

His eyes held hers. 'Please believe what I say. I care for you. But I don't wish there to be any misunderstanding. The likelihood is that if you marry me, you'll be a widow within the week.' He looked at her sadly, remembering the effect she'd had on him when he had first met her, standing up for her brother, talking animatedly of justice and right, making him think for the first time in his life that he might have met a woman worth the knowing. But the German shell had blown all that away. His fingers clenched and unclenched. 'Sylvia, you don't know how much it grieves me to say this but, whether I live or die, what I am proposing will be a marriage of convenience.'

'I don't understand.'

'I assure you, Sylvia, even the prettiest young nurse has failed to make any effect on this cursed body of mine.'

'Oh.'

'The shrapnel is lodged near the base of the spine,' he said gruffly. 'My eyes appreciate, my imagination formulates... and my body... makes its apologies and leaves.'

54

He wanted her to give an answer straight away, but she couldn't do it. She sat for nearly an hour outside the hospital, as the bright morning faded to a cloudy afternoon, unaware of the cold, or the concerned looks from passers-by. Lorries and ambulances came and went, picking up convalescents, delivering more broken bodies to be patched up. She wished she could be at work: she thought better when she was active. But she was banned from driving for a week, because of the blow to the head from the Jubilee Park riot.

Thoughts buzzed around her mind like angry bees. Max's

predicament...the children....his mother....her mother.... So many conflicting thoughts. How could she possibly decide what to do?

Marriage was something she had put firmly out of her mind, but would it really be such a terrible problem for her to consider it again? She'd always enjoyed male company - being brought up in her family had made that inevitable - and she only had to remember the scene in Octavius's rooms to realise that the warmer feelings she'd suppressed after Hugh's defection had not gone away. Even with Eddie Seymour...and Max himself....

She sank her head into her hands. Poor Max! To have to face that when he was still a comparatively young man. She remembered the VAD nurse in Kent telling her of the man who had screamed for two days after being told of his misfortune. If she did marry Max, it would be an end to all such feelings. For life.

Assuming Max had one.

And then there were her principles: married women, not being ratepayers, had been excluded from just about every suffrage bill ever put before Parliament. But how could she think of such a thing when Max's life was in danger?

She went in to take her leave of him, as she'd promised, but was refused admission until after the specialist's visit. She couldn't return to Ardingley House until she'd spoken to him. Instead of pacing up and down the corridor, she set off to find someone who could tell her about the forthcoming operation.

A VAD nurse directed her to the Roentgen Ray Department - once again it helped that she was in uniform and she was happy to let the nurse believe she was there on duty. The technician was about to go to lunch, and over poached eggs and toast in Lyons' Corner House, he explained to her how the vast and bulky Westinghouse electro-magnet she had seen in the department, newly arrived from Pittsburgh in America, was used to probe for shrapnel in newly-wounded men. Powered on 4000 watts and operated on 70 volts, he said with pride, *and* it came with different shaped poles for different applications - though there were barely half a dozen men in the country who could operate it.

'Less painful than the usual probing, and pretty powerful. But it's not so easy when the wounds have healed. Scar tissue's a lot harder to get through, see. So we take two X-rays, something like a stereographic photograph, if you follow me, by slightly moving the bulb that sends out the X-rays.' He drew a sketch on a paper napkin. 'The new probe can send a rattle to my telephone headset when it contacts metal. All very clever.'

But the risks were enormous, especially when the metal was lodged near vital nerves or, as in Max's case, alongside the spine. In such cases paralysis or death could not be ruled out.

When she was finally admitted to the side ward in the late afternoon, Max was looking even worse than before. Sweat stood out on his brow and his skin had the colour and texture of cold porridge.

'It was a bit of an ordeal,' he said through gritted teeth, in answer to her question. 'Couldn't put me out, you see. Had to see the reactions...'

She wiped his forehead with her handkerchief, brushing his hair out of his eyes. 'They won't let me stay. They want you to sleep.'

He put out a feeble hand to detain her. 'Something I must say.' She sat at the bedside, holding his hand as though she could infuse warmth and health through her grip.

'Occurred to me...might think I want to marry you just because I want you to look after the children.' He took a deep breath. 'You may not like children. I never asked. Mother's not young - you must think you'll be saddled with them for ever.' She tried to speak, but he waved her to silence. 'Only until the war ends. My sister Charlotte - in Canada - she'll give them a loving home. Atlantic crossings - not advisable - just now.'

She shook her head in confusion. 'Where does Imogen come in all this?'

'She doesn't. Just a case of battling it out with the Graysons.' She was pleased to see that a little colour was coming back into his cheeks. 'I meant it when I said we were unlikely to see her again.'

'Actually, the children aren't a problem,' she said, and was surprised to realise that she meant it. 'But I can't pursue the case - I'm no lawyer.'

'It's all set up,' he said. 'My partners will show you the papers. It's just a case of - Good God!'

Sylvia followed his gaze. A tweed-suited man, with a heavy moustache familiar from countless caricatures, bounced through the ward doors, followed by Eddie Seymour.

Max struggled to sit up, but she pushed him back against the pillows.

'Sir, I'm honoured. To find the time at such a busy period...'

'Just now I'll take any excuse to get away,' said the visitor, in a lilting Welsh accent. 'What do you say, Seymour? This is a fine way to avoid all the in-fighting, isn't it?' He patted Max vigorously on the shoulder. 'Perhaps they could find a bed apiece for us until it's all blown over?'

Sylvia could have taken the opportunity to slip away, but she was rooted to the spot. First the Prime Minister, now the Chancellor. What circles she was moving in! Lloyd George was shorter than she'd expected, but there was vitality in every inch of him and a sparkle in his eyes that made him look much younger than his fifty years and twice the man that Asquith was.

'May I introduce...'

'Introductions are unnecessary, Mr Bryson,' said Sylvia, regaining her composure. 'I can recognise the Chancellor of the Illiberal Party.'

Eddie bit off a laugh. Max rolled his eyes to the ceiling. 'Sir, may I introduce Miss Sylvia Shaw....the lady I hope will consent to become my wife.'

Lloyd George's eyes twinkled. 'Going for the sympathy vote, eh?' He reached his hand across the bed, then hesitated as he saw the badge on her coat. 'Perhaps the young lady does not wish to shake hands with the enemy?'

'But if Max thought you were worth saving...?' Her lips twitched. 'If I *should* decide to marry him, it wouldn't do to start married life disputing with my husband.'

'Hah!' said Max.

The Chancellor smiled as he took her hand and shook it vigorously. 'You mustn't believe all you hear, Miss Shaw. It was not me he saved, but a young captain. He threw him at me and knocked us both in the mud. Although the way the shrapnel came across immediately upon my ignominious descent, I can tell you I was a damn sight safer in the mud than out of it.'

She lingered only a moment after their departure, but when she emerged she found the two visitors waiting for her.

'May we offer you a ride home to Ardingley House, Miss Shaw?' said Eddie. 'I hear you're not driving at the moment.'

'Banned for a few more days.'

An elegant motor was drawn up to the pavement, driven, Sylvia saw, by a woman. Sylvia leaned back against the cushioned seats and as they drove through the streets, Lloyd George quizzed her about her work, showing an unexpected familiarity with the voluntary services.

'They've rallied magnificently,' he said. 'Driving lorries and ambulances, working on the railways, and even in the munitions factories. The nation is grateful to the women.'

'It needn't be,' she replied with spirit. 'We *are* the nation - half of it, at least. Even if you don't deem us worthy of a vote.'

He looked at her quizzically. 'As I said before, Miss Shaw, you shouldn't believe all you hear. I didn't oppose every franchise bill.'

'You opposed the only one which came close to being passed!'

'Because it only gave the vote to propertied widows and spinsters. It would be a very foolish Liberal who chose to give the vote to Bath widows and not to the wives of working men. You might as well tell the Tories they can govern for perpetuity! And remember that many working men still don't have the vote themselves. I want universal suffrage or nothing.' He leaned back against the cushions and closed his eyes.

'And when is that likely to happen? This century or the next?'

Seymour intervened. 'We were on the point of negotiating towards that when the war broke out...'

'Talks about the possibility of talks?' Her voice was full of scorn. 'The first debate was in the eighteen-sixties! You could have negotiated at any time instead of flinging us all into prison!' In spite of herself her hand went to the scar at the side of her mouth.

'But you must agree, you Suffragettes gave due cause - '

'I am a *Suffragist,* Mr Seymour. There is a difference. I threw no stones, broke no windows, fire-bombed no houses. I canvassed support and helped draw up petitions...but you put me in prison nonetheless.'

Lloyd George opened his eyes again. 'After the war you shall have your vote, Miss Shaw. But what use would it be to give you the vote now? Or give the Irish their independence? The Kaiser could still take it all away again. No, you'll have to wait till we've won the war. And that, for the moment, is my only priority.'

55

Sylvia put her head on one side and surveyed the bowl of spring flowers in the centre of the table. 'Something else I can't do,' she said wryly to Lady Alice, who had joined her downstairs for the first time in days. 'It looks as though I stood on the far side of the room and threw them at the vase. A few landed in the right place, purely by chance.'

'Don't spoil my illusions,' said Lady Alice briskly. 'I'm sure they look perfectly good.' She patted the seat next to hers. 'Come and sit by me a moment, my dear. I want to talk to you about Max.'

Sylvia hesitated. She wasn't sure she wanted to talk to anyone about Max until she'd made her own mind up what she was going to do, and that, after a long and wakeful night, was still far from clear. She'd cancelled her duties for the next few days, in case Lady Alice could be persuaded to return to the hospital, but that only left her more time to think.

Out in the hall the telephone shrilled and they both looked at each other.

'News?' said Lady Alice, her face pale.

'Can't be,' said Sylvia briskly. 'The operation isn't until tomorrow.'

'Mr Seymour, your ladyship,' said Maisie. 'For Miss Shaw.'

Sylvia hurried out to the phone. She skipped the polite greetings. 'Is it Max? Is something wrong?'

'No. But he wants to see you.'

She let out her breath in a sigh. 'We can be there in fifteen minutes.'

'Not Lady Alice. Just you.'

She dropped her voice, conscious of the half-open door behind her. 'Surely his mother...'

'They're not allowing any visitors in this morning. Only you. The operation has been brought forward to this afternoon. This is your last chance to see him before they put him under.' There was a pause. 'He hopes you'll give him your decision.'

'I see.' She swallowed hard. If she was to agree to marry Max, it had to be now. 'But why doesn't he want - '

'Stop dithering, Sylvia,' said Eddie crisply. 'Come now, or there's no point in you coming at all.'

'I'll be there as quickly as I can.' Only after she'd put down the phone did she think how difficult it must have been for Eddie to carry out his friend's commission. It hadn't escaped her notice that Mr Seymour had taken a shine to her.

Lady Alice was in the conservatory, talking to the gardener about summer bedding, and accepted Sylvia's story that she was taking the car out on business for Max. Sylvia hated to deceive her, but she still didn't know what she was going to do when she reached the hospital. She could do without two of them trying to persuade her.

The whole hospital seemed to be in a state of barely subdued excitement when she arrived. The little nurse who had let her into Max's room the previous day called out to her as she passed the nursing station, but she had no time to stop and chat. As the door to the side-ward swung beneath her hand she saw a group gathered around Max's bed, and for a moment she felt sick and giddy. Matron was there, with the hospital chaplain beside her. Was Max dying? Would she have to break the news to his mother? Then she saw that Matron was looking as pleased as punch, and gradually her breathing returned to normal.

The room was cramped. She wondered that Matron had allowed so many in. There was Lloyd George, sandwiched between two officers in dress uniform. The man closest to her turned his head, and her jaw dropped as she recognised King George.

From that moment everything seemed to pass in a dream. Sylvia was introduced to the king and informed that his own surgeon was to assist in the operation, to observe the new equipment. Had she remembered to curtsey? She couldn't be sure.

She was passed along to the head of the bed. Max held out his hand and she took it. The hospital chaplain said a prayer, King George touched Max's shoulders with a dress sword, pinned a medal on Max's striped silk pyjamas and said a few words, then everyone bowed and curtsied and the royal party was gone.

She wanted to pinch herself as the door swung closed behind the last equerry. She looked down at the shining medal on the striped navy silk cloth, but there was no sense of excitement or exultation. Her heart lurched as she realised the significance of that brief ceremony: they were all expecting Max to die. Tears pricked her eyes and she brushed them away with her free hand.

Eddie Seymour looked at her across the bed, and she thought he was about to speak, until he moved away, breaking the spell.

'I can only give you ten minutes, Max,' Lloyd George called from the doorway. 'Expected in Downing Street.' He turned back to talk to the king's doctor. The chaplain, face jowly and mournful as a bloodhound's, gazed up at the ceiling, as if seeking divine guidance.

Max was propped against the pillows, almost as white as the sheet he lay beneath. 'LG and Eddie have offered to be witnesses,' he said through parched lips. 'That is, if you will consent to marry me.'

'Not that you want to put pressure on me...'

Eyes still locked with hers, he shrugged. 'This is all the time there is...'

She wasn't conscious of having come to a decision, but she found herself standing by the chaplain, repeating the words of the marriage ceremony, shortened for use in emergencies. Max was almost too weak to push the ring over her finger and she had to help him. On impulse she snatched off her father's ring, which had been made smaller to fit her, and gave it to the minister to bless.

'My dear lady, there is no provision in the service for you to give the groom a ring.'

'Bless it,' said Max harshly. He smiled up at her as she slipped it halfway onto his finger, stopping at the knuckle.

'I'll have it made larger again.' She looked him straight in the eye. 'We'll check it for fit when you're a little stronger.'

When he'd signed the register with a shaking hand, Matron gestured to a nurse to give Max the sleeping draught. The witnesses signed the register and Sylvia found herself at the door, propelled by Seymour's hand on her elbow. She broke away and hurried back to the bed. 'I'll be here when you come out of the operation, Max,' she said in a low voice. She hesitated, then bent to kiss him on the cheek. 'I'll be waiting for you.'

'I'll try not to disappoint you,' he said in a thread of a voice.

56

Mopping her eyes, she almost didn't see the Chancellor, chatting in the shadows with a one-armed man in a wheelchair.

'I've sent Seymour ahead to tell them I'm on my way. I hoped you might give me a lift, Lady Bryson, if it's not against your principles.'

'What? Who? But I'm not - '

He smiled at her confusion. 'The king tapped his sword on Max's shoulders. If he's been knighted, then you're Lady Bryson. I hope *that's* not against your principles.'

'Right now I'm more concerned about Max than my principles.'

'He's a strong lad. Not bred up in idleness, like Seymour.' He patted her arm. 'He'll come through, you'll see.'

She hadn't intended to leave the hospital, but the drive would fill some of the dragging time. 'I'm sure you're used to much more elegance,' she said, looking doubtfully at the little green car parked by the pavement, 'but our Lanchester has gone to the front.'

'For some general to swank in, no doubt.'

Fortunately she managed to start the car at the first attempt, and he chatted away sensibly, not demanding anything of her, which gave her a chance to marshal her muddled thoughts and concentrate on the traffic. In spite of herself she found herself liking him more than she could ever have expected.

It was as if he'd read her mind. 'You see, I'm not such an ogre,' he said as they drew up in Downing Street. 'Though I'm not always as polite as I might be. Or so Seymour tells me.'

'I was not terribly polite myself. And I don't suppose you find yourself in the car with Suffrage campaigners very often.'

'Something I tend to avoid, as the last one got in purposely just to hit me on the head. Though that was a *Suffragette*, of course. Not one of yours.' He smiled winningly. 'I don't always consider other people's sensitivities, you see, because I have only one thing in my mind, and that is to win the war.'

The policeman on the doorstep of Number Ten hurried across to open the car door. 'For someone with a knock on the head you drive very well,' the Chancellor went on. 'They tell me I should have a second driver. Perhaps you'd care to apply for the position?'

She shook her head. 'I shall be too busy. Max...m-my husband...'

'Of course. It will be a long haul. Perhaps you may know of another Suffragette - I beg your pardon, *Suffragist!* - who would be suitable.' He tipped his hat. 'I look forward to meeting you again, Lady Bryson - under happier circumstances.'

57

The heavy downpour ceased as abruptly as it had begun and a solitary thrush began to sing in the nearby yews, trilling up and down the scales, unperturbed by the leaden and overcast sky. From the far side of the glade another joined in, an inappropriately joyful background to the droning of the minister's voice.

The undertakers' men shuffled forward, picked up the hessian bands and lowered the coffin into the damp, cold earth.

The minister fell silent. All eyes turned on Sylvia, standing stiffly at the graveside. Oblivious to their presence she stared ahead through her black veil, transfixed by the crystal drops of water dripping off the edge of the black umbrella held above her head. The cold and damp seeped through even the sound buttoned boots she was wearing.

A shudder ran through her rigid body. Would she ever feel warm again?

The minister cleared his throat. A voice in Sylvia's ear said 'earth, Lady Bryson'. Starting at the still unaccustomed name she stumbled forward, picked up a handful of earth from the grave spoil and let it fall into the abyss. Gritty earth rattled on the metal plate and scattered into the shadowed corners. Pools of water gathered, slid in shining beads across the polished wood of the coffin and dripped onto the welling mud. 'Goodbye,' she muttered, and then, as she stepped back, 'I'm sorry. But I did my best.'

'Earth to earth, ashes to ashes, dust to dust...' Damp earth clung to her black gloves. She should be in tears by now. That was what people did at funerals. Recent events had left her in a state of numbed exhaustion, and though her eyes were sore and swollen, no tears would come.

At last it was all over. Someone took her arm and led her away from the graveside, down an avenue of weeping stone angels. Drooping evergreens gave off strong odours in the rain, pungency matched with the sourness of decay. A few meaningless words of comfort from the minister, and the little party trudged back to the station, to the train which had brought them from London's overcrowded burying grounds to the spacious acres of the Surrey cemetery.

The three women hardly spoke on the journey back. Words were superfluous. Each was eager to be in London once more, praying that nothing had changed while they'd been away.

Piet was waiting for them at the London terminus, and drove them back to Ardingley House. Eager as she was to get back to the hospital, Sylvia would not go to Max's sickbed wearing mourning.

In the hall she drew off her muddy gloves and turned to Lady Alice and Nanny Armstrong, who had been her mother's only other mourners. 'Thank you both for all you did. I know she wasn't easy....'

'It was just the illness,' said Nanny Armstrong bracingly. 'We wouldn't any of us like to be remembered on how we were in our last days. Pain and drugs do terrible things to the kindest of souls.'

But her mother had never been the kindest of souls, reflected Sylvia as she hurried up the stairs to change out of her damp clothing. Not to her, at any rate. Any enthusiasm she'd felt for her firstborn was swiftly displaced by the birth of the son and heir. And when Sylvia showed more desire to join in Freddie's games than to sit obediently in the parlour in a clean lace-trimmed pinafore, mother had looked on her as if she were a changeling. There had been a brief truce when the first beaux began to show interest, but that hadn't survived Sylvia's association with the Suffragists.

She'd almost achieved redemption with her engagement to Hugh, but arrest and imprisonment had been the last straw. From then on, for her mother, she was simply beyond the pale.

Nanny Armstrong had hoped that news of Sylvia's marriage and unexpected title might heal the rift, but it all came too late. Eithne Shaw's last words to her daughter were spoken in criticism; after that she ignored her, talking instead of Freddie and Pip as if they were still alive and about to walk through the door.

Coming on top of the rushed marriage and her fears for Max, it was all too much for Sylvia. Dashing from sickbed to deathbed, plagued by returning nightmares in the few hours when sleep overtook her, she withdrew into her shell once more, functioning only by habit.

58

She woke with a start. Damnation! She hadn't intended to fall asleep. She turned up the fob watch: half past three. The newspaper, with the latest news of the second battle for Ypres, lay unopened at her feet. She lacked the concentration to read the reports, with their news of advances and reverses, the unvoiced stories of more broken bodies and lingering deaths...and the still raw reminder of Freddie, who had fallen in the first battle for Ypres.

The room was not cold, but she shivered. She slipped on her jacket, shook out her crushed skirts and took a turn around the room to restore her circulation.

She paced back across to the bedside and looked down at Max in the dim illumination of the nightlight. Heavily drugged since the operation, he was still strapped face down, surrounded by sandbags to stop him moving. She thought inconsequentially: he'll have a stiff neck when he finally wakes up.

She was by the window, cooling her forehead against the panes, when sister brought the night team in to change the dressings. As the orderly unstrapped the belts that pinned his body, she was reminded of the hessian straps by which the undertakers' men had lowered her mother's coffin...and the straps they had used to hold her down in the punishment cell. She began to shake.

'Why don't you go home and get some sleep?' said sister, as she'd said every night since the operation. 'You've had a difficult time...'

'No. I promised I'd be here when he woke up.'

'Who can tell when that will be? Well, if you're determined to stay, at least go along to the nurses' station while we change the dressings. They'll give you a cup of tea.'

'You'll call me if he wakes?'

'Of course.'

She was by the window, cup in hand, watching the pink streaks of dawn lighten the pale grey of the sky, when she heard movement from the bed. She hurried to the bedside, wrinkling her nose against the penetrating smell of the Eusol they soaked the dressings in, and found Max fighting against the straps.

'Don't, Max.' She knelt by the bed and put her hand over his. 'Lie still. You must lie still.'

Recognition came slowly into his pain-filled eyes, and he stopped struggling against the restraints.

'How long have I been here?' he asked. Then, 'Bloody Hell, my neck hurts.'

59

She took the steps of Ardingley House two at a time, eager to share the news. Flinging her hat on the hall chair she crossed to the drawing room, but there was no sign of Lady Alice. She passed through to the conservatory, then down the steps into the garden, but her employer was nowhere to be seen.

Drawing off her gloves she rang for Maisie and asked if Lady Alice had gone out.

Maisie shook her head. 'The Countess is in her room, miss.' She raised her eyes to the ceiling. 'Thought you would've heard it.'

The last booming notes of a Tschaikovsky symphony reverberated around the room over their heads, and there was a brief pause before the needle was dropped back at the beginning of the record and it started all over again.

Her heart sank. 'How long?' she asked.

'Since last night,' said Maisie. 'It must've all got too much for her. The waiting and that. All over again.'

Sylvia took the staircase at a run and hammered on the door of Lady Alice's dressing room. Annie came to the door, took one look at Sylvia's face and, closing the door behind her, dragged her down the landing.

'You've got some news?'

Sylvia nodded, the words jamming up behind the sudden tightening in her throat. She tried to speak, but the green Celtic knots of the wallpaper began to swim before her eyes, and the crimson carpet was coming up to meet her.

Annie grasped her above the elbow and dragged her into an empty bedroom. 'Here, sit down. You look all in, girl.' She pushed her down into a chair. 'Stick your head between your knees, that's the way.' She whisked a small flask out of her pocket and waved it under Sylvia's nose. 'Shouldn't have left you alone all these days, but I couldn't leave her...'

The acrid fumes made her shudder. With a choking cough she raised her head and looked at Annie. 'He made it through,' she said hoarsely. 'He woke up and recognised me.' Then, quite unexpectedly, she burst into tears.

She felt Annie's arms go around her shoulders and leaned helplessly against her, crying into the black wool.

'There, there. You're all right now,' said Annie soothingly. 'I should never have let you stay all hours in the hospital. Not after your ma and all. Look at you: you're dead on your feet.'

Sylvia sat up, wiping the back of her hand over her face. 'So sorry,' she muttered. 'Didn't mean to fall apart. Must go and tell - '

'Will he live?' came a hoarse voice from the doorway. 'Will he walk again?'

Neither of them had heard the door open. Annie abandoned Sylvia and hurried across to Lady Alice's side, only to be brushed aside.

'Will my son ever walk again?' she repeated. She looked like a ghost.

Sylvia rose, clutching the back of the chair for support. She swallowed. 'Max knew me. He could speak. His upper spine is fine. They don't know about his legs yet. They won't know for some time, not until the bruising has subsided.'

'I see.' Sylvia took a step towards her, but Lady Alice looked at her as if she was a stranger. 'I'd rather be alone just now. Thank you.'

Annie followed her mistress out. She turned in the doorway. 'You should sleep, miss,' she said. 'Lie down before you fall down. Ring for Lizzie and I'll come along and see you later.'

Sylvia started down the corridor, her feet placed one in front of the other without any conscious effort from her. From behind the closing door came a howl that made the hairs stand up on the back of her neck. 'I can't stand it,' cried Lady Alice. 'Hasn't God taken enough from me? Oh, Annie, I can't go through it all again.'

60

Max opened his eyes to see a figure by his bedside, dressed entirely in black. As he twisted his head, his gaze travelled from the knees up to the cadaverous face. For a moment he thought he'd died and gone to hell.

He blinked and opened his eyes again. The man was still there. 'Good day to you, Max,' he said. 'Thank God that He has brought you back to us.'

'John Groom?'

'Yes.' The minister squatted down at Max's eye-level. 'Your mother asked me to visit.'

'She's not coming herself?' The minister hesitated. 'Be honest with me, John...as you were with Esmond.'

'She can't face it. Not at the moment.' Groom sat, crossing his long legs in front of him. 'Part of her longs to be at your bedside; the other part is quite terrified to get up her hopes...'

'...in case she loses me too.'

'Sister tells me that's unlikely. The doctors say progress is as good as can be expected at this stage.' He raised his eyebrows. 'Part of their optimism appears to be based on the fact that you cursed and swore when they tried to turn you yesterday.'

'I never pretended to be a saint. Though oddly enough, it isn't the pain where they operated - that's only just starting to come through. It's the stiff neck that's driving me mad.'

'Sister says they hope to turn you on your side tonight.'

'Oh, the small things that bring joy to our heart...' muttered Max.

'Speaking of joy, I must congratulate you on your marriage,' said the minister. 'The nurses tell me your new wife has been at your bedside constantly.' Then, unable to suppress his curiosity: 'An arrangement of long standing? I must have missed the announcement of your engagement.'

'A spur of the moment decision. I thought I was on my deathbed. But I have known the lady for some years. She - '

As if on cue, the door opened and Sylvia came in. She looked exhausted, almost as bad as when she'd first come to Ardingley House, with black circles under her eyes and no spring in her step. Was she regretting the charitable impulse that had driven her to accept him? Did she think it was all to waste, now that he had so unexpectedly survived?

'We'll spare Max the introductions,' she said, before either of the men could speak. She advanced on the minister with a smile. 'Sylvia Shaw...'

'Lady Bryson,' muttered Max.

'Reverend Groom, ma'am, at your service. I'm on several committees with Lady Alice.'

'The silk flower workshops for blind girls...I've heard much about your work from Lady Alice.' She tried to compose her face. 'I'm afraid she couldn't accompany me this morning.'

Before they could do more than exchange polite formalities, the nurses came in to change dressings and both visitors were shown the door. As they left, the minister was called back to the bedside where Max muttered something in his ear.

'If you could explain...' he said. 'Don't want her to think badly...'

Groom patted his shoulder. 'I'll do my best.'

Sylvia and Reverend Groom sat side by side on an uncomfortable bench in a waiting area, where the VAD nurse promised to find them when the dressing was done. Someone had left a copy of the *Daily Mail* on the bench and as the minister moved it she saw the headline: *The Tragedy of the Shells. Lord Kitchener's Grave Error.* How cocooned she had become from the real world, hurrying from sickbed to deathbed. From the ward nearby came a low keening and sobbing from the latest batch of wounded boys from the front.

'Wh-what did Max want you to explain?' she asked, though in her heart she was sure she knew the answer.

'You must have wondered why Lady Alice has not come in to visit her son?'

She shrugged. 'It's not my place to have an opinion on the matter. I'm merely an employee.'

'Hardly. As Max's wife, you are a member of the family, Lady Bryson.'

Lady Bryson. The name didn't seem to have any connection to her. The hurried marriage ceremony seemed only a fleeting memory, as if it had been acted out on stage with two perfect strangers taking the lead roles.

'You've heard of Esmond, Lady Alice's younger son?' said Groom, breaking into her thoughts.

'Harry and Emily's father?' She looked bewildered.

'It's just about a year now since his death. Do you know anything about him?'

'I - I never liked to ask. It seemed like a closed subject.'

'Esmond was much more of a country boy than his half-brother. I suppose in many ways each took after his own father. Lewis Bryson was a talented advocate, while the late Earl was a country gentleman through and through. It was Esmond's love of horses that led to his death. He had a young stallion in the stables at Whitefields for which he prophesied great things. During a fierce summer storm - year twelve, as I remember - he went to check on the horse. It shied at the lightning and knocked him down. We think the horse must have kicked him in the head, although there was no obvious sign of injury.' He sighed. 'The family went through a long and agonising period of waiting. Not unlike this waiting now.'

'But Max isn't going to die...is he? They told me he'd come through...'

'Esmond didn't die immediately...which was almost worse. The family were prepared to lose him then - as prepared as one can ever be. But he survived, although he was never the same man. At first he seemed not much older than his own children, which is often the case when the brain is injured. And like a child he had to learn to do everything all over again.' He clasped his hands, as if asking for the strength to go on. 'I took him to one of our farms in the country - we have many such cases there.'

'Was he happy there?'

'He seemed so - even when his wife abandoned him. I'm not sure he really understood - then - that she was not coming back. Little by little he began to return to us, to be more like his old self. And we rejoiced. But as he healed, he began to remember what he'd been like before the accident, and to realise that he would never be quite as he had been. He became increasingly irritated - with others, with himself, with his own clumsiness. Then, one day, he set a horse to a gallop and found he could no longer control it. That was the end for him: he walked across to a neighbouring farm, took up the farmer's rifle and shot himself.'

She made a strangled noise deep in her throat.

'Some can cope with not being the person they once were. Others seize on the chance to start afresh. Esmond - couldn't cope.'

'So that's why Lady Alice won't come.'

'She can't put herself through all that again - for fear she might lose another son. Max wanted me to tell you, so that you wouldn't judge her too harshly.'

'I could never do that. But you don't think - ?' Her face blanched. 'I thought he was making progress?'

The minister patted her clenched hands. 'Dear Lady Bryson, Max is not Esmond. Even if he's forced to spend his life in a wheelchair, he'll find a way to turn it to good account. And we can thank God that his mind seems to be unclouded. I think that's the most important thing for Max.'

The minister left her with a great deal to ponder, and she was deep in thought when they called her back in. Max was lying face down once more, his head now propped on his forearms. The room was acrid with the smell of Eusol. The sandbags were still in place, but they'd reduced the number of straps holding him rigid.

She couldn't see whether his eyes were closed, but she thought it likely. He was often exhausted when the dressings had been done. She was debating whether to tiptoe away when she thought she heard her name.

She came closer to the bed. 'Max?' she whispered.

'I missed you this morning.'

'I had to go to the Register Office.' To register a marriage - and a death. 'Anyway, how would you know? Most of the time when I'm here you're fast asleep.'

'I can tell,' he said, a smile in his voice. 'I can hear you breathing.'

'That's probably Ellen, the little VAD nurse: she sits with you when I'm not here.' She caught sight of his face, which hadn't been shaved for over a week. 'Goodness,' she chuckled. You look very swashbuckling with that beard!' She went to the bottom of the bed. 'The wounds must be healing well: they haven't bothered to change the sheet this time.'

'Bled a lot, did I?'

'Like the proverbial stuck pig,' she said cheerfully.

'I say! You're not peeping, are you?' He tried to turn his head, but only succeeded in twisting his neck again. 'I don't know whether I've got anything on under this sheet.'

'You haven't, but don't worry. The dressings preserve your modesty.' She chuckled. 'Anyway, I'm your wife. It would be - ' She whirled back to the head of the bed. 'How did you know what I was doing?'

'I felt the draught on my legs as the sheet moved...' He dropped his arm and turned his face sideways. 'Sylvia, I felt it.' For the first time there was hope in his eyes.

'Oh, Max.'

He caught at her hand and held it tight.

'Do you think - ?'

He interrupted her, afraid that she would start building hope where there might still be none. 'Do you think you could rub the back of my neck for a few minutes? It gets devilishly stiff lying like this.'

She massaged the tense muscles of his neck and shoulders until they relaxed a little, finding the movement oddly relaxing herself.

'I'm very tired,' he said at last. 'I think I'll go to sleep now.'

61

Each day she could see changes: at first only small ones, such as the removal of the straps, then the removal of the sandbags. As they cut down on the morphine he was awake more often, although frequently in pain. The day that they turned him over onto his back was a milestone for him. 'At least now I can look the world in the face,' he said with a beaming smile.

She found it easier to deal with him once he was propped up in bed; they slipped effortlessly back into their old relationship, part friendly, part argumentative. It helped that there was so much accumulated correspondence to go through: there had been an avalanche of letters following the announcement of their hasty marriage: letters from ministers, Maharajahs, old schoolfriends and total strangers. While they were dealing with those, there was no time to touch on more sensitive matters.

A brief article about the new operation brought in another wave of letters, this time from soldiers who had been crippled in the fighting, telling him that life in a wheelchair wasn't half bad once you got used to it. Those she kept back and answered herself: Max didn't need to look that in the face until he had to.

They both knew that the real challenge would come when he was allowed out of bed. Reacting to draughts was one thing; walking would be quite another, and no one was prepared to say what the likelihood was of that ever happening.

62

Sylvia was in the drawing room opening the latest batch of letters when Eddie Seymour was shown in.

'It's good to see you again,' she said, taking his outstretched hands in hers.

He stood for a moment too long with her hands in his before bending over to drop a kiss on them. Colour high in her cheeks she withdrew from his grasp and crossed the room to ring for refreshments.

Maisie brought the tea tray out to the conservatory, where they could make the most of the sunshine. As Sylvia poured the tea she turned the talk to politics, begging him for the latest news. 'Without Max, we don't hear what's really going on, and the papers can't tell rumour from fact, it seems. Is it true that they've set up a Ministry of Munitions at last? Lloyd George must be very pleased to have his suggestions vindicated.'

'Yes and no. You see, they've put him to head it and he's very gloomy at having to leave the Exchequer. He still had so much to achieve there - pensions were only the start of it. And he still has Kitchener to contend with. Strictly between us, the Premiership was his for the taking, if only he could have nerved himself to turn out Asquith, but that could have split the Party. In the end he thought a coalition government would be better for the war effort, so some of the Conservatives have come in too.'

'And is it true Fisher's gone?'

'Gone without a word of thanks from the government. Kitchener, who hasn't done a thing right since the start of the war, is to have the Order of Merit, and poor Jackie Fisher's got the order of the boot.'

'And Churchill is to be demoted to the Duchy of Lancaster.'

'The papers are behind the times. Winston's out of the government - probably for good. His treatment of Fisher on top of the terrible losses in the Dardanelles...'

'I thought he was the great hope of the party? A future leader?'

'A number of us think very differently. And not just because he started off as a Conservative...I mean, Winston is all very well for those death and glory moments – though he's messed up tremendously in the Dardanelles – but I've never seen him as a true liberal. I can't imagine him putting his political career on the line to fight for pensions and better medical care for the poor, as LG did in his People's Budget.'

'That's the difference between being the grandson of a Duke brought up at Blenheim Palace, and being brought up in a two room cottage....'

'Quite. Winston's whining to everyone, of course. He cornered LG the other day and accused him of not caring about Winston's reputation. "No, indeed," says LG. "I don't even care about my own reputation. Our prime business at present is to save our country." '

Seymour didn't stay too long, which was just as well. Her marriage lay unspoken between them, an unbridgeable barrier. It was not until he was taking his leave that he mentioned it.

'I blame myself for this marriage,' he said. 'I should never have telephoned you, however much Max asked me to do so. I never thought you'd go through with it. Such folly! If they hadn't all been there, I would have stopped you. I should have told you: even if he walks again he can never be a true husband to you. He - '

'Max has already told me - everything. I was under no illusion when I married him.' She couldn't tell him about the conflicting feelings the news had aroused in her. 'Max was quite plain about the prospects.'

'Of course. I should have known he would be open about it.' He bit his lip. 'He's my good friend, but...I'm sorry for it. You were worth more than that.'

She withdrew her hand. '*He* was worth more than that,' she said softly.

63

In the first week of June she arrived at the hospital and found Max's bed empty. For a moment she stood disorientated in the doorway, frightening thoughts tearing through her mind. The nursing station was unmanned and she fled through the wards, desperate to find anyone who could give her news.

In the right hand annexe to the main ward, men lay in their beds, staring blankly at the walls, twitching and contorting their faces at the slightest sound. In the left-hand wing there was an overwhelming stench of Eusol and putrefaction. Many of the beds had the tented covers that marked the occupants as amputees. In the central ward most of the casualties were sitting on their beds in their hospital blues or making their way up and down the ward on sticks and crutches, cracking jokes with one another. She recognised one or two faces. They must have been here some time, for she hadn't driven for several weeks.

She was wearing uniform - she couldn't bring herself to come in wearing mourning, even though black ties and armbands were now as common on the streets of London as khaki - and some called out to her, asking if she was going to drive them to their convalescent homes in the country.

Enquiries about Max were initially met with blank looks, until someone remembered that two of their number had gone down to be Pageted. 'Per'aps he's gone down wiv 'em,' suggested a bouncy little Cockney with a heavy bandage around his head and over one eye.

'Pageted?' she queried blankly.

'Therapy,' explained the nurse, coming up the ward behind her. 'The Almeric Paget masseuses are working on some of the men in the day room...those that are due for discharge soon. Come along. I'll show you.' She turned to the little Cockney. 'And you, Bertie Bradstock, you'd better be back in that bed by the time I get back. No one's given you permission to be out of it that I know of.'

The sight that met Sylvia's eyes in the day room was completely unexpected. Two young women in white skirts and blouses were working their way down a line of seated patients, massaging muscles and demonstrating exercises for stiffened arms and shoulders; to her left a pair of parallel bars ran the length of the room and three men in hospital blues – the cardigan suits issued to the walking wounded for ease of dressing and undressing - were working their way up and down the room with various degrees of success, supported by the bars and aided by the orderlies. One of them was Max.

For the first time since the operation he was clean-shaven and sweat was pouring down his face as he turned to make his way back towards the door. It was painful to watch: it must have been agonising to do. Even his stronger leg was feeble after being immobile for so long, and the right leg seemed to have no strength in it at all. He made as much progress as a child learning to walk, but his centre of gravity was so much higher that a fall would be both painful and damaging. Halfway down the bars he paused with a muttered curse, looked up and saw her standing in the doorway. For a brief moment he relaxed his grip, and if the orderly had not caught him, he would have toppled over.

'That's enough for today,' said the masseuse briskly. 'Help them into their chairs,' she instructed the orderlies. 'I'll be with you shortly; the rest of you go through your exercise routine again.' She turned to Sylvia. 'If you'd care to wait in the ward...?'

'That's my husband,' said Sylvia, nodding to Max, who was being half-carried by two of the orderlies to one of the wheeled chairs. 'Could you teach me how to help with the exercises?'

64

She settled Max in the corner opposite his mother, and made sure that the rug was tucked in around him. The short journey from hospital to railway station had pulled him considerably and she'd had to give him a sedative against the pain. Now he dozed in a corner, opposite his mother. The wheeled chair had been taken to the guard's van.

Leaving them to Annie's care, she stepped out into the corridor and put her head out of the window to cool it. For someone who had rejected with loathing the idea of nursing, she'd ended up doing a great deal of it. First her mother, then Max, not to mention Lady Alice, who had fretted herself to the brink of a nervous breakdown. She could only hope they'd pick up with a little sea air and a great deal of care.

Originally the plan had been to go down to Brighton, where many convalescent hospitals had been opened, including the Prince Regent's Pavilion, now full of Indian wounded. A team of Almeric Paget masseuses was working in the resort, but when Max heard that Cynthia Asquith had installed her children in Brighton, and often stayed there herself, he'd flatly refused to go.

'The wretched woman came to visit me yesterday, just after you'd gone home,' he'd complained. 'Stayed a whole hour. When she wasn't rambling on about how badly Asquith had been treated, she was giving me a blow by blow account of who's died.' They'd deliberately kept from him the news about Julian Grenfell, Ettie's son, and others from Max's schooldays who had been killed at Ypres and Aubers Ridge. 'And then she launched into this wretched tale about her and Diana Manners having themselves taken along the promenade in Brighton in wheelchairs, pretending to be cripples.' He shook his head in disbelief. 'And the blasted woman expected me to laugh with her at this tasteless escapade!'

Sea air having been prescribed, Bath and Cheltenham were dismissed out of hand; Eastbourne was too close to Brighton and Ramsgate too close to the continent, so they'd finally settled on Torquay. The engine had steam up and the guard's flag was raised when she saw Eddie Seymour running down the platform towards her, clutching a large bouquet of flowers.

'Just - snatched a moment from work - when I heard you were leaving,' he gasped, while the guard huffed and puffed behind him, looking conspicuously at his turnip watch. 'Just - wanted to say - to apologise for what I said before. Quite uncalled for.'

She smiled down at him. 'I've already forgotten all about it.'

'Max is a good friend - and I hope you will be too, Lady Bryson.' He shook her hand and pushed the bouquet at her. 'Oh, and tell Max - LG says there'll be a place for him when he's fit to come back to London.'

'Heaven knows when that will be,' said Sylvia wistfully as the guard blew the whistle and the train chugged slowly out of the station.

65

Sylvia stood on the balcony at the back of the hotel, looking over the gardens and across the bay to the pine-clad islands off the point. The sun was warm on her skin through the silk blouse and for a while she was content to listen to the gentle splashing of the waves on the rocks and the occasional clip-clop of the horses' hooves as they drew delivery carts and carriages down to Meadfoot and back up to the main town.

She'd never been to Devon before: if she'd known just how steep the area around Torquay was, she would certainly have turned it down as a suitable place for Max's convalescence. Nonetheless it was a popular centre for recovering wounded, thanks to the pine clad cliffs, the sea air and the presence of doctors and masseuses at the large houses which had been requisitioned as convalescence homes.

They'd managed to secure a ground floor suite in the hotel, level with the front drive and close to the main public rooms, and the masseuse at Torre Abbey had prescribed Max a gruelling regime, which was already showing results. At least the path that edged Meadfoot Bay was flat, as was the elegant palm-tree lined promenade in the centre of Torquay, tucked in close to the little fishing harbour. Since they went everywhere else by carriage or cab, they had coped so far. And life itself was never going to be flat and even, not for someone like Max Bryson.

She tapped the letter she was holding against the back of her hand. Should she put it aside for Max's attention, or just answer it like any other letter?

And yet she knew it was not just any other letter.

It had looked so innocuous, in among the pile of letters of congratulation. True, this one was addressed only to Max, but so were a number of others, and she'd been opening and answering them all, at Max's request, while he was in hospital. She'd thought it a rather familiar letter for a female to write to a man not related to her, particularly with its coy ending of 'for old times sake', but even the frank of St John's Wood would not have alerted her to its true meaning, had she not gone the following day to Charles Street.

While the valet was packing Max's trunks for a prolonged stay in Torquay she'd opened the desk drawer to find Max's address book, in order to satisfy herself of an ill-written address before sending off the customary polite reply. In the right hand drawer she found the Morocco-bound book, and beneath it a bundle of letters, tied in red ribbon, all in the same handwriting, and posted, like this one, in St John's Wood.

The significance of the ribbons was not lost on her: those letters were from a lover and she was damned sure they too had been signed 'Rosie'. Just then the valet had come back into the room, his eyes widening as he saw her at the desk. With one fluid movement she drew a sheet of paper over the letters and closed the drawer.

'Now I'll be able to answer those last few ill-penned cards and letters,' she said, calmly rising and crossing the room with the address book. 'One thing less for Max to fret about.'

'Yes, m'lady.' Hoskins regained his customary calm. 'Will you and Sir Max be dining out in Devon? Should I put in his evening dress? Country tweeds?'

'We plan to have a very quiet time, Hoskins. But there may be occasions when we can't avoid going into company.' She followed the valet to Max's rooms but stopped abruptly halfway down the corridor. On one wall was an early eighteenth century painting of a riotous Roman scene, with one buxom lady very definitely hogging the attention of the carousers, clad - if that was the right word - in a fraction of toga. In a few short moments her concept of the icily competent and unemotional man she'd married was undergoing a drastic reassessment.

'One of our family treasures,' said Hoskins, gazing at the ceiling. 'An Italian artist, I understand.' He cleared his throat. 'It is widely believed that the main character is a portrait of an earlier Lady Ardingley. Most ladies at the time were content with Kneller or Gainsborough, but she was very proud of her - ahem - attributes.'

'As well she might be!' In spite of herself Sylvia could not help laughing.

'One of the few matters that the Dowager Countess and Lady Imogen agreed on was that it must go. But the young Earl - Master Esmond - could not bring himself to sell a family treasure, and asked his brother to look after it for him.'

'Protective custody, as it were.'

'Quite so, m'lady.'

'It's a large house for one man to live in,' she observed, peeping into doors as she followed Hoskins down the hall.

'It was originally purchased in the expectation of a family house being required,' said Hoskins repressively.

'What happened?'

'The young persons decided they were not suited.'

'How long ago was this?'

'Year two, or was it year three?'

Max would have been in his early twenties. 'And he hasn't contemplated marriage again since?'

'The house was divided up some years ago,' said Hoskins, as if she had not asked the question, 'and we only occupy the middle portion. I believe we have Belgian refugees in the upper portion of the house. With children.' He closed his eyes and shuddered. 'If your ladyship is intending to make this your main residence, it would necessitate giving the van den Baerdts their notice...' He didn't look as though this would grieve him greatly.

'Time enough for those decisions when we come back from Torquay,' said Sylvia hastily. But other decisions would not wait, and Rosie's letter was just one of them.

A cloud scurried across the sun. Sylvia returned to her hotel room and took up her pen. For a moment she wished she'd fallen back on ready printed cards: under the circumstances such a step might have been excused. In the end she decided to write to Rosie as she would write to a brigadier, or a friend of Lady Alice: politely expressing her gratitude for their best wishes and giving the latest guarded news of Max's recovery.

At eleven o'clock the car arrived to take them into town for Max's treatment. When she went to his room she was surprised to find him dressed, not in his usual hospital blues, but in a light summer suit.

'I don't want to look like an invalid for ever,' he said, as she picked up the bag with his hospital blues in. 'One of the waiters helped me dress.'

It seemed a great deal of trouble to go to, when he would have to change again at the hospital for his exercise session, but she passed no comment. For him to take control of even so minor a part of his life was another step towards recovery. She pushed the chair down the ramp which had been laid over the steps, but when she would have called the chauffeur to lift Max from the chair, he put her gently to one side and pushed himself up from his seat. While Sylvia hovered anxiously at his elbow he made his way on sticks to the open door of the car and lowered himself into the front seat.

'You've been practising!'

'In my room.' He looked up at her with a boyish grin. 'Wanted to surprise you.'

'You've certainly done that.' She bent forward to tuck the car rug around him, and told herself she'd imagined the feel of his breath warm on her neck and his lips on her hair. One glance at the broad grin on the face of the chauffeur as she straightened up told her otherwise. Briskly she instructed him to put the wheelchair on the back of the car and whisked herself into the back seat with glowing cheeks.

Sometimes she stayed for Max's treatment at the country house on the other side of town which had been requisitioned for use as a convalescent hospital, but today her nerves were jangling and she couldn't face the sight of all the broken and mutilated bodies. When Max had been dropped off, the chauffeur drove her back into town. She bought some toiletries for Lady Alice and went on to the main Post Office. She hesitated, hand half-in and half-out of the red pillar box, but someone came up behind her in a hurry and she let the envelope fall. What else could she have written, after all? That *old times' sake* was all there was? All there ever would be? No, that was for Max to tell.

66

Max's buoyant mood endured through the next few weeks. The new therapist, a Chartered Paget masseuse with twenty years' experience, was very pleased with his progress. She had put him on a strict diet of fresh fruit, vegetables and ginger tea to purify the blood, and given him a new set of exercises to build up weakened muscles. As he grew stronger the pain grew less and after a few weeks he was beginning to feel as if he could take on the world.

The sun was glinting on the waves as they turned onto the seafront road and he shifted restlessly in his seat. He was sick of the endless shuttling between hotel and hospital, and Sylvia's assumption that they would head straight back to the hotel for his afternoon rest incensed him.

'Drop us off at the harbour,' he instructed the chauffeur. 'We can take a cab back later.'

'I can wait if you like, sir. You might need that chair - '

'Take the damned thing back to the hotel!' he snapped. Then, more calmly: 'Please tell them we won't be back for lunch.' As the car pulled up outside the Pavilion he turned to Sylvia. 'I feel the urge for some fresh air. I hope that doesn't put you out?'

'Not at all.' Pleasant and amenable as ever, but with that note of formality that sometimes crept in. Then it was as if she'd erected a wall between them: he was permitted to approach so far but no further. 'Though you're unlikely to lunch as well down here.'

'I can bear it.'

The seafront was bustling as ever, with invalids in khaki and blue limping up and down the promenade, or being wheeled along in bath-chairs by family or uniformed VADs. Resolutely he turned his eyes away from them and concentrated on making the strengthening muscles obey his will. He still had to lean on two sticks, but he made it round one side of the harbour before he had to stop and rest. Sylvia showed her concern when he slumped against the harbour wall, but even then she didn't fuss over him, only observing mildly that perhaps they should have hung onto the chair a little longer.

The proprietor of the nearby restaurant, who had been standing in the doorway contemplating the unloading of the fishing boats, hurried forward to offer a seat.

'Fine day, sir. You don't want to rush it though. Slow and steady, that's the way, and those cobbles can be hard on the feet. Will I have the boy bring you out a chair?'

Max realised that Sylvia was holding her breath and reached out a reassuring hand.

'Or perhaps you'd care to step inside for a brandy, sir...Still a bit of a breeze in the air. No obligation, I need hardly say.'

Sylvia confessed herself quite peckish, and they were shown to a table with a view across the harbour.

'I hadn't realised my temper was that uncertain,' said Max, sipping the brandy and relishing the feel of it coursing through his veins.

'What?' Sylvia looked up from the menu, where she was trying to decide between turbot and sole.

'That poor man - you were expecting me to bite his head off.'

'He wouldn't be the first, would he? What about the general?'

'I say, be fair! It was only when he asked me for the sixth time whether he should send his man to fetch my wheelchair....'

'Third, actually. I was counting. But he has forgiven you. He said it was the pain speaking.'

'Well, it wasn't. I'm just bored with the role of invalid. And I feel great pangs of guilt when they talk to me as if I'm one of England's heroes. I'm *not* a brave soldier and I feel a perfect fraud.'

'Not everyone who was injured was necessarily going over the top at the time,' she said. 'One of the poor souls I took down to Sussex last month was in his dugout reaching for a packet of cigarettes when they were shelled. But he was there serving his country, as you were, when it happened...'

'I know, but - '

'Why can't you just smile and accept their congratulations? If not for yourself, then do it on behalf of those who can't.'

He knew she was thinking of her brothers. Whatever he did for her, he could never bring them back. She was struggling to blink back the tears, and he gazed out across the harbour until she had regained her control.

One positive aspect of this enforced visit to Torquay was the way they'd managed to put some sort of relationship back together again. In the early days of his convalescence they'd fallen back into the same part friendly, part argumentative relationship they'd enjoyed when they first met, when he was fighting to clear her brother's name. She'd treated him then just as she treated Freddie, scorning his opinions if she thought they deserved it, arguing with him on all points. It had been a salutary experience, and quite new to him, but one he'd missed terribly when she vanished out of his life. Now he could acknowledge, if only to himself, the real reason he'd pursued her trail so vigorously: certainly not just to deliver a letter of condolence.

Since they'd come down here, she had been friend and companion, even nurse. He'd found that hard to cope with at first, being an intensely private man, but he'd been deeply touched when she'd learned massage to help with his leg muscles. While his mother had been forced, to some extent, to make her own way, Sylvia had spent much more time with him and he felt they were moving beyond friendship to a deeper understanding - even if occasionally she still put up that wall between them.

She was mopping her eyes surreptitiously. He gave her a moment longer. The view of the pretty harbour was one to savour, though the boats bobbing at anchor were no longer the *Saucy Sally* and *Merry Dancer*. All names had been painted out by Admiralty orders, and each now bore only a regulation number on the prow. Quite how that was supposed to confuse the enemy he couldn't understand.

'Until I came down here I hadn't realised how much I miss the sea,' he said, when a glance under his lashes showed that she had herself back in hand.

'I tend to think of you as a city boy. I forget you were brought up in Scotland.' She returned to the topic when they'd placed their orders. 'Lady Alice had no thought of returning there when her second husband died?'

'Scotland was never my mother's home. She hates the place.'

'But - I thought - You told me you spent your early childhood in Scotland.'

'With my guardians. My father's elderly Scottish cousins,' he said heavily. 'When my father died they took me away from my mother. She was ill for a brief time, and they made out that she was an unfit guardian. They could do that then, you see. That was the law. And the canting bigoted Puritans made the best use of it for their own means.' His mouth twisted in bitterness. 'In four years I saw my mother only four times, and then only when my guardians were present. She was in Gloucestershire; I was in Scotland. It took so long – and she might never have got me back at all if it hadn't been for Ardingley.'

'Max! How dreadful for you both.' Her hand went out to him across the table.

'History, you see, has a habit of repeating itself. That's why I would do - did do - anything, rather than let Harry and Emily suffer what I had gone through.'

'Marry me, you mean? *Merci du compliment!*'

'I'm sorry. I didn't mean to be offensive.'

She shrugged. 'I knew what the situation was. You were quite honest.'

He was still holding on to her hand. One lock of curly hair had escaped from under her hat - much simpler hats this summer, not nearly as inspiring as the wonderful creations she had worn before the war! - and he was almost tempted to reach out and touch it. *Then* he'd show her 'what the situation was'.

Not yet, he told himself. Not yet. Time enough for that when - if - the improvements continued. Too early yet to say if there was any permanent change. Too early yet to raise his hopes - or hers.

67

June faded into July with everyone bemoaning the fact that the summer of 1915 was not a patch on the previous year. The theory about the gun bombardments on the continent having disturbed the weather patterns was trotted out once more, only to be pooh-poohed by the General and his cronies. Sylvia, who had seen no more of the previous glorious summer than a square of blue sky high up in the wall of her cold, bare cell, lowered her eyes to her book and let the discussion rage about her.

The invalids made good progress, and when Sylvia was not sitting in the hotel with Lady Alice and her new circle of friends, she was taking the air on the promenade with Max, or helping with the Swedish massage which was slowly bringing the strength back to his legs and reducing his dependence on opiates.

Some good might come of Max's sufferings, after all. Without it, Lady Alice might have clung to Sylvia, believing herself incapable of managing life without permanent support. That was down to Henrietta Jennings. But now, while Sylvia was looking after Max, Lady Alice was making friends among the summer guests, sitting in on bridge parties, even taking a cab into town occasionally with Mrs Cunningham, a gentle but energetic widow of Lady Alice's own age, to shop and take tea at the Pavilion.

The only fly in the ointment was that Max was in a rush to return to London. As he emerged from the first few weeks of drug-ridden stupor, the petty concerns of the elderly residents of the hotel began to wear on his nerves. Eddie Seymour was a regular correspondent and it was clear that Max was missing out on some exciting times.

'No hurry, surely,' said the General, when a return to London was spoken of. An inveterate snob, he was enjoying the company of the Countess, even if she could no longer play bridge. 'London will be empty, and who wants to spend the summer in the city? Much better stay down here till September.'

'Unfortunately the Germans are not taking the summer off, sir,' said Max coolly. 'Nor is the War Office, nor is the Minister for Munitions. And if Lloyd George is in London, then I should be there too.'

'You won't be any use to him if you're not fully mended,' said Sylvia one evening, as she massaged his tired calf muscles. 'You've been overdoing it these last few days.'

'Dammit, don't tell me what I can and can't do!' he said. 'Don't treat me like a child!'

'Then don't behave like one!' she snapped back. 'The doctor said you were to practise on gentle inclines, and work against a light resistance. And the masseuse agreed. So what do you do as soon as my back's turned? Bully the attendant to take you on one of the steepest cliff paths in the area. *I'd* think twice before doing it, but you know better.'

'It was foolish.' His bad temper faded as quickly as it had come. 'And if I've hurt my back then I deserve it.'

'You didn't tell me. Would you - ' She swallowed hard. 'Shall I see if I can ease it for you?'

'Please. Otherwise I shall never sleep.'

She averted her eyes as he removed the collar studs and drew off his shirt. By now she ought to be inured to embarrassment, but massaging a man's bare back was a different kettle of fish to rubbing his leg muscles through his clothes.

When she turned back he was lying on his front on the bed, head propped on his arms. He looked just as helpless as he'd been in the hospital.

She struggled to remember what she'd learned from the masseuse and soon fell into the rhythm, rubbing in the liniment, kneading the strained muscles around the shoulders and spine. Whenever the reality of what she was doing began to intrude into her consciousness, she forced herself into the masseuse's position and tried to see this as just another task.

It became more difficult as her hands moved further down his back. With shaking hands she eased the high waistband of his trousers a few inches down, massaging more carefully as the ridged scars were revealed. When she could bring herself to go no further, she slumped back against the bed post. From his deep breathing it sounded as though Max had fallen asleep. She felt a little envious of him as she leaned back, eyes closed, tired hands limp at her sides: *she* would have to drag herself back to her own room before she could put her head down and sleep.

She was gathering her strength to move when she felt Max stir.

'I thought you were asleep,' she said, forcing her tired eyes open.

'Just getting my breath back.'

She summoned up a smile. 'It's me that's exhausted, not you.' She leaned forward, half-expecting him to kiss her cheek, as he often did when they parted.

'I hope you'll think it's worth it. My dear, you've brought me back to life.' He caught her hands and drew her towards him, eyes shining. 'I had to be sure before I said anything. But it's true.'

'What is?'

'It's happened again.' He jerked her down alongside him and her eyes widened at the excitement in his eyes and the warmth from his half-naked body. 'I wasn't going to say anything yet, but I can't wait any longer.' He rolled his body across until he was looking down at her.

When she still didn't speak he rolled a little closer, until there was no space between them. 'Can't you guess?' he whispered, gripping her wrists tight.

She heard the metallic clank of the prison door. The room whirled around her, and the man's hot gaze burned into hers, his face only inches away. All she could feel was the tight grip on her wrists and the pressure of his body.

Close the door Mr Nash. Turn the key....

His aroused body grinding into hers...

She screamed and whirled into a dark vortex of terror.

68

'Welcome back, Lady Bryson.' A warm voice with a soft Devon burr. 'I told your husband there was nothing to fear.'

She tried to turn her head to where the voice was coming from, but it eluded her. 'I'm very tired,' she murmured. 'My head...'

'That will be the sleeping draught they gave you. Not what I would have recommended, but then, no harm done.'

Her eyes were heavy, the lids almost stuck together. She forced them open. She was in her own room, in her own bed. The light summer curtains were blowing in a gentle breeze. From the position of the sun in the sky, the day was well advanced. She turned her head back into the room and saw two men at her bedside; one was Max, the other a stranger in a dark frock-coat.

'Sylvia, my dear, this is Doctor Sarret.' Max put his hand over hers, lying limp on the counterpane. She pulled it back, shrinking away from him. The blood drained from his face and he moved away from the bedside. 'Doctor Sarret wants to examine you. Shall I call Annie?'

Receiving no answer, he crossed to the door and went out. Annie swiftly took his place.

She tried to explain that she was fine, that she didn't need, didn't want, *couldn't abide*, a doctor, but the words wouldn't come. The doctor already had his stethoscope against her nightdress. She turned her head away, tears running silently down her cheeks. At least she knew Annie would not desert her post, and she supposed the sleeping draught must have dampened down her screaming nerve endings. At last the doctor put away his stethoscope and pronounced himself satisfied.

He was halfway to the door when he turned back. 'One question I should have asked. You are not increasing, are you, Lady Bryson?'

She looked at him as if he had run mad.

'I mean – could you perhaps be with child?'

Annie muttered something to the doctor that Sylvia could not hear. 'Ah, I see. You mustn't fret over that, Lady Bryson. You and your husband have been through a difficult patch. Motherhood will come all in its own good time. I'll prescribe a strengthening tonic. And I recommend a couple of days in bed. So often in these cases we care for the injured and forget to look after the carers. Good day to you.'

Annie closed the door behind him and crossed to plump up the pillows. 'What a turn you gave us, my dear, to be sure. Such a scream as'd go right through your vitals. I thought it was my lady, but there she was in the summer room, happily sitting at bridge with the General and Mrs Cunningham.'

Sylvia coloured up. 'Did everyone hear?'

'Couldn't help but. Oh, don't you fret now. We all have nightmares.' She looked at her charge curiously. 'Nothing else on your mind, is there?' She settled down in the chair and patted Sylvia's hand. 'If you want to talk, I'm here. Nothing you say will go any further.'

Sylvia was almost tempted to tell her, to confide in her those things she had told no one, not even the Suffragettes who had looked after her when she'd come out of prison. But to do that she would have to face it herself and she wasn't ready to do that. Not yet.

'It's very strange,' she said sleepily. 'But I don't really remember...'

69

Max returned from his treatment at the hospital in dark mood. He couldn't decide who he was more angry with: Sylvia for cringing away from him like that in front of the doctor, or himself for having frightened her in the first place. It didn't help that Annie made him wait until late afternoon before allowing him in to see his wife. 'Rest the doctor prescribed, and rest she shall have,' she insisted. 'Go and sit with your mother and I'll fetch you when she's fit to be seen.'

Mrs Cunningham was reading the newspaper to his mother in the elegant conservatory, but he couldn't be diverted even by the news from Brussels.

'It was the Belgian National Day, and the Germans had banned the poor Belgians from showing their flag. So they all wore red and yellow flowers on their black coats and dresses. So they *were* the national flag, you see, each and every one of them...'

His mind was not on his company: he couldn't stop his thoughts racing, wondering about the events of the previous evening.

With hindsight it had been foolish to surprise her as he had. It must have been a shock, to be sure, to find out that his powers had returned so dramatically, after all he'd said to her at the hospital, but her behaviour had been beyond belief. What the devil had happened to Sylvia to make her react like that?

Last night, lying alone in his bed, angry and wakeful after they'd sedated her, he'd wondered about Hugh, the man to whom she'd once been engaged. Had he harmed her? If he had, he would personally kill him. But then common sense prevailed: even when they'd broken off the engagement, he'd seen, even through his own desires, what they had once meant to each other. But who else could it be? Not Jeremy Lang, surely? No. Hadn't the fire.

In the early hours of the morning it came to him: the Hyde Park march. She'd said she'd been mauled about and had struck out at her assailant. But perhaps she hadn't told him the whole truth. It would be interesting to review the files of her arrest, which he could do very easily, with his government contacts. But first he must speak to Sylvia herself...when he was allowed to.

His temper was further frayed by an afternoon spent with the General and his circle, and he was not feeling very charitable when at last Annie came for him. But when he saw how pale and exhausted Sylvia looked he forced himself to curb his anger.

'I won't stay long,' he said. 'Annie wants you to rest. But I'd appreciate a word in private.'

With a sniff, Annie left the room, closing the door behind her.

'I don't know what happened last night, but I don't believe that anything I did, however unmannerly it may have been, should have caused you so much distress.' He bit his lip. 'Sylvia... tell me what's going on.'

She forced herself to look him in the face, to remember that this was Max, not...anyone else. 'I was just - overtired. It won't happen again.'

'If you find my presence so upsetting...'

'It's not that.' She dragged a smile from somewhere. 'No really. I'm fine.'

'That is manifestly untrue.' He dropped his voice again. He wouldn't put it past Annie to be listening at the door. 'We need to talk. I - I apologise for my crass behaviour. I had - foolishly - thought you would rejoice with me ... '

She gazed blindly past him. 'I'm sorry.'

'Well, no more of that.' He couldn't bear to look at her, so pale and wan with her beautiful hair tumbling over her shoulders, glinting in the shafts of late afternoon sun. He took a turn around the room, fiddling with the trimmings on the chair in front of the dressing-table, lining up the bottles and jars. 'You have my word that I won't force myself on you. Had I known how distasteful you would find my attentions...'

'I'm sorry.'

'So you said.' His throat was hot and tight and it was a struggle to keep his voice level. 'For better or worse, we are married. There are proprieties to be observed...I'll limit myself to those. Can I rely on you not to cringe away again and show me up in public?'

'I didn't. I - '

'God, you don't even realise you're doing it. But please spare me a repeat of last night, or everyone will have me down for a wife-beater.'

She sank back against the pillows when he had gone, her hand rubbing at the scar by her mouth as she wondered how she was going to cope with this new and wholly unexpected situation.

'What have I done?' she whispered as the tears began to fall. 'Oh, Heavens, what have I done?'

70

Sylvia sat on the platform fiddling with the black tassel on her parasol. Two restless nights considering her problems had shown her no way out of her dilemma, but until she could find a solution she could only continue with the role fate had assigned her. Perversely Max seemed quite unperturbed by their problems, sitting beside her with a smile on his lips.

'I wish you'd tell me who we're meeting,' she said pettishly. She'd intended to return to the hotel for a much-needed afternoon nap after Max's treatment, but Max had borrowed the car from the chauffeur and asked her to drive them to the railway station.

'But that would spoil the surprise.'

'Eddie Seymour?' He shook his head. 'Lady Cynthia? No, you wouldn't be looking that pleased. The Chancellor? Lloyd George, I mean. Of course he isn't the Chancellor any more...'

'No.'

'You really can be the most infuriating - Good heavens, it isn't the children?'

'Harry and Emily?' The smug look was replaced by a frown. 'No. I had a letter only last week from the Graysons. The summer visit will not take place. Apparently it would distress the children too much to see me in my present condition.'

She cursed herself for having brought up the subject. 'I'm sure it would do them the world of good to see you now: they could stop worrying straight away. You look the picture of health.' It was true: the strained look around his mouth had faded as the worst of the pain ebbed and his eyes - No. She mustn't look into his eyes and see the condemnation there. She wasn't ready to cope with that yet.

'Not quite ready to run the marathon, I daresay, but well enough to think about moving on. I've had as much as I can take of hospitals and nurses, not to mention retired generals. Could you be ready to move to Gloucestershire at the end of the week?'

'Of course. But why not straight back to London?'

'You're as eager to get back to work as I am, I can see. But I want to stop off at Stancombe - '

'Is that your house in the country? I remember you mentioned it once.'

'I've neglected it for far too long. I may put it on the market when the war's over and I'd like to have it in prime order before then.'

Her reply was lost in the noise and smoke of the Portsmouth train.

'There he is,' said Max, heaving himself to his feet as the doors opened and the passengers alighted. Among them were a number of soldiers, one of whom looked scarcely big enough to carry his kitbag. 'Little fellow over there.' Leaning on his stick he made his way along the platform. Sylvia followed in his wake.

'Private Jacob Harrison?' he said. 'Jake?'

'That's right. Well, Corporal Harrison now.' He pointed to his sleeve. 'Mr Bryson?'

'And my wife.'

'Welcome back, Mr Harrison,' she said.

'And glad I am to be back in Blighty, Mrs Bryson, believe me.' He turned back to Max and asked eagerly: 'Any news about Lily?'

Max consulted his watch. 'In precisely five minutes, the London train will arrive on the other platform. All being well, Lily Parker will be on it.'

'God bless you, guv'nor,' said Harrison, his tanned face wreathed in smiles. He hoisted his kitbag onto his shoulder. 'I been desperate to put things right with Lil ever since I heard. I never would've gone off if I'd known - '

'It's Lily you've got to convince,' said Max, handing over an envelope. 'Otherwise that special licence will go to waste. Now don't rush her. There's plenty of time, and a car here to take you to the church.'

While they waited in the hired car, giving the couple some privacy for their first meeting, Sylvia bombarded Max with questions. He explained how he'd traced Jake through the army lists, and arranged for him to have compassionate leave. 'By the time it was all sorted, there were Zepps over London, so Nina Doncaster arranged for them to come down here.'

'You could have asked me.'

'You already had enough on your plate. Besides, I used to see Miss Doncaster regularly at the Mission Hall, where she made it *her* mission to nag me about Lily and Jacob. I was happy to turn the travel arrangements over to her.'

He disappeared behind his newspaper, putting an end to the conversation. They could discuss Jake and Lily, but it seemed neither of them was ready to discuss their own problems.

It was ten minutes before Lily and Jake emerged from the station, but the time had been well-spent. Jake was gazing adoringly down at the shawl-wrapped babe in his arms, and Lily, dressed in a smart navy tailor-made with a spotted silk blouse, was smiling equally adoringly at Jake. A porter came behind with the kitbag and Lily's shabby suitcase. Sylvia was surprised to feel a pang of envy.

Lily was profuse in her thanks, but Max shrugged it off, insisting that others had done the hard work, from army officials to his own clerks, not to mention the Doncasters.

As Sylvia drove them through Torquay Lily looked around her in wonder. 'I haven't never seen the sea before,' she explained.

Jake Harrison only had eyes for his bride-to-be, although he did look up briefly as they drove along the promenade. 'Blimey, guv,' he exclaimed. 'Palm trees in England? They won't believe this when I tell 'em back in Wipers.'

'Don't, Jake,' said Lily with a shiver. 'Let's not think about the war for a few days at least.'

The church ceremony was brief, and the baby cried throughout, provoking heavy sighs from the reluctant clergyman and embarrassed grins from Jake and Lily. He fell asleep at last on his mother's shoulder while Max and Sylvia witnessed the register, then both the luggage and the sleeping baby were left at Mrs Norton's family lodging house while the little party went on to the photographers. Lily was shocked to discover that the Brysons had no wedding photo of their own, and insisted that they should have one done there and then, before they set off in the car for a wedding lunch at the harbourside restaurant. They didn't linger: Lily was anxious about the baby and Jake couldn't wait to be alone with his little family.

'He's so small,' said Sylvia as she let in the clutch and drew away from the seafront lodgings.

'The baby?'

'Jake Harrison. Far too small and skinny to be a soldier, surely.' She lowered the visor to shield her eyes from the setting sun, flaming out across the pearly summer sky as it dipped towards the western horizon.

'That's what our army has to rely on these days. It's also the main reason why LG was so reluctant to give up the Exchequer. It's a disgrace that so many of our working men are so undersized and underfed. Some volunteers are too unfit even for the Bantams. And those that do scrape in, put on weight and height even on the basic army diet. What does that say about their home conditions?' He shaded his eyes against the setting sun, darting a glance at Sylvia. 'What do you think about our love birds?'

'They seemed very happy. Though they'll have little enough time together.'

'Three days. It was the best I could manage.'

'You've worked miracles to bring them together at all.' Privately she was amazed at his tact. He'd even held the baby while a blushing Lily was handed in to the car by her groom. Seeing him looking down into the little face Sylvia had been racked with guilt: a man in his thirties would be eager to set up his own nursery, especially one who'd thought his opportunity snatched away from him. And she was depriving him of that chance, even though she'd never set out to deceive him.

71

At the end of the week the Torquay party broke up. Jake left for Portsmouth and the front, Lily and baby Alfie returned to London. Lady Alice had decided to stay a little longer with Mrs Cunningham, to give Max more time with his new wife. Mrs Cunningham and the general had promised to escort her safely back to London.

The station car was waiting at Charfield to meet Max and Sylvia off the Bristol train and the elderly man drove them away from the station through lush green fields. Ahead of them, over to their left, the last finger of the Cotswolds thrust forward, the monument on the tip penetrating the August haze.

'That's Tyndale's monument,' said Max, turning sideways in his seat to look at Sylvia. It was the first time he'd emerged from behind the newspaper or dispatches since they left Torquay. The last few days there had been spent in a flurry of packing and leave-taking and they'd had no time alone.

'William Tyndale? Translated the Bible?'

'That's the fellow. He was tutor to one of the local families before he very unwisely strayed into the wrong part of the Continent and got himself burnt at the stake.'

'Very unwise.' She peered through the side window. 'Is that a cotton mill? I thought they were all in the north.'

'Wool mill. The South Cotswolds made cloth for army uniforms. The Napoleonic wars were boom time for the district, but many of the mills have fallen out of use. It used to be Stroud for scarlet and Uley for blue uniforms. Now, of course, it's all khaki.'

At a small castellated lodge just beyond the mill, they turned onto a potholed roadway. 'Not too bumpy for you sir?' The old man hunched over the wheel as he overtook a pair of Land Army girls with a cartload of timber and a plodding carthorse. 'I could've gone round by Wotton if you'd rathered. Only the old motor, she don't go so well up that last hill.'

'This will do,' said Max, shifting his position as the wheels bumped over the rutted surface.

'How far is it to Stancombe?' asked Sylvia. Max had made good progress, but she didn't want him to be too shaken up. There was no longer any danger of the wounds breaking open, but the masseuse was in Torquay and the last thing she wanted was a repeat of the scene in his hotel room. Without Lady Alice she felt exposed and unprotected.

'A few miles away, just beyond the monument,' said Max, 'where the Cotswolds meet the Severn Plain. I'm prejudiced, but I think it one of the most beautiful spots in the whole of England.'

At North Nibley, just below the monument, they turned a bend and began to run alongside a wall built of the mellow golden stone of the Cotswolds. 'This is Stancombe land,' said Max. 'That's Stinchcombe Hill beyond, and if you look to the left you can see the River Severn.' He cleared his throat. 'I hope you're not expecting anything like Taplow or Whitefields. Stancombe is a small estate, lived in by a succession of country squires and vicars. Very modest.'

The car turned off down a curved drive which swept up to a neat two-storied house in palest cream stone. It sat on a rise, with the ground falling away on one side to grassland studded with tan-coloured cattle. Further down the small valley could be seen the chimneys of the home farm and behind it all rose the magnificent wooded hill, the leaves of the oak and beech trees a lush and heavy green in the shimmering air.

'Why, it's exquisite.' Sylvia spoke with genuine enthusiasm. She'd been fretting at the thought of acting as chatelaine in a vast house where she'd be at the mercy of unknown servants to find her way around. But this was manageable.

A small woman came bustling out of the door. 'It's well time you came back to see us, Master Max,' she said, her lined face wreathed in smiles. 'And brought your lovely bride with you too. Lady Bryson, let me be the first to welcome you to Stancombe. I hope you'll love it as much as Master Max do.'

'This is Mrs Terrett,' said Master Max. 'She's been at Stancombe since my father first came here.'

'I have that. And seen 'em all through their foolish years: Miss Charlotte and Master Max, and poor dear Master Esmond.' She sighed deeply. 'Well, come you in and make yourselves comfortable. The trunks have all come these last few days, and Hoskins come down last evening from London, with a lot of papers and goodness knows what to fret you with. I've brought in a couple of lasses from Nibley to wait. Can't get the staff these days. Won't be what your ladyship is accustomed to, I'm sure. But there, as they say, there's a war on.'

It wasn't at all what her ladyship had been accustomed to, thought Sylvia, looking appreciatively at the glowing velvet curtains and freshly painted walls: not that long ago her ladyship had been scrubbing floors and washing sheets in a rundown tenement.

72

August was slipping gently towards September and although the gardens were beyond their best, the late summer bedding plants still provided a riot of colour. Sylvia stood at the top of the formal Italianate gardens, looking down at the house framed between the two exclamation marks of the columnar cypresses.

Max was at work in the gazebo, as he had been all week, engrossed in papers sent him by his officials in the new Ministry of Munitions. Lloyd George had had the inspired idea of sending groups of trade union leaders to the front, to see how desperately their munitions were needed; responsibility for organising them would fall on Max on his return.

Their lives had run on parallel lines this last week, meeting only at mealtimes, where they chatted like the acquaintances they were, parting at the head of the stairs each night with a chaste kiss on the cheek. If Hoskins or the maid thought it odd that the honeymoon couple had separate rooms, and that the dividing door was always shut, they kept their concerns to themselves.

Sylvia spent her days playing at lady of the manor, receiving visits from local landowners and farmers, politely declining pressing invitations to dinners and fund-raising receptions, while Max struggled to prepare himself for the imminent return to work.

She wished she were back at work too. She missed the daily routine of the depot, the freedom of the steering wheel in her hands, mistress of her own little mobile domain. She'd always known she wasn't cut out to be a lady of leisure, even when she'd lived at home with her parents and that was all they'd ever wanted her to be. Torquay had been a pleasant interlude, and the improvement in both Max and Lady Alice so striking that she could not regret the time spent there, but as Mrs Terrett never tired of saying, there *was* a war on, and now that Max was on the mend, she wasn't contributing anything to it.

There was nothing for her to do in Stancombe House. The rooms were well-furnished and comfortable, more homely and relaxed than either of the London houses; they had been decorated in warm colours some years before, with the occasional touch of Russian influence to bring it up to date. The two of them made few demands, and they weren't entertaining; even with the reduced staff, Mrs Terrett ran the house perfectly well, and certainly didn't need any assistance from Sylvia.

Yesterday, the anniversary of her release from Holloway Prison, she'd spent alone on Stinchcombe Hill. Breathless after the stiff climb she'd sat for an age gazing across the valley and plain to the glittering swathe of the River Severn and the Bristol Channel, revelling in her new-found strength and fitness - much of it, no doubt, due to pushing Max's wheelchair around Torquay in the early days of his convalescence.

Today, however, was much too hot for walking. She'd passed the morning in the conservatory reading the papers, with their customary reports of advances and consolidations which seemed mysteriously to make no change whatsoever to the front line, and now she was reduced to dead-heading summer blooms in the neglected Italian garden.

Still, on a day like today, even that could be pretty tiring. Foolish to have come out without a hat. At the top of the garden she paused gratefully in the shade, then spied a little path that led her through the shrubbery to the edge of the rise. From this new vantage point she gazed down across the parkland, where even the huge Cedars of Lebanon and the sweet chestnuts were drooping in the heat. The little lake at the bottom of the valley looked delightfully cool and she had a sudden childish urge to go down to the ivy-covered bridge and dabble her feet in the cool water.

Instead she followed round the loop of the path and saw, beneath the dappled leaves of the lime trees, a swing she hadn't noticed before: a remnant of Max's childhood, no doubt. With an impetuous movement she kicked off her shoes, ran across the grass in her stockinged feet and threw herself onto the wooden seat. She stepped back on tiptoes until the swing would go no further, let go and swooped forward and back, kicking herself high into the sky, revelling in the half-forgotten sensation until she was breathless with it all. For the first time for weeks she felt alive and exhilarated.

As the swing reached the top of its arc and began at last to slow down, she felt someone start to push it higher again. Startled, she half-turned, but the soft cloth of her skirts slipped slightly on the wood and she had to concentrate to keep her seat.

'Steady!' said Max, sharp concern in his voice. 'Do you want to stop?'

'No. Just - you startled me. I hadn't realised you were there.'

She stayed on the swing for a few minutes longer, but Max's arrival had subtly changed the tenor of the day and she was content to come gradually back to earth once more.

'How long have you been here?' she asked, smoothing her skirts and wondering how much he had seen of her hoydenish behaviour.

'Oh, I just strolled up,' he said casually. Then, as she made to rise from the swing, he dropped his hands onto her shoulders. 'Stay there. You complete the picture. House, garden, park, all framed by the ropes and your beautiful curls. Gainsborough would have fought to paint you. Or Watteau, perhaps.' She froze as she felt his breath on her cheek, but before she could react, he released her and took a step away. 'To tell the truth,' he went on, 'I've had about as much as I can take of shell specifications and inter-departmental disagreements. No doubt I'll find out what's going on quickly enough.'

'You still plan to return in the next few days?'

'Mmm. Though it will be hard to tear myself away from all this.'

'It is beautiful here, isn't it?' she said, uncomfortably aware of his presence close behind the swing, close enough to touch but no longer touching. 'Why didn't you come here for your convalescence?'

'Mother won't stay here. Too many unhappy memories. Both her husbands died here and she was here alone when I was taken away.'

'And you?'

'It's all I have left of my father.' He came round to sit on the grass at her feet. 'When I was in Scotland, I used to dream of it. I remember thinking that if only I could run away and find the train that would bring me here, everything would be all right again.'

She reached out her hand to him in swift sympathy and he took it, held it a moment, then raised it to his lips. Then, with one fluid movement, he drew her down on the grass beside him and before she realised what he was going to do, kissed her full on the lips.

For a brief moment he thought he'd broken through the barrier, but then she began to pull away. Quickly he released her and lay back full-length on the grass, his hands clasped behind his head.

'Don't panic,' he said with more calmness than he was feeling. He'd seen the suspicion on her face as she pushed away from him, poised between flight and fright. 'I'm hardly likely to throw you on the grass and make love to you in full sight of the house, am I?' As if on cue the dumpy figure of Mrs Terrett emerged from the side door and crossed the courtyard between the house and the dairy. 'Even if it was in my nature to force the issue.'

She sat up, half-turned away from him, and caught her breath on a sob. He watched under his lashes as she struggled for control, wiping her eyes with the back of her hand and leaving dark smears on her cheek bones.

'Even if it was in my nature,' he repeated, more sternly.

'I know. At least I think....'

'We'll get nowhere if you're in any doubt about that.'

'We'll get nowhere anyway. Look, Max, you might as well face it - I'm a lost cause. Let me go, and you can get on with your life.'

'That's for me to decide. Obviously you've had a bad experience, but - '

She made a strange sound, somewhere between a cry and a despairing laugh.

'Tell me what this is all about, Sylvia.' He knelt in front of her, careful not to lay a finger on her. As her drooping head came up he said: 'You must tell me. I've already promised that I won't force the issue.'

'I - ' She shook her head. 'I can't talk about it.'

'I think you owe me that much. As your husband.'

'I never should have married you.'

'And I never should have put you in such a position. Forgive me.'

It was almost easier to deal with him when he was being unsympathetic: when he was so understanding, it left her with nowhere to go. She made the mistake of looking in his eyes and saw only compassion in them.

'You know I was imprisoned in Holloway?' It came out in a great rush, so fast he had to strain to make out the words. 'They treated us like the lowest of the low. We were put in the third class of prisoners - like the very dregs of society. As third class we were forced to wear prison clothes - stained and foul and germ-ridden. Even the Irish Fenian bombers were first class politicals, allowed to wear their own clothes. *We* couldn't even keep our own undergarments.' She shuddered at the memory. 'It wasn't right. If we were anything, we were political prisoners.'

His face darkened. 'You didn't go on hunger strike?'

'What else could we do? No one would listen to us.'

'I never thought...Oh God.' He closed his eyes in horror. 'They didn't force-feed you?'

'Every day for nearly two weeks.' She pointed to the scar at the side of her mouth. 'This was tidied up after I got out of the prison hospital but it's one of my mementoes of force-feeding. You were a Member of Parliament. You must know how it works.'

'I – I never...I know McKenna...the Home Secretary...was questioned on it. I read his statement in Hansard.'

'Of course. Just the words *Women's Suffrage* would be enough to empty the Chamber.'

Actually he had been away from London at the time, comforting Esmond's children after their mother had bolted for India, but he wasn't going to say so: it sounded too much like special pleading.

'McKenna said that no one was hurt. That it wasn't painful...'

'And you all believed him, like little obedient lambs!' she said scornfully. 'Well, this is how it works, Mr Bryson! They ram the metal gag in your mouth to hold it open...ratchet your jaw so wide...you wouldn't believe how wide they can force it...so they can push the tube down.' She almost choked at the memory of the metal on her mouth, the blow that had knocked away half a tooth, the sickening, burning sensation of the slimy tube being forced much too far down her gullet. The memories had been bottled up for too long, but she couldn't stop now. 'When it touches your throat, you can't help but cough it up, but he...he just pushed it back down.'

He had to strain to make out the words. 'Don't, Sylvia.' It was a struggle not to reach out, to take her in his arms and comfort her. 'It's too painful for you to remember. Don't...'

She didn't hear him: she was in a world apart and the memories came tumbling out, now that the box had been opened. 'The first time they did it, they stood me up too quickly. I was sick all over him and the wardresses. But he...he took it as a personal affront.' She cupped her cheek. 'He slapped me *so hard*...my ears were ringing. And then after that he wouldn't let me alone.' Her voice dropped to a whisper. 'They took three of us down to the punishment cells. There were over two hundred of us arrested in May and he - he knew no one was keeping track. He had *carte blanche* to do what he wanted. Down there they changed the team, you see...and...'

She swallowed hard. 'They always left the doors open, so we'd hear each other... crying and pleading...Not my door though. Never mine. Every day he slapped me again. Even when I wasn't struggling. He got the wardresses to strap me down...and then he sent them away and he...oh God....he....'

'Who was this?'

She didn't answer. Her eyes were focussed on another time and place: another life.

'You're saying he abused you?'

'Yes.'

'Raped you?'

'Yes. No.'

'You can't be that naive.' In spite of himself his voice sharpened. 'You must know whether he raped you or not.'

'You're a man!' she spat out. 'How could I ever have expected you to understand?'

Before he could speak she leaped to her feet and ran down the garden, across the gravelled drive and into the house.

She was gone before he could stop her and it took him an age to cover the same distance. By the time he reached the bottom of the stairs he was out of breath and panting, his legs barely supporting him. How he made it up the stairs he never knew, but his legs were like lead as he crossed the landing. He reached her bedroom only to find Hoskins and the maid in the doorway.

'You'll have to ask Mr Hoskins to get the trunks down, ma'am,' the maid was saying nervously as Sylvia swept brushes and cosmetic pots off the dressing table and hurled them onto the bed, tears pouring down her face unchecked.

'Sir Max has given me no instructions...' said Hoskins.

'Out!' Max held the door wide. 'Downstairs, both of you.'

He waited until the footsteps on the stairs had gone. 'Now,' he said, turning back to Sylvia, 'would you be good enough to tell me what the devil this is all about?'

'I can't be here with you anymore,' said Sylvia, pulling out the contents of the chest of drawers with shaking hands. 'I'm going back to London.'

He made a show of consulting his watch. 'The last connection to London leaves in five minutes. Even if you had a car here, you wouldn't make it.' He stepped forward and staggered as pain shot through him. 'Damnation!'

She started across to his side, then stopped. Max swore ripely and clutched the foot of the bed until the pain receded.

'You shouldn't have run after me.'

'You didn't leave me much choice, did you?' he said savagely. He eased himself down onto the bed, among the pots and pins that spilled across the counterpane. 'Hell, Sylvia, I think I've twisted it again.' He winced. 'The usual place, just to the right...'

'You don't expect me - ? Now? You really think *I* - ? Dear God, you just don't understand, do you?' She crossed to the bell and pulled it until the maid came running. 'Tell Hoskins Sir Max needs his assistance,' she said.

The valet arrived hot on the maid's heels. While he helped Max out of the room, she stayed by the window, gazing blindly out across the gardens.

73

Max lay on his bed watching the orange and pink of a spectacular sunset and wondering whether he could be bothered to dress for dinner. It would be so much simpler to have a tray sent up.

Sylvia was right, he thought. So foolish to have run after her in that mad headlong fashion. No wonder he'd jarred his back. And in his pain he'd said the first thing that came into his mind and the last thing she needed to hear. Asking her to massage his injury? What had he been thinking of?

When he swung his legs off the bed he was relieved to find that the pain had subsided - no thanks to Hoskins' useless attempts at easing the strained joints. The valet returned with hot water, looking so woebegone that Max finally consented to dress for dinner. Besides, a tray in his room would be too reminiscent of his invalid days. When he descended the stairs, however, he found his gesture was in vain: the dining room was empty.

He dined in solitary state and drank far too much. He was standing out in the rose garden drinking brandy and wishing that Sylvia was there with him when he was struck by a sudden insight. Of course, he never *had* dallied in the moonlight with Sylvia, or walked through scented gardens hoping for no more than to be allowed to kiss her hand. She'd found herself wife to her employer's son, with no mention ever having been made of love, of caring, of sharing. *That* was what she needed, especially after her terrible experience - whatever it might have been. He would find the truth of that if it took him a twelvemonth. Meanwhile he would embark on a delayed courtship. He could wait. He'd waited this long.

Congratulating himself on his insight he hurried up the stairs to tell her, but when he found she'd locked the dividing door, he had the sense not to force the issue.

'Good night, Sylvia,' he called. 'I hope you feel better in the morning.'

There was no answer, but he could hear her pacing up and down on the other side. With a heavy sigh he loosened his tie and collar and untied his shoes. Tomorrow, he promised himself. Tomorrow would be time enough.

74

Max experienced a brief moment of panic when his wife failed to appear at the breakfast table. Mindful of Sylvia's propensity for disappearing, he sent Mrs Terrett to her room with a tray.

'Tired out, she is, poor lady,' said the housekeeper, popping her head back round the dining room door. 'Small surprise, with all the running round she's been doing after you and your mother these last few months. And losing her own mother and all...' She paused to replenish the teapot. 'You'll need to cherish her, Master Max. There's more than one of you needs to recoup their strength.' She gave a roguish smile. 'Especially at this delicate time.'

Ye gods, thought Max helplessly. They're all expecting me to set up my nursery before I've even had the honeymoon! He had a sudden desire to take Sylvia away to a deserted island and shut the world out until they could resolve their problems.

There was little enough chance of that. He had spent a great deal of the morning on the telephone to London, much of it speaking to his secretary, an elderly civil servant brought out of retirement for the duration of the war, who lived in daily fear of being called on to make a decision in Max's absence. He'd just put the earpiece back on the stand when Sylvia came into the dining room, and he had to admit she was not looking her best.

'You should have called me. I never meant to sleep so long.'

'There's no rush. I've put off our departure.'

'But I *want* to go back to London.'

'You can 'phone for a taxi at any time. The operator will connect you to the station.' He crossed to the sideboard and poured two glasses of sherry, resisting the temptation to bring up what lay between them. 'My dear, I don't think either of us is quite fit for the journey yet.'

'But Lady Alice - '

' - has gone to Brighton, with Mrs Cunningham.' He pressed a glass into her hand. 'Mother's favourite pianist is giving a concert there tonight, and she hopes to persuade him to play for her fund-raising evening next month.'

Sylvia's face was a mirror of conflicting emotions. 'A few more days won't make much difference,' he said, as casually as he could manage. 'We could both do with a little more peace. You'll be busy enough once you get back - as I will.'

'Oh, very well.' Hardly the most gracious capitulation, but it was enough for him. Today she seemed a little calmer: at a guess the bad memories had been boxed up once more, put to the back of her mind....until the next time.

Best not to think too much about that now. Wait till he had the information he was seeking... His mind began to formulate plans for the afternoon.

'Your back is better?' she asked, after she had sipped at her sherry in silence for a few moments. 'You seem to be moving more freely than - than before.'

'It will do.'

'Then Hoskins fitted the bill?'

'Hardly. It was like being massaged by a kitten - more irritation than relief.' The guarded look returned. 'Don't fret. You're excused duties. I don't propose to do any more running, and once we return to London I can find another Paget masseuse.'

Over lunch he asked what plans she had for the rest of the day.

'I could start packing, I suppose....'

'Leave it to the maid. I want to show you another part of the estate. I think you'll like it. It's where we played as children, Charlotte and I. Esmond too when he was older.'

She frowned. 'You didn't grow up at Whitefields?'

He shook his head. 'The old Earl was still living there then. He fell out with his son when he married my mother: she was a lawyer's widow, not a very good match. They were only reconciled on the old man's death bed.'

'What a waste.'

'Indeed. But it meant that we grew up here, for which I will be eternally grateful.'

She went upstairs to change into something more suitable for a country ramble. She couldn't face the maid after yesterday's upset, so she dressed herself and twisted her hair up in a simple knot.

When she came down, broad-brimmed straw hat on her head, Max was nowhere to be seen. She paced impatiently back and forth across the shadowed hall, longing to be out in the fresh air. It was a little while before she noticed the envelope on the table.

Her name was on the front, in Max's bold handwriting. Intrigued, she slit it open and found a small card with instructions. *Go down the valley, keep to the right bank of the lake and follow the ribbons. If you get lost, just whistle!*

It was absurd, but still it brought a smile to her lips. This was the kind of game she might have played with Freddie. As she stepped out of the door the warm sun kissed her skin and her spirits began to lift. She strolled down the valley, resisting the temptation to linger at the bridge over the lake. The meadows were loud with the hum of insects and the gentle munching of cows in the lush green grass. Somewhere down the valley she could hear the clack-clacking of a harvester.

Beyond the lake the scenery changed. Ahead of her lay a wilderness of rhododendrons and azaleas, magnolias and other shrubs that she didn't recognise. This would, she thought, eventually bring her to the old carriage drive, which had been abandoned with the advent of the motor car. The path appeared to veer to the right, but just as she would have turned, she caught sight of a pale ribbon fluttering from a branch to her left. Changing direction she saw a flight of steps which had been hidden from view. Intrigued, she set off down them, looking for more ribbons as she went.

She found the next tied round a stone font, set with a fragment of mosaic from the Roman villa Max had told her about, dug up in the valley in the previous century. This ribbon led her off to the side, down more steps. Over to her left was a second small lake which she had not known existed.

If it hadn't been for two ribbons, tied close together, she'd never have found the steps to the shell-lined grotto, which appeared to have been dug out under the carriage drive itself. A huge stone dog guarded the entrance to the grotto, a third coloured ribbon tied around its neck. She felt quite envious of Max growing up in such a wonderful place: this would have been the best hide and seek ever!

She stepped carefully through the grotto, for the floor and walls were a little damp, but soon emerged into dappled sunshine again. The path led her on through a long tunnel of vines which skirted the edge of another, much larger lake. Emerging at last from the tunnel she saw a cluster of buildings. The largest structure was an Egyptian-style temple with a broad flight of steps leading up to it. And there, at the bottom of the steps, sat Max.

He looked up at the sound of her gasp. 'Welcome to the secret garden, Sylvia.'

She looked around, eyes wide in astonishment. Grassy lawns sloped down to the glinting waters of the lake, in which swam large silver and golden carp, rising occasionally to snap at vivid blue dragonflies that skimmed across the surface. Exotic trees clustered around, screening the garden from the rest of the estate....screening it from the rest of the world. 'The magical garden,' she whispered.

He studied her face for a moment, but saw no signs of alarm. 'Care for a row on the lake?' He indicated a boat, rocking gently at the bottom of the steps. At one end was a broad rattan seat with comfortable cushions, at the other a plain board for the oarsman.

'Are you up to rowing?'

'I usually just push off and drift around the lake,' he said with a disarming smile. 'The only rowing you need is when you're ready to come back. Even I can manage that.'

When she still hesitated he said, 'It's deliciously cool out on the water. I tried it earlier, to make sure the boat was still sound.' With an easy movement he descended the steps and fished out a bottle which had been cooling in the water. 'Champagne,' he said. 'Can you think of a more delicious way to spend a hot summer's afternoon?'

She couldn't. In a couple of days they would be back in the noise and smoke of London: why not enjoy the last of their summer holiday?

Max handed her into the boat, smiling as she subsided onto the feather-filled cushions with a sigh. 'Take these,' he said, handing her the bottle and glasses. Now came the difficult part: stepping in himself without staggering and swamping the boat.

He stepped in, not elegantly, favouring his weaker leg, then hesitated.

'Sit down, Max!' She grabbed the painter and held them to the bank. 'You're rocking the boat.'

'May I sit beside you? The board will be a bit hard.'

There was a sharp intake of breath, then she moved over to make room for him. He reached across to cast off, then pushed them away from the bank with one of the oars.

They drifted out into the middle of the lake. He took a knife out of his pocket, eased the cork out of the bottle with a satisfying plop and poured out two glasses. Somewhere among the trees a bird sang.

'I think I could get drunk as quickly just on the air.' She sipped her drink. 'But champagne still tastes good.'

'A perfect day.' He let his arm fall behind her along the back of the seat, but made no move to touch her. 'I'm glad you like my garden,' he murmured, closing his eyes.

She must have drifted off to sleep, waking with a start at the touch of leaf fronds on her face. Then the boat bumped into the bank and she felt Max's arm tighten around her shoulders.

Max opened one eye. 'I was relying on you to keep us safe,' he teased, catching her hat just before it would have fallen in the water.

'And there was I thinking *you* had sworn to cherish *me*.' She flushed as he pulled her hat on over her curls again. What a thing to say, after all that had happened! 'Sorry. I didn't mean that.'

'You're still half asleep.' He let go his grip on her, moved carefully across to the central board, took up the oars and rowed them out to the centre of the lake. 'I think I can promise not to drown you. I haven't capsized a boat since I was ten.' He pointed to the little Gothic cottage alongside the temple. 'An old gardener used to live there. Actually, he was a hopeless gardener: Ardingley kept him there solely to fish us out of the lake if we fell in.'

Sylvia let her hands drift in the cool water and gave herself up once more to the magic of the day.

'There are medical people who specialise in these things,' said Max softly. 'Have you ever talked to a doctor about these...nightmare memories?'

She jumped, and he thought she wasn't going to answer.

'Lady Harriet took me to a specialist,' she said after a moment. 'Soon after I came out of prison.' Her mouth twisted and she gave an ugly laugh. 'He had a solution. A certain cure, he promised. He would cut out the feminine parts of me - my womb and - and all my other female parts. Then I'd never have any more problems.'

Max swore softly. She looked at him under her lashes. 'Don't look so shocked. It's the standard treatment for hysterics, didn't you know? Although most of the women die during the operation, or bleed to death soon after, so it's hard to know whether it really helps...'

'You know as well as I that you are not an hysteric. After what you've been through these last two years....' He pulled on the oars. 'We all have times when our mind is overset. If you'd seen me last year when they told me they couldn't get the shrapnel out...that I might never walk again. I went through hell....'

She bit her lip and said nothing.

'Was there never a time when you....might have overcome it yourself? No man who tempted you to...'

Her face flamed and she began to tremble. 'Don't!' She held out a hand as if to ward him off.

'You're down there and I'm up here,' he said in a steely voice. 'And you will recall my promise? Yes?'

'Yes.' She reached out to refill her glass. The bottle chinked against the rim as her hand shook.

'*Was* there ever a time....?'

'Once.' It was as if the words were being wrenched from her. 'I was exhausted. Mother had kept me up half the night. I'd worked a long office shift in the morning, then a long shift driving. I hadn't eaten. Foolishly I drank some wine and...Nothing happened,' she said hastily. 'I came back to my senses. But...I didn't feel scared.'

Octavius Jameson? Most likely, but he knew better than to ask. This was not about his jealousy. It was enough that he'd persuaded her to talk at last.

But it looked as though she'd said all she was going to say for the moment. 'Let me fill your glass,' she said, the social smile back on her face.

'Finish off the bottle.' He leaned back into the oars. 'Plenty more in the ice house.'

She was still lost in her own thoughts as he brought the boat back into the bank, but she didn't cringe away when he held out his hand to her.

'Would you like to know the story of the temple?' he asked, spreading the cushions from the boat under the trees.

She slanted an anxious glance up at him. 'Shouldn't we be getting back to the house?'

'We're not expected for dinner.' He opened another bottle and filled the glasses. 'Mrs Terrett put up a hamper. We can have a picnic before we go back...if you'd like.'

She didn't answer. He didn't press her. Leaning back against the steps he told her the story of the vicar of North Nibley, who had built the temple a century before for his gypsy mistress, and planned such a narrow pathway to it that his plump and indolent wife would never be able to find her way to the hidden garden, even if she could summon up the energy.

'Were they happy together, the vicar and the gypsy?'

'History doesn't relate, alas. But I like to think so. There's such a happy atmosphere here.'

'Poor wife.'

'It was the custom then, when couples were so ill-matched. Women didn't have the choice about who they married.'

'Huh! And now they're so much freer?'

'Come on, Sylvia. Be honest. If you'd really hated and loathed me, you'd never have considered marrying me - under any circumstances.'

'I only did it for the children.'

He let that pass.

It was a hot afternoon and they drank another glass of wine. 'Much more of this and I shall be tipsy,' she said drowsily.

'I don't believe it. You have an unusually good head for drink - '

'For a woman? That's from spending time with Freddie and all his fast friends.' She looked down at the lake. 'He would have loved this,' she said softly. 'What a long time ago all that seems.'

It seemed like a good time to fetch another bottle. 'Goodness! Is that a door?' she said as he descended to the ice house. 'What a strange door-frame.'

'This? Jawbone of a whale. The unfortunate creature turned left at Land's End instead of right - and became stranded in the River Severn.' He carried on chatting as he disappeared into the ice house, but by the time he re-emerged, she'd dozed off. Obviously she'd had as little sleep as he had last night. He rescued her hat, which was in danger of being crushed, poured himself another glass and stretched out on the rug nearby.

She was still sleeping when the sun began to sink behind the trees. A cool breeze rippled the surface of the water. He knelt down beside her and brushed the hair off her face.

She stirred and stretched like a cat. Without thought he lowered his head and kissed her gently at the side of her mouth. She opened her eyes and smiled at him.

'You see,' he murmured. 'You don't really hate me.'

'No. I don't think I ever hated you.' As she came back to her surroundings, her face grew a little more guarded.

'Don't let it take you over again,' he whispered, stroking the side of her face, but taking care not to get too close, so that she could get away if she really wanted to. 'Relax. Why not just...give in to it?'

Why not? It would be good to have another human being who cared about her: it was such a long time since anyone had.

'I don't dislike it - you kissing me,' she said, her voice still slurred with tiredness. 'It's just that - I'm afraid of what might follow.'

'Then may I kiss you again?' he asked. 'Just - kiss you? No more.'

In answer she turned her face up to his. As his lips met hers in a slow and gentle kiss, she gave herself up to the warmth and sensuousness of the moment, closing her mind to harsher memories. This, after all, was no more than the time in the boathouse when she and Hugh had come so close to passion....

A shiver went through her. Instantly he drew back, forcing himself to breathe steadily and keep his control. 'What is it?'

'I was remembering - no, not that.' The strain around his eyes disappeared. 'When I was engaged to Hugh.'

'Ah. Well, you see, there are good memories as well as bad.' He began to gather up the blankets and cushions. 'Shall we go inside? I brought you a shawl, but the air's cooling down.'

75

She was not prepared for the sight that met her eyes as she entered the temple. The place had obviously not been inhabited for some time, and paint was peeling off the elaborately moulded plasterwork in the main room, but the light of a flickering fire concealed the worst of the neglect. The last golden rays of the setting sun shone down through a stained glass cupola, casting jewelled colour onto a faded Oriental carpet.

In front of the fire a substantial picnic had been laid out on a low table set on a thick rug. Cushions and quilts were scattered liberally around. It looked like something out of the Arabian Nights.

She stopped abruptly in the doorway, but Max passed on and began to light candles and lamps. 'Come right in, or we'll have all the moths in Gloucestershire joining us.' He darted a glance at her over his shoulder. 'This isn't the prelude to a seduction. I just need my comforts more than I did when we stayed here as children.'

Still she said nothing.

'You can go back at any time,' he said gently. 'With or without me. I swear it.'

'I am...quite hungry.' Her voice was unexpectedly hoarse. 'All that wine...'

He let his breath out in a sigh of relief. Crossing the room he put a record on a gramophone that she had not previously noticed.

'I thought it would be good for us to have some time together, just the two of us. We may have known each other for some time, but we've been catapulted into intimacy without ever really getting to know each other. It's my fault,' he said, as the strains of syncopated piano music filled the room. 'I should have had the good grace to die under the knife, as everyone expected.'

'Max, don't say that!'

He shrugged. 'You can't deny it would have made life a deal easier for you. All the advantages of a society marriage without the inconvenience of a husband.'

'That wasn't why I did it! You *can't* think that.'

'As you said - you did it for the children.'

'I wanted to put your mind at rest...'

'And you did.'

'I didn't want you to die, Max. Sometimes you can be the most infuriating man of my acquaintance... but don't ever think I wanted you to die.'

He saw the distress in her eyes and cursed himself. 'I was jesting, Sylvia. A poor jest, and in poor taste. I never really thought that.' He crossed to her side and took her hand in his. 'I woke up once, you know, just after the operation, and I heard you crying. I thought then: Good God, perhaps she *does* care if I live or die.'

'You're imagining it. You didn't wake up for days. They kept you drugged.'

'Oh, I couldn't speak, and it was only for a moment. The doctor was there. He handed something to you and you started crying.'

She put her hand to her mouth on a sharp intake of breath. 'I'd almost forgotten. It was the shrapnel...'

'What?'

'The shrapnel they took out of you. The orderlies string it together and present it to wives and sweethearts.' She wrinkled her nose. 'Apparently they have it made up into necklaces, but that seemed a bit gruesome to me.'

'That's why you were crying?'

'There was so *much* of it. I thought you couldn't possibly recover from so much damage.'

He bent his head over her hand and kissed her fingers. 'Bless you, my dear,' he murmured. 'It helped to know that you cared. And I've always cared for you too,' he said, drawing her over to the fire, 'even when you were engaged to marry another man. Can't we try to build on that?' He stroked her hand. 'Even if we can't manage complete intimacy....some couples never do.' A muscle twitched at the side of his mouth. 'But there's always tender friendship - it has much to recommend it.'

'I want to try, Max. Truly I do. But - ' But if it didn't work, and if he couldn't accept it, then she knew she couldn't stay with him. 'I can't promise anything.'

'Tonight I'll settle for that.' The intense light went out of his eyes and he slipped back into the role of perfect host, as if the deeper discussions had never taken place. He pressed her to eat and they dined sumptuously on cold salmon, new bread, golden cheeses and summer fruits, all washed down with more champagne.

At last she lay back on the cushions with a sigh of satisfaction. 'Sir Max,' she said, 'that was the most magnificent midnight feast I have ever had.'

'Lady Bryson, my heart warms to hear you say it.' His lips twitched. 'D'you know you have peach juice all over your face? I believe a visit to the lake is called for.'

They sat on the steps in companionable silence, watching the moonlight on the lake and listening to the slap-slap of the water against the side of the boat.

'It's just like warm silk,' she said, letting the water fall in sparkling droplets through her fingers. 'Max?'

'Yes?'

'Have you ever swum in the dark? Just floated on the water, looking up at the stars?'

'One mad summer. In the south of France. I'd just come third in one of the big motor races. Might even have been my last Paris to Bordeaux. Year two, it was, or maybe year three. A group of us got very drunk and swam in the sea. Madness, really: we were lucky none of us drowned. It was very clear, just like tonight. God, it seems like a lifetime away.' He looked sideways at her. 'And you?'

'Never considered it before.' Her voice grew husky. 'But tonight I feel as though I could lie on my back, gazing at the stars, and - just float away.'

'Not in this lake. There are too many lilies and the roots can drag you under. There was an old bathing pond here that was fed from the lake, but I don't know what condition it's in now.'

She shook her head. 'It was just a crazy idea. With the stars so clear...and the moonlight. And with the water so warm....'

'I'm almost tempted to risk it for the joy of seeing you rise from the water like Venus from the waves. But I wouldn't be able to save you if you got caught up. I'm still too feeble.' He lifted her hand to his lips and kissed it. 'And you, my dear, have drunk far too much champagne to save *me*.'

After a while they went back into the temple. She crossed to the gramophone and put on a record. As she turned, Max was close behind her. 'May I have the pleasure of this dance?'

The room was a haze of golden light and in his arms she felt warm and safe. 'One day,' he murmured in her ear, 'one day when this wretched war is over, I'll take you to the south of France and we'll swim under the stars.'

She turned her face up to him like a flower and he lowered his head, almost holding his breath for fear of frightening her and spoiling this golden moment. Her face moved a little closer to his and they kissed, a long and satisfying kiss.

'Sweetheart,' he murmured, 'I've wanted to do that ever since we first met.'

She drew away from him with a shuddering breath, but this time he knew it was not the shudder of rejection.

They danced a little longer, until the gramophone ran down. Neither of them made a move to wind it up again, but stood hand-locked, only inches apart. 'I'd like to kiss you again,' he murmured.

'Would that be wise?'

'We can do it as much as you want. There's no risk of going any further.'

'Are you sure?'

He grinned. 'It's very early days. My physical responses are far from reliable.' He twirled her towards the cushions. 'Which is why I became so rudely enthusiastic the other day. But as for tonight - rest easy. I've drunk far too much.'

It wasn't strictly true, but above all tonight she needed to feel safe.

As the logs crackled on the fire, and the candles guttered, and shafts of silvery moonlight spilled through the glass cupola, she relaxed into his arms. They chatted drowsily, about the past, about the war, about the children. He teased her and as she shook her head her hair, disarranged through the day, tumbled over her shoulders.

'I don't suppose that among all your efficient arrangements you included a comb and a mirror?'

'No. And I'm glad I didn't.' He reached out and rescued a handful of falling hairpins, tossing them into her discarded straw hat. 'Let me be your mirror,' he said, running his fingers through her tousled locks. She gave a soft sigh as he drew her hair down the side of her face, smoothing out the tangles. 'I love the feel of your hair,' he murmured.

He continued to run his hands rhythmically through her loosened curls until she relaxed against him. After a few minutes he realised that she had fallen asleep. Settling himself among the quilts and cushions he drew her head down onto his chest.

The fire crackled as the logs settled. A tear squeezed from under his eyelids and ran down his cheek.

76

Hobbling after the VAD nurse, the sitter leaned on his makeshift crutch and turned to wave goodbye. Sylvia waved back. She stacked the steps back into the lorry, closed the rear door and swung the hasp across. Suppressing a yawn with some difficulty, she climbed up into the driving seat and turned over the engine. Fortunately it fired the first time, avoiding the necessity of cleaning the fuel lines yet again.

She'd been so eager to get back to work - and it certainly beat nursing into a cocked hat - that she'd overlooked how physically tiring it all was, especially as her absence had lost her the automatic right to the self-starter motors. Today she was lucky, and her old vehicle was available, because many of the drivers would not work on Sundays: even after nearly eighteen months of war they still clung to the proprieties. For Sylvia, however, work was an excuse to avoid the oppressive sanctity of the Sabbath: today Max had the joy of escorting his mother and Mrs Cunningham to church.

It was late afternoon before she finished her duties, and her feet in the heavy boots and puttees were hot and sore as she hurried out of the depot and along Holborn. Turning into the Kingsway she saw the back of the tram disappearing down the tunnel. She swore softly - it would be a long wait for the next one, on Sunday timetables. She could take a cab, if there were any to be had on a Sunday, or walk. She'd done it before, but today the prospect made her feet rebel.

While she was making up her mind, a sleek black car drew up alongside.

'Sylvia? Lady Bryson?' Eddie Seymour leaped out of the car and hurried round to hold the door open. 'May I give you a ride home?'

Her mother would have been appalled at her daughter, unchaperoned, in a car with a single man, but she was damned if she'd let that stop her.

'I'm going to Ardingley House.'

'Not Charles Street?' She saw the curiosity in his eyes, but she couldn't satisfy it.

They'd arrived back at Stancombe House after the idyll in the secret garden, to find an official letter waiting for Max. He'd been summoned to join Lloyd George and Seymour on a tour of a new, secret explosives factory in the Forest of Dean. They'd parted, with so much still to be discussed between them, and she'd returned to London alone, wondering whether she would be expected to go back to Lady Alice's service, or move into her new husband's house. She'd failed to decide which would be harder. After that night in the secret garden, she felt a growing warmth towards Max, and gratitude for his understanding, but in her present state she was nothing but a burden to him.

'Max is spending the day with his mother,' she said calmly. It wasn't the whole truth, but it was as much as she was prepared to tell Eddie. 'I promised to join them there. But if it takes you out of your way...'

'At your command, dear lady.'

Traffic was light and they soon drew up outside Ardingley House. She was surprised when Seymour invited himself in. 'I promised Lady Alice my assistance with her gala charity evening,' he said smoothly. 'I must enquire about our progress.'

Max had fallen into the habit of dining at Ardingley House, before going to his club, and from there back to Charles Street. While Sylvia stayed in her old rooms at Ardingley House it was a mockery of married life, but the time was not yet right to rock the boat. His smile of welcome dissolved into a frown when Eddie Seymour entered the drawing room on Sylvia's heels. But he soon composed himself, shook Seymour's hand and, when he'd made his bow to Lady Alice, introduced him to the rest of the company.

'Mrs Cunningham, a friend of ours from Torquay. Mrs Brewer, a distant cousin of Ardingley's. And her daughters, the Misses Brewer.'

Sylvia wondered whether she was the only one to notice the stress on the word 'distant'. She shook hands with the elderly lady and the two daughters, as old-fashioned and staidly dressed as their mother. Ensconced by the fireside, they looked as if they were there for the duration.

'We met Constance and her daughters by chance in church,' said Lady Alice in neutral tones. 'We've been talking about old times over lunch.'

'Such a delight to see you again, dear Lady Alice,' gushed Mrs Brewer. 'Family is so important, don't you think, and to have left you unsupported....I blame myself for not being *au fait* with the situation, but of course I don't get about quite so much since my poor dear husband died. Had I known that poor darling Imogen was no longer with you - I can't imagine why Henrietta Jennings did not think to inform me! - either Gertrude or Penelope would have been only too delighted to have come to you, to be your eyes.'

Her own beady eyes, reminiscent of a bird of prey, moved around the room taking in the quality of the furniture and the ornaments. 'Indeed, when Mrs Cunningham returns to - Torquay, was it? - she will be eager to get home again, after being away for so long - my girls will be only too delighted to step in to be your guiding hand. I need only one of them at home and can easily spare you the other.'

Sylvia was on the point of excusing herself, to go to her room and change out of her uniform, but seeing Mrs Cunningham blush with embarrassment at the suggestion she had outstayed her welcome, she leaped into the breach. 'We hope Mrs Cunningham can be prevailed upon to extend her visit.' She smiled reassuringly at the widow who had succeeded so well in bringing Lady Alice out of the doldrums. 'I don't know how the gala evening can possibly go ahead without her. She's worked so hard for it.' She turned to Lady Alice. 'Mr Seymour was hoping to discuss the arrangements with you both this evening. I'm sure Mrs Brewer will excuse us if ....'

But on this occasion Seymour let her down. 'No urgency, I assure you, Lady Alice. I can call another time. Perhaps you or Mrs Cunningham will ring and let me know when would be convenient?'

Sylvia muttered something in Seymour's ear and he answered, equally *sotto voce*. She would have followed him out, but Mrs Brewer turned her gimlet gaze on her. 'I did not see *you* in church today, Lady Bryson,' she said.

For a mad moment Sylvia toyed with the idea of announcing that she was a Mahometan or a follower of the Buddha, but she overcame the impulse. She gestured to her uniform. 'As you see, I've been on duty.'

'One must admire your dedication.' She surveyed Sylvia from head to toe, taking in the military style jacket, the culottes, boots and puttees. 'Though I should not wish to see my daughters in such very unfeminine attire.'

Propped against the fireplace, Max turned a snort of derision into an unconvincing cough. Mrs Cunningham looked down at her hands, but Lady Alice rose from her chair in a swirl of skirts.

'There are so many things women can do for the war effort without having to wear uniforms,' she said. 'I'm glad to hear you can spare the girls: when Mrs Cunningham and I next go to the Mission Hall, we'll be delighted to take one with us.'

'What an excellent idea,' said Max. 'They always need volunteers to make tea.'

'But not on the Sabbath,' said Mrs Brewer, desperately fighting a rearguard action. 'I insist on proper Sunday observance. Indeed, I find it strange, Max, that you should permit your wife to work on the Sabbath.'

'It's not for me to tell my wife what to do or not do.' He looked at Sylvia with warmth in his eyes. 'I'm very proud of her and all she does.'

Sylvia knew she was blushing, and hurried into speech. 'Doctors and nurses don't stop work on Sundays,' she pointed out to Mrs Brewer. 'Nor do the German guns. Would you have us shunt hospital trains into the sidings at midnight every Saturday? Our casualties would be even worse than they are now.'

Mrs Brewer was not to be robbed of the last word. 'You missed an excellent sermon today, Lady Bryson. One can always rely on Reverend Curtis to find the right words for a nation in mourning. He spoke very movingly about victory over death - '

'There is no victory over death!' snapped Sylvia. 'When will people understand that? *There is only death!* High-flown words and sermons won't bring the dead back again!' She banged her fist on the back of the chair in frustration and ran out of the room.

Mrs Brewer did not give up so easily. The echo of her sepulchral tones pursued Sylvia across the hall. 'Such a comfort as the Reverend Curtis is to those who have suffered. But one can hardly expect the heedless young to understand.'

'For Heaven's sake, Constance,' snapped Lady Alice. 'She lost two brothers in the service of the country!'

'We each deal with our losses in our own way, Mrs Brewer,' said Mrs Cunningham, pouring oil on troubled waters.

Sylvia hadn't realised that Max had followed her out. 'Take no notice of that old battle-axe.'

'I don't.' She turned on the first step. 'Bigots like her aren't worth the argument.'

He put his hand over hers on the banister. 'What were you whispering about with Eddie?'

'I hadn't expected him to rat on me. If he'd taken my lead we could have got rid of the Brewers.'

'Oh?' He didn't sound convinced.

'He said he wasn't up to the task. Said Mrs Brewer reminded him of his Aunt Hermione and he kept expecting her to ask him to recite his catechism.'

Mrs Brewer's voice boomed out once more. 'Very odd behaviour, to run out of the room like that when you have guests.'

Max rolled his eyes to the ceiling.

As she approached the door, Constance Brewer dropped her voice to what she fondly believed to be a confidential whisper. 'I suppose she must be breeding. She left it very late to marry - it's to be hoped she's up to it. Dear, dear. Poor Max. Such very odd ideas these emancipated women have.'

77

Sylvia returned late from an evening duty to find that Max had already left for his club and Mrs Cunningham was in her room catching up on correspondence.

Lady Alice lifted the needle from the record on the gramophone. 'Would you pour me a brandy, my dear? And whatever you would like.' She leaned back in her favourite chair with a sigh. 'I'm glad we have this opportunity to talk. It's been so long.'

'We've been at sixes and sevens ever since that wretched May Fair.'

'Almost five months. Hard to believe...'

'I know I've neglected you. If you want me to give up my work at the depot - '

'Do you know, I don't believe I do. These last few months, while you have been caring for Max, I've managed quite well.'

Sylvia turned cold. 'I always knew you could.'

'I probably never needed you in the first place - or perhaps only to tell me what a pathetic fool I was making of myself.' She chuckled. 'I put that down to Henrietta Jennings, compounded by my worries about the children. But finding you was a blessing. Without you I'd never have learned to cope for myself.' She overrode Sylvia's protests. 'It's a misfortune that I can't see, and I don't suppose I'll ever completely recover from that shock - especially coming as it did among so many others - but I'm coming to terms with it. You helped me to reclaim my life, but I realised in Torquay that I no longer need you as a crutch. I probably never did.'

'In truth you did more for me and my mother than ever I did for you,' said Sylvia warmly. 'You gave us a roof over our heads when we needed one...'

'But you no longer need this roof, Sylvia. Your place is in Charles Street with your husband.' Lady Alice rose from her chair and held out her hands. 'You and Max have to build your own life together. I don't want to stand between you.'

'But who will do your correspondence for you?'

'You or Max can read my letters out to me. I trust you will still drop in occasionally?'

'As often as possible. But your committees...?'

'You, when you have the time, or John Groom, or that nice Mr Doncaster. But a great deal of writing can be avoided if I can learn to be more at ease with the telephone. Dora is helping me with that. I've invited her to stay on for a while longer, but as a friend, not a crutch.'

'She can't drive.' She knew she was clutching at straws.

'I know. It's a bore that I can't drive myself, but I can afford cabs. Even the Graysons can't take my financial independence away.'

'You've found a good friend in Mrs Cunningham.'

Lady Alice pressed her hands. 'And in you I have quite unexpectedly found a dear daughter.'

78

Max had great hopes of Sylvia's removal to Charles Street, but they both seemed to spend more time out of the house than in it and were rarely at home together. The summer offensives around the Ypres salient, and the battle for the huge crater which had once been Hooge Château, had sent wave after wave of wounded back to England. Many of them were from Kitchener's Army, some badly burnt from the liquid fire the Germans were now turning on the trenches. When Sylvia wasn't working extra shifts at the depot, she was at Ardingley House helping out with the arrangements for Lady Alice's gala evening in aid of blinded servicemen.

Max too had plenty to occupy his time, establishing himself once more in the team of economists, railway builders, chemists and manufacturers Lloyd George had gathered about him at the Ministry of Munitions. After such a long absence he felt the need to show that he could pull his weight as well as the others and often worked late, either at the Ministry in Whitehall Gardens or in Lloyd George's rooms in the House of Commons.

One night Sylvia came in from duty to find Max standing in the dark by the uncurtained window, watching the spotlights quartering the clear starlit sky. Her breath caught in her throat at the sight of him. She'd woken in the early morning light at the temple to see him standing at the door, silhouetted against the lake and the misty trees, his profile stern as a granite statue; now he stood in the same rigid pose, unaware of her presence.

'Max?' She stepped into the room, tray in her hand, and kicked the door to behind her. 'Close the curtains. I want to turn on the light.'

'Good evening, stranger,' he said, closing the drapes. As she flicked the switch and flooded the room with light, he crossed to take the tray that she was balancing on one hand. 'I thought I heard a Zeppelin. But it's all gone quiet now.'

'No action that I could see.'

'I didn't hear you come in. You're late.'

She shrugged. 'The trains were delayed.'

'I don't like you driving about the streets of London by yourself late at night like this.'

She bit off a sharp retort. She knew he was thinking about the Zeppelin raid shortly after their return to London, when five bombs had torn up the city between St Paul's and the Mansion House. The papers had only been permitted to print the Press Bureau's unfortunately worded statement that a London district had been 'visited' by a Zeppelin and some bombs dropped, but the cold reality was that forty people had lost their lives, ten of them on a motor omnibus heading for Liverpool Street Station. The last bomb had fallen close to Bart's, only a few hours after she'd driven away from the hospital.

'Stop worrying. I'm safe.'

'I suppose there's no point in me asking you to give up these night duties?'

'Not unless you want this tray around your ear!' she said fiercely. 'Look, Max - if I'd known you were going out to the front line with Lloyd George, I don't suppose I'd have been too keen about that either.'

'You're right.' He dropped a kiss on the top of her head and she started. 'As Mrs Terrett says, there *is* a war on. I'll try to stop worrying.'

With an effort she pulled herself together. 'Have you eaten? I can ask cook to bring you up a tray.'

'I dined with Sir Herbert.'

She dropped her fork with a clatter. 'Progress with the custody case?'

'I hope so. Fortune is looking our way at last. The government wants to requisition Whitefields for a convalescent home. For men with neurasthenia.'

'Shell-shock?'

'That's what the men call it. The Medical Officers think it's best to nurse them apart from the other wounded men, who have a tendency to call them malingerers and lead-swingers.'

'Unless, of course, you're the P.M's son. Then nobody turns a hair when you take four months' leave for a shrapnel graze.'

He shrugged. The continued presence of Lady Cynthia's husband in England was in sharp contrast to most shell-shocked soldiers who were granted only the shortest of Blighty leave - sometimes not even that - before being sent back to the front. 'I can testify to the shock of having just one shell go off close by. God alone knows what it must do to the men out in the trenches, under shell-fire day in, day out. They deserve the best care we can give them, and Whitefields will be an ideal location.'

'I suppose the Graysons are resisting the move?'

'Tooth and nail. Frankly, I can't think of a better use for the place. These huge mausoleums of houses have had their day. You saw how impossible it was to heat it.'

'And you, as the children's guardian, would be quite prepared to hand it over. Thus showing yourself a better patriot than Grayson.'

His lips twitched. 'I'm sure Sir Herbert will find a way to show it in its best light.'

'Not that you want to influence anyone, of course.'

'There's nothing I wouldn't do to get the children out of Grayson's grip.' He shrugged. 'And a word in the right place never goes amiss in the legal world.'

'Will I be summoned to court?'

'No. Why should you be? You're not cited as guardian.'

Sylvia stopped with her fork half way to her mouth and wondered why she should feel so hurt.

'I told you I wouldn't put that burden on you. Mother and I are the appellants, for the children to stay on the estate, but to live at the Dower House with Mother until Charlotte can come back from Canada.'

'Or Imogen from India?'

'In theory, yes. But it will never happen.'

'And your mother? Will she cope?'

'She'll have Mrs Harmitage, and of course she knows the Dower House well. She lived there when Esmond and Imogen were first married.'

'Will Mrs Harmitage speak in your favour?'

'She's already done so.'

She caught his hand. 'Oh, Max, I'm so delighted - for all of you!'

'It's still early days.' He held her hand in his for a moment, his eyes smiling into hers. When at last she looked away, he dropped her hand, lifted a finger of devilled toast from her tray and sank his teeth into it. 'But I'm optimistic enough to open up the Dower House right away.'

That night, unusually, they both went up together. Since she'd moved here from Ardingley House, he'd taken great care not to alarm her. Each time he offered only a chaste goodnight kiss; each time he hoped she would make another move towards him, however small; each time he was disappointed. They smiled at each other at breakfast, they asked after each other's concerns and welfare, but even his proposition of passionate friendship seemed at times too great an ambition. It was almost as if the interlude in the temple had never happened.

Tonight he sensed a subtle difference. As he bent his head to kiss her goodnight, she moved into his arms. Resting her hands against his chest, she turned her face up to his. Taking care not to hold her too tight he kissed her lips and, as she responded, kissed her again, a long slow kiss. His breathing quickened and he struggled to hold himself in check, keeping his hands lightly on her shoulders. He pressed a chain of kisses across her cheek and let his mouth stray to the soft skin under her ear, the khaki of her jacket rough against his skin. She gasped and swayed a little and his arms went around her.

'Don't ring for Lizzie,' he said, struggling to keep the need out of his voice. 'Let me come in for a while.'

'I don't know.' She buried her face in his shoulder. 'This isn't fair on you.'

'Let me worry about me,' he said. 'Passionate friendship...no more than we did in the temple.'

'You won't...?'

'Hurry you? No.' He sought for the right words to say. 'Sylvia, sweetheart, we have all the time in the world...'

79

Max had just enjoyed an excellent lunch, marred only by the fact that Sylvia had to hurry off immediately afterwards for an emergency run, taking casualties from the boat train and transferring them to the London hospitals. Still, she would be back early this evening. She had promised.

He settled in a comfortable armchair with papers at one elbow and a large brandy at the other, but instead of turning to his work he found himself day-dreaming about the feel of Sylvia's curls between his fingers and the silky skin of her shoulders beneath his hands as he undressed her down to her satin under-garments, caressing her, kissing her, yet at the same time holding himself firmly in check.

He tried not to think of the moment when he had dragged himself from her side and crossed the hall to his own room. A new tranquillity was building between them which made worthwhile every minute of the frustration he presently endured. Even if they had to go on like this for a six month, it would be worth it in the end. After all, they had their whole lives ahead of them.

Out in the hall the telephone shrilled, jarring him back to the present with a start. Sunday was Hoskins's free day, and Lizzie was visiting her mother. He rose from the chair, stretched, and picked up the receiver.

His heart sank when he heard Eddie's voice. He'd persuaded Sylvia to sign off evening duties tonight - was he going to be called in to the Ministry?

'Max? I think you'd better come over straight away.'

'Damn it, why do they always choose Sundays for a political crisis?'

'I'm not at the office.' There was a long silence. 'I can't discuss this over the telephone. Come to my flat. And you'd better bring Sylvia.'

But Sylvia was driving her ambulance and couldn't be reached. Max spent an uncomfortable few minutes alone in the cab wondering what Eddie felt unable to discuss over the phone. They'd dined together on Friday, in the Parisian Café at the Berkeley. What could have blown up in less than forty-eight hours?

His friend had the brandy poured and ready to press into Max's hand the minute he arrived at the apartment. When he told him that a prominent artist had hung a nude in his exhibition, and was letting it be known that it was modelled on the new Lady Bryson, Max at first refused to believe it.

'It's true, my dear fellow. I had it from Cynthia Asquith the other night - ran into her and Diana Manners at the Four Hundred Club. Knocking back the gin fizzes and cherry slings and dancing the bunnyhug with a succession of officers on twenty-four hour leave. She's quite close to Octavius Jameson...'

'Jameson! My God, it had to be him!' Sylvia had already confessed to drinking with Jameson and coming close to letting down her defences - had she told him the whole truth? Would he ever be able to trust her again?

In a brief instant, Seymour had unwittingly shattered the serenity that had begun to build between them. 'Jameson's painting Cynthia's portrait. I wondered if she wasn't just a tiny bit jealous...'

'Whether she was or not, it's hardly the action of a friend to spread such rumours,' said Max indignantly. 'I'll have words with her...'

'Worst thing you could do, old boy. Give the gossips even more ammunition. I wouldn't have said anything, but you don't need this just before the court hearing. I know Lady Bryson's not in the case, but it could colour the old judge's view on you as a suitable family.'

Max sank his head in his hands. 'Then what the devil am I going to do?'

Eddie's insistence that the only way to stop the gossip was to face it out did not go down at all well with Sylvia. 'But, dammit all, Max, I don't *want* to go to Octavius Jameson's exhibition!'

'There isn't any choice in the matter!' snapped Max 'You may be happy to have London pointing fingers at us, but I am not!' The question trembled on his tongue: '*Did* you sit for him in the nude? *Did* you - ?' But he had the sense not to ask.

'If people want to gossip, why should we care? Oh.' Her face fell. 'I suppose this is the last thing you need just before the court case.'

'If you really think that's all I'm worried about...'

Eventually the combined entreaties of Max, Eddie and Lady Alice overrode her qualms. She was not in the best of moods when they drew up outside the gallery in Cork Street.

Max reached across to squeeze her hand. 'You look beautiful, my dear.'

'I don't feel it. I feel positively haggard.' She turned huge, beseeching eyes on her husband. 'Max, I don't want to go in there. Everyone will be looking at me and - '

'Just follow my lead. Come on, smile. We have to face this out or it will haunt us.' He reached out and tilted her chin up. 'Courage, my dear. We'll show them you have nothing to be ashamed of.' Then, '*Smile*, dammit,' between his teeth. 'Ah, good. Here's Eddie and Dora Cunningham waiting for us.'

There was a sharp intake of breath from a group by the door as the little party entered the gallery, but they ignored it. With a smile for the proprietor they passed into the gallery, joining the other parties drifting around the panelled room, examining and discussing the portraits and landscapes.

As if they had all the time in the world they lingered in front of the new portrait of Lloyd George, exchanging views on whether it was better than the more formal portrait of the previous year. Dora Cunningham argued strongly in favour of the recent photograph of the former Chancellor in his regalia, but was outvoted by Max and Eddie, who still felt that a good canvas was superior to a photographic plate.

Sylvia moved through the exhibition like an automaton, responding only to the pressure of Max's hand in the small of her back. This was a nightmare. However much Max smiled and joked, she knew it was all a show. He was livid with her for putting him in such an embarrassing situation, so close to the vital court case, and the ease that had begun to grow between them was vanishing as if it had never been.

By the time they reached the alcove where the painting of the nude hung, they'd accumulated quite a few hangers-on, all eager to see how they would react. At first Sylvia could scarcely bring herself to raise her eyes but, stung by an ill-concealed snigger behind her, she stiffened her spine and looked at it. It was a three-quarters view from the rear, and could have been of any woman of her age, build and colouring. The face, half turned away, could have been hers, could have been anyone's, but the clinching factor was a small head and shoulders study alongside, which clearly *was* of her.

Seeing her colour up, Max instantly lowered his head and whispered in her ear. 'Pretend I've said something saucy to you,' he said with a grin. 'A mutual joke between newly-weds.'

She gritted her teeth and smiled up at him. 'Such as?' she murmured.

He kept his lips at her ear. 'Such as...he hasn't caught the voluptuousness of your figure at all. Your breasts are much riper.' He looked down at her with unconcealed lust in his eyes. 'And he certainly hasn't done justice to the lush curve of your hips.'

She wished she hadn't asked.

Without waiting for an answer Max turned to Eddie Seymour. All eyes were on him, which was what he'd intended. 'I don't see it at all,' he said, running his thumb along Sylvia's shoulder. 'No doubt the artist has a vivid imagination, but - ' His lips twitched. 'But he lacks a certain first-hand knowledge.'

His *sangfroid* had the desired effect. News of their visit to the gallery flew swiftly around town and when it became clear that this was not a marriage about to crumble in a welter of scandal, the gossips lost interest and moved on to other victims. The dashing young society women who frequented the new London night clubs gave the scandalmongers plenty to get their teeth into, dancing with other women's husbands, home on forty-eight hour leave, while their own husbands were still away at the front.

Now it was Max who spent most of his time away from the house in Charles Street. He had set Thurrock onto the Graysons and, with only a fortnight to go before the custody case was due to be heard, the detective found evidence that, as Max had suspected, Grayson had been fiddling the Whitefields accounts and milking money from the trust fund. Confronted with the prospect of a trial for fraud and theft, Grayson capitulated. To the disappointment of the newspapers and scandalmongers, a custody case which had engaged the best legal brains for over a year, and promised a juicy and long-running court hearing, was hastily concluded in twenty minutes in the lobby of the Law Courts.

Within days, the children, Lady Alice and Mrs Harmitage were installed in the Dower House, the Graysons had decamped to Scotland

and the Army Medical Corps was busy turning Whitefields into a hospital for shell-shocked officers.

As Max said to Eddie, it had been an exciting few weeks.

80

'My dear Sylvia,' said Mrs Cunningham, 'I had not expected to have so much of your time, as busy as you must be.'

'Evening duties have tailed off. With Lady Alice down at Whitefields I thought you could do with some help....'

'Make no mistake, I'm very grateful.' She looked round at the young ladies folding programmes together and the off-duty soldiers hanging flags at the back of the concert hall. 'You know all Lady Alice's contacts.' The carpenters resumed their hammering on the staging and she had to raise her voice. 'But shouldn't you be spending the time with Max?'

Sylvia brushed Dora Cunningham's concerns aside with a cheery line: she could hardly tell her Max made every effort not to be in the house alone with her. She'd signed off evening duties deliberately, in the hope of making matters right again between them, but ever since the visit to the gallery Max had been avoiding her. One night he hadn't come home at all. He'd offered no explanation and she could hardly demand one: they were scarcely on that kind of footing. She could only think that he was seeing Rosie again. And why not? He would find a warmer welcome in St John's Wood...

'The Territorials have volunteered to set out the chairs on Thursday,' said Dora, consulting her timetable. 'The officer is coming to see me at five today, but that's when the caterers are due.' Her voice rose. 'And Margot Asquith is threatening to come too, with her suggestions of tableaux, which Lady Alice says we are absolutely *not* to give in to...'

'I can deal with the Territorials for you. You can have Margot.'

Dora wrinkled her nose. 'How kind!'

'Just hope that Margot will be late; she usually is.'

Just before five Sylvia saw a figure in khaki wandering about at the side of the stage, where the orchestra was tuning up to practise the opening item, to feature a solo by a blind cellist. Leaving Mrs Cunningham to discuss refreshments with the hired caterers, she hurried to his side. 'Good afternoon.' She held out her hand. 'I'm Lady Bryson. I - '

The officer turned and Sylvia's voice died in her throat.

81

'Sylvia?' The words came out with a croak.

'C-Captain Osborne?'

'Major.' He gestured to the sleeve of his uniform.

'I - I thought you were at the front.'

'I was.' He drew her into the side room, away from the mournful strains of cello and orchestra. 'I'm home on leave. My colonel was gassed - blinded. He's to be a guest of honour at the gala concert - so our men volunteered to help.' He studied her face for what seemed like an eternity, while she struggled to think of something - anything - to say.

'By God, Sylvia, I've missed you these last three years,' he said softly. He raised her hand to his lips. 'I must have been mad to let you go when I loved you so much.'

She snatched her hand back. 'You didn't love me, Hugh. At least, not enough to stand up to your uncle.'

'He only wanted what was best for me - for us. The way your father defied the government was making your family the mock of all. And that was reflected - '

'Onto you. I know.' Her heart was slowing down to something nearer its proper rhythm. 'But those marriage vows we were going to take, Hugh, they say *for better, for worse*. Right then, with the case against the Admiralty and everyone refusing Pip a fair trial, that *was* my worst. That was when I needed my fiancé's support - and you couldn't give it.'

'Come on, old girl.' He'd recovered something of his customary hearty equilibrium. 'Fault wasn't entirely on my side. You could have talked your father out of his insane obsession any time you wanted.'

'But I didn't want...'

'Quite. So it's a bit thick to load everything onto me.' He squeezed her hand. 'Sylvia, darling Sylvia, the last thing I want is for us to quarrel. I've looked forward to this meeting for so long.' He brought her hand up and laid it against his cheek. 'You know I only ever loved you.'

She thought: *what about your wife?* But she didn't trust herself to say it.

'Do you remember the night my father gave an engagement dinner for us?'

'It's burned into my memory,' she said. 'You walked me home - '

' - the long way round - '

' - and we stood by the pool in the moonlight and you recited your vows to me.'

'By Jove, so I did! Love, honour and cherish, for richer, for poorer...'

'....for better, for worse,' she said softly. 'To me, that meant everything - more than any vows in church. That's why - if it - if it *had* happened in the boathouse...I considered us bound together already.'

He took her hands in his and held them close to his chest. 'I've been a fool. To have wasted all these years! Can't we fulfil those vows anyway? I still have five days leave before I go back to - '

'*No*, Mrs Asquith.' Eddie Seymour's voice cut in on them and Sylvia jumped. With a jolt she became aware that the music from the hall had stopped. 'We're most grateful for your offer, but it's quite impossible to put anything more into the programme.'

Hastily Sylvia snatched her hands out of Osborne's grasp. While she and Hugh had been talking, Max and Cynthia Asquith had come in with Eddie and the Prime Minister's wife.

'Lady Bryson,' gushed Cynthia. 'We wondered where you had gone. Hiding away in here with *such* a dashing officer - '

Max came forward, his face pale and drawn. 'Osborne, isn't it? It's been a long time.' She wondered how long he'd been standing there, how much he had seen...or heard. If he'd been angry with her at the gallery, then this scene would have put the tin lid on it all.

Margot Asquith was looking from one to the other, barely able to restrain her curiosity.

'Hugh Osborne,' said Max. 'An old friend of my wife's family.' Hysterical laughter bubbled up inside Sylvia's throat and she had to dig her fingernails into the palms of her hand. 'How is your wife, major?' asked Max. 'And your children? You have three daughters, I believe?'

'That's - that's right. All well, I'm pleased to say.' Hugh blinked hard. 'So...that's agreed, then....L-Lady Bryson. My men will be here at four on Thursday to set out the chairs. And just one centre aisle.' He bowed in the general direction of the ladies, crammed his cap back on his head and marched briskly out.

82

She didn't know whether to be relieved or disappointed that Eddie Seymour was waiting to drive them home in his car. One look at Max's face as they alighted from the car decided her: she pleaded a headache and asked Hoskins to send her dinner up on a tray.

She spent a restless night, thoughts in her head going round and round like mice on a treadmill, giving her no peace. When she came down to breakfast, heavy-eyed, the next morning, Max was behind his newspaper. He emerged only to wish her a gruff 'Good morning' and then immersed himself again in the bad news from the Dardanelles. But if she'd thought that would be an end to the matter, she was to be disappointed.

He waited until the maid had put a fresh pot of tea on the table and Sylvia had poured herself a cup. 'Always interesting to see old friends again after such a long time,' he said as the door closed.

The cup rattled in the saucer. 'Yes, it is.' She bit into a piece of toast, but it tasted like sawdust in her mouth and she had difficulty swallowing it. There seemed to be a permanent lump in her throat these days.

'You spent a great deal of time talking with him. Dora had quite lost track of you. '

'We had a few years to catch up.' Her voice grew steely. 'Though I'm surprised you noticed. You must have been busy yourself, catching up with Cynthia Asquith. Quite one of her devotees. What is it she calls you all? Her male *conks*.'

He lowered the paper. 'I was one of her conquests once,' he said levelly. 'Diana Manners had her flying ace, Cynthia trumped her with a racing driver – although by then it was only a holiday sport.'

'You were actually a racing driver? I know you mentioned it briefly, but I was never sure how seriously - '

'At one stage I almost gave up my legal career for it. Hard to believe now, I know, but I was quite a success. Won a few road rallies....' His grey eyes fixed on her face. 'I had my moments - in my salad days.'

'You and Cynthia must have made quite a pair,' she said sweetly. 'Did she break your heart when she married someone else?'

'No. Oh, perhaps I thought so at the time - for at least three weeks

- but I soon realised I'd had a lucky escape.' She raised one eyebrow. 'She has a great deal of wit, but there's no fun in her. She never makes my soul lift with laughter as you do.' She shivered, desperately hoping Max hadn't witnessed too much of the scene with Hugh. 'She has no lust in her - for life or lovemaking. She works hard on the theory but shies from the practice, as all her beaux eventually discover. That won't do for me.'

She was feeling oddly breathless. 'So you became engaged to someone else?'

'I made a mess of that too.' He folded his newspaper. 'I seem to make a habit of falling in love with the most unsuitable women.'

She wanted to cry out: no, it isn't true! But could she say that, hand on heart? Could she make him happy, or was she destined to ruin his life, just as Goring had ruined hers? Her thoughts were running wild again, muddling her head until she could hardly think straight. I shall grow as mad as Emily Davison, she thought. Oh, save me from that! She pushed her plate aside and hurried out of the room.

Max looked after her in helpless despair. If he'd hoped his frankness would provoke an equal openness in her, he was disappointed. He was a fool to have expected otherwise.

83

Over the next few days Sylvia threw herself into her work and drove herself hard. She put herself down for early morning shifts and late night duties, anything to keep her out of the house. She would have a whole day off on Thursday, to help with the last minute preparations for the gala evening, but in the meantime she had to keep herself busy so she wouldn't have to think about the mess she had made of her life. Above all, she wouldn't have to face Max.

She was fast coming to the conclusion that the best thing she could do for Max was to take herself out of his life. She'd proved nothing but an embarrassment to him: first Jameson and that terrible nude painting and then the very public encounter with her former fiancé. All that on top of her complete failure as a wife. Small wonder that he'd turned to Rosie once more.

She never allowed her troubles to affect her work: driving was a dangerous enough occupation and the patients she transported deserved the gentlest ride she could give them. But at night, when there was nothing to distract her mind, the thoughts ran round and round again in circles, becoming ever blacker.

The lack of sleep inevitably caught up with her. Driving back the night before the gala concert, after delivering a batch of burn casualties to a large house in the wooded Hertfordshire countryside, she found her eyes closing in spite of herself. She should have stopped to eat earlier; now all the teashops were closed. It didn't matter so much on the side roads, but when she picked up the Great North Road, the evening traffic was quite busy. The second time she drifted into the pavement she drew off the road: she had no desire to kill a cyclist or a pedestrian in the course of her duty.

She had to have some coffee to wake herself up. If she'd been doing her usual run on the Old Kent Road, there would have been plenty of coffee stalls and pie stalls open, but here there was nothing but public houses. Decent women didn't go into public houses, certainly not alone. She knew if she thought too much about it, her nerve would fail, so she marched straight in, through the crowd of men, and up to the bar.

'Buy you a drink, darling?' said one of the men, undeterred by her uniform. 'What'll it be? Port and lemon, eh?'

She could feel the colour washing over her face, and was furious with herself. What did she have to be embarrassed about? She was doing her duty, after all. If they had time to lounge about the pubs, why weren't they out at the front fighting for their country? She began to see why people were so vicious towards men like Mark Doncaster and his pacifist friends.

Ignoring the voices and the curious looks, her gaze passed along the bar until she caught the faintly scandalised eye of the barmaid. 'Could I buy some coffee?' she asked.

The barmaid passed down the bar, silencing the men with practised wit.

'Coffee, is it? Don't have much call for that here.'

'Tea, then. I've been driving an ambulance all day and I - '

She swayed on her feet and in a flash the barmaid was at her side. 'Come on, ducks, I'll take you through to see the missus.'

'The missus' turned out to be a vastly overweight woman, the owner of the pub, who sat Sylvia down by the fire in the back room and made her a pot of strong tea and a round of thick beef sandwiches. She refused to take any money for it. 'Lost me only boy at Saint Julien, I did,' she said, wiping away a tear with a handkerchief the size of a small tablecloth. She passed Sylvia a silver-framed photograph of a smiling young man in his twenties. 'Them ambulance boys out there, they brought him out under fire....done all they could to save him.' She sniffed. 'No, ducks. You got money to burn, you put it in a ambulance fund. But this here is on the house, so get it inside of you. You got an important job to do.'

With a promise to drop in again any time she was passing, Sylvia finally managed to get away. The delay had set her back and it was past nine o'clock by the time she turned off to the depot. Overhead the sky was clear and brilliant with thousands of stars, visible now that the streetlights were extinguished or painted over. As she rounded a bend, she saw searchlights playing the sky, over to the south, towards the river. For a moment she thought she saw a silver shape against the star strewn sky, but then tall warehouses blocked it from view. Over to the west the great gun in Green Park began to roar, shells bursting with a percussion she hadn't experienced before. Men spilled out of the public houses, tankards still in their hands, to see what was going on.

She doused her lights, panic welling up inside her. Caught up in a raid, just as Max had feared! What did one do in a raid? No one had ever said. Should she abandon the vehicle and take shelter? But the building might be hit. Drive on? What?

A white-haired Special was haranguing the onlookers, ordering them to close the pub door and douse all the lights. He stepped out in front of the slow-moving vehicle, holding up his hand. 'That's right, douse your headlamps. Now get this vehicle down a side road. Oh no. Damn. It's an ambulance. What depot?'

'Kingsway.'

'Oh, dear. Perhaps you'd better - ' The rest of his words were drowned in a frightful grinding roar, followed by an enormous explosion that hurt the ears. Then another, then a third in quick succession.

After the third explosion palpable waves of silence came at them, and she felt painful popping sounds in her skull. Ahead of them a pillar of flame rose above the buildings, curiously graceful.

'Better get back to your depot,' said the Special. It seemed madness to drive back towards the bombing, but he was insistent. 'They'll be needing all the ambulances they can get. Drive on, missie.

That's an order.'

With a fatalistic shrug Sylvia stamped on the clutch and let in the gear. Screwing her eyes up against the glare she steered the lorry round the corner. Just as she was about to emerge from Gray's Inn Road into Holborn there was a clap of thunder and a blinding light and the ambulance was picked up and flung across the road.

84

The last of the explosions died away, and the naval gun in Green Park, which had been firing at the Zeppelin, fell silent. Max had stayed in tonight, waiting for a call from Thurrock. Fresh from his success with the Graysons, the detective was now looking into the circumstances of Sylvia's arrest and imprisonment. Max risked a glance out from behind the curtain and saw a graceful silver shape drifting across the night sky towards the East End, explosions and flashes bursting in its wake as bombs and incendiaries fell to earth. Suddenly Thurrock's information was not so important.

He ran downstairs and picked up the telephone, barking out the number of the depot. The operator came back with the same answer as before. 'I'm sorry, sir. Still getting no response at that number. I'll keep trying for you.'

He told himself to stay calm. Sylvia's usual evening run was to the south, and all the bombs had been north of the river this evening. She would phone shortly, to let him know she was all right. He forced himself to return to the drawing room and pick up the papers he'd been working on, but after a few minutes he realised he hadn't taken in one word he had read.

85

Someone was shining a torch in her eyes. She reached out feebly and pushed it aside.

'You O K in there, miss?' said a voice close to her ear.

'Yes.' The side window had been blown out and the torchlight sparkled on broken glass. 'Yes. I think so.'

'Easy does it. Let's have you out of there.' Willing hands drew her out of the cab and set her on her feet. The torch passed up and down her body. 'No damage that I can see,' said another Special.

'What?' She had to strain to hear him. 'Where are the fire engines?'

'No fire engines here, miss. All round at the Aldwych. Three bombs fell there.'

Eddie Seymour had invited them to join his party at the Aldwych, to see Hall Caine's popular play *The Prodigal Son*. Was that this evening? She couldn't remember.

'Missed the theatres by inches, they say. But one of 'em got a gas main. That's the burning you can smell.'

'I knew they were nearby. I heard the bells.'

He looked at her oddly. 'No bells, miss. Don't need 'em, see. Hardly any traffic.'

She shook her head like a dog shaking off water. 'But I can hear - '

'That's the percussion, miss. Got my ears too the last time. Go on for weeks, that will. Drive you half-mad. Still, you had a lucky escape. My Gawd, you did!'

She followed his gaze across the street. The bomb had fallen between Holborn and Chancery Lane, leaving a huge crater. Shop fronts had been blown out, and there was glass everywhere. The pavement had been torn up for some yards, and in the middle of the road, close to the crater, bodies were being carried off an omnibus that was tilted drunkenly against a wall.

'You fit to drive, miss? If we can get your bus back on the road?'

Climbing back into the ambulance was the last thing she wanted to do. If she could just lie down quietly in a dark corner and stop the ringing in her ears....There was a scarlet mist before her eyes and a dragging pain in her chest...

Two men carried a limp body off the omnibus: the boy looked no older than Esmond's son Harry. 'Need to get this kiddie to a hospital smartish,' came the cry.

Through the scarlet mist her brain snapped back into action. 'Get the stretchers off the shelves as quick as you can. I can take six lying, or ten sitting.'

86

Twice in the course of the night Max found himself with his coat on, ready to leave the house, but each time common sense prevailed. He could hardly trail the whole of London, looking for his wife. He had no idea where she'd been during the day or even if she'd returned to London. He could go to the sites where the bombs had fallen, but he'd only get in the way. And what if she telephoned and he wasn't here?

He almost wore a groove in the Persian carpet, pacing up and down. By five in the morning he could bear it no longer, and telephoned Scotland Yard, pulling rank to get the information he needed. The depot had not been hit, his contact told him, but several bombs had exploded in the vicinity and the telephone lines around Holborn were down. The officer went off to get hold of a list of casualties and came back with the news that an ambulance had indeed been caught up in the attack at Holborn, and that the driver had been ferrying the dead and injured to Charing Cross and Bart's Hospital.

Slamming the earpiece back on the phone, Max grabbed his coat and hurried out to the cab rank in the next street, where he roused a driver from the shelter and offered double fare to take him across London with all possible speed.

87

It was late in the morning when Sylvia opened her eyes and saw Max peering anxiously down at her.

'For God's sake, why didn't you phone?' he grated. 'I've been out of my mind with worry.'

'As you phoned me last week, when you didn't come home?'

'Not the same thing at all. Good God, you might have been killed!'

She was stiff and her head hurt and she was in no mood for an argument. She'd managed three runs during the night, and after the third, to a temporary hospital in the back streets behind Euston, her legs had buckled beneath her. The nurses, with more immediate concerns, had pushed two chairs together in the day room and left her there.

She moved, and every muscle protested. 'What is it?' he said. 'Are you badly hurt? Why the devil hasn't the doctor come to see you?'

'What?' The ringing was back in her ears again, making it hard to hear. He repeated his words slowly, and by watching his lips she could just about understand him.

'Doctor's seen me. Nothing he can do about my ears. And the rest is just bruising. Max, please, just take me home.'

His own doctor confirmed that all she needed was rest. 'No driving for the next couple of weeks. Bed rest for the next few days. I'm afraid the ringing in the ears could go on for weeks.'

'You heard him, Max. All I need now is some sleep. You go to work.'

'I'm not expected today.'

'Oh, Lord, I'd forgotten. It's the gala, isn't it? I won't be much help like this...'

'Out of the question.'

'You go. Lizzie will look after me. I just want my bath and my bed. Come back for me this evening.'

She slept the day through but it was all she could do to drag herself out of bed that evening. Her hearing was a little better, but her mind seemed to be buzzing in time with the ringing in her head. Lizzie dressed her hair and chose her outfit. Sylvia couldn't bring herself to care what she looked like.

They took a cab to the Bechstein Hall - or the Wigmore Hall as they must now learn to call it. As she stepped out on Max's arm, a man stepped forward and exploded a flashlight almost in her face. She winced and recoiled.

'Not now,' said Max edgily, and hurried her into the foyer. Before she could ask what was happening, they were surrounded and people started clapping enthusiastically. There was Hugh Osborne with his blinded Colonel, Lady Alice, Dora Cunningham...She found herself shaking hands with people she didn't know, whose names escaped her in the general hubbub. As they walked into the hall, some in the audience too rose to their feet and began to applaud. She stopped abruptly, her head reeling as the noise burst in waves over them.

'The late editions had your picture on the front page,' said Dora proudly. 'My dear, you're the heroine of the moment.'

She held back in the doorway. 'That's nonsense. I only did what I - '

Max interrupted her. 'Sylvia, my love, listen,' he said into her ear. 'The news from the Dardanelles is as bad as it can be, and Loos is turning into a disaster. Huge losses. A home grown heroine is just what everyone needs right now.' He drew her on into the hall, her bruised eardrums cringing under the assault. 'Come on. Smile. Don't disappoint them.'

'Why didn't you warn me?' she hissed, as they took their seats alongside Lady Alice in the front row.

'Because you wouldn't have come.'

'But it makes no sense,' she protested, as the orchestra struck up the first notes of the national anthem. 'I only did my job.'

'Remember what you said to me in Torquay?' Max squeezed her hand as they rose to their feet. 'Smile and accept their congratulations. If not for yourself, then do it for those who can't.'

So smile she did, throughout the gala evening and for three whole days after that, though she pointed out tartly that the newspapers wouldn't have made so much fuss - certainly wouldn't have published the pictures - if she'd been a balding middle-aged *male* ambulance driver, many of whom had performed acts of equal dedication to duty.

'She'd throw a fit if she knew the full extent of it,' Max told Eddie when he turned up with a huge bouquet of flowers. 'Just as well the doctor told her to rest her eyes. We've banned newspapers.'

'All that jingoistic rubbish they've made up about her hatred of the Hun - '

'And calling her the Avenging Angel. She'd hate all that.'

'Could have been worse, though,' said Eddie. 'The Sketch tried to match the Mirror with a picture of a woman driver from another depot. Photographed her in her uniform and called *her* their Knickerbocker Glory!'

Sylvia refused Max's suggestion that she should stay with Lady Alice at the Dower House in Whitefields, and she was greatly relieved when the newspapers moved on to the next patriotic story. But the oddest people seemed to think they were entitled to turn up on the doorstep and demand to speak to her, and she soon instructed Lizzie to say she was not at home.

Her ordeal, while keeping her from the work she needed to keep her sane, at least gave her an excuse to deny herself when Hugh Osborne came calling. Max had reluctantly gone to visit Professor Weizmann in Manchester, where the Professor had devised a new system for producing acetone for explosives from horse chestnuts; she wondered what Max would say if he heard that her former fiancé had come calling in his absence.

She paced up and down her room, unable to sleep, unable to settle to anything. Hugh's words kept ringing in her head. What had she ever done to make him think she would start an affair with him, when they were both married to other people?

But perhaps Hugh had seen what a sham her marriage was. Perhaps everyone could see it. When Max failed to arrive home on the day he was expected she knew she had to talk to someone - but who? Certainly not Hugh. If Lady Alice had been in London - but no, Lady Alice had her own demons to deal with, and a full-time task settling the children into yet another home.

Lady Harriet? No. From what Nina's friends had said at the May Fair, being *one of Lady Harriet's* meant you'd pretty much had it - physically or mentally - and she wasn't ready for that yet.

She tried Nina, but she was in Lincolnshire, with her brother. Then she tried Gwen, but the housekeeper said she was visiting friends in Yorkshire. As she put the receiver back on the stand, a voice spoke in her head: *Rosie*, it said.

It was vital that she spoke to her. She didn't know why: her thoughts were too wild these days. She hadn't felt this bad since they'd carried her to the prison hospital. If she didn't talk to someone soon, she'd go mad, like Emily Davison. If only she could remember the address...she thought about raiding Max's desk once more, but Hoskins was always hovering about the hall.

Her life here with Max was over. The nude picture, then the scene with Hugh, on top of her unsatisfactory performance as a wife, had turned him completely against her. That was why he didn't come home. If he preferred to be with Rosie, then she must give them her blessing, and get out of their lives.

The next morning she woke up with Rosie's address clear in her mind, in letters of green against the red mist. She didn't ring for Lizzie, but quickly dragged on her clothes, lest she change her mind or lose her nerve. In her haste she tore one of her stockings and had to root about in her drawer for another. She spent so much of her life in uniform these days she hadn't noticed the shortage...She made a mental note to send Lizzie out to Selfridges...but no. If she was leaving Charles Street, there would be no need.

True to form, Hoskins materialised at her elbow as she headed for the door. 'Shall I call you a cab, m'lady?' he enquired. 'Shall you be visiting Ardingley House?'

'No thank you, Hoskins. I think I shall walk.'

'Shall I summon Lizzie to accompany you?'

Her fingers tightened around her umbrella. If he didn't get out of her way soon.... With an effort she brought her raging mind back under control.

'That won't be necessary, thank you, Hoskins.'

She took a cab from the stand at the end of the next street, giving the driver the St John's Wood address. She stared blindly out of the window, seeing nothing of the journey, struggling to keep the discordant jangling inside her skull under some sort of control. The driver had to speak to her several times before she realised that they had arrived.

88

She paid off the cab and looked around her, bewildered. She'd built up a mental image of exotic settings with lush Oriental carpets and silken drapes, something between Monna Vanna's boudoir and the ballet Russe, an eastern harem in the verdant acres of north-west London. The rows of neat white-washed villas didn't quite fit the picture.

As she stood between the capped white gate posts a voice in her head, overriding the singing and the bells that had haunted her since the Zepp bombing, asked her sharply what the devil she thought she was doing here? Doggedly she pushed the question aside. She had to talk to Rosie while Max was away at work, and that was that.

She walked down the gravelled drive past beds of straggly roses in their last autumnal flowering, mounted the steps and wielded the dolphin-shaped doorknocker vigorously.

A motherly looking maid answered the door, yet another element which hardly fitted with Sylvia's ideas of illicit sex.

'I've come to see - ' As the woman winced, Sylvia realised she was shouting. 'So sorry. Only I must see...' Her voice trailed off. 'That's odd,' she said, putting a hand to her forehead. 'I can't actually remember her surname.'

The woman put out a strong arm and caught her round the waist as she swayed. 'Better come on in, dearie.' She closed the door in the face of an inquisitive delivery boy coming up from the basement steps, and led Sylvia into a room decorated in homely chintz. 'There you are. Now sit down before you fall down.'

Sylvia collapsed into the sofa cushions, her head swimming. There was a swishing of silken petticoats. 'Better give her a brandy,' said a distant voice.

Sylvia took a sip, coughed a little, and came slowly back to her senses. As her vision cleared, she saw an elegantly dressed woman in her early thirties, plump and fair-skinned, looking down at her in some puzzlement.

'So sorry,' she murmured. 'I'm - '

'You're Sylvia Bryson, aren't you?'

'Well, I'll be damned,' said the maid.

'Only if you breathe a word of this to anyone else,' said Rosie, qualifying her words with a grin. 'Go on, Elsie. Clear off, there's a good girl. And bring us in that pot of coffee. Good and strong. Max always preferred coffee, though I'd peg this one for a tea drinker.' She raised her eyebrow as Sylvia choked again. 'It *is* Max you've come to discuss, isn't it? I don't expect you came all this way just to enquire after my health.'

'I don't know why I came, to be honest.' Sylvia passed her hand wearily over her eyes. 'I've been a bit confused recently.'

'Quite a crack on the head, they said. I read the story in the papers. Anyway, it doesn't matter why you've come. Somehow I always knew you'd turn up one day, after that bloody letter you sent me. Thought I was sending congratulations, like all the others, did you?'

'Or condolences. Depended on which announcement you'd seen.'

'Hadn't seen either. I'd been away. It was just a friendly letter after Max and I - went our separate ways.' She took the tray from the maid and closed the door in her face. Efficiently she eased Sylvia's coat from her shoulders. Shaking it out she saw the badge in the lapel. 'One of the sisters, are you?'

This wasn't going at all the way Sylvia had planned. 'I don't suppose you have much time for Suffragists.'

'Because women like me have our own ways of getting what we want out of men? You're a prime one for jumping to conclusions. I pay my rates and taxes and I reckon I've as good a right as any male householder to choose the colour of the government that taxes me.' She saw the look of surprise on Sylvia's face. 'This is my own property, right enough. Though I've never been averse to letting my gentlemen friends contribute to household expenses.' She poured out two cups of coffee. 'Here, get some of this down you. I can't have a conversation with a corpse.'

Sylvia shuddered as the heat from the coffee coursed through her veins.

'I suppose you're thinking of setting up your nursery,' said Rosie, waiting in vain for Sylvia to open the conversation. 'Come to check it's all over between Max and me?'

'It isn't, is it? He stayed here the other week. And again on Sunday...'

Rosie blinked. 'I don't know what Max is up to, if he's up to anything. But he's not up to it here, I promise you. Haven't seen him in over two years. Well, let's be honest, I saw him about eighteen months ago. But not in the way you mean. Here, you aren't going to faint, are you?' She took the cup out of Sylvia's hand. 'You in the family way already?'

'No. We haven't...that is, we can't...'

'Ah, don't tell me...not Maxie? Oh, poor man. His injury, I suppose. He did so love it. Knew how to share it too, if you know what I mean.'

'No. Not him.' She flushed. Why was she telling this woman everything? She didn't know. 'Oh, at first...after the operation. But now it - it's me. We haven't even...'

'I see.' Rosie refilled their cups before she spoke again. 'Not one of these man-hating Suffragettes, are you? What was their daft slogan? *Votes for Women and Chastity for Men*?'

Sylvia winced. 'No.'

'Good. Because he deserves better. I'd never have broken off our arrangement otherwise...'

'Arrangement?' Sylvia's green eyes widened.

'That's what it was. He'd had his fill of society girls. I'd just buried one husband and was in no rush to get hitched again.' Her blue eyes sparkled. 'Very merry widow I was. I like men, you see. But I am choosy.'

'You *chose* Max?'

'I had a few introductions. My friends knew what I was looking for. Not all of us loose women are exploited and downtrodden, you know. I chose this way of life. I'd been married to a man old enough to be my father - matter of fact, he *was* a friend of my father's - and after that I wanted a bit of fun. Don't look so shocked. Women have needs too.'

She put her head on one side. 'You haven't got to your age without working that out?'

Sylvia remembered that evening with Octavius. And creeping into the boathouse with Hugh. 'There were times...' She felt the colour stain her cheeks.

'Well, that's something. At least you're not a completely cold fish. And you couldn't ask for a better lover than Max. So if you're not a man-hater, then....Oh, Christ.' She rolled her eyes to the ceiling. 'You're one of life's casualties, aren't you?'

Sylvia drew in on herself. 'What do you mean?'

'I've seen plenty of them.... One man's forced himself on her and too often it ruins her for life. They decide if men are going to exploit them, then they'll do a bit of exploiting in return. Hard-faced bits they turn into.' She frowned. 'That's what happened to you, isn't it?'

Sylvia nodded miserably.

'I thought I knew Max better than that.'

Sylvia hastened to correct the misapprehension. 'Max has been a perfect gentleman. The rest - that was all before I met him. I should never have married him. That's why I have to leave him. I wanted to tell you that... Because he still needs....'

'Not me, dearie.' Rosie picked up a silver-framed photograph and showed it to Sylvia. 'Now I know I said I'd had enough of marriage, but that was before I met my Antonio. Very fiery. In the grocery business, but it still leaves him plenty of energy, if you know what I mean.' She smiled coyly. 'We're getting married next month. I shan't be seeing Max again. That chapter's closed.'

'I've made a complete mess of it. Everything.'

Rosie shrugged. 'If you want to live in the future, then you've got to get over the past. Show him you care. And you do care, else you wouldn't be here.'

'It's too late. I've turned him away too many times.'

'It's never too late. Sort it out, dearie, or someone else will do it for you. And then you'll have lost him forever.' Rosie stood up and walked around the room, running her hands slowly over the silk cushion covers. 'D'you know why men like to come here? To St John's Wood? They like to enjoy sex. Don't blush. I'm telling you something important here. And you're not a kiddie any more. Too many of them are married to women who view carnal relations as a duty. And duty is a killer. But a woman who likes sex and shows it, who loves her man without making him feel like a dirty beast - she has a price beyond pearls, my dear. A man will travel far beyond St John's Wood to be with her.'

'Then you think Max - '

'Has to be worth a try. But you'll have to go halfway to meet him....'

'I should never have come here.' Sylvia stood up distractedly. 'I have to go.'

'Elsie'll call you a cab,' she said. 'Now, you sure you'll be all right?'

She nodded.

'Right then. I don't s'pose I'll see you again. Doesn't really do for a lady like you to come calling here. And Max wouldn't like to think we've been talking about him behind his back. So we'll just keep this between ourselves, right? After all, I shall be a respectable married woman before long. What a turn-up for the books, eh?'

The cab was at the gate by the time Sylvia had her coat on again. 'One thing you never asked,' said Rosie, walking down the path with her.

'What?'

'How I knew who you were.'

'The papers.'

'I knew before that.' She smiled. 'I saw you in court. When Max took your brother's case on he couldn't stop talking about you. I knew then that he'd fallen. It's taken some time, but it's nice to be proved right at last.'

89

When she left Rosie's, Sylvia knew exactly what she was going to do. But by the time she reached Charles Street her mind was racing again, thoughts tugging her this way and that, ravelling her brain up in choking tangles until she was sure she was going mad.

'You're looking very tired, m'lady,' said Lizzie. 'You should tuck back into bed for a while.'

Sylvia nodded weakly. She was finding it hard to speak.

Lizzie was upstairs running a bath for her when the phone rang. 'I'll answer it, Hoskins,' said Sylvia, startled out of her daze. 'It will be Lady Alice.' Or Max, saying why he hadn't been home.

She waited until the valet had left the hall, and picked up the receiver. She nearly dropped it again when she heard the voice at the other end.

'Sylvie my dear. How are you?'

'Mr Jameson?' She shrank into herself. Was there a malign fate hovering around her? Only that afternoon she'd recalled the scene with Jameson when she had drunk wine and behaved in such a scandalous manner, and now here he was, popping up like some malevolent jack-in-the-box to do her more harm.

'Octavius. After all, between such old and dear friends...You telephoned me a few days ago.'

'No!' Her voice was shrill and she struggled to control it. 'I telephoned Gwen. How - how did you know it was me? I left no name.'

'The housekeeper recognised your voice.'

'I don't know how you have the nerve to speak to me after that disgusting picture. How dared you make people think - '

'That you'd posed for me? Why not? People were very impressed. And envious.'

Her voice dropped to a hoarse whisper. 'How dare you?'

'I'll wager we've kept that staid husband of yours guessing.' The voice was gleeful, gloating. 'Does he still think it's all my wonderfully vivid imagination?'

'You *know* that's all it was.'

'Now you're married, I thought you might look on my company more favourably. Sylvie, darling, do come to my party on Saturday.'

She swallowed hard, fighting back the bitter, angry words. 'If I paid you,' she said at last, 'would you take down the painting?'

'Bryson must give you a large allowance if you can pay me enough to end the jest.'

'It may be a jest to you, but to me it's my marriage.'

'You can do better than that stick-in-the-mud, darling Sylvie. Come on Saturday, and I'll introduce you to all sorts of jolly fellows...But I'm afraid I can't let you have the painting. It's already been taken down. I sold it. To a Mr Edward Seymour of the Albany. He'll be panting over it right now. Sylvie? Are you still there?' He paused. 'Ah well, never mind. I'll telephone again. In the evening perhaps, when I might even get to talk to your esteemed husband. He'll be delighted to hear that the picture is no longer hanging in the gallery....'

She sat for fully five minutes by the disconnected telephone, her face white as a sheet. So even Eddie had let her down, after all his promises of friendship. As soon as Max heard about that, the marriage would be over before it had even started.

No one could be counted a friend now. She wouldn't wait for the axe to fall: she would pack her bags and leave today.

PART II

Winter, 1915 - 16. Northern France.

She dragged on a cigarette, listening to the strains of 'Silent Night' floating out of the nearby huts where German prisoners were being nursed. The ringing had almost gone from her ears now, and the sweetness of the singing made her head reel.

'Brings tears to your eyes, doesn't it?' said the little nurse standing next to her, huddled in her cloak, puffing surreptitiously on a forbidden cigarette. You could tell she'd been out here for some time, unlike the newest wave of VADs, for the regulation ankle-length skirt had been hitched up to calf-length, the only practical solution for a woman who spent her day lifting and bending. 'I've hated the Hun ever since the war started and my cousin was killed at the Marne, but when you're face to face with them, they're not that different. Specially the young ones: they're just frightened boys like our own lads.'

'That must make it difficult to nurse them.'

The nurse shrugged. 'Only way you can get through, whether they're Huns, Belgians, British or Indians, is to forget they've got souls and just concentrate on patching the bodies back together. Least, it's the only way I can get through.'

Sylvia ground the cigarette stub under her heel. She'd started smoking again almost as soon as she came out here. It gave her something to do, to stop her mind wandering back across the Channel. 'Better head back to Eetap, I suppose, before the snow sets in again.' She tucked as much of her hair as she could into the leather helmet, strapped it under her chin and drew on her fur-lined gauntlets.

'Pip-pip,' said the nurse. 'Take care. See you again. D.V.'

D.V. God willing. Out here everyone tacked it onto the end of their good wishes, for fear of offending the Lord. And what an armoury He had for showing His displeasure: mines the size of oil-drums from the *Minenwerfers*, gas, liquid fire, gangrene, pneumonia - it all made a bolt of lightning seem rather tame. Sylvia, whose belief in the randomness of fate had been confirmed long before her arrival in France, couldn't be bothered with such superstition. A God who could look on while men were torn apart, drowned in shell-holes, gassed, or spitted on barbed wire to die slowly and hang in death like rotting washing on a line, was not one she cared to propitiate, not one she cared to consider at all. Especially while the rival armies called on Him as a justification for their barbarity: *God on our side; Gott mit uns.*

She fastened her goggles, kick-started the motorbike and wove her way through the tents and sheds until she picked up a track which would lead her back to the main military road. Gripping the handlebars she set the machine at what passed for a hill in this region; from its slight eminence the British forces encampments were laid out before her, strung out behind the coast from Boulogne in the north through Dannes and Camiers and south to Le Touquet on the banks of the Canche.

Clustered pinpricks of light signposted the hospitals and barracks that fringed the vast grassy area behind the sand dunes which the soldiers called the Bull Ring, where new recruits trained, day in, day out. Strange to think that the great Napoleon, whose statue dominated the port of Boulogne - albeit facing entirely the wrong way - had encamped his invasion forces here only a century before. Strange to think that the ten thousand British troops now in the Bull Ring were coming to the aid of their former enemy.

Only not, as yet, to much purpose: the German line was still pretty much where it had been since the Battle of the Marne almost seventeen months before, when Galliéni and the Paris garrison had sallied forth in their commandeered taxis to save the city from General Kluck. A similar stalemate extended pretty much all the way along the line, from the Channel to Switzerland. Freddie might now lie under the German lines or the British, or in the desolation of No Man's Land. No one would ever know.

She turned left at the broken tree stump, half-covered by dirty snow, revved up the motorbike and set it at the coast road, thrilling in the feel of the icy wind in her face as it whipped over the sand-dunes, teasing the strands of hair that tore out of the embrace of the long khaki scarf wound close about her throat. The clean sharpness of the frosty wind, though it numbed her face and hurt her lungs, was a welcome change to the sleet and rain that had persisted since her arrival from England. Close to the coast there was very little snow but the road was muddy and pitted with puddles just crusting over with frost and ice. Twice she had to pull over for a convoy of lorries, and once the motorbike was almost shaken off balance by the slip from a large grey-painted Staff limousine, speeding north and almost blinding her with its glaring headlights.

She throttled down as she approached the precipice over the

railway line where King Manoel of Portugal had almost come to grief not so long ago, when his car had had a contretemps with a horse and cart, but once past the danger spot, she speeded up again.

The night was clear and starry and she could see Le Touquet ahead of her, across the Canche estuary. The golf links among the pines, where she had played before the war, when she and Freddie had been guests of the Merryweathers for one glorious summer week, were now home to the Machine Gun School. Here the cavalry, reluctantly parted from their horses, were being retrained, for even the most hide-bound general had to concede that there was no immediate prospect of punching large enough holes in the enemy's lines for the cavalry to ride through to Berlin. But while Kitchener's New Army amateurs had had only a few weeks to familiarise themselves with the machine guns, the professional soldiers of the cavalry had already spent months at the training school.

She followed the road to the left, and there, spread out before her in the moonlight, was the huge sprawling camp, almost a shanty town, which had quite swallowed up the fishing village of Etaples. Hundreds of men from the front passed through Etaples on their way up to Boulogne, for embarkation for home leave, but it was also a magnet for those who were only being stood down for a day or two from front line duties.

A clutter of hospitals had grown up here, part tents, part huts shipped over from England and erected on site. They were run by a variety of agencies: Royal Army Medical Corps, Queen Alexandra's Imperial Military Nurses, British Red Cross, Women's Suffrage Units, Australian and American units, Canadians with the maple leaf picked out in stones in the front of the tents, all mixed in higgledy-piggledy with quartermaster's stores, ammunition dumps, canteens, petrol stores and remount lines. If the Zepps ever drifted this far south of the Channel ports on their way over to London, it would not bode well for the hospitals to be so intermingled with what were, after all, legitimate military targets.

She coasted the last few hundred yards, not wanting to disturb the residents, many of whom would have been up before the dawn, and propped the bike against the outhouse. Peeling off her gauntlets, she pushed the door open and went in.

The welcoming warmth hit her at once. Her mouth watered at the smell of coffee - even the French had to admit that the British Soldiers'

Buffet made good coffee - although these days she hardly ever drank it. It kept her awake, and anyone who worked at the buffets was likely to be hoofed out of bed at all hours of the day and night to provide refreshments for passing messengers, a busload of men going home on leave or, on one memorable occasion, an entire shipload of men disembarked and sent back down the line because of submarine activity in the Channel. That sort of adaptability, and Lady Angela Forbes's connections in government, were the reason her Soldiers' Buffets were still in business; General Headquarters was constantly trying to close her down.

A morose elderly Frenchman was swabbing the floor, working around the occupied benches. One of Angela's titled hunting friends from the Scots Greys was behind the buffet, his elegant uniform covered by an apron. At the sight of Sylvia he picked up the teapot and poured her a cup. She took the tea gratefully, scooped up a wad of sandwiches from the counter and subsided onto a bench with a sigh.

'No action this evening?' asked an elegant young man with a monocle, playing patience on the far side of the room.

'No. The guns have gone very quiet.' She looked at Freddie's wristwatch. 'Dawn in a couple of hours. Then it'll start up again.' The scalding tea, strong and stewed, burnt her wind-numbed lips, bringing them back to painful life.

'Awfully brave of you to do the run,' he said.

It hadn't been brave at all. It had been a challenge, the kind of dare Freddie would have appreciated. After all, it was he who had taught her to ride a motor-cycle. Not that her family had ever known...

She tried to remember who the elegant young man was, but his name escaped her. The well-bred young men who came up here from HQ for diversion could be useful when the staff at the buffet were rushed off their feet, but they made her uncomfortable. If all these British staff-officers and attachés had the time to come up here, after spending their mornings playing tennis or endless rounds of golf - or polo in the case of the cavalry - then there must be too many of them. She couldn't help feeling they would be a lot more use up the line, where the fighting was.

'How's the dispatch rider, Pearl?' she asked a stout middle-aged woman who had just come in with a pile of plates.

'Angelina reckons it's only a twenty-four hour bug,' said Pearl in her soft Scottish voice. She set the plates down with a crash. 'He'll be wanting his bike back come the morning. Did you get all the requisitions?'

'Every last one. All ready to go over to HQ in the morning. Though it seemed a bit pointless bringing them all back here. I could just as easily have taken them over to Boulogne: I was practically there.'

'That would have raised a few eyebrows,' said Pearl with a grin. 'You on a dispatch bike and all the generals going off in an apoplexy...'

'Would have been worth it, just to see their faces.' She carried her plate and cup behind the buffet to the sink. 'Any hot water left in the bathhouse?'

'Afraid the Canadians took the last of it.'

'Then I'll have to stay filthy a little longer. I'm turning in now. It's been a long day and I'm on again mid-morning.' She was racked by an almighty yawn. 'Don't call me out before then for anything less than a trainload...'

In her icy little room, divided from the others by a plywood partition, she took off Freddie's wristwatch, a precious item normally issued only to military personnel, and laid it under her pillow. Hanging her outer layers on the nail that served as a hook, and pausing only to brush her teeth, she tumbled into her 'fleabag' in her underclothes and was fast asleep in minutes.

2

Christmas passed quietly, due to Lady Angela's frequent absences in Boulogne, where she was chivvying those in charge of the quayside buffets. A vigorous campaigner for the ordinary soldiers, who without her buffets would often have gone hungry and thirsty away from their billets, she was a bit like a wasp at a summer picnic, constantly forcing her presence on the company, impossible to ignore, and with a distinct sting in the tail if annoyed. She reminded her rather of Margot Asquith.

Lady Angela had welcomed Sylvia with open arms, even though her letter of introduction was from one of the Suffragettes, of whom she heartily disapproved. The government had clamped down on the waves of aristocratic women who had hurried out from England in the first year of the war, many of them eager to do their bit, others using it as an excuse to look up their relations. Now only those who committed to a minimum of four months service were allowed out.

Recent government regulations meant that Sylvia had had to apply for one of the new passports before she was allowed to leave the country. Lady Harriet's friends had had to arrange it all for her, as the inoculations against typhoid and other assorted ills had brought her even lower than before. Fortunately no one had yet given it any more than a cursory glance, since it was for Eithne Sylvia Summers, using her mother's maiden surname and place and date of birth, with only the year changed to match Sylvia's age. They had taken the precaution of making the original application in Edinburgh; it would be some time before the paperwork made its way down to London.

Passports were so new that no one over here had ever asked to see it. She'd simply introduced herself to Lady Angela as Sylvia Summers and proceeded to take her turn on duty, day or night, spreading bread for sandwiches, brewing tea so strong you could stand a spoon in it, stirring vats of porridge or frying hundreds of eggs for the early morning rush. It didn't take the physical strength that ambulance driving did, but it was hard enough, and served to take her mind off her own concerns.

At New Year she went to the YMCA canteen, where one of Lena Ashwell's concert parties was performing. The troops loved every minute of it, and demanded endless encores of Mr Novello's *Till the Boys Come Home*, the hit of the season. Most of the canteen staff were in Le Touquet, where the celebrations were loud and often drunken, particularly among those on leave from the front. They'd passed through the previous year unscathed, but didn't hold out much hope for their future survival. They were determined to seize the day and let the devil take the hindmost.

As she left the concert, to make her way back to her own canteen through the dark and the rain and the mud with a group of off-duty nurses and VADs, the audience were singing the chorus for possibly the twentieth time. *Keep the home fires burning, till the boys come home.* How many of the singers would ever make it home again?

That night, for the first time since leaving England, she dreamed of Max and woke to find her pillow wet with tears.

New batches of men arrived daily in the camp, bright and enthusiastic in their brand new khaki, on their way to training in the Bull Ring, or to replace the reserves who had been shunted up to the trenches to fill the gaps caused by the carnage of the previous autumn. Fresh from England, the new soldiers passed through the canteen full of bluster and jollity, eager to get to grips with the enemy. Occasionally they came face to face with a busload of mud-caked, exhausted men travelling in the opposite direction, looking like ghosts with the chalky slime of the trenches adhering to them. Then the jollity was muted.

Winter rain set in again, falling steadily and unrelentingly. In Etaples the meadows either side of the military road were waterlogged and at the front the trenches were engulfed in a sea of mud such as only northern France could produce.

For those serving men who lived beyond London or the Home Counties, and for whom a twenty-four hour leave was not enough to get home and back again, Eetapp, as they called it, was an island of sanity in a world gone mad. London omnibusses and furniture vans brought them the twenty or thirty miles from the front – the railways that ran close by being reserved for supplies and munitions - and they homed in on the various canteens, where they could be sure of good food at reasonable prices. The smell of tea and coffee would arouse the exhausted, mud-caked Tommies from their stupor and then the buffet would ring with gruff voices asking for 'three Woodbines, please miss', 'any tea left?' or 'some more o' them sandwiches, ma'am?'

In the YMCA huts, the Salvation Army canteens, or the British Soldiers' Buffets, concerts, boxing matches and theatricals were laid on for them, and any slim, fresh-faced young man was liable to find himself dragooned into playing the heroine on an improvised stage, accompanied by his comrades playing on the various instruments that Lady Angela had conjured up from her contacts.

A few, knowing the next operation could see them lying dead in a shell-hole, went further afield, to look for companions more wholesome than the Red Lamp brothels in Béthune could provide, or to try the various *estaminets* and get gloriously drunk. All too often they missed their transports back, and some of them returned to their regiments in the less than kindly grip of the military police, with field punishments awaiting them at the other end.

Officers generally went on to Le Touquet. They all had money to burn, and not just army pay. Whenever a platoon went into action, it was the custom for officers to empty their pockets into the trench kitty, and on their return the survivors would share it out. The dead had no use for money, the wounded were only too glad to be out of it and on the way home, and the survivors needed a celebration.

The sole ambition of the younger officers, after months in the company of their men, was to go *Paris-Plaging* with a pretty young nurse or VAD. Paris-Plage, on the edge of Le Touquet, was a small beach resort, with little restaurants and hotels secluded in the woods, happy to turn a blind eye to unmilitary manouevres and forged hotel registers. If caught, the nurses and VAD girls would be sent home in disgrace, but some still took the risk. Officers would get off scot-free: loss of career and character was all heaped on the women.

Sylvia was not exempt from their attentions, even before the groove in her ring finger began to fade. She learnt quickly how to deal with British officers, who felt their leave was incomplete without a girl on their arm, but the Australians and New Zealanders were particularly hard to shake off. One South African even said he couldn't see what Sylvia was making such a fuss about; being attached to no particular organisation, she wouldn't be risking her job if she were caught.

'Don't be too hard on them,' said an American voice, after she'd sent the South African off with a flea in his ear. She turned to see one of the Harvard doctors propping up the counter, his broad shoulders straining at the cloth of his uniform.

'Why can't they take *no* for an answer?' she said, more shaken than she realised. 'Our men at least don't press one so.'

'Your men at least have the prospect of an occasional leave to see their nearest and dearest. Even those who have to wait for a four day pass. Think what it's like for an Australian - or a South African...even a four-day pass is no good to him.'

She looked at him cautiously: as an American the same must apply to him. But all Dan Tripp wanted was to talk about his wife and three children. When he showed her the family photograph he always carried, she knew a brief pang that it wasn't her and Max and their children. But that could never be. She had tried, and been found wanting.

It wasn't hard to lend a sympathetic ear. Over the next few weeks she found herself looking out for his tall figure. She even joined him and two of his American nurses for an omelette in the Hotel restaurant when she was in Le Touquet for supplies, and offered them all a lift back in the rusty old Ford delivery van.

'Thanks, but we still have some shopping to do,' said the younger of the two nurses.

'You drive this delivery van?' asked the other, in a syrupy deep Southern accent.

'Yes.'

'Then you're wasted in the canteen. The ambulance service is crying out for drivers. Last week we had to fetch in a couple of old Frenchmen, and they drive like maniacs: even been known to throw the patients out of their stretchers.'

'I used to drive an ambulance once,' she admitted. She felt Dan Tripp's eyes on her and became aware that she was rubbing the place where her ring had once been.

'Well, then, honey, why don't you - '

'I - they - ' She didn't want to talk about this. 'Not strong enough any more. Those ambulances are deuced heavy, you know.'

She expected Dan to pass some comment, but he spent the journey in light conversation about nothing in particular. As they drove across the bridge, almost back at the camp, there was a sudden loud explosion behind them. The wheel jerked, the low winter sun became a column of fire, the sodden road and the pine trees disappeared and all Sylvia could see in front of her was the bomb crater and the Holborn shop-fronts exploding out towards her in slow motion.

'Hey, steady there, lady!' cried Tripp, as the tyres slewed on the wet grass and the old delivery lorry began to mount the bank on two wheels, tipped at a crazy angle. He reached across to grip the wheel, fighting to control their progress along the grass bank. 'Brake! Brake! It's only the gun range. Steady does it!'

When they finally came to a halt she was shaking uncontrollably. Dan reached over to switch off the engine and put a comforting hand around her shoulders. 'C'mon, it's only the new gun over at the range,' he said, dropping his hand as she flinched away. 'They're trying out some new mortar, or something. That's all it was.'

'My God!' she exclaimed bitterly, head in her hands. 'That's all I damned well need!'

'What is?'

If she hadn't been in a state of shock she wouldn't have said anything at all. 'Memories,' she said in a choked voice. 'Sort of living memories where the same scene goes over and over in your mind...like moving pictures...'

'Flashbacks. Lots of soldiers get them. When they hear a shell land, takes 'em back to a previous battle, where perhaps they were hit or saw a friend killed. Sometimes they don't even need to have been hit: just being knocked unconscious is often enough.'

'Oh.' She looked up at him, blinking nervously. 'Doesn't seem half so bad when you explain it that way. I - I thought I was going mad again.'

'Again?'

'It's happened before. These sort of images...memories.' There. Now he would know she was completely insane. Probably try and have her locked up.

'You were driving an ambulance at the front?'

'Gosh, I'm not that brave. No, it was in London. A Zepp raid. Knocked my ambulance sideways. Killed a lot of people on an omnibus.'

'Talking about it often helps,' he said quietly. 'It's like a wound, you see. In your mind. It takes time to heal. But running over it again and again inside - or having flashbacks, as you do - well, that's like picking at the scab. Stops it healing up.'

As she grew calmer, he began to question her gently and she told him about the bomb crater, about the shop-fronts blowing out towards her and being pulled out of the ambulance through all the broken glass.

'Don't hide it away, my girl. Let the moving pictures run. But instead of remembering the fear, you've got to tell yourself the really important thing, over and over again.'

'And what's that?'

'That you survived. All that, and you survived it. That makes you pretty special.'

She smiled weakly. 'No harm in trying, I suppose. How quickly does it work?'

'Fresh memories don't take too long, if you deal with them straight away. But the older ones, they're often harder to shift. Months? A year? Hard to say. Different people...'

'I don't have that much time, do I?' she said. 'It won't be long before the fighting starts up again.' As if to echo her words there was a low rumble over to her right. It sounded like thunder, but they both knew it was the guns. '*That's* not practice, is it?'

'No.'

The brief lull was over and soon the broken bodies would start pouring in again from the frontlines. 'You need to get back to camp,' she said, with a sudden pathetic attempt at briskness. 'Would - would you care to drive? I - I don't think I'm quite up to it.'

'That'd be the easy way out, but it won't help you in the long run. Here.' He took a small silver flask out of his breast pocket. 'A small nip.'

His eyes twinkled. 'Strictly for medicinal purposes. No, that's enough, or you'll have us in the ditch, for sure.'

She shuddered as the brandy burnt its way down her throat, but still made no move.

'I've got to clear out my tents - send the Blighty ones home, make room for the next lot. I hear the Zepps bombed Dunkirk again last night, so we can't send casualties there. We'll get their hospital trains as well as ours. C'mon, girl, I'll bet you a stale bun and a cup of coffee you can't get me back there in ten minutes.'

She gave a watery laugh, but she started the engine and let in the gears. By the time they reached the camp she was almost herself again.

Tripp paused as he swung himself down from the van outside his hospital unit. 'You know, no one would blame you if you went back home,' he said softly.

'I can't go home.' She bit her lip. 'I no longer have a home to go to. And anyway, home is where the worst ghosts are.'

3

Max opened the door and stepped into the hall. Even in the short distance from cab to front door, his coat had been soaked by the driving rain. While Hoskins carried it off to dry, he stood in the hall, oddly reluctant to penetrate further into the house.

It was as well that he had so much work to occupy him, even at the weekends, as the Ministry struggled to send sufficient munitions to the front for the next big push. Coming home was a nightmare, however late he left it. Sylvia had been here for only a few short autumn months, hardly long enough for them to become at ease around each other, too short a time to recapture the happiness they had known so briefly at Stancombe, and yet the scent of her, the feel of her, seemed to pervade every room.

He went into the drawing room and poured himself a stiff brandy. Dropping the stopper back into the decanter, he felt he had only to turn and she would be there, elegant in a silk evening gown, clinging to her figure, or smart and energetic in the khaki uniform that deepened her eyes to a muted green, the puttees that emphasised the line of her calf...

But in the latter days there had been no glow in her eyes, only pain and trouble. He cursed himself for a fool: he should have found the time to talk to her, to dig out what it was that troubled her. Instead he'd put it all down to the accident, and allowed unwarranted suspicions to fall on her meeting with Hugh Osborne.

His first thought, when he found she had gone, had been to confront Osborne and demand to know where she was. But he knew he was in no state to talk rationally to the man; instead, he'd harnessed the mixture of fear and anger that threatened to overwhelm him, and sent Eddie to make more subtle enquiries.

His mother, Osborne, Octavius Jameson, all had been suspected and eventually, reluctantly, abandoned. He'd visited the Doncasters, Gwen Jameson, even Lily Harrison. Wherever Sylvia had gone, she had left no trace that even Thurrock could find.

At first he'd hoped for another letter, to say she'd gone away to sort out her problems, and that she would soon be back, but after a few weeks all hope had passed from him. The cold fact was that she had left him. He had pressed her too hard, too often. When Christmas passed with no word, he could no longer pretend, to himself or anyone else, that she would be coming back.

He drained his glass and picked up the heavy silver frame with the only photograph he had of the two of them together. It had been taken in Torquay on the day that Lily and Jake were married. The newlyweds, discovering that he and Sylvia had no wedding day photograph of their own, had chivvied them into posing too. Sylvia had chosen the frame, heavily chased with snowdrops. When Max hired an architect to transform his bachelor's rooms into a family home, he'd commissioned him to repeat the motif in the drawing room.

The architect was long gone: there was no longer any point in rebuilding or redecorating. Max crossed the room and poured himself another brandy. Standing in front of the fire he drew out the letter she'd left him and read it again, although he could easily have recited it from memory.

Dear Max, I'm so sorry. I can't make it work and it's simply not fair on you. It's best if I go away, out of your life. You can divorce me in Scotland, then you can still remarry. I remember someone telling me that. I hope you will one day be happy again. You deserve to be. I wish it could be............but it can't.

I will always think back with happiness on the months with you and Lady Alice. Try to explain to her for me. I can't write any more, Sylvia.

There were a few words on the fourth line which she had scribbled out. He liked to think they were: *I wish it could be with me, but it can't.* That way he could at least hold on to the brief moments of happiness they had once known. It was all he had left.

4

In February the snow returned to Etaples, and the bitter cold. One evening the wind from the sea blew open the window of Sylvia's sleeping compartment and she had to scrape snow off her bed before she could get into it. Condensation gathered on the plywood roof of the sleeping cabins and dripped down onto her at night. Drusilla, consulted by Lady Harriet, had advised her to buy her own 'fleabag' - an eiderdown sleeping bag with oiled silk waterproofing. These days she slept in the butchered men's combinations that were her underclothing; she had to remember to take her uniform shirt into her fleabag with her - it was the only way to stop it freezing stiff overnight.

It had been enthusiastically asserted all along the line that the promotion of General Haig as commander-in-chief of the Western Front in place of Sir John French, would swiftly bring about a change of direction. Six weeks on, it seemed to have made no difference at all. Trench warfare was still as terrible as ever, and the worst fighting brought only the slightest advance, which was almost invariably reversed over the course of the following few days. When news came that the French were getting it hot in Verdun, further to the east, sympathy was tinged with hope that Fritz might withdraw some of his men from Béthune and Loos, and take the pressure off them for a while.

People said it was the bitterest winter in memory: it was certainly the first winter that hundreds of thousands of men had spent out in the open with nothing but trenches and dugouts to protect them. It was impossible for troops to stay on watch for more than a few hours: men were found at the change of duty frozen on the firing steps. Trainload after trainload of infantry reserves were sent up to the frontlines to allow the fighting troops to fall back to billets in the rear, to thaw out and sleep in the comparative comfort of shelled cottages and roofless barns. The cavalry, however, was still at the Machine Gun School, its officers still comfortably billeted in Le Touquet.

The men passing through the Etaples canteens were grateful for the warm food and drink provided, although some of the officers acted as though it was their divine right to have women running around after them, taking no more notice of them than if they were statues. As she poured tea and handed out plates of bacon sandwiches Sylvia could hear one in particular, an officer in his late thirties, making his way down the queue, complaining loudly to his companion about the way women were getting into everything.

'A damned clerk in Boulogne - a woman clerk, ye gods! - told me I couldn't take my hunting dogs back with me on leave. My papers weren't in order. Told me to get them in by that evening, or my leave pass couldn't be stamped. I gave her a piece of my mind, I can tell you. These days the bloody women are getting into everything. I hear Lloyd George has even promised them the vote when this show is over!'

Sylvia glanced at Pearl, busily filling the sandwiches from the mountains of bread which Estelle, the little lame French girl, had spread. Pearl looked as angry as Sylvia felt.

'You won't be wanting these, then,' said Sylvia, who'd been about to hand sandwiches to the complaining officer. 'Not if they've been made by *bloody women*...'

'What the devil - !' The captain looked at her with as much astonishment as if the tea urn had spoken. When she handed his share to the next man in the queue he couldn't believe his eyes. 'I suppose you're one of these wretched Suffragettes,' he hissed. 'Do you know who I am?'

'No,' said Sylvia. 'And frankly I don't care.'

'We'll see what Lady Angela has to say about your insolence! I'll damn well make sure you're on the next boat home!'

5

He came round the buffet towards her and she backed away, white-faced, until she was brought up short by the boxes of supplies at her back. She could see the officer's lips moving, but his threats were lost in a chorus of 'Oh, I say - !' and '*We* appreciate you, missus!' from the waiting soldiers. She'd never had any trouble from the ordinary soldier, though they served far more of them than officers. If the canteen had been fully staffed she could quite easily have walked out and never come back, but they were short-handed and she couldn't leave Pearl in the lurch. Besides, she'd done enough running away.

Pearl abandoned the sandwiches and planted herself between Sylvia and the angry officer. 'Don't let the miserable bastard get to you.' She gave Sylvia a swift hug, splodging margarine on her shirt collar, while her free hand brandished the bread-knife.

Sylvia blinked. She'd always thought of Pearl as a proper little mouse.

'*We* think you're doing a grand job!' The chorus gathered strength. 'Little heroines they are.' 'Aye. Proper angels.' 'No call for Captain Butler to speak to ladies like that.'

She took a deep breath and pushed past the officer, back to the counter. 'Just common courtesy - that's all we ever ask. Now - who's next?'

Butler came under attack from all quarters. Embarrassed at having shown himself up before his men, he flushed, muttered something that could have been taken for an apology, and slunk out of the line. As her anger subsided Sylvia started handing out the 'doorsteps' once more, to a round of hearty applause. Out of the corner of her eye she saw a young second-lieutenant hand his ration to Butler and slip back into line for his own.

When the rush died down, the others tried to persuade her to go and lie down. 'I can see he's upset you, the miserable toad!' said Pearl. 'Take a cup of tea with you...'

'Thanks, but we're far too busy.' She glared at Butler, furious that she'd let him affect her so. She'd stood in for a dispatch rider, been blown up in an ambulance, and yet none of those could equal the terror of a well-bred pillar of society who had turned violent. But she'd known that ever since the mauling she'd received on the abortive march to Buckingham Palace.

Butler and his companion were still there later when she was cleaning down the American-cloth covered tables, ready for the next onslaught. She had, in a gesture of defiance, taken her Suffrage prisoners' badge from her blouse and pinned it on the outside of her apron. She'd even thought about washing down the floor and making a crack about being in her proper place, but she'd resisted the temptation.

Butler stood up and spoke to her. 'Awfully sorry. Never meant to cause offence...'

'You did,' she snapped back. 'Not just to me, but to all women. If you're firing a shell, you don't ask whether it was made by female munition workers; you still send your dispatches, even if there's a woman on the motorcycle. Most of you officers will have been driven at some time by female staff drivers. And if, Heaven forbid, you catch one, I'm sure you won't object to being driven by a female ambulance driver, or having your life saved by a woman doctor.'

'I grant you that. Women make wonderful nurses and we all think that they're absolutely splendid...'

'Providing they don't claim to have an opinion, or to speak with any authority.'

'My point was that they shouldn't meddle in administration, or in politics - '

His lieutenant came to his aid. 'Yes, politics is quite a different matter. After all, you Suffragettes can't even make up your mind which party you support! You can't deny that Mrs Pankhurst has changed her allegiance twice and - '

'That surely is the whole point, lieutenant,' she said wearily. 'When we have the vote at last, we won't want anyone - man *or* woman - to tell us who to vote for. Strange as it may seem to you, not all women feel a need to support the same party. As Mr Gilbert says in *Iolanthe*: some of us are born little Liberals and some of us little Conservatives. And some, much as it may shock you, may even be little Socialists.'

As she turned away to wipe down the next table, she reflected that the wretched Pankhurst family was looking as if they might in fact manage to be all three between them - not that she would have admitted as much to Butler or his ilk.

'I say, Miss!' An officer had been hovering nearby, ready to smooth over further trouble, should it arise. 'Someone over by the door, trying to attract your attention.'

A handful of men had appeared in the doorway, their mud-streaked faces and crumpled faces testimony to their recent arrival from the front lines.

'Coupla bus-loads more to come, miss,' called the sergeant in charge. 'Heading for the Boulogne train. Can you cope with us?'

'Willingly. Pearl – best send a runner down for more supplies.' She turned back to Butler. 'If you'll excuse me, *gentlemen?* We need your space more than your company.'

One of the mud-stained soldiers, a jaunty little corporal, was still waving. Her eyes widened as she recognised him.

'Good Heavens - Jake?'

'My God! Fancy seeing you out here, miss! Did y'know Sir Max went to see Lily? Wanted to know if - '

The departing officers were looking at her curiously. 'Not now, Jake. Not here. And please don't tell anyone you've seen me.' A harried glance showed that Pearl had started refilling the urns.

'Sorry, miss. Didn't mean to - '

'I have to get back to the counter, Jake. Or no one will get fed. We'll talk later. Lily and the baby are well?'

'Last I heard. See for meself soon.'

'You've got home leave? That's wonderful.'

'Forty-eight hours.' Jake smiled broadly, his teeth pale in his muddy face. He dropped his voice. 'But the sergeant's going to put in for an extension. See, I haven't had any leave since the wedding, early August. And I was ten months out before that....'

More and more men were pushing their way in behind the Bantams, and the hubbub was growing. 'I must get back now. We'll talk later.'

There were five busloads of men to be fed and warmed. She lost count of the number of times she refilled the urns. Her wrists ached from lifting the heavy metal teapots.

All round the buffet and in the adjacent rest rooms, under a haze of cigarette smoke, men slumped in various stages of exhaustion. Some chatted, others propped their head on their arms and slept. When there was a brief lull she sent Estelle to put her feet up and went to find Jake, taking a couple of packets of Woodbines from behind the counter. She was admiring the photograph of Lily and the baby which Jake drew out of his pocket and fielding his hesitant questions about why she hadn't told her husband where she was, when a stentorian voice came from the doorway. 'First, Third and Eighteenth?'

Three duty officers leapt to their feet.

'Right. Get your men back on the transports. There's another show on and you're standing-to for the trenches.'

There was a ragged chorus of moans and complaints.

'Hard luck, boys,' said the sergeant-major. 'But Fritz is misbehavin' hisself.'

'Thought he'd gone to say 'bon jaw' to Verdun!' shouted someone at the back.

'Which is why they're pullin' the French out from our trenches,' the sergeant-major muttered to the nearest duty officer. 'So now we've got to cover for the damned frogs as well as run our own show.' He turned back to the men. 'Now, come on! You've had your orders!' he bellowed. 'Shift yerselves! Any complaints, take 'em up with the Kaiser!'

'Well, there's a lousy piece of luck.' Jake stood up, his face white and exhausted under the layer of mud. 'Bang goes my leave - again.'

She pressed the Woodbines into his hand, wished him luck, and watched him stomp to the door. She waved, but he didn't look back. Someone started to whistle *Tipperary*. Within seconds, they'd fallen into line and set off back through the camp.

6

By early March Sylvia had been several months in the canteen and the monotony of the work was beginning to get on her nerves. The distant booming of the guns was an ever-present feature of their days, along with the waves of reinforcements being entrained south from Boulogne, and then east in any vehicles to hand, to fill the gaps left by the withdrawal of the French armies to Verdun.

One day she came on duty late, after a night disturbed by everyone from messengers to the exhausted performers of the latest concert party, to find Lady Angela, newly returned from Boulogne, making tea for one of the Lines of Communications brass hats. Lady Angela spent a lot of her time pleading and cajoling with them, for it was through the LOC that permits were issued for volunteer workers to come out to man the buffets. This time, however, the brass hat was moaning to Lady Angela.

'I can't keep count of the number of dispatch riders we've lost this last week,' he complained. 'This spotted fever has gone through my young men like wildfire. I've sent for replacements from England, but it could be weeks before they get here. And what am I to do in the meantime? It's the devil of a problem.'

Sylvia paused with her apron in her hand. Then, with a smile, she tossed it on the counter. 'One volunteer, colonel. At your service.'

Lady Angela looked up from the teapot. 'You? Oh, no. I can't spare you.'

'For a few weeks, surely. You could find plenty of friends to take my place.' She didn't specify the officers at the Machine Gun School, not in front of Brass Hat, but Lady Angela followed her drift. 'You're so clever at rustling up volunteers,' she went on, laying on the flattery with a trowel. 'Sometimes I think you can conjure them from the air.'

Brass Hat came unexpectedly to her support. 'She's amazing, isn't she?' he said, patting Lady Angela's hand. 'Don't know how she does it, really I don't.'

Lady Angela preened herself.

'To be honest,' said Sylvia, pressing home the point, 'if I see another fried egg, I may well make a bolt myself, and run screaming back to Boulogne. Unless I could take over the supply run for you...?' She knew her employer would do anything rather than give up the supply run, which gave her the opportunity to get away from the canteens and catch up with all the gossip, preferably at HQ, which was staffed with all Lady Angela's aristocratic friends from pre-war days. 'Or let me do this instead - just for a couple of weeks until they fetch replacements from England.'

'Out of the question, my dear young lady,' said Brass Hat regretfully. 'You don't know your way around. And a young lady on a motorcycle...'

'But she did it when Victor was ill,' said Lady Angela. 'Do you remember, Bernard, the poor boy was taken ill and we had to keep him here until his temperature fell - '

'You are not telling me that this charming lady was his replacement?'

'Indeed she was.'

'I know my way around,' said Sylvia. 'I've even got my own uniform. London Auxiliaries.'

Shock and admiration warred for supremacy. 'Well, what can I say?'

'Further protests would seem futile,' said Lady Angela, who could never resist scoring a point, even though in the long run this one would be to her detriment.

'We can only use you well behind the lines, of course, my dear Miss - ?'

'Summers. Sylvia Summers,' said Lady Angela, answering for her.

'Behind the lines, Miss Summers. And entirely at your own risk.'

Sylvia smiled. 'Just lead me to the machines.'

7

Max sank his head in his hands and groaned. Thurrock's letter fell from his nerveless fingers. The detective's notes, together with the Home Office report that he'd acquired through devious means, added up to a hideous story, of abuse of power and cover-up in high places. It was a struggle to keep his emotions under control as he recalled the conversation with Sylvia in the garden at Stancombe.

'You're not saying he raped you?'

'Yes. No.'

'You can't be that naive. You must know whether he raped you or not.'

'You're a man! How could I expect you to understand?'

He understood now, when it was too late.

If only she'd told him...But to expect a woman brought up by Eithne Fletcher-Shaw to discuss something like this with a man - any man, even one who loved her - was unrealistic.

His lawyer's eye had quickly ripped through the weasel words of the *unofficial* and *confidential* hearing to the heart of the matter. Three doctors and a Home Office official had dealt with the unnamed complainant, shutting him up and shifting him out with merciless swiftness.

At one stage they had been on the point of dismissing the accusations entirely, and the devil might have got away with it, but there had been another witness to previous crimes. His Christian conscience, said the second witness, would not allow him to lie under oath. Max wondered what had happened to his Christian conscience while he had stood by previously and done nothing.

Nothing to be gained by bringing the matter to public gaze, they had decreed. *Not right to make those poor women relive their unfortunate experiences.*

And that was that. No further action to be taken. Not then, not now. He cleared the reports into his desk drawer and tried in vain to bring his mind back to his work.

Half an hour later Eddie Seymour stopped in the doorway. He looked at his friend with compassion. Staring into space, as he often did these days, Max was unaware of his visitor. Far too pale, with dark circles under his eyes, he didn't look as though he'd slept for months.

‘Morning, Max,’ said Eddie, shutting the door behind him. ‘Brought those papers you wanted.’ He dropped two box-files on the desk. ‘Is the old man giving you a hard time?’

‘I’d rather be busy.’

‘He’s lined up yet another outing of trades unionists and factory managers for the front. Actually, I thought you might appreciate the change of scenery. Go in my place.’

‘I’ve no desire to go back to France if I can possibly avoid it,’ said Max grumpily. ‘Unless...Eddie, what if she’s gone off to join the VADs?’

‘We tried the Voluntary Aid Detachments,’ said Eddie patiently. ‘Along with the Women’s Medical Units and just about every ambulance unit there was, including Malta, Egypt, Serbia, Italian front...’

‘I know.’ He passed his hand wearily over his eyes. ‘But she might have used a false name...’

‘She chose the wrong time for that. Once the new passport scheme came into place, she couldn’t have got away with it. We checked every Bryson, Shaw and Fletcher, and any combination we could think of.’

‘I know. Just clutching at straws.’

Eddie wished he could offer words of comfort. But women who went away just to think things through generally didn’t leave their entire wardrobe behind, and their wedding ring on the dressing-table. At least, not if there was the slightest chance of them coming back again.

‘If this American scheme comes off, the whole show could be over in a matter of months, and all the ambulance drivers will be out of work, thank God.’

‘What terms were settled on with President Wilson’s man?’ For the first time for weeks Max showed some of his old enthusiasm.

‘Belgium and Serbia to have their independence restored, of course. Alsace and Lorraine to return to France, with Germany gaining overseas territories to compensate.’ Eddie marked them off on his fingers. ‘Adjustment of the Italian-Austrian border to release the occupied Italians; Russia to be given an outlet to the sea, and of course, guarantees against any future catastrophes like this one.’

‘And if Germany doesn’t agree...?’

‘The Americans to come in immediately on the Allied side – though I have my doubts about that. Wilson will still have to sell it to Congress and they’ll probably spend the next eighteen months talking about it.

Meanwhile LG and Kitchener are to go to Russia to sell the idea to the Czar.'

Max raised his eyebrows. 'Together? That should be an interesting voyage. Kitchener hates civilians having anything to do with the war effort.'

'And he particularly hates LG. His brilliant mind makes Lord K look slow and stupid. Mind you, everyone has something against LG,' said Eddie. 'The King's nervous of him because of his social reforms, and his own Liberals snipe at him for working with Conservatives. He can't win.'

'But the thought of what will happen if he loses is too horrible to contemplate.'

'Trenches in Peckham, and the German Imperial Navy steaming past Tilbury...'

They sat in silence for a moment, thinking the unthinkable. When the orderly brought in morning tea, Eddie changed the subject. 'How's your mother bearing up?'

'Better than I am. She's with the children and Mrs Harmitage at Whitefields, and a happier little household you can't imagine. It helps her come to terms with losing yet another daughter-in-law. The children are her life now. She's already making plans to take them down to Torquay in April to visit Mrs Cunningham.'

'Which leaves you moping around Charles Street by yourself. Look, why don't you come to the theatre with us tonight? I'm taking Mary and Diana; thought we'd take in supper at the Savoy afterwards...'

'Thank you, but I'd be poor company. I'm better left to grouse on my own.'

8

Being a dispatch rider was a different life all together. After so long shut up in the canteen, Sylvia revelled in the fresh air and the feeling of independence. It wasn't all fresh air and freedom, however. As she progressed back and forth along the cobbled backroads of northern France, often only a mile or two behind the lines, she saw a side of the war that had so far been hidden from her.

She needed her wits about her all the time to avoid the new, unmapped, narrow-gauge railways that threaded across the countryside, like model trains, seemingly built overnight, to carry fuel and shells to the front. Each day she roared past pioneer companies burying men in mass trenches, for although there had been no major battles in this sector since the autumn, what the authorities described as the 'normal wastage' of trench warfare meant men were still being killed and mutilated in their thousands. Halfway up a tree, among the tightly furled green buds of spring, hung the rotting corpse of a horse, blown there the previous year by an explosion.

Every day she woke to shell and mortar fire and every day, when one came too close, she remembered the time when the Zepp had almost taken her ambulance out, and her with it.

She often carried requisitions from the hospital tents and Dan Tripp would give her coffee and encourage her to talk about her experience in High Holborn. The flashbacks of the bombing came less often and less vividly; by telling herself that she was a survivor she managed to keep it boxed up in the back reaches of her mind, where it couldn't harm her. Perhaps, one day, she could do the same with that other memory, which still came out to terrify her at night.

After the claustrophobic nature of the canteen, where she'd lived, worked and slept under the one roof, she welcomed life in the open. As spring came, the clear and frosty days increased, and even in this devastated quarter, pock-marked with shell craters, there was the green haze of new grass, or catkins on a tree, to raise her spirits.

The authorities wouldn't use her for the really important dispatches, but she did the bread and butter work which freed up a more experienced man for work closer to the front. She carried communications between the string of châteaux, twenty or thirty miles behind the lines, where the Generals and staff officers lived in gilded luxury while they decreed the fate of men in the squalor of the trenches.

She took food or medical requisitions down to Boulogne, fighting her way through the log-jam of supply wagons unloading hospital trains onto the boats, or loading supplies from the boats onto troop and ammunition trains. She wove her motorcycle through sidings where trains waited their turn to leave the port on the inadequate dock loop, to head south to Etaples, or north for Flanders, where supplies were urgently wanted. Sometimes she even went as far afield as Arras, with its grand arcaded squares, or Amiens, the major railway terminus on the Somme which was a constant target for German bombing.

Each night she slept in a different place, sometimes back in Etaples, or at the buffet on the sidings in Boulogne, occasionally in an ambulance depot, where the volunteers' lives were regulated by a heartless commander with a whistle, known to them all as Mrs Bee Itch. Life at the canteen had been punctuated by the distant army bugles, it was true, but Mrs Itch's whistle was altogether more penetrating and urgent, not to mention much closer by.

'For Heaven's sake,' groaned Sylvia, as the whistle sounded again before dawn. 'What now?' The guns had been going all night and there was a distant yellow glow on the skyline where shells were falling. 'Another stand-to? You've only just got to bed.'

'Roll-call and uniform inspection,' said one of the girls, who could hardly stand straight for tiredness, having been out all night meeting hospital trains. She'd only got back in at five and hadn't had the energy to get undressed. 'She's bound to moan about the state of the ambulances. We'll have to scrub them out after breakfast and polish them until you can see your face in the bonnet. Then we have to start on engine maintenance...With luck we'll get that done before the first afternoon train comes in.'

Sylvia dragged herself out of the borrowed fleabag, thinking about the depot in London with its staff of mechanics and cleaners. She hadn't realised how fortunate she'd been: all she'd had to do there was drive.

A large-boned woman climbed out of her camp-bed, dressed in a double layer of men's long combinations. 'Phew. What's the stink?' She recoiled theatrically across the room. 'Someone smells like a newly-scrubbed public lavatory.'

A girl gestured to a coughing heap in the fleabag nearest the door. 'That's Hettie. Poor kid had three spotted fever cases last night. Got spray-disinfected three times.'

'God! On a cold night like last night! Probably be double pneumonia by next week. She should stay in bed.'

'I know. But last time I sneaked her in a cup of tea, I got double duties for a week.'

'How do you stand it?' asked Sylvia as the whistle shrieked again. 'I've only been here one night, and already I feel like shoving that damned whistle down her throat.'

The large-boned woman shrugged. 'If we argue with her, she'll send us back in disgrace. Our parents will be mortified: they won't be able to boast that we're *doing our bit* - '

' - and theirs too!'

' - and they'll replace us with girls who've never driven at night. Last time that happened, a new girl drove her ambulance off the road on a moonless night. Killed the lot.' She pulled up her uniform collar to hide a crumpled shirt and checked her tie knot in the cracked mirror. 'By the way, if you're ever here for dinner, don't.'

'We rather suspect dead dog,' wheezed Hettie.

'Then what do you live on?'

'Well, we eat their bread and tea, on the basis that they can't get at that. And cocoa in the evening, except that Mrs Bee Itch insists that twenty cups of cocoa go into thirty ambulance drivers. Other than that, food parcels from home. Biscuits and potted meat. Sometimes - oh joy! - Bovril and chocolate - '

' - so if the post's late, we go hungry.'

In the dining room there were postcards of the depot for sale, to send home to Blighty, showing bowls of flowers and smiling VADs fussing over the drivers. The women reckoned they must have been photographer's models hired for the occasion.

As Sylvia wheeled out her bike, the drivers were disinfecting their lorries with buckets and large brooms, or hunched under their bonnets, cleaning fuel pipes and clearing choked carburettors with chapped and ulcerated fingers. The Commandant was behind them at every turn, whistle at the ready. It was a sobering thought that women in authority could be just as awful as men, but then she'd found that out eighteen months ago, with Canning. Three cheers for the likes of Lady Angela, thought Sylvia, kicking her bike into reluctant life...though neither she nor Lady Angela would last two minutes in this organisation.

9

The spotted fever outbreak was worse than at first suspected, and at the end of her second week no one thought to recall her. Every time she reported in, someone had another job for her, so she got back on her motorbike and did it, and kept on doing it.

On her third Sunday she was stood down, halfway through the day, at one of the posts behind the lines, where a motley crew of front-line ambulance drivers, senior orderlies and stretcher-bearers were taking a well-earned break.

In the sandbagged cottage - the door long ago blown off its hinges, and propped drunkenly across the frame - some were grabbing much-needed sleep upstairs, while others sat over a fire, frying omelettes with eggs from the half-ruined village less than a mile away. In what had once been the parlour, under the malevolent glare of a stuffed owl in a glass dome, two Quakers were reading the Bible while the rest of the men smoked and played cards.

The card-players looked up with interest as Sylvia took off her helmet and her hair came springing out in its customary disorder, but when she failed to respond with anything more than politeness to their remarks, they left her alone. She drew out her Woodbines, and passed them round before she smoked one herself, taking care not to offer a third light to anyone. Even behind the lines no one would run the risk of lighting up third in a row; that was the sniper's light: one to note, two to aim, three to fire.

She bagged herself an armchair in the corner and stretched her legs out on a wooden box, ignoring the occasional splinter that tried to work its way in through her puttees. With luck she could catch up on some sleep while she waited for further orders.

Less than a mile away the shells started falling again - a bizarre way for two Christian nations to spend their holy day.

There was a wind-up gramophone in the opposite corner and every few minutes, or so it seemed to Sylvia, someone would come in and put a record on. Then someone else would come in and say: 'My God, this is a dreary dirge. Why don't we have something cheery for a change?' and replace it. Then *he* would get called out to the kitchen to eat, or to take a message on the field-telephone, and another would come in and say: 'Who in blazes put this cheap rubbish on?' and change it once more.

As the afternoon light began to fade, three female ambulance drivers came in, absolutely exhausted. Sylvia gave up her chair and went into the kitchen to make them a pot of tea and something to eat.

She was handing round the chipped and handle-less cups when the field telephone rang. 'Drivers?' said the orderly down the mouthpiece. He winked at his mate. 'What sort of drivers do you want?' He cast his eye over the women in the parlour who were yawning and stretching, trying to wake themselves up for another spell of duty. 'Front row of the chorus or titled lady - we stock them all here.'

This was regarded as a very good joke, and every man chortled happily.

Not long after the ambulances departed, a shell, fired long, struck the ruins of a nearby cottage. As the walls of the post shook, the loose door shot aside and a man with a red-cross armband hurtled through the gap, just as a second shell whistled overhead.

'Close the door, Mr Nash,' said the wit, and the obligatory sally of laughter followed. In the hope of a second round of applause he repeated himself. 'Do come in, Mr Nash. But close the door behind you.'

With a strangled cry Sylvia leaped to her feet. In front of her, his face as white as a sheet, stood Mr Nash. The last time they'd met had been in Holloway Prison.

10

She woke reluctantly, still half in and half out of her dream. Someone was whistling, close by.

'If you were the only girl in the world,
and I was the only boy...'

She opened her eyes. Pale grey light filtering through. Was it dawn already? Max must have woken before her and put on that record again. She looked at the door, expecting to see his stern profile, with the trees and the lake behind him, still shrouded in early morning mist.

A deep voice joined in, singing the second line.

Nothing else would matter in the world today.
We could go on loving in the same old way...

Other voices took up the refrain. She rubbed her eyes and looked again. There was no sign of Max in the doorway, only an orderly with a sad face, his drooping moustache curving in line with the deeply-grooved wrinkles on his face.

'Good, you're awake. I'll tell Doctor Delahaye.'

Bewildered, she propped herself up on her elbows and looked around her at the grey canvas walls. A tent, then. Not the temple - that must have been the dream. Unsteadily she reached out a finger and touched the canvas, needing confirmation for her disordered senses. As she passed her finger over the rough weave, water seeped through, gathered in a bead, and trickled down to puddle on the oilcloth floor. It must be raining again.

The orderly reappeared with a cup of tea and two ginger biscuits, which he set on the cupboard beside her, tender as a ladies' maid. When he'd gone, she pushed back the rough blankets and saw she'd been sleeping on something slatted, like a steamer chair with the extension pulled out. As her eyes began to focus she saw that she was in an annexe to a larger structure, probably a nurses' night room, with a small trolley covered in dressings and implements. The locked cupboard by her side probably contained the drugs. She wrinkled her nose at a strange smell she hadn't come across before – and goodness knows she'd encountered a multitude of strange smells as she'd moved around the camp hospitals, fetching and carrying orders and casualty lists.

Shivering, she buttoned up her uniform tunic, in which she appeared to have slept. Her greatcoat was flung over her, on top of the red blankets. She was groping for her puttees and boots when a slender figure appeared in the doorway.

'Good morning.' What she'd thought was a slight youth was a grown woman in trousers, military shirt and jacket, her hair cropped short. The voice was measured, almost cold. 'I hear you've stopped being sick.'

'Y-yes.' It was a struggle to remember the previous night's events till her eye fell on a bucket beside the bed. 'M-made a bit of a fool of myself. Must have been the eggs.'

'Odd that Archie took so queer too.' The woman approached the bed, not taking her eyes off Sylvia. 'He wasn't at the post long enough to touch the food. They evacuated within minutes of his arrival, on account of the air attack.'

'Very odd.' Sylvia groped under the bed for her puttees, desperate to evade that piercing scrutiny. 'I don't quite recall - '

'But of course he *had* just missed being blown up.'

'That would account for it, then.' Was it her imagination or was there an air of disapproval, even hostility, about the woman at her bedside? 'Do you know where they put the rest of my uniform?'

'I took away the puttees. Bad for your circulation, and you had them wound far too tight. That's half the cause of trench foot, you know. Leads to blood clots too. I'm preparing a paper on it for the Academy back home.'

'But I can hardly ride a motorcycle in a skirt!'

'You're right there. But your bike's under lock and key for the time being. When I think you're ready to leave, I'll let you have a pair of trousers. We must be about the same size, I should think.'

'Trousers?'

'Much the most practical solution. If there was anything to be said for skirts, men would still be wearing togas.' She nodded at the ribboned badge. 'As a Suffragette – '

'Suffragist.'

' - I wonder you hadn't thought of trousers before.'

'I wore culottes or knickerbockers in London. But my superiors out here would go mad if they saw me in trousers! It's as much as they can do to cope with knickerbockers and puttees.'

'Had the same problem with Matron at first. Last year I was the only one not in ankle-length skirts, but it's amazing what a winter of mud can do to change priorities. I'll write you a doctor's letter: that should do the trick. Oh, I didn't introduce myself, did I? Annie Delahaye, doctor in the Imperial Australian Medical Services.'

'Sylvia S-Summers. Pleased to meet you.' Sylvia held out her hand. After an initial hesitation it was taken, and vigorously shaken. 'If I could have those trousers...' She glanced at Freddie's watch. 'Only I'm late on duty as it is.'

'You and Archie are officially stood down. For observation.'

'But I'm perfectly well!'

'Wouldn't do to go careering from camp to camp if you *do* have food-poisoning, would it? Or anything more serious? I understand spotted fever is going the rounds of the dispatch drivers. Look, I'm due on ward rounds now - I'll be back in about an hour. We'll talk then.'

'But I've got to go!'

'You're not going anywhere without a bike - not to mention trousers and boots.'

A word with another, younger, orderly produced an all-enveloping coat, a pair of slippers and a nurse to take Sylvia across to the ablutions, a lean-to hut in the middle of the tents, reached by a row of duckboards above the mud. The nurse stayed with her while she went into the cubicle, washed her face and hands, and combed her hair.

'Time I was getting back to Etaples,' said Sylvia, dragging her broken comb through her hair. 'Haven't had a bath in a week.'

'You could have one here if it wasn't so damned cold,' said the nurse. 'But in this weather you could catch pneumonia crossing the yard with wet hair.'

'How do you manage?'

'We go into Boulogne on our leave day and hire a bedroom between five or six of us. With a bathroom attached.' The nurse smiled. 'The greatest joy is just walking back and forth across the carpet in our bare feet.'

'Carpet!' said Sylvia. 'Wouldn't that be bliss after mud and tarpaulin? Oh, no.' She leaned over the tin basin, shoulders slumped. 'Oh, hell and damnation!'

'What is it? You're not going to faint again, are you?'

'I'm not that delicate. No, don't come too close: I've got crawlers.' She wiped angrily at her eyes. After all she'd been through, it took this to reduce her to tears.

'Grey backs or fleas?'

'Grey backs. I must have picked them up when I overnighted at the ambulance depot. Damn! The bedding must have been lousy.'

'We've all had the same problem,' said the nurse, pulling off her cap to show a neat head of hair cropped into the nape of her neck. 'Half the men coming up from the trenches are lousy. They can't help it. But it's murder trying to get them out of long hair.'

'Especially curly hair. Ugh! it's so disgusting!' She picked up one of the old newspapers waiting to be cut up into squares and drew out her trench lighter. 'Ah well, only one thing for it...'

11

Max shifted restlessly, trying in vain to stretch his legs out in the cramped pew. The minister was still droning on, but he'd long ceased to listen. It was a small congregation; he doubted whether religious observance would ever be the same as it had been before the war. Now that military service was no longer a choice, and every fit man was liable to conscription, would those fortunate enough to return from the front lines still cherish a belief in a benevolent God? It didn't seem likely.

He was pretty sure Sylvia felt the same way...

He pulled himself up short before his treacherous mind could wander down that path. Too often he found himself thinking, *I'll talk to Sylvia about that; I wonder if she feels the same way...?* But they had lost the opportunity for talking, and it would never come again.

On the wall to his right shone a new brass plaque, commemorating the son of the lord of the manor, who had died in the horror of Churchill's Gallipoli campaign. Too many young men from the local villages had died on the battlefields but most parents couldn't afford brass plaques: black armbands and crepe-ribboned hats marked their mourning.

He held the children's hands while his mother spoke to the rector on the way out. The Whitefields congregation was made up of the young and the old, with barely a handful of men his age, and he couldn't help but feel conspicuous. Only the other day on his way to work he'd been waylaid by an elderly harridan waving a bunch of white feathers at him. He refused to go about London wearing his medal, or his exemption armband, or leaning on his stick when he had at last reached the point of dispensing with it, but he rather thought he might have to start carrying it at least.

12

Sylvia woke with the strong feeling that she was being watched. Blinking in the weak afternoon sunlight she saw the doctor adjust her expression to one of professional observation. But Sylvia had seen the unguarded look of hostility.

'Am I allowed to get up yet?' She felt at a disadvantage, lying here with the other woman looking down at her.

'Not yet.'

Sylvia bit back a protest. 'How's the stretcher-bearer? Mr - Nash, was it?'

'He's a medical orderly.'

'I'm sorry.'

'And he's called Archie Nash, as you very well know,' snapped the doctor.

'I - I didn't...'

'You're telling me you've never seen him before?' Anger rippled through her as Sylvia remained silent. 'Then why has he shut himself up in his tent since you came on the scene, and won't even speak to me?'

'I'm sorry, I don't - '

'He said I should ask you.' She paced across the floor of the tent, her fingers twisting the buttons on her uniform until one of them fell off in her hand. 'So don't you dare tell me you don't know!'

'I don't see what concern it is of yours...'

The doctor thrust her left hand under Sylvia's nose. 'Archie Nash is my fiancé. We're supposed to be married next month. It's taken me a year to get him to this point, and I'm not having him go to pieces on me again now.'

'Again?'

'Archie had a bad time just before the war. Threw in his medical studies. I didn't know him then, and he's never told me why, but if you had anything to do with it, then I want to know.'

Sylvia opened her mouth, but no sound came out.

'Tell me what's going on!'

She sank her head in her hands. 'It never occurred to me that it would affect him too.'

'And you still haven't told me what 'it' was.'

'Sorry.'

'*Stop apologising!* You bloody English are all the same! "Frightfully sorry, old thing. Awfully sorry, old boy." But do they stop doing whatever it was that upset you in the first place? Do they hell!'

'I'm sorry.' She rubbed her tired eyes. 'I mean, yes, I suppose you're right.'

The doctor resumed her pacing. 'The ones who really stick in my throat are the ones who fawn all over you to your face and then spit in your bloody eye when your back's turned.'

There was an explosion of laughter from the bed. 'Good trick if you can do it.'

'What?'

'Spit in someone's eye when their back's turned.'

In spite of herself, the doctor's lips started to twitch and soon she too was engulfed in laughter. 'I do get carried away,' she said at last, mopping her eyes. 'My language leaves a lot to be desired. My Grandpa Joshua always threatened to beat me whenever I swore. And it sends Matron into an apoplexy. She prays for me every Sunday.' The laughter disappeared as suddenly as it had come. 'Now - you had something to tell me.'

'It's hard to know where to start.' Sylvia looked down at her entwined hands. 'I've tried so long to forget it. I was in prison, you see. In Holloway.'

'With the Suffragettes?' Sylvia nodded. 'I've heard about your campaigns. But of course women have had the vote in Australia for a good ten years. Were you on hunger strike?' She nodded again, and Annie saw her hand creep to the small scar by her mouth. 'Something Archie said - '

'Yes. But this - what it was that - ' Her hands writhed and she swallowed hard. 'It wasn't just the force-feeding, though God knows that was bad enough.'

'Worse even than force-feeding?' There was a sharp intake of breath. 'Archie? You're telling me that Archie - ?'

'No, not him.' The pain and bewilderment on the doctor's face was too much to bear. She launched into her story without any further delay.

13

They always knew when Doctor Goring was coming by the wailing, groaning and even more horrible noises that accompanied his progress through the punishment cells. Doctor Goring, a dapper middle-aged man with a carefully waxed moustache, was in charge of force-feeding in these isolated cells, and to say he enjoyed his work was putting it mildly. Morning and evening, as she heard him working his way down the corridor, Sylvia would start shaking, knotting her hands together, desperately praying that she would have the strength to hold on.

It had seemed the right thing to do when they were refused the privilege of wearing their own clothes: one of the older Suffragettes passed the word when they were briefly together in the exercise yard. 'We shall refuse all sustenance until the decision is overturned. We shall refuse all prison work.' And in her fury at the stained flannel drawers and kerchief she was forced to wear, that might have come from goodness knew what diseased or lousy body, she'd needed little persuasion to go along with the rest of them.

She wasn't a radical Suffragette, but a peaceful protester, a Suffragist, and they should never have put her in prison, but now she was here she couldn't let the side down. Nevertheless it was a shock to find herself separated from the others and taken down to a row of cells in a dank basement. There were only three of them down there, and one wardress, in an isolated area that was littered with timber, showing every sign of being in the process of rebuilding. Dressed in the coarse prison dress, so much patched that it looked like a delivery sack, she was permanently cold even though it was summer. The plank bed was nailed to the ground, but in the day-time the wardress took away the bedding, so she had to lie on bare planks. None of the windows opened, though several of the small panes in her cell window had been knocked out. It wasn't enough, however, to take away the constant stink from the metal can in the corner which served as a lavatory.

A number of the Suffragettes had boasted of breaking their window glass, either for air or just as a gesture against the authorities, but she'd asked the wardress to take note that the panes in her cell had already been broken before she was brought down.

The dank, stale air had its effect on prisoners and wardresses alike: every one of them had a hacking bronchial cough. 'Why they brought you three down here I can't understand,' said the night wardress. 'This lot've been out of use these six months. They were going to do them out, but that won't happen now till after the War. Mind you, with two hundred and seventy coming in one wave, I s'pose they're a bit pushed for space.'

Hers was the last of the three cells, and the doors of the first two were always left open so that she had to listen to the crying, the howling, the choking of the previous two prisoners being force-fed, knowing that her turn was soon to come.

Goring was always accompanied by a medical student. Someone had to carry the jugs and funnels and tubes, and two pairs of hands were better than one when holding a woman down, particularly if the prisoner had backed herself into the corner of the cell, arms crossed across her body, fingers locked over mouth and nostrils. This was the position recommended by the older women, who had been through it all before. It made it doubly difficult to pin you to the bed, they said.

To every new medical student, Goring trotted out the same joke. 'The younger women are a much more enjoyable challenge; force-feeding the older ones is a little like stuffing turkeys.' The medical students laughed on cue, and while the wardress turned the key on the weeping occupant of the first cell, Goring stopped outside the second door, speaking deliberately loudly. 'Plenty of young ones in this time. I think this little filly has been disowned: she gets no visitors.' He had a cackling, tuneless laugh. 'Mark my words, all she needs is a strong man to take her in hand. A good seeing to would soon settle all her nonsense.'

Until it came to the point Sylvia hadn't appreciated the full horror of what she'd so blithely agreed to in the exercise yard. She'd thought herself a strong enough young woman, but after days without food they had no problem throwing her on the bed-frame and fastening her hands to the sides with the straps.

The sensations of the metal bar jammed against the teeth and cutting into the gums, the rubber tube thrust in, coughed back up and then thrust again for a third or fourth time too far down the gullet into the stomach, the liquid poured too fast down the funnel...it would all stay with her until the day she died. This was how it must be to drown, the burning and choking as breathing and swallowing became inextricably confused by the panicking body. After the first time, Goring and his apprentice torturer stood her up far too swiftly, and at the pressure of the student's hands on her breasts 'checking her heart rate', she vomited it all back over Goring's coat and highly polished shoes.

After that first day, she was marked out for special treatment. As the wardress set out the instruments, the jug, the funnel, the gag, the tube far too thick for its purpose, Goring ordered the removal of Sylvia's outer dress, 'in order to save on the laundry'. Then he found fault with one of the jugs, or the funnels, and sent the wardress to scrub it in the sink at the far end of the corridor. She left with a look of sympathy for Sylvia, knowing as well as anyone that it was a patent excuse; the tube used was always third or fourth hand, sufficient to start the victim gagging at the mere thought of it, and no one ever suggested washing that. As her footsteps retreated down the corridor, Goring turned to the student and said: 'Close the door, young man, and turn the key.'

With the wardress gone, the torment of the gag and the force feeding was made doubly horrifying by two pairs of hands that roamed unchecked all over her body as they held her down. On the third day the medical student, being called on to check her heart, thrust his hand down her chemise and listened through his stethoscope for no more than two beats of her heart. 'Oh, ripping. Splendid heart!' he exclaimed, squeezing her breast painfully as he withdrew the stethoscope. He pushed her back down on the bed and while Goring pinned her down the student thrust the gag into her mouth, tearing the gum, ripping the edge of her mouth so that she could feel the blood running down the back of her throat.

Her struggle to free herself from the restraint only seemed to arouse her tormentor. Confident that the wardress would not disturb them, Goring sent the student to the door, unbuttoned his trousers and lowered his length on top of her, rubbing and grinding himself against her lower body while his mouth slobbered at the neck of her chemise. With a gag in her mouth it was impossible to scream; it was as much as she could do to go on breathing. After what seemed an age, Goring started to pant heavily; his face went crimson, he made a choking sound and one more obscene stain was added to those on her chemise. And then they started on the forced feeding, and once again she was horribly sick, all over herself, her hair, the bed, the walls.

The next day she begged the wardress to stay, but the wretched woman was too scared to stand up to the doctor. She said she'd tried to bring Sylvia in a bowl of gruel early that morning, before doctor's rounds, but had been forbidden. 'Tell them you're off the hunger strike,' she urged. 'Give up your protests, dearie. You're only storin' up trouble for yerself.'

Sylvia retched at the thought of food. 'I thought they'd stopped force-feeding, since the Cat and Mouse legislation,' she said, when she could speak again.

'Letting 'em out when they get too weak? Works with most of the doctors. They don't want to do this – who would? But you chose the wrong month to go on hunger strike, girl, with the Governor sick and the prison so overcrowded. This one don't miss his chance. Not ever. He picks out one for his special attentions. And it ain't no use you complaining,' she said, her red-rimmed eyes mournful. 'I'd be bound to say I was in 'ere all along, else I'd lose me job. I'm a widow. I got three kiddies and an old mother to look out for - without my wages, we'd be out on the street.'

It went on for twelve more days, with the medical students mauling her about, thrusting their hands under her chemise, and the doctor repeating his obscene ritual each time before he commenced the force feeding. Doctor and student laughed and joked together as they left her weeping in the stinking cell, and with each passing day she had less and less strength to fight them. No wonder Emily Davison had gone mad and thrown herself in front of the King's horse. Sylvia knew she hadn't the courage to go on that long. When she heard them outside her door on the thirteenth day, she just leaned against the wall and wept. She no longer had what it took to resist.

14

'And that day it was Archie?' Annie Delahaye had forced herself not to interrupt till now.

'That day it was Mr Nash. Yes. *Close the door, Mr Nash, and turn the key.* That's what Goring said. And started - doing what he did.' She looked up at Annie, the tears streaming down her cheeks. 'But Nash refused. He *refused.*' He said he'd heard rumours about Goring, and he could hardly believe them, but now he knew they were true, and he would make sure everyone else knew too. I'd forgotten that. You see, when I dream of it - and God knows, it comes back to haunt me often enough - I always wake up at the worst bit. Until I saw your Archie Nash, I'd forgotten...Not the words, but certainly him...and what he did.' She shook her head. 'How could I have forgotten that?'

'What happened...afterwards?'

'I was carried to the hospital ward and sedated. They stitched my mouth up.' Her hand went to the scar. 'I don't remember a great deal after that until they opened the gates and let me out. By then, the war had started. But those words stayed with me. And - and then, in that outpost yesterday, it all came back.'

By time she finished telling her story she felt as though she had been wrung out. There was not a drop of energy left in her tired body and all she wanted to do was sleep. Outside the tent it was growing dark. Annie Delahaye was called back into the ward to see to a dying man, then an ambulance arrived with another batch of wounded from the trenches. When an orderly brought Sylvia in a cup of cocoa and two white tablets from the doctor, she was happy to take them and drift off to sleep again.

She woke in the middle of the night, her dreams so vivid that she found herself looking round for Freddie. It took a while for her to come back to the present, to remember that Freddie was dead.

On the other side of the inner canvas wall a dim glow from a night lantern shone on a nurse, bending over a bed, talking quietly to a wounded soldier. There was that strange pungent smell again, hovering on the borderline between pleasant and unpleasant - she kept forgetting to ask what it was.

The night was bitterly cold and she slid down the bed, bunching the blankets around her ears. She tried to remember what it was that Freddie had said to her, but the harder she tried to drag it out of her dreams, the faster it retreated.

15

She dozed until the early morning light and woke with a start to find Archie Nash putting a cup of tea on the bedside table. He backed away with a nervous expression on his face.

'I didn't mean to startle you. Look, I promised Annie that I wouldn't upset you. I just wanted to - '

'I'm not upset. God, what *is* that smell?' She wrinkled up her nose. 'Like nice herbs with a touch of mothballs that someone dropped into a swamp.'

'Oh, that?' He grinned. '*Melaleuca alternifolia,* to give it its Latin name. The ti-tree...but quite a different plant from the tea that we drink...that's *camellia sinensis.* Annie says this ti-tree is a native remedy in Australia. Cleans wounds and helps them heal. Good on trench foot too. We started using it when there was nothing else. You hardly notice the smell after a day or two. A few tents along there's an English doctor using marigolds on wounds that won't heal. Then there's another team somewhere clapping mouldy bread over gunshot wounds - now there's a stink for you!'

'Marigolds? Mouldy bread? Why?'

'It all started when we ran out of antiseptic some months ago - but we're still using our alternatives to eke out supplies. Results are extremely good. The French think we're insane, of course, though I did hear of a French doctor up the line putting crushed garlic dressings on open wounds...'

'Phew! And the men?'

'The poor bloody infantry? Just bloody grateful that we're putting them back together....' He bit at his thumb-nail. 'When you woke up you looked really sad.'

'Was I? I'd been dreaming about my brother. He died early in the war. First Ypres.'

'I'm sorry. And then I barged in again. The last person you want to see.'

'You're wrong. It was a shock coming face to face with you in that outpost, but it must have frightened the life out of you too. Please - don't go. I wanted to see you before I went back to Etaples. I wanted to thank you for everything you did for me in Holloway. And to hear the rest of the story.'

'No, look, I swore to Annie I wouldn't upset you.'

'I'm not upset. Yesterday was the first time I'd spoken about it, really - and - ' there was a sense of wonder in her voice ' - and last night was the first time I didn't dream about it. I just - I need to know how it ended.'

'With Goring?' His face darkened. 'They wouldn't prosecute, even with my evidence. Even when I found someone who'd witnessed the same terrible things - some years before, in an asylum and in an orphanage – even then, they still wanted to hush it up. Oh, they drummed him out of the prison service, early retirement they said, but essentially he got away with it. I failed you.'

'No, you didn't.' She reached out her hand and he came forward hesitantly and took it. 'Without you, it would have gone on and on. With me and with others too. You saved me, and for that I will be eternally grateful.'

'It gave me a hell of a shock to see you,' he admitted, 'but I must say, to know you came through it all has bucked me up awfully.'

Out of the corner of her eye Sylvia saw the tent flap go back; Doctor Delahaye stood in the opening, watching them with a wary expression.

'They carried you off to the prison hospital, you see.' He was stroking her hand, unaware of the third presence. 'They didn't think you'd make it. Said your mind was quite overset. And, of course, once I started to go against Goring, they wouldn't have me back in the prison.'

'I *was* a little mad, Mr Nash. At first. But as you see, I survived. It can't have been easy for you.' She nodded at his uniform. 'What happened?'

'I threw in my studies. Goring's cronies were making life a little uncomfortable.'

'I'm so sorry. I never wanted my problems to spill over onto you - '

'But then, when we went to war, I found my country needed me after all.'

She patted her overcoat. 'Just as it needed its ex-prisoners. But surely you haven't given up your medical studies for good? It seems such a waste.'

Archie's face lit up as Annie Delahaye joined them.

'I reckon I'll take him back to Australia with me after the war,' she said with a conspiratorial wink at Sylvia. She linked her arm with Archie's. 'He'll finish his studies out there - if I have any say in the matter.'

16

Sylvia returned to partial duties the next day, riding dispatches in a mixture of volunteer and medical uniform, for her shirts and underclothes had been taken away to the steriliser and she was forced to borrow from Dr Delahaye. At her suggestion, Sylvia based herself for the next eight nights at the field hospital, where she slept on a camp-bed in Annie's quarters – once a nurse had sorted out the 'crawlers' with a mixture of olive and ti-tree oils and a fine tooth comb. The two women spent each evening talking through all that had happened to Sylvia, sometimes well into the night.

'I still don't understand why he did what he did – Goring, I mean,' said Sylvia one evening. 'He could easily have bought any woman he wanted - '

'You're right. Expensive brothels in every big city...Prostitutes two a penny...'

'He could have kept a mistress...'

'There are some men – prosperous men – who seek out really poor prostitutes...the more sordid the better. I guess Goring must have been one of them. Hard to believe, I know, but it's a fact. *Nostalgie de la boue*, they call it. A desire for squalor or depravity. I read a paper on it by some French psychiatrist when I was working in the women's hospital back home.'

'Sounds bizarre.'

'After a few months in the women's hospital, the terrible things some men do to women soon lose their initial strangeness,' said Annie sadly.

'But why us? What did we do to deserve such abuse?'

'You did nothing. I can't be certain, of course...but for him, finding this little trio of vulnerable women - good, clean young women from a decent background, who just happened to find themselves in sordid circumstances – it was a perfect situation. You said yourself that you gave a false name...'

'I did. Called myself Charlotte Corday.'

'French Revolution? The woman who killed Marat, in the hope of ending the executions?'

'Much good it did her. Much good it did me. Nobody knew who I really was until I was at Lady Harriet's after they released me from hospital. The woman in the next cell told me that she was an orphan. She only had elderly aunts, and they lived in Derbyshire. I don't know about the third one, but she never had any visitors either.'

'There you are then. Nothing any of you could have done about it. He was the one rotten apple in the barrel. Some sick bastards can only do it when the women are tied up...'

Her eyes widened. 'Dear God!'

'I'd led a sheltered life, like you,' said Annie, 'until I started working in the women's hospital. Then my eyes were opened, I can tell you!'

'I suppose some French psychiatrist has written papers on that too!' said Sylvia, with a ghost of a smile.

'Too true!' They both fell silent for a moment. 'He could have got away with worse,' said Annie, 'so you were fortunate in that at least. You can't undo what happened, but if you let it colour the rest of your life, then the bastard has won. You've got to talk it out of your system,' said Annie, 'not let it fester in your heart and soul. There are some doctors who keep their patients talking about it forever, but there's no need. Once you've stopped it festering, you get on with your life.'

It seemed to work. By the end of the week Sylvia's sleep was deeper and more peaceful, and for the first time since before Pip's trial, she awoke refreshed.

One night she woke from her dreams with a clear vision of Freddie. What was it that he had said to her?

Move on.

She could still see his smiling face. *Move on,* he'd said. *You're the last one left. You've got to put all this behind you and get on with your life.*

She snuggled down under the blankets. I will, she thought. I'll put it all behind me. If only Max were here. I'd like to tell him...though it's too late for that now.

'Little by little the bad memories will go, you'll see,' said Annie Delahaye. 'Find yourself a nice kind fellow like Archie - if there are any left after this bloody war! - and you'll find it simply doesn't matter as much anymore.'

'I had a nice kind fellow,' said Sylvia sadly, rubbing the base of her finger where her wedding ring had once sat. 'He tried to help me through it all, but I drove him away.' Tears welled up in her eyes and spilled down her pale cheeks. 'I'll never have that chance again.'

17

'You know, I fought here in the *first* war,' said the orderly with the drooping moustache, as he placed a bowl of stew and two tablets in front of her.

'The – the *first* war?' said Sylvia, taken aback equally by his words and the fact that he had spoken in faultless English. After eight days with no response to her greetings, either in French or English, she'd been convinced that he must be Flemish. 'But – but we've never fought the Germans before.'

'*I* did,' said the orderly, his chest swelling with pride. 'Fought with the French in eighteen-seventy, when the Germans brought up their damned great guns and laid siege to Paris. Only seventeen, I was. Working as a clerk for a London business, in their Paris branch. Fancied a bit of travel and adventure.' He chuckled wheezily. 'Got more adventure than I'd bargained for. Ended up eating cats and dogs and rats, and fighting in one of the French volunteer brigades.'

'I didn't realise that we were involved at all in that war,' she said.

'Over five thousand British in Paris at the time of the Siege, they reckon. Mind you, not every one of them was in the fighting. I said then, and I say it again now: if Gladstone had done his duty and come to help the French give the Kaiser a bloody nose back then, Fritz wouldn't have dared take us on again.'

'But when Serbia assassinated the Austrian duke - '

He shook his head sadly at such ignorance. 'Just an excuse,' he said.

'But then when the Kaiser marched through Belgium...'

He shook his head again. 'The Germans have been waiting forty years to flatten France for good. Aye, and the French have been waiting forty years to get their revenge. It could all have been avoided if that Gladstone had done his duty...Mark my words...' He stomped off, sunk once more in silent gloom.

'It's being so cheerful that keeps him going,' said one of the nurses, who had come in for medicine and heard his rant. 'Mind you, he only speaks once a week, so you were honoured!'

'Bewildered, more like,' said Sylvia, returning to her stew. 'Did he really fight out here in eighteen-seventy?'

'Oh yes. Got a bullet wound in the side of the head, which probably accounts for a lot. Mind you, he's as gentle as a lamb with the wounded men.'

The next afternoon Sylvia was summoned back to Etaples and when she'd made her farewells, she was officially discharged from the field hospital. She would never forget Dr Delahaye and Archie Nash. Thanks to them, she felt she could at last close the door on the horror and put the dreadful memories into a part of her mind where they did not obtrude on her daily existence.

An orderly had sponged down her great-coat and she was bundling the last of her sterilised and laundered shirts into her saddlebag when Archie Nash came hurrying across.

'You're wanted on the field telephone,' he said, and she could see from his face that it wasn't good news.

It was Lady Angela on the other end. 'I'm on my way back now,' said Sylvia. 'I was stood down at the Field Hospital for a few days and - '

'It's not that, my dear,' said the tinny voice. 'It's your young corporal, the little fellow.'

'Jake Harrison?' She looked across the tent at the canvas wall, but all she could see was Jake and Lily at their wedding day. She shivered.

'Harrison. Yes. Jacob, that's it. One of his friends came here looking for you. Though he insisted you were called Miss Shaw. But we have never had any other Sylvia here, so I suppose he really meant Miss Summers...do you think? I'm not quite sure what it was all about. Pearl spoke to him.'

Then put Pearl on the bloody phone! thought Sylvia. It was infuriatingly typical of Lady Angela not to let Pearl make the call herself. She always had to be at the centre of everything, even when it was nothing at all to do with her.

'She said something about a charge of cowardice, but I'm not sure she has that right. No, that can't be right, surely. Such a little fellow, of course he'd be frightened. What on earth do they mean sending men like him to - '

She cut ruthlessly through her employer's ramblings. 'What's happened?'

'Pearl says there's to be a Field Court Martial. If they find him guilty, they'll shoot him. My dear, he seems to think you can get someone to help him? A Mr Bronson?'

'Bryson,' said Sylvia from a parched throat. She took a deep, steadying breath. 'Please get a message back to Jake. Tell him I'll get help out here as soon as I can.'

18

Max huddled in his greatcoat, the bitter wind numbing his ears and threatening to lift his hat from his head. The little ship was vastly overcrowded, carrying about twice the number of people it was equipped for. With the sinking of the *Sussex* earlier in the week, the service from Newhaven was reduced to one ship to cover both directions. A German torpedo had sheared off the bows of the *Sussex*, killing diners and stewards, so most of the passengers today had opted to stay on deck, each with an eye on a lifebelt and lifeboat, like over-sized children in a game of musical chairs.

There was not a great deal of logic to this, as most of the survivors of the *Sussex* were those who had stayed with the stern of the ship; most of those lost had drowned in capsized lifeboats or, like the famous composer Granados, been washed by the waves from their life-rafts.

A group of nurses returning from leave had perched themselves, wrapped in thick cloaks, on wooden boxes full of medical supplies;

around them clustered a large contingent of new recruits for the American Field Ambulances, disgusted that their country still remained neutral and determined to 'do their bit'. The rest of the travellers were civilians, families going out to visit wounded soldiers and a horde of journalists eager to get to Boulogne and interview the survivors of the *Sussex*.

A collective sigh ran around the deck as the grey bulk of the coastal patrol dirigible, which had hovered above them since they left the harbour, began to fade back into the mist. Now they really were on their own. The ship began another of its zig-zagging tacks, which would make the journey take twice as long, but hopefully deter any submarine sniffing out a second prey in the cold grey wastes of the Channel. Carrying only civilians and with no escort of destroyers, she should have been safe from attack, under the Hague Convention - but that had not saved her sister ship.

Some of the journalists passed along the deck, asking the passengers how they felt, now that the coast of England had been left behind. Max moved away, bracing himself against the yawing of the ship until he found himself a quiet nook on the sheltered side. He let his mind run forward to the reception that would be waiting for him in France. That Sylvia had felt it necessary to address letters to him at his office, his home and Ardingley House, showed the urgency she attached to the case.

It had not been easy to extricate himself from his commitments; Lloyd George was not best pleased to lose one of his right-hand men, especially as Max had been back at work barely six months.

'Never does to become too involved, man,' he'd said brusquely. 'Interferes terribly with your work. Look what happened when they made me go and see that boy with the terrible head wound - I couldn't work properly for days! Court martial...an unfortunate necessity, I admit, but...If we want to do our best for the boys at the front, we have to stay detached and get on with our job here.'

'Awkward questions are already being asked about courts martial in the House,' said the Minister's secretary, Miss Stevenson, looking up from her notes. 'So far the War Office has failed to come up with satisfactory answers. What if you were to instruct Sir Max - as one of our most eminent lawyers - to *review* the findings of this particular court-martial? He could fit it in with a visit to the front.' She flicked rapidly through the desk diary. 'We have two parties of munitions workers due out in the next month.'

'But we want those munitions workers back in one piece,' jested Lloyd George, 'and Max is a veritable magnet for shells.'

Max wasn't in the mood for joking. 'I can't turn my back on this man, sir,' he said. 'Lady Bryson and I are godparents to his child. And from what Lady Bryson tells me, he hasn't had anything approaching a fair trial. How could I face his widow - and my godson - if I hadn't done all I could to make sure he received justice?'

'Lady Bryson is involved in the case?' Lloyd George looked up from his papers, eyes sharp.

'So it would seem.' He shifted uncomfortably. Everyone knew by now that his wife had left him, but he didn't relish having to discuss it with his superior. 'She wrote to me from France.'

'Well, well. This puts a different complexion on the matter,' murmured Lloyd George, drawing a sheet of paper towards him. 'How could I face Lady Bryson if I'd refused her your assistance?' He twinkled up at Miss Stevenson, formerly his daughter's governess, and now Lloyd George's personal assistant both in the office and out of it...and considerably more, if rumour was to be believed. 'The wrath of that woman is a thing to be avoided. She's a Suffragette like yourself, my dear. Actually, a Suffrag*ist*, but very dedicated to the cause. You know, Max, I once had to talk to Christabel Pankhurst. It was like going to a lunatic asylum and talking to the patient who thinks he is God. Lady Bryson is entirely different, of course.'

'Any permit for Sir Max to become involved would have to be in the strongest terms,' said Miss Stevenson, drawing him back to the matter at hand. 'Tthe Army command will see it as interference...'

'Yes, they will, won't they?' A positively gleeful expression crossed Lloyd George's face and he began to scribble rapidly. 'You'll need a clerk, to take notes.'

'Not if I have Lady Bryson.'

'Right. If we're going to put backs up, may as well do it thoroughly, eh?'

The letters from Lloyd George were in Max's inner pocket, together with the letters from Sylvia. She must have been desperate to turn to him, after all that had gone before.

He must not let her down. Further than that he couldn't think. First he had to cross the Channel without being torpedoed, and then get himself from Dieppe to Etaples in one piece.

19

Sylvia stood in the doorway, blinking in the sudden gloom after the bright sunlight. There were so many off-duty officers in the little café that it was difficult to pick one out from the rest. She unbuttoned her gloves while she surreptitiously scanned the faces. There he was, at last, the man the sentry had described to her: a young lieutenant, sitting apart from the others, curly fair head sunk in his hands. Not in the main part of the room, which would make it difficult to set up an 'accidental' meeting, but as she drew off her leather helmet, she saw behind him a row of coat hooks.

He seemed so sunk in his gloom that she thought it would be impossible to catch his attention, but in the event it was surprisingly easy. Hanging up her overcoat and gas mask, she contrived to drop her dispatch bag, and the papers spilled out onto the floor. Roused from his misery, he leaped to his feet and helped her to collect them. Then it was the most natural thing in the world, under the envious glances of the other officers, to invite her to join him. As the waiter hurried over with coffee and wine, the gloom temporarily lifted from the lieutenant's face.

He looked at her across the table as she peeled off her gloves and helmet and leaned back, eyes closed, as the wine warmed its way through her. A Suffragette, no doubt: who else would have cropped that glorious hair? Immodest, his mother would have called her, and a forward hussy, but then what young officer on the front - who never knew when his last day might come - cared much what his mother might have said?

As she sipped the scalding coffee he introduced himself - Lieutenant Robert Duncan – and asked hopefully whether she was based in Arras. It was a long time since any of them had seen a young Englishwoman who wasn't under the petty rules and regulations of a hospital matron.

She shook her head. 'Just on a special. Back to my base at Etaples this afternoon.'

'A pity, Miss - ?'

'Summers. Sylvia Summers.'

'You brighten the place up no end,' he said gallantly.

'Goodness only knows it needs it. Everyone's going around with such long faces....' The lieutenant's mouth quivered and she half reached out to him, then withdrew her hand. 'Sorry. I shouldn't have said... Was it a very bad show?'

'Something like that. Only it's not the Germans...'

As his voice trailed off again she looked at him with a sympathetic smile. 'Oh dear. Is it the court-martial?' He looked at her with a frown. 'Everyone at the depot was talking about it. Is the man in your platoon? That's awfully bad luck.'

At her expression of sympathy it all came pouring out. 'I've let him down. The poor fellow....I was supposed to be prisoner's friend, you see. But the adjutant ran rings around me.' He covered his face. 'I just wish it was all over.'

'They told me it was.'

'It should have been. But it's gone for an appeal. Don't know who's intervened there, certainly not the authorities. *They* just want an example to be made - don't care who it is. With all the new recruits...' He looked up at her, eyes wide. 'I say, you're not a journalist, are you?'

'Dispatch rider - temporarily. Usually I work in Angelina's in Etaples - the British Soldiers' Buffet.' She wrinkled her nose. 'Do they *have* female journalists?'

'Probably not. But I shouldn't be talking of such things to you.'

'Not if you don't want to.' She raised her glass and sipped it. 'But you look as though you need to talk to someone. My brother used to talk to me when he was troubled. His name was Freddie. He was killed at Ypres.'

The information seemed to act as a passport. For a moment she felt guilty for taking advantage of him, but then she thought of Lily and the baby and turned her mind grimly back to her task.

'Of course I'm glad for him, at least I will be if the appeal works out. But it means I've got to go back to that ghastly cell, and look him in the face again, and know that he knows I failed him.'

'He must know you did your best.'

'Don't think he knows anything anymore. Poor beggar, he's been so ill. When I examined his records he's only had four days leave in eighteen months. And they're such little fellows, both of them.' Both of them? She pricked up her ears, but didn't interrupt him. He was musing aloud, relieving himself of the thoughts that tormented him, almost as if he'd forgotten she was there. 'I sent them to be padre's servants, to keep them out of the firing line. It's often done. But the wretched God-botherer sent them back - said they weren't quick enough on their feet. Of course they weren't! Being buried in a trench would addle anyone's brains.'

'Dear God.' She reached out a hand and touched his briefly. 'When was this?'

'Barely a month ago. Just before they - '

'You too?'

'Just missed me. I was one of the l-lucky ones. But I saw it after the b-bomb b-blew it in. Believe me, it will haunt me to the d-day I d-die.' He couldn't tell her the full horror of the hands moving at either end of trench, of the earth shifting as they tried to get out. But each time it shifted, the trench settled deeper. They'd dug them out, but it had taken two hours and some of the men hadn't made it. The expression of horror on the dead faces lived with him still.

Sylvia turned his hand over and looked at the broken nails and shredded fingertips only just healing over. 'You helped to dig them out?'

'We had m-miners in our company. They knew what they were doing. I allowed them to supervise the operation.' He shook his head glumly. 'I got bawled out by my c-captain for that too.'

'But shouldn't you all have been sent back to recuperate? After such a great shock?'

'We lost so many when we tried to take the salient. And then with the shelling and the c-cave-in.....No more m-men could be spared. All leave was c-cancelled.' His hands were shaking badly: he could not be far from a breakdown himself.

'Why am I telling you this?' he said wretchedly. 'You won't repeat it, will you? Don't know why I - '

'We all need to let down our guard some time.'

'Yes, but a fellow can't lose control, you know. After all, you're doing your bit.' He looked admiringly at her uniform. 'Dispatch rider - and *you're* just a woman.'

She decided to let that pass.

He put his hand out across the table. 'You don't despise me, do you?'

She took his hand and pressed it, watching the torment ease a little. 'I think you're all frightfully brave. And, look, you shouldn't blame yourself for things that are outside your control, really you shouldn't.'

'Chin up, eh?' He managed a half smile.

'That's the ticket.' She scratched around for a less painful subject and ended up telling him about the ti-tree oil treatments, the mouldy bread, marigolds and crushed garlic at the field station, in such a way that she soon had him laughing. At that she rose to fetch her greatcoat. 'Look after yourself, won't you?'

'G-going so soon?'

'I must. Dispatches, you know. But I've enjoyed talking to you. Thanks for the coffee - and everything. See you again some time.'

'DV,' he said, returning to contemplation of his damaged hands.

'DV,' she said softly.

As she rode out of town there was a huge explosion to her left: the brief lull had come to an end. She hoped Lieutenant Duncan wouldn't have to go back to the killing too soon.

All along the lines, only a few miles behind her, the guns barked out their death-dealing blows. She could recognise most of the bombs and shells now: Jack Johnson's, with their great clouds of black smoke and huge craters; canisters that sounded like the day of judgement and scattered maiming shards of scrap metal through the dug-outs; trench-mortars and Stokes mortar guns that could put four or five mortar shells in the air at once. The men called them Lloyd George's shells, convinced that his arrival at the Ministry of Munitions was responsible for the improvement in the calibre of the armaments being sent out to the front. She must remember to tell Max that, she thought. Her stomach lurched. He'd probably be waiting for her when she got back to Etaples.

20

The boat had been delayed by its zig-zagging journey across the channel, and the train for Etaples had already departed by the time they docked. His business at the local military HQ was soon dispatched, along with his heavier luggage, and he returned to the station with just a light case, only to be held up again for hospital trains steaming up from the front. It was late when they came within sight of the silvered waters of the Canche.

It was a quiet day in Etaples. For once the Square was not blocked with military vehicles. According to the porters it was a quiet day at the front too, as no guns could be heard. They still experienced strong ground tremors, vibrating up through his shoes, evidence that the death-dealers further along had not fallen completely silent.

He found a car to carry him up from the station, but the driver professed ignorance of the different canteens and dropped him off just short of the tented encampment of hospitals. In every direction as far as the eye could see were wooden huts and large tents haphazardly sited among the pines. Ambulances and staff cars wove their way up and down the sandy tracks; nurses in white, grey and navy, soldiers, orderlies and messengers in khaki, hurried back and forth between the temporary buildings. Looking for one woman amongst these seething masses would, Max felt, be an impossible task.

Over to his left a church service was taking place in a large marquee: he'd quite forgotten it was Sunday. From behind the canvas walls, eerily muted, came the strains of a hymn.

The Day Thou Gavest, Lord, is Ended. The hymn was fast becoming a requiem for the lost: did no one ever sing anything else? The mournful chords sent shivers up his spine. He picked up his case, turned his back on the church and made his way towards the largest of the hospital tents. The sandy track twisted and turned between stands of pines, and brought him out at the back of the tent, where two large ambulances had drawn up to take on coffins. As the orderlies heaved the last ones on board, and draped the flags, the two female drivers stubbed out their cigarettes in the mud and climbed wearily on board. He caught them in time and asked for directions.

'British Soldiers' Canteen?' said a perky little red-head, smiling down at him. 'Which one's that? Y.M.C.A.? Sally Army? Young Christians? Angelina's?'

The first three seemed unlikely, bearing in mind Sylvia's scathing views on religion, so he decided to start with the other.

'I can give you a lift,' she said, patting the passenger seat. 'It's on our way to the cemetery.'

Max declined hastily, declaring that the walk would do him good. It was a foolish decision, given that the brief hours of sunshine which had warmed him through the middle of the day had vanished, and that grey clouds were scurrying across the sky like a grubby blanket, accelerating the fading of the light. He stood a moment watching the ambulances out of sight, mocking himself for his superstition.

'That's eight more telegrams,' muttered the orderly, fastening up the flap again. 'Eight more poor buggers gone west.'

Eight more bereaved families. As Max picked up his bag and took the fork that led away from the hospital tents, following the directions to Angelina's, he thought of the heartbreak in store for those eight families. Never again would they see the telegram boy cycle up the road without reliving the anguish. At least I've been given a second chance at life, he thought. Who knows, maybe even a second chance with Sylvia.

The canteen turned out to be a large hut, or series of huts, in a clearing in the woods. He arrived just as the light was failing, to find the buffet heaving at the seams. Making his way through lines of mud-streaked men he could see no sign of Sylvia and it was some time before he could attract any attention from the three women behind the counter, frantically buttering bread and frying up eggs.

'Sylvia?' said Pearl, wiping the back of her hand wearily across her forehead. 'No idea where she is at the moment, but she's generally back here on a Sunday for a bath and clean clothes. If you want to wait, put your case down over there. I'll fetch you a cup of tea across when it's a bit quieter. Unless...?' She gestured towards the surging lines of exhausted men, all 'gasping for a cuppa an' a couple o' Woodbines, missus' in a variety of accents.

'Point me to the teapot,' he said, taking the hint. 'I think even I can manage that.'

And manage it he did, until the counter was briefly empty and the buffet and the adjoining rooms full of cigarette smoke and the buzz of contented conversation.

But each time the canteen emptied, another detachment would march in from the darkness, muddied and tired, to be fed and watered. Still there was no sign of Sylvia.

Relieving him of the heavy teapot at last, Pearl thrust a plateful of sandwiches at him. As he took his cup and plate across to one of the benches, he heard her ask one of the other women what duty Miss Summers was on that week?

Sylvia Summers, he thought. He'd lay odds on that being her mother's maiden name. Why the devil hadn't they thought of that?

'Still standing in for the dispatch riders, last I heard.' Max schooled his face not to react, but his mind was already visualising the dangers. Accidents, enemy fire, capture. The Germans had executed Edith Cavell, and she was only a nurse. There were other, equally terrible stories of German atrocities....

'Spotted fever went through 'em all like a knife through butter. But there was a new batch of dispatch riders out from Blighty last week, and they must be trained up by now. Angela was expecting her back this week.'

'She'll find canteen life a wee bit boring after all that excitement, I'll be bound.'

When there was a lull, Pearl led him to Sylvia's sleeping compartment. 'Leave your kit here. It'll keep it from getting underfoot. Her fleabag's cold,' she said, looking around, 'and all her spares are gone. She's not been in for a while, I'd say.'

He waited in the canteen until the last of the leave embarkations had gone. 'It's getting very late,' said Pearl. 'She may not make it back tonight. Perhaps you should find yourself a bed in Eetap?' He could see she was bursting to ask what his connection was with Sylvia, but he was not eager to enlighten her.

'I've come this far. If I leave now, I might miss her.'

'Better stay then. You might as well bunk down in her bed. Doesn't look as though she'll be wanting it tonight after all.'

He could imagine what Sylvia would say to such presumption and he wasn't going to give her the chance to berate him in public. He stretched out on one of benches, with a blanket thrown over him. It wasn't at all comfortable and he was wakened from time to time by all the comings and goings - first a couple of Red Cross drivers, then a French gendarme, then a colonel of the Scots Greys who unfortunately knew him. They exchanged a few words and he saw eyebrows raised all round at his name and title.

Feeling unable to answer their curiosity until he'd spoken to Sylvia, he went outside for some fresh air. There, outside the canteen, was a double-decker bus with its lights dimmed, and *Kensington High Street* writ large on its front destination box.

He blinked and rubbed his eyes. When he looked again it was drawing away, soon lost to sight in the misty night.

'Did I imagine that?' he asked. 'Could have sworn it was a London bus!'

'It *was* a London bus,' said a voice at his elbow, from a man propping a bicycle against the canteen wall. 'They use 'em to take men on leave from the trenches to the coast for embarkation. And back again too. Frees up the trains to take supplies and ammo to the front. The other day I looked out and it was a Harrods' removal van!'

He was woken again in the early hours. In the canteen someone was sharing news in what they fondly imagined to be a subdued whisper. 'She took her bus over the edge, they say...Fully loaded. All her patients killed. New ambulance driver, probably never driven at night. And one of their dispatch rider stand-ins has failed to report in too. Maybe she went over with it....' Max's back had grown stiff on the bench and by the time he found his feet, the informant had gone, leaving behind the smell of vehicle exhaust hanging on the damp pre-dawn air.

'Sorry you heard that,' said Pearl, hurriedly closing the door. 'Clem likes a bit of drama to cheer up his miserable existence. But don't worry: dispatch riders are often late reporting in; they're a law unto themselves. We don't know it was Sylvia.'

'He said 'she'. How many female dispatch riders are there?'

Pearl bit her lip and her silence was his answer.

'Look, we'll know soon enough,' she said at last, 'so stop your fretting. Why don't you catch a few hours sleep on the bed? We'll call you if there's any more news.'

If he returned to the bench he'd be fit for nothing by morning, so for the few remaining hours he stretched out on Sylvia's bed. He imagined he could still smell her perfume on the pillow. June Roses, that was it. He drew the sleeping bag closer around him, curling his body up in complete misery. What if he'd left it too late? What if he never saw her again, never got the chance to put things right between them?

Just before the dawn, as he was drifting in and out of sleep, he heard the sound of voices. Dragging his jacket on he hurried through the restrooms to the buffet. In the half-light he could just make out a woman in a dressing gown, leaning over the sink, washing her hair. 'We had to turn the bath house into a bake house,' she was saying, her voice muffled. 'Just can't get enough bread, so we've had to start baking it ourselves.'

'I hadn't realised I'd been away so long,' said a voice from the shadows, and his heart lurched. 'Don't use all the hot water. I could do with some myself. God knows when I last washed my hair.'

He leaned back against the wall, relief at the sound of Sylvia's voice making him feel quite weak. Outside the canteen another double-decker disgorged its weary cargo.

'More customers,' he said softly. 'Your hair will have to stay unwashed a little longer, Sylvia.'

She turned to him, face white. Her leather motorbike helmet was half on and half off and the beautiful curls he loved to run his fingers through had all been cut off.

He couldn't move. This was the moment he had wanted for so long, ever since the dreadful day when he'd come home from the office and found her gone. He'd visualised it all so differently, imagining himself sweeping her up into his arms, showering her with kisses, and promising her all that her heart desired. Instead he found himself in a cold canteen kitchen, with the smell of yesterday's fried bacon lingering on the air, regarded with intense interest by several pairs of eyes.

All he could think of to say was: 'You've cut off your beautiful hair.'

She shrugged. 'I had no choice. It was lousy.'

The woman at the sink winced. 'Won't you introduce us, Sylvia?' she said, gathering her wet hair into a towel.

'This is Sir Max Bryson,' said Sylvia. 'Max, Lady Angela Forbes. She runs the British Soldiers' Buffets, here and in Boulogne. Pearl Stone - '

'We've already met.'

'Gertie Major, and Estelle and Alphonsine Picard.'

He made a brief bow towards the group of women.

'You're attached to the War Office, I suppose,' said Lady Angela. 'Have you come to close us down?'

'Max is here on - other business,' said Sylvia, when Max didn't answer.

'Then let us go into my office.' Accustomed to taking charge of a situation Lady Angela was halfway out of the door when Sylvia interrupted.

'Thank you, Lady Angela, but I'll take Max to my room. We need to talk.'

'To your room, indeed.' Lady Angela smiled archly. 'I'm not really sure that I ought to permit - '

'I don't need anyone's permission. Did I not say? Max and I were married.'

Were married, thought Max. Not *are*. But he let himself be led back to the room where he'd been sleeping.

Sylvia closed the door in the interested faces and gripped Max's hands. 'You got my letters.'

He wanted to take her in his arms and hold her close to him, but he hadn't the right. After a moment he regained his self-control. 'And came straight away, as you requested.'

'You'll do all you can for Jake, won't you?'

'Of course.' His voice roughened. 'Did you doubt it?'

'No.'

'I'll do my best for him, but I can make no promises. Army law is a thing apart.' She became aware that she was still holding onto his hands. Colouring, she dropped her hold and crossed to the window.

Dawn was just breaking, spilling silver light over the pines, catching the edges of the previous season's pine-cones and reminding her heart-breakingly of Christmas trees. Then the pounding and shaking began again as the guns to the east opened up, and all thought of home and Christmas trees was driven from her mind.

'And when this is all over,' said Max softly, 'you propose to slip away again?'

Silence.

'Ah. I perceive you require notice of that question.' She looked hurt. 'Forgive the tactlessness of a mere man,' he said in a brittle voice. 'Let us return to the matter at hand.'

Succinctly she gave him all the information she had picked up from the young lieutenant. 'He'll be hurt when he discovers I used him, but I can't help that. Jake's life is more important than Duncan's feelings.'

'And Jake himself?'

'I don't know. The lieutenant says he's been ill. I tried to get in to see him, but I never got near the barracks. The colonel had me turned off the camp.'

'It will be interesting to see his face when you turn up again as my assistant.'

'I don't know how we'll get there. I have to give the motorbike back.'

'No you don't. I've just requisitioned it.' He waved the sheaf of letters. 'Courtesy of LG - who sends his good wishes, by the way. So - room for a pillion passenger?'

21

It was the oddest sensation, speeding across the hinterland on the back of Sylvia's motorcycle. He had to hold on tight, his hands clamped tightly about her waist, his body curved into her back, but there was not the resistance that he'd expected. As for himself, if he had thought himself resigned to his wife's loss, his body soon put him right. There had been neither time nor water for her to bathe and there was an earthy, musky smell about her that excited him almost as much as June Roses had done. He could only hope she remained ignorant of his arousal through the thick layers of uniform she was wearing.

The Bull-Ring was covered with spring grass, wiry enough to resist even the attempts of the British soldiers to push it back through the muddy earth with their endlessly tramping feet. Early spring flowers peeped through here and there and the water-filled dikes were beginning to drain. The green buds on the trees had burst into pale leaf and their verdure softened winter's harsh landscape.

Speech was impossible with the wind rushing past your ears and snatching the words out of your mouth, but when they stopped for a belated breakfast in a small French town - its ruined church and shell-damaged cottages evidence that it had once formed part of the disputed front line - they took the chance to catch up.

She was glad to hear that Lady Alicia and the children were safely settled into the Dower House, even though Imogen's threatened return had proved no more reliable than previous announcements, but there was little leisure for domestic news.

'Do you think you'll be able to obtain Jake's release?' she asked, tucking in heartily to omelette and fried potatoes.

'I don't know,' he said truthfully. 'If he's been as ill as your lieutenant says, then it should be possible...but if he's that bad, I can't see how they could put him on trial in the first place. And if there are two of them, that could complicate matters even further. We'll just have to wait and see.'

'What will happen to him - to them - if we can't get them released?'

'You know that already. The army will take them out to the abattoir at Mazingarbe at first light...and shoot them.'

She disappeared into the garden at the back of the inn and when she returned he was searching through the panniers, which had been attached over the wheels of the motorbike. 'I dread to think what state my papers will be in when I dig them out,' he said, looking in exasperation at the canvas bags, into which everything had been so hastily stuffed. 'Not to mention my shirts.'

'Someone will press them for you,' she said. 'Plenty of service wherever we stay. War has put an end to any other occupation for these poor people.' She thrust a bunch of flowers into his hands and pulled the helmet on over her curls, conscious of his scrutiny, hoping that he wouldn't say anything more about her hair. It still shocked her every time she caught sight of herself in a mirror. 'Besides, you don't want to turn up looking too neat and clean. The Army despises anyone from Blighty who looks as though they've just stepped out of a bandbox.' She climbed onto the bike and kicked it into life. Over her shoulder she said: 'I hope you've brought your medal.'

'What?'

'The medal the king gave you, and your wound ribbon. With them on your jacket you'll carry more weight with the top brass.'

'In with the rest of my luggage.' He looked at the flowers, bemused. 'I phoned ahead and it's being sent on. Along with my stick.'

'You seem to manage perfectly well without it.'

'I do. But I thought it would add to my *gravitas*.'

Her reply was lost in the roar of the engine and they were off once more, hurtling down the road.

On the crest of a gentle slope above the little town they stopped, close to where the side of the road had been scoured away by tyre tracks.

'This is where the ambulance went over?'

'You knew about that?'

'Someone called Clem came to tell Pearl.' His face grew pale as he recalled the shock of that moment. 'He seemed to think you might have gone over with it.'

'We stopped to see if we could help. Me and another dispatch rider from further north. But there was nothing anyone could do. Poor girl. She'd only been out here one day.'

She walked out to the tyre tracks. After a moment's silence she tossed the flowers one by one over the edge, to where the remains of a shattered vehicle lay on the valley floor.

When she came back to his side there were tears in her eyes, and his hand went out to her. For a moment they stood there, together and yet apart.

'The regular drivers *said* this would happen,' she said angrily. 'There wasn't a big push on: they could have let her drive around for a few days to get her bearings. But they sent her out at night, with no lights, the minute she arrived. She'd probably never driven further than the local market town, and that only in the daytime. This war is being run by *fools!*'

He wanted to comfort her, but she turned away. With an angry sob she pushed past him and picked up the bike. The minute he was on board she pulled her goggles down and set the bike at the road without a backward glance.

22

The barred door clanged shut behind Max, but the small hunched figure at the window didn't stir.

Jake, more alert, stood up smartly and saluted the escort. His eyes moved on to Max and remained fixed there. 'You came,' he breathed. His dark brown eyes glistened with unshed tears. 'She said you'd come, did your lady. I never thought you'd spare the time, but her message said you'd come. *He'll be here, Jake, come hell or high water.*'

'Of course I came.' Max shook his hand firmly. He took in the bare room with its barred windows and two low wire beds. 'I'm sorry to see you in this situation, Jake.'

'Not half as sorry as I am, sir.' Jake's brief smile disappeared as swiftly as it had come. He struck his forehead with his fist. 'Oh, God, how's Lil going to take all this? She were that thrilled about the recommendation, and now this....'

'What recommendation?'

Jake didn't answer. At the mention of Lily, his mind seemed to have drifted off into another world.

'Jake were put up fer a medal,' said the little man in the corner, turning away from the window, where he'd been feeding left over bread crumbs to the birds through the bars. He was smaller even than Jake, and hardly looked old enough to have left his mother. For a brief moment the lad's simple face shone. 'Jake was a hero. They said so. When we was still with our old crowd he saved the sergeant from drownding in a J.J.' He smiled at the blank look on Max's face. 'Thass a Jack Johnson,' he explained. 'A gurt great shell-hole.'

'Good Lord!' Till now the junior officer, who had been put at Max's service, somewhat against his will, had looked almost as glum as the prisoners. 'Never heard about that. But I suppose I could check up on it.'

It didn't take Max long to question the prisoners, not that there was much to be got from Tommy Shepherd, surely the smallest Bantam soldier ever enlisted, and the most unlikely. Within half an hour Max was back out in the fresh air once more, breathing deeply.

He turned to the young officer. 'I want you to find out about their service with their previous unit. Everything there is to know. I'll be pursuing that at the hearing. I assume you'll be in attendance?'

'Yes.' Another glum look. 'But, dammit, sir, this isn't what I volunteered for. I didn't expect to come out to this.'

'Your first commission?'

'Yes. But God knows I came out to fight the Hun, not shoot poor souls like them.'

'No one's going to shoot them if I have anything to do with it.' The young man seemed to be irredeemably sunk in his gloom and made no move. 'Come along, what are you waiting for?' snapped Max. 'Brace up, man! I've given you something useful that you can do. Get on with it.'

'Yessir.' He drew himself erect, responding instinctively to the voice of command.

'I'd appreciate that information as soon as possible. Oh, and chase up the notes of the original Field Court Martial. I want them in my rooms as soon as they turn up, even if it's gone midnight. Understood?'

'Understood, sir.'

'If you meet any resistance, let me know.'

23

As the light faded Max made his way along the muddy track back to the town, following Sylvia's directions. His hands in his pockets - for the wind had grown chill - he walked along deep in thought, teasing at the few facts that he knew about the case, worrying at them to find a way out for the two men. And at the back of his mind, for he was only human, he wondered how he and Sylvia were going to manage to rub along together for the duration of the hearing.

At the hotel recommended by Lady Angela, where Sylvia had arranged to meet him, all the rooms had already been taken by Generals and their associated officers, in town to argue the direction of the next proposed advance. In the dining room two junior officers were hotly debating the various options, while a languid captain tested out his charms on a young French waitress.

Max tapped the captain on the shoulder, stepping between him and the young woman as he turned to see who was accosting him. 'Do you think that's appropriate behaviour from your subordinates?' said Max softly, nodding to the two young men, whose voices were growing louder as they embarked on yet another bottle of wine.

The Captain bristled. 'And who are you, sir?' he demanded haughtily.

'Bryson. Special Delegation. And a patriot.' He nodded to the waiters hurrying in and out with wine, coffee and meals for the various tables, and the porter lounging in the doorway. 'Let us hope they are patriots too...and that they don't have a German cousin a couple of miles down the road...'

He left while the captain was still looking for a cutting reply.

Due to the forthcoming conference, added to the recent influx of officers from England, and their desire for comfortable billets while they awaited their posting, there were no rooms available at any of the central hotels, set around the two squares at the heart of Arras. As Max followed Sylvia's trail from one establishment to the next he was becoming aware that the chances of two rooms in the same establishment were slim.

The best that Sylvia had been able to find was a fair-sized L-shaped corner room above an *estaminet,* just off the central square, with two windows and a large walnut table which took up most of one wall. When Max arrived the landlady was supervising the stacking of his boxes, which had been forwarded with his luggage from the army camp. Only Lloyd George's requisitions and orders had saved them from being caught up in the general backlog of deliveries.

The room was large and airy, with the vast table, an equally vast double bed and a shiny leather couch by the screen in front of the dressing alcove. He wondered how much that couch had influenced Sylvia's acceptance of the room, but forbore to comment.

Sylvia had taken advantage of his absence to take the long-awaited bath. She was in her shirt-sleeves in front of the fire, kneeling on the threadbare carpet while she fluffed up her damp hair. There was a lingering perfume of lavender soap.

'This will do us very well,' he said to the beaming landlady. 'We shall be working late this evening, so we'll take our dinner up here, on trays. And coffee. Lots of coffee.'

'There's not much time to get our case together,' he said, loosening his neck-tie and collar as the landlady departed. 'Thank God for Mrs Cunningham.'

'What on earth has Mrs Cunningham to do with it?' demanded Sylvia, rising to her feet and buttoning up the cuffs of her khaki shirt.

He'd forgotten how splendid she looked in khaki. It brought out the depth of colour in her green-brown eyes, jauntily framed by the cropped curls, to which he was gradually becoming resigned. He realised he was staring, and dragged his gaze away. 'Her late husband was a general. She dug out his training books, so I was able to do a deal of preliminary work while I was waiting for my official papers and passes.'

He drew two heavy tomes out of his box. 'These have been my bedtime reading since I first received your letter. Quite an eye-opener, I must say. I've managed to establish - ' His voice died away as the room shook with the percussion of a large shell to their rear. He gripped the table. 'Dear God, does that go on all the time?'

'You get used to it,' she said with a pale smile. 'If you know you're out of range, that is. Sometimes you even stop hearing it unless there's a particularly large impact. Do you want me to take this down?'

He nodded, watching her settle at the table, straightening papers and unscrewing the cap of her pen.

'Notes, or verbatim?'

'Notes. Ready?' He started to pace up and down, pausing only occasionally to glance at the book on the table, or to turn a page. 'In the Clode report, published in 1869, the author found not a single case of capital punishment for desertion or cowardice since 1803.'

'Nothing since 1803.'

'That is, much of the Napoleonic Wars, all through the Crimean War and all the Colonial wars. And that doesn't change, up to the end of the century. Sentences range from a few months' imprisonment to ten years' penal servitude. For cowardice, again, ten years' penal servitude, but this was often commuted to a lesser period.'

'What about the Boer War?'

'While Lord Roberts was in command, that is 1899 and 1900, still no executions. Even under Kitchener - and he has an unrivalled reputation for brutality and ruthlessness - there were only two death sentences in 1901, and one of them was for murder. Then in 1902 two Colonial officers were executed for reprisal killings of Boer prisoners. Most sentences for desertion, cowardice, sleeping on post, even one for murder, were commuted to short terms of imprisonment. So - barely a single execution for what Jake's accused of, in over one hundred years.'

'Lieutenant Duncan, the one who acted as prisoner's friend at the court martial, said they had to make an example. I asked him, why now, after so long?'

'All the people who didn't volunteer in the last two years, for whatever reason - career, family, politics, religion - will be forced into the army now the government's decided on conscription. Conscripts may lack the enthusiasm of the earlier volunteers, so there's a need to show them something they fear even more than facing the enemy.'

'My God. If I didn't already think that war was hell...'

'Quite so.'

Once Max was absorbed in his work, he ceased to notice the passage of time, and Sylvia found herself swept along, following up a connection here, chasing down a precedent there. Her ink-stained fingers ached with all the writing, but she wasn't going to ask him to slow down. He would be accustomed to the best clerks, at his chambers and at the Ministry, and she wasn't going to let the side down by failing to come up to scratch. Besides, it was the only way that she could help Jake and Lily.

Only the arrival of the landlady's buxom and bold-eyed daughter with a laden tray forced a halt. They stopped briefly for dinner, once more the ubiquitous omelettes and fried potatoes, but this time with a good soup before and an excellent fruit pie to follow.

As soon as the girl had set the coffee pot on the table Max returned to the books and papers, picking out instances which might help their case: two officers charged early in the present war with surrendering a sound position to the enemy without due cause, who had merely been cashiered; two death sentences on privates during the retreat from Mons which had been commuted to two years' imprisonment 'in recognition of previous soldierly bearing under severe hardship'. Late into the night they picked sections out of the official records and the Manual of Military Law, and Sylvia dutifully noted and annotated them. He was pleased to see, looking over her shoulder, that she took clear and concise notes, quite speedily.

'I never thought all those boring hours in Miss Canning's office would bear fruit in quite this way,' she said, leaning back in her chair and rubbing her eyes. She opened her eyes to find him leaning over the back of his chair, regarding her closely. 'What is it?'

'Nothing.' He ran his fingertip across her cheek and lightly flicked her nose. 'You've got ink all over your face.' Outside a bugle sounded and the street filled with the tramp of marching boots. He flung himself down into the easy chair with a sigh. 'Nearly midnight. Why don't you go and change for bed? I'll order more coffee.'

'Aren't you going to - I mean...'

'Eventually. But I've got some more thinking to do, and that's best done in silence.' He stood up and shrugged himself back into his jacket. 'I'll fetch us up some brandy.'

He could have rung the bell for brandy, but she realised that he was giving her some privacy. Once more he was showing good manners in an awkward situation. She wasn't sure, under the circumstances, whether she appreciated that or not.

There was a washstand behind the screen in the corner and it didn't take her long to wash and clean her teeth. By the time she heard Max's footsteps on the landing she'd already struggled into the voluminous flannelette night-dress she'd been forced to borrow. She was accustomed to sleeping in her underclothes - or, rather, the men's combinations she now wore for underclothes - with her uniform close at hand for a midnight shout. She'd lost track of the pyjamas she'd brought with her to France, but then her plans had not included sharing a room with her former husband.

As the door opened she suddenly felt very vulnerable, in spite of the acres of flannelette. She grabbed one of the quilts off the bed and drew it around her shoulders.

Max appeared in the doorway laden with a bottle of brandy, glasses, coffee pot and a spirit stove. 'It will save disturbing the night porter. I have a feeling this night is going to require a great deal of coffee.'

She wondered whether he was referring to the work or the situation, and decided she was not going to ask. She perched on the leather couch, drawing the quilt around her, looking across at the comfortable bed with its pile of snowy quilts. If only...

But what could she say? 'Look, Max, things have changed. I've talked it through with a doctor and I think I've come to terms with what happened. Maybe I'm not so scared any more. Are you willing to give it a try?' It was out of the question. It was neither the time nor the place. Tonight there were far more important concerns.

Max's voice broke into her thoughts. 'Will you have some?'

'Coffee? No, thank you.'

'Damn. I forgot. You're a tea drinker. I should have asked - '

'There's no point. They make tea like dishwater, and it's always lukewarm. I'll have a brandy.'

He brought it across to her, stopping in front of the couch and looking down at her with a baffled expression in his eyes.

'I'm not expecting you to be noble,' she said swiftly. 'Your back must be troubling you after that bike ride: besides, you need a good night's sleep. You get the bed.'

'It's not that. I just - ' He stopped, for once in his life quite unable to find the words to say what he wanted to say, without causing offence or a lasting breach.

'You're vital to this exercise,' said Sylvia, with a sleepy smile. 'I'm just a hanger-on. I'll take the couch.'

'There's really no need. It's a large bed and - '

'I wouldn't want to disturb you.'

He'd gone as far as he could; it just wasn't the right moment. He poured himself another brandy and paced the room with the notes in his hands, deep in thought once more.

When she'd finished the brandy, he came across to take the glass. Seeing the couch properly for the first time, he could barely suppress a grin. It was a sturdy piece of furniture, covered in highly polished leather, broad and long enough for a bed, but so overstuffed that it rose to a high curve in the centre. Hard enough to sit on, let alone sleep on, he thought. Ah well, we shall see.

He was along the corridor in the bathroom when the dispatch rider arrived just after midnight with the records of the Field Court Martial. Unfortunately it was a rider Sylvia knew from her recent service.

'You clerking for this lawyer bloke, then, Miss Summers?' said the dispatch rider, when Sylvia opened the door, shrouded in the quilt. 'Turn up for the books, that. I thought you'd gone back to Eetapp.' He looked over her shoulder into the room. 'Coo. Bit embarrassing, this, isn't it? Can't you put in for a male clerk to take your place?'

'Not really,' said Sylvia, gathering her quilt and her dignity about her with equal difficulty. 'The lawyer bloke is my husband.'

Max returned then, and she wondered how much he'd overheard. Ernie was an inveterate gossip: news of her altered status would be around the base camps in a flash, if Lady Angela hadn't got there first.

Max promptly buried himself in the papers, dismissing all offers of assistance. Discarding jacket, waistcoat and shoes, he spent the next hour pacing up and down in his stockinged feet reading the court-martial records.

She'd thought it would be impossible to fall asleep with someone else awake in the room, but she must have done so, for the next thing she knew was a strong and alarming sensation of falling, which ended only when she landed with a bump in a heap of bedclothes on the floor.

'What the devil ? Who...?'

Then it all came back to her. Max, in shirtsleeves and braces, was looking down at her, the initial concern on his face belied by a malicious spark of laughter in his grey eyes.

'Goodness! Energetic dreams,' she said, shaking off his helping hand. She picked herself up with as much dignity as she could manage under the circumstances, and deposited herself and her quilt back on the couch.

She wriggled about, trying in vain to find some sort of purchase on the shiny curved surface. 'Have you made much progress with the court papers?' she asked, turning at last on her stomach.

'No. In the end, they were a waste of time.' He yawned hugely. 'They told me nothing new, just confirmed the total incompetence of the system...if it needed confirming.'

'You should sleep.' She'd almost said, you should come to bed. She flushed, and shifted uncomfortably.

'You're right. I'll turn in soon. I can read these notes again in the morning.'

She fell asleep again long before he turned the light out. She dreamed that she was flying through the night on her motorcycle, with Archie Nash on the pillion behind her. Then Doctor Delahaye stepped out into the road in front of her, and she tried to come to a halt, swerving around the doctor, losing control of the motorcycle, which soared out over the hillside....

She landed with a thump, swearing beneath her breath. Someone was shining a light in her face.

Max tried to help her up off the floor, but they both became entangled in the quilt. 'Dammit, stop fighting me,' he said in some exasperation. 'I'm only trying to help you up.' She blinked owlishly up at the tall figure bending over her, clad in a pair of elegant maroon silk pyjamas. 'In case you're as bemused as you were before, you're in the *estaminet*. You are on the couch, or rather, *off* it, keeping us both awake.' He crossed the room and pulled back the quilts. 'I'm in this bed,' he said, climbing back in. 'It's a very large bed. Very comfortable. Unlike that damned couch. We could both get some sleep if you would come and use it.'

The figure on the floor stopped struggling and went very still.

'I'm very tired,' he went on. 'And I have far too many important matters on my mind to...to worry about anything else.'

There was a long pause, then a shuffling, and he felt the mattress dip as she climbed in on the other side. The light went out, and then there was silence.

'Good night, Sylvia,' he said. 'I'll see you in the morning.'

24

When she entered the public rooms next morning after a hasty toilette, Max was already there, at a table in the window, tucking into a large plate of grilled ham. The hum of conversation died for a moment as the others in the restaurant, mostly officers from the nearby camp, looked around to inspect the latest arrival. Some, recognising her, half-stood, bowed and then put their heads a little closer together for a muttered conversation. Others, seeing only the uniform, didn't stir until they saw Max rise to hold out her chair for her.

'You've confused them,' he said with a grin. 'They always rely on the skirts to tell them when to get up.'

'Then I don't know how they're going to manage when the war ends,' she said crisply. 'If ever it does.'

'You intend to keep your trousers, then?'

'Certainly when I'm working...though how long that will be, I don't know. I've a feeling that when the soldiers come back - if there are any left to come back - we women will be put out of our posts before you can say knife.'

She turned up her nose at the offer of ham, and ordered hot chocolate and croissants. She was relieved when Max passed her the report to read: she felt awkward in his presence this morning. Waking in the night she found she'd huddled her body close against his in sleep, curled into his back. She had rolled away, hot with embarrassment, hoping against hope that he had slept through it all.

It was only a short stroll to the hotel in the next square, where the court-martial had been convened the previous month, and where they were summoned to appear at half past ten. A military aide came to carry their papers and books down the road, but Max declined the offer of transport.

'I have no intention of sitting here twiddling my thumbs and waiting on the army's pleasure,' he said, adjusting his necktie while Sylvia scurried round collecting up pens, pencils and notebooks. 'We shall arrive at a time of our own choosing.' There was a light in his eyes which she remembered from the time he had taken on Pip's case. Max Bryson was back in his proper milieu and enjoying the challenge.

'I would offer you my arm,' he said to Sylvia as they stepped out into the fresh spring sunshine, 'but if an elderly colonel were to espy us from the rear....'

She spluttered with laughter. 'The temptation is irresistible.' Linking arms with him she noted with approval that he was wearing his wound ribbon and the medal he had been awarded by King George. He was using his stick, but hardly leaning on it at all. She told him it was an affectation.

'*Gravitas*, my dear Sylvia. *Gravitas*.'

They arrived after the officers, which she was quite sure was not by chance, and the ill-suppressed annoyance of the Colonel, Captain and four or five other officers waiting for them showed her precisely why he had done it. Not that his careless apology helped matters at all: laying his stick across the table which had been provided for his use he murmured something, rather mournfully, about forgetting how much longer even a short distance could seem nowadays. The Colonel, who was looking pointedly at his watch, and had been about to say something very sharp, was forced to swallow his words. It was all game-playing, and point-scoring, of course, and thus very petty, but it was nonetheless fascinating to watch an expert like Max at the game.

Colonel Powell, a red-faced individual whose elegant and well-pressed uniform could not disguise the fact that his head was too large for his short torso and squat legs, explained that he was here from HQ to see that everything went according to military rules. The three officers who had constituted the original Court Martial were here and Major Gawston, who had been in charge, would clarify any queries there might be. This morning there would be no prisoners present. 'It would hardly be conducive to military discipline, as I understand you are to question the authority of the Court Martial.'

'Not its authority, sir,' said Max, stretching his legs out before him with a grimace. 'Its competence.'

The Colonel began to make choking noises, and the Major intervened hastily. 'You will find, sir, that the FGCM was set up in accordance with all due procedures as laid down in the manual. My superiors are quite satisfied ...'

'I'm sure they are, Major. But you must bear with me as I endeavour to elucidate some clarification of the procedures followed last month, so that I may report back to *my* superiors.'

'You're on Lloyd George's staff?' barked the Colonel.

Max bowed. 'I have that honour. I am required by Government authority to review the evidence of the FGCM against Harrison and Shepherd. I would remind you all that you are on oath to give a true rendering of the evidence, and that charges may be levelled against anyone who does not do so.'

It was then that the Colonel's eyes fell on the clerk. Sylvia, not wishing to attract any attention, had slid quietly into her seat at the table. Head down, she was busy setting out the papers and making sure that everything was to hand.

'And this fellow you have brought with you? What regiment...?' Then, as Sylvia raised her head: 'Good God, it's a woman!'

From somewhere behind the Colonel came a burst of ironic laughter, quickly broken off as he turned to glare at the perpetrator.

Major Gawston rushed into speech. 'Sir Max, I really must object...A court-martial is no place for a lady. The things she must hear....'

'Major, the lady has been employed as an ambulance-driver and a dispatch-rider. She is more inured to the sights and sounds and horrors of war than I am.'

'But she is a woman!' growled the Colonel.

'I think we can all agree on that. But at the moment all that need concern the court is that she is here as my clerk.'

Thank you, Max. Was it too much to hope that you might have said 'my trusted clerk' or 'my efficient clerk'? But this had nothing to do with what was between her and Max, only with her function as the lowliest being in the courtroom. She would do well to bear that in mind.

In spite of his insistence that he was there only as an observer, the Colonel was on his feet again. 'She cannot possibly stay,' he protested. 'Absolutely out of the question.'

Max let him run on for a few more sentences, then he rose to his feet and held out his hand in a bored manner, not even looking at her.

'The Military Manual, if you please.' She picked up the tome and put it in his hands. 'Colonel, I read to you from the Manual of Military Law, 1914, with which you are, I am sure, familiar, and which we can all agree is the relevant authority for today's proceedings. I quote: *"The court can deliberate in private, and may either withdraw for the purpose or cause the court to be cleared; but at other times the court must be open to the public, military or otherwise, so far as the room or tent in which the court is held can receive them. It is not usual to place any restriction on the admission of reporters for the press - "* '

'The Press? Good God! That's all we need!' The Colonel looked as though he were about to burst a blood vessel.

'I don't think we need concern ourselves with reporters, colonel. As yet.' Max cast his eyes speakingly around the large public room. 'No problem with space for members of the public here, I think you'll agree. Major?'

Gawston shook his head.

'And you will also agree that no mention is made that all those members of the public must be male?'

Gawston nodded.

Someone muttered something about the fabric of civilisation collapsing, now that women got into everything. Sylvia looked up at Max. This would be a good moment to cut in, surely, and say something about the fabric of civilisation collapsing when a shell-shocked, brave little man who had overcome physical problems to fight for his country was threatened with a firing squad after a travesty of a trial...

But Max didn't take the bait.

'I'm sure we could provide you with a clerk if you need one,' said one of the captains, seizing the opportunity to pour oil on troubled waters and ingratiate himself with the colonel. 'Plenty of men outside who could - '

'I need *detailed* answers. *Detailed* notes.' Max's voice hardened as he picked up the cue he had been waiting for. He banged the papers down on the table in front of him. 'These notes were taken by an army man - I tell you, major, these notes are a disgrace. These notes are all but incomprehensible.'

A young second lieutenant stumbled to his feet. 'Sir, I did my best.'

'Of course you did.' Max's voice softened. 'You are not a trained clerk, and so no blame attaches to you. But is your best good enough when a man's life is at stake?'

'I know it isn't. But they didn't slow down enough for me to take the notes. Last time I had to do it they slowed down so I could write it all out...'

'I understand. I repeat, no blame attaches to you, lieutenant....?'

'Jessup, sir.'

'Ah, yes. Second Lieutenant Jessup.' He looked down at his notes. 'No, don't sit down, lieutenant. Perhaps you could clarify something for me. Is it customary to use a witness to take down court martial proceedings?'

'I wasn't called as a witness, sir.'

'Not...called...as a...witness?' said Max, measuring each word. 'Then we had better swear you in, young man, as you are certainly a witness now.' While the lieutenant took his oath on the Bible, Max made a show of consulting his notes. 'Now, although you say you were not called as a witness, yet you had had some dealings with both Jacob Harrison and Tommy Shepherd, had you not?'

'Yes, sir. They were in my unit.'

'In fact, you were the duty officer the day after the cave-in, were you not? The day after the trench was blown in.'

'Yes, sir.'

'Now, the day after the cave-in, you had occasion to give instructions to Harrison. Would you tell us in your own words what happened.'

'He couldn't stop shaking, sir. So Lieutenant Duncan and I agreed to send him to the rear.'

'You covered him with a blanket and told him off duty for the day? What was your authority for that?'

'Common sense. The man was shaking too much to hold a gun.'

'And Shepherd?'

'He wasn't there, sir. He'd been sent up-line to have his hand stitched.'

'I see. So one man was shaking too much to hold a gun, and the other had been sent away to have his injuries seen to.' He paced across the room, apparently deep in thought. 'Were you the officer in charge when the trench was blown in?'

'No, sir. That was Lieutenant Duncan.'

'No doubt we shall hear from him shortly.'

'No, sir. They sent him home.'

Max leaned forward on the table, his eyes wide in disbelief. 'Sent him on leave when he was a major witness in a legal hearing?' He turned his gaze on Major Gawston, who stared rigidly ahead, a tic in his cheek the only sign of his discomfort.

'You wouldn't have got any sense out of him, sir,' said Jessup. 'He was quite raving in the end. They've sent him to a special hospital.'

Max turned away from Jessup and walked across the room to the three who had formed the original court martial. 'I must beg your assistance, major. I want to be quite sure that I am under no misapprehension. The officer who saw the trench blow in and supervised the digging out has suffered a nervous collapse and been sent home for specialist hospital treatment?'

'That is correct.'

'But two of the men who were actually *buried* in the cave-in have been offered no special treatment, but instead put on trial for their lives?'

'You don't understand, sir,' said the older of the two captains. 'Duncan was raving...He was spouting Latin all the time and breaking up the *estaminet* - '

'So if Jacob Harrison had started raving, and spouting - let us say, Hindustani - then he too would have been sent back to England, to hospital?'

'Not up to me, sir. You'd have to ask the MO.'

'So if he had started raving, you would have sent him back to the Medical Officer. But because he suffered in silence, because he broke down quietly, you assumed he had no problems, and demanded of him that he return to duties.'

'He's not a sensitive man, sir, like the lieutenant.'

'I put it to you, Captain...?'

'Hartley, sir.'

'I put it to you, Captain Hartley, that it was more a case that you recognised the sensitivities of the lieutenant, who had been brought up as you have, educated as you have, trained in the same academies as you have. While someone like Jacob Harrison is assumed to have no sensitivities, simply because you don't recognise them.'

'I've always done my best for my men, sir. I resent your - '

'You can resent all you like, captain. No one is planning to take you out and shoot you.' He crossed back to his desk and picked up the Military Manual. 'Gentlemen, I crave your indulgence once more.' His eyes ran along the line. 'It is not entirely clear to me which of you is serving as judge-advocate, as set out in the Manual of Military Law...?'

The embarrassed silence was broken at last by Major Gawston. 'As the colonel has already informed you, sir, I am the President of the Field General Court Martial, with Captains Hartley and Smith in support.'

'Am I to conclude that none of you has the necessary legal training to constitute himself judge-advocate?'

Gawston licked his dry lips and cast a harassed glance at the colonel, but there was no help from that quarter. 'You are correct in your conclusions, sir.'

'You are telling me that two men were condemned to death at your Field Court Martial, Major Gawston, without benefit of *any* legal advice to either the panel of judges, the prosecution or the prisoner's friend? And yet to my certain knowledge the proportion of barristers and solicitors joining the colours is at least as high as in any other profession. Why did you not avail yourself of their assistance?'

'Dammit, sir, we could not go outside the regiment.' The colonel was on his feet once more. 'We have no wish to share our disgrace..... '

Max turned on the colonel, his face as white as the officer's was red. 'So you weighed regimental pride against a man's right to a fair trial, and you decided regimental pride was paramount.'

'All very well for you civilians to take offence, but matters are different out here!' said Major Gawston, coming to his superior's rescue. 'We have to abide by military law.'

Max's voice dropped to a dramatic whisper. 'But you didn't, did you, major? By your own admission you didn't.'

25

Sylvia watched Gawston drop back into his chair, seeming to shrink by the second. They wouldn't have any more trouble with him, she decided.

Max walked slowly back to the desk and picked up another bundle of papers, with Sylvia's hasty annotations on it. 'Now, Captain Smith, as I am unable to consult Lieutenant Duncan, or the adjutant who acted as prosecutor, who has, I understand, been sent up the line, I shall have to turn to you for the events leading up to the day in question. Is it in fact the case that Lieutenant Duncan went against your orders and *did* send both Harrison and Shepherd to the MO?'

'Yes, sir.' Captain Smith ran a finger round his collar. He too was beginning to sweat. 'They were both complaining of aches and pains, and so forth. The usual lead-swinging.'

'The usual lead-swinging.' Max turned on Sylvia. 'You have that?'

'Yes, indeed.' She smiled at the officer. 'I have Captain Smith's words verbatim.'

'According to records the Battalion Doctor could find nothing wrong with either man.' Smith was becoming aggressive. 'He prescribed a tonic and sent them back for duty.'

'A tonic for a man who had only a few days before been buried alive in a blown-in trench? Dear me. That seems rather inadequate, does it not?'

'How do I know?' growled Smith. 'I'm not a doctor.'

Max tapped the papers against his hand and said in an almost musing voice: 'When I was blown up in a trench, I was ordered several months' hospitalisation. I am most grateful that I was not in the tender care of your battalion doctor.' He turned away and paused for a moment, looking over Sylvia's shoulder. The captain, thinking himself off the hook, took out a large handkerchief and mopped his brow.

'Now,' said Max briskly, turning back to the top table, 'when the MO sent the two men back, what happened then?'

'I have no idea,' said Captain Smith through gritted teeth.

'Lieutenant Jessup?'

The young officer rose to his feet again. 'Lieutenant Duncan still couldn't see they were fit for duty, so he detailed them off to be padre's servants.'

'In order to take them out of the firing line?'

'Yes, sir.'

'We can assume that the man who saw them being buried alive had more notion of how it would have affected them than the rest of the officers.'

'Yes, sir.'

'So he sent them to the Padre - that is, the chaplain. What then?'

'Padre sent them straight back.'

'Ah, yes.' Once more he made a show of consulting his notes. 'Here's what the chaplain says: "Harrison in particular was shaking all over, stammering so much that I couldn't understand him. He wanted to sleep all the time. He was unsteady on his feet." ' He looked up. 'Habitual drunkard, was he?'

'No sir.' Jessup was indignant.

'In fact, he had a reputation for sobriety when he was made up to Lance-Corporal. I have seen it noted in the records.'

'He doesn't drink at all, sir. Not that he would have the money for drinking anyway. He makes an almost total allocation of his wages to his wife and child.'

'Quite so, lieutenant. I'm glad your impression of Jacob Harrison matches with mine. I did not think the man could have changed so completely in the six months since last I saw him.'

Even the Colonel sat up at that.

'Now, Major,' Max went on smoothly. 'We have heard the reasons why the lieutenant is not here to help us in our enquiries today. With hindsight, given his problems, was Duncan the right man to be entrusted, as prisoner's friend, with the lives of two men facing a court martial?'

'What choice had we?' said the major irritably. 'Jessup had only just joined us. Duncan was the only one who knew them.'

'Ah.' He crossed the room, seemingly sunk in thought, and stopped in the shaft of sunlight that came through the window. 'He was the only one who knew them....'

The Major realised what he had said. 'Well, when I say he was - '

Max turned to him, a smile on his face. 'Thank you, Major. I think we have established that point. Lieutenant Duncan was the only one who knew them. Which makes sense of the fact that he tried twice to send them back up the line after their shocking experience. And twice was effectively overruled, first by the MO then by the padre. Did the padre give evidence on the men's behalf, by the way? Evidence of the - er - shakiness, stammering and confusion?'

'No. He wasn't called.'

'Dear me. He was, presumably, ready to do his duty by the condemned men and attend them on the night before they were to be executed, but he wasn't prepared to come to the trial?'

'He wasn't called. He - '

'I think we have established that, for whatever reasons, not in any way clear to me, the padre wasn't called,' said Max, interrupting the major. 'Now I'd like to move on. I'd like to ask you about these documents which were sent on to the higher authorities, with the recommendations for mercy.'

Behind him, Sylvia cleared her throat. When he turned, she pointed to her wrist.

'My clerk has pointed out to me that we have already reached the point in time which marks the end of the original court-martial.' He sat down on his chair, his long legs stretched out before him. He steepled his fingers beneath his chin. 'I think you will agree with me, gentlemen, that we have barely begun to establish the characters of these unfortunate men, let alone discuss the events of the day which were the cause of their appearance before you. And yet we have already taken up the time in which the original hearing concluded that it had reason - good reason - to condemn these two men to death by firing squad. Dear me.'

The major rose to his feet, struggling to keep the anger out of his voice. 'As your clerk has pointed out, sir, we have already passed midday. I propose that we break for lunch, and reconvene here in two hours.'

26

Back at the inn Max ordered coffee and light refreshments to be brought to their room. While Sylvia disappeared behind the screen he took off his jacket and stood at the open window, breathing in the warm spring air. A moment later a convoy of army lorries chugged out of the main square, sending up clouds of dust, and he closed the panes with a startled imprecation.

'Dust is nothing,' said Sylvia with a chuckle. 'You should have been here earlier in the spring. I've never seen such a place for mud. I used to have to crack it off my uniform every night.' She saw him stretch and wince. 'Are you in pain? Oh, Max! You shouldn't have spent so long on your feet.'

'Just a little stiff,' he admitted. He lowered himself carefully onto the bed, looking at her from under his lashes. 'It's nowhere near as bad as it was, but I'm missing my regular massage. I found a very good Almeric Paget masseur in London. Perhaps I should ask the landlady's daughter...?'

'I doubt if you're strong enough for the landlady's daughter,' said Sylvia with a scornful laugh. 'She'd reduce you to nothing in no time. And Jake still needs you.' She crossed to the side of the bed. 'Come on, then. Turn over. Slip your braces off and undo your shirt.'

'I don't wish to put you under any pressure,' he said, as she rearranged the bolsters.

'You're not,' she said briskly, unbuttoning her cuffs. 'I'm doing this for Jake - '

'Ouch.' He winced as she dug her fingers into the tense muscles around his shoulders.

' - and to save you from the landlady's daughter.'

27

When at last Sylvia turned away from the bed, Max let his breath out on a long sigh and muttered his thanks. Declining anything beyond a cup of coffee, he turned onto his back and flung his arm over his eyes.

'Sleep, I think,' he muttered gruffly.

Sylvia crossed the room and opened the window, disturbed to see that her hands were trembling. She inhaled deeply into her lungs until her breathing had steadied, then shuttered the window. She watered down some coffee and nibbled on a little bread and cheese, but she didn't have much appetite either.

'Come and lie down,' said the voice from the bed. 'It's going to be a long day. Snatch some rest while you can.'

She hesitated.

'No more nonsense with the couch,' he said. 'I need some sleep, and so do you.'

'But we might both fall asleep and - '

'I've asked the landlady's daughter to wake me,' he said. Then, with a wicked grin, 'She has to be useful for something.'

She lay beside him stiffly, with no thought of sleep, until the softness of the quilts and feather bolster began to weave their magic. After a few moments she drifted off into a half-sleep, curling up unconsciously into her usual sleeping position. An arm fell around her shoulder and she tried to roll away.

'Lie still,' said Max. 'Sleep.' Then, as she shifted again under his touch, he said edgily: 'Stop fretting. It's the same conditions as at the temple.'

She looked up into his face, sighed, and went back to sleep.

She was woken by the softest of kisses on the top of her head only seconds before the knock fell on the door, and she was on her feet and shrugging herself into her jacket before Max had even sat up.

She pulled a face as Max drank a lukewarm cup of coffee, declining to wait for fresh. When he'd straightened his collar and tied his necktie, they went downstairs. Jessup was waiting for them with an urgent message.

Max read the note intently, then turned to Sylvia who was adjusting her cap in the mirror. 'My apologies to the court,' he said briskly. 'I will be a trifle delayed. I have to take instructions from my clients.'

She turned away from the mirror. 'I can't tell them that,' she said, eyes widening in panic. 'They'll eat me alive.'

'Clerk's duties, my dear.' He smiled encouragingly at her. 'Don't be apologetic, whatever you do. Just state our case. Every lawyer is entitled to consult with his client.'

28

This time it was Jake who was staring out of the window. Tommy Shepherd was lying on the bed in a deep sleep, with a beatific smile on his face. He didn't stir as the escort fell in around Jake and marched him and Max to the outer room.

The adjacent cell was occupied by a drunken soldier, sleeping it off.

'They tell me it's the custom to get the condemned men drunk,' said Jake, as they passed. 'So drunk they don't rightly know what's happening. If it comes to the worst, sir, I just wanted to say - don't let 'em get me drunk, sir. No blindfold neither. If they're determined to murder me, I want 'em to look me straight in the eye while they do it.'

The sentries pushed him down into his seat, towering one on each side of him until they stepped back, rifles at the ready. 'Promise me, sir. Promise me you'll see to it.'

Max suppressed a shudder. 'Let's make sure it doesn't come to that. I'm here to advise you, Jake, that it would be in your best interests to opt for a separate trial.'

'What? Not be tried with Tommy?' He peered intently into Max's face, as if trying to read his mind. 'Is that what you're saying? But we're both on the same charge, sir.'

'You come into the charges from different starting points, however. I've just heard that Shepherd already has a suspended sentence.'

'I know about that. But it wasn't for anything bad, nor intentional,' said Jake. 'He wasn't being disobedient. He just didn't understand what they were telling him to do.'

'Nevertheless it will count against him. For a second infringement they'd feel justified in demanding a stronger penalty. I don't want you to be tarred with the same brush. My best advice to you is to demand to be tried separately. You have the right.'

For a moment Jake gazed into the distance, then he turned back to Max. 'Thank you for your advice, sir. I know you mean well and to do the best you can for me. But I can't separate from Tommy now. He only copied me, like he's always done. I told him, see, do as I do, Tommy, and you won't come to harm. That's what he did and that's why he's in here alongside of me. So how can I abandon him now?

29

Max made his way back to the hearing deep in thought, barely aware of the columns of new soldiers being marched through the main streets and towards the front lines. The devil was in it now and no mistake. In the course of the morning he'd devised a defence for Jake and his friend, but whether it would be enough to sway the court-martial panel when one of the accused was already on a suspended sentence, he wasn't quite so sure.

He had hoped to have Jake at least brought to the court in the course of the afternoon, for cross-examination, but the opportunity never arose. Instead the afternoon was spent in a long and wearisome discussion of red tape, in particular the B122 - the soldier's conduct sheet - which had been sent to the commanding officer, together with the court martial papers, and on which the Commander-in-Chief in his turn had to base his judgement as to whether a condemned soldier was worthy of reprieve.

Time and again Max asked why there was nothing about Jacob Harrison's earlier faultless service, no mention of his recommendation for a medal, nothing about the trench-shelling which had left the two men buried alive. All anyone could say was that the two men's earlier service was not known to them. They had only come into the regiment when a number of battalions which had been pretty well smashed up at the Battle of Loos had been recombined into a new fighting force.

On and on and round and round the questioning went, until by the end of the afternoon Sylvia's right arm felt as if it were on fire from shoulder to wrist, and her fingers could scarcely grip the pen.

Fortunately there was a battalion mess-dinner in the general's château some way behind the lines, and the review hearing broke up early to allow the officers to don mess-uniform and make their way to the rear. As Max and Sylvia left the hearing, Lieutenant Jessup came running after him, bearing a proposal from the court.

'You are now the colonel's messenger boy?' asked Max, raising his eyebrow.

'More like his whipping boy,' said the lieutenant ruefully. 'My name's mud, as far as he's concerned.'

'I can't see why,' said Sylvia.

'Always has been. Well, for a start, I'm a grammar-school boy.' He shrugged. 'If it was good enough for Shakespeare, it's good enough for me, but Powell thinks it an insult to the regiment to have to accept officers like me. *Temporary gentlemen*, they call us. And then, of course, he's hopping mad that I admitted making a poor hand of taking the notes at the first FCMG.'

'A job you should never have been burdened with in the first place,' said Max acidly. 'If it's any consolation, you're one of the few in this whole sorry business who has acted honourably throughout. I shall be sure to commend you to the War Office.'

'That's kind of you, sir - under the circumstances.'

'So, tell us, what is this proposal?'

'Colonel Powell has offered a deal. That's not how he put it, but it's what it comes down to. If Harrison and Shepherd will admit to cowardice, the colonel won't press for the death penalty on the charge of casting away arms.'

'And in return for this dubious advance - which will still leave them at the mercy of the Commander-in-Chief?'

'Reduction to the ranks and dishonourable discharge.'

But when it was put to Jake, he shook his head.

'Can't do that, sir. We never did anything wrong. Dishonourable discharge? How could I look Lil in the face with that to my name? And how could I face my Alfie when he grows to be a man? I know you think I'm a poor figure of a man, sir, but I have my pride.'

'You're a brave man,' said Max, shaking his hand. 'If I could hold onto my dignity as well as you have under these circumstances, I'd be a proud man too.'

Sylvia, waiting impatiently for him outside the prison, was not at all surprised to hear that Jake had refused the offer.

'But we have them on the run,' said Max with a triumphant smile. 'Why else would they start bargaining now?'

30

'Enough,' said Sylvia, casting down her pen and stretching her arms above her head. 'I cannot write a single word more.'

'Writer's cramp?'

'*Par excellence*. You'll have to do the rest yourself. I'm going to soak in the bath,' she said, gathering up her towel and soap from the washstand. She turned in the doorway. 'This clerking isn't all it's cracked up to be,' she said, stretching her fingers with a grimace. 'Bob Cratchit deserved every penny.'

'If this is a hint that I have been taking your services for granted...' he began, reaching for his wallet.

'Don't be ridiculous, Max. Besides, I'm not doing it for you; I'm doing it for Jake and Lily.'

'And you'd be wise not to forget that,' he muttered as the door closed behind her.

When she came back from the bath, Max had the spirit stove going merrily on the hearth, making tea for her.

'Ah, this is nectar,' she said, as she sipped the hot brew. 'But where did you get it?'

'Army QM stores. Bit stronger than Mother used to make, so I used a little less.'

'Perfection,' she sighed, sinking back into the chair.

She was holding the cup in her left hand and still flexing the stiff fingers of the right. He watched with a frown as she rubbed the front of her shoulder.

'It's not just the writing,' she said in answer to his questions. 'It's been stiff for some time.'

'Since the accident with the ambulance, if you're honest.'

'I suppose so. I had quite a struggle with the motorcycle, I can tell you!'

'Will you be able to cope tomorrow? There'll be more notes to be taken...'

'I won't let you down.'

'Why don't you lie on the bed and I'll return the favour.'

Her eyes widened. 'Which favour?' she asked cautiously.

'I've learned a great deal from watching the Paget masseuses,' he said coolly. 'I'm sure I could ease your shoulder, just as you eased my back.'

At last she allowed herself to be persuaded. 'Shall I change first?' she said, having slipped her shirt and trousers back on over her spare set of underwear when she came back from the bathroom.

'Good heavens, no!' He looked at the offending nightdress, hanging in voluminous folds from her hand. 'I wouldn't be able to *find* your shoulder under all that cloth. Shirt off too, or the massage won't make much impression.' When she hesitated, he took the nightdress from her and tossed it over the screen. 'You could rent that out to the Canadians,' he quipped. 'I understand they're short of marquees.'

The embarrassment of the moment dissolved in a burst of shared laughter and she turned her back and unbuttoned her shirt. She felt very exposed, lying on the bed clad in nothing but her trousers and vest - actually the top half of a pair of men's long combinations - but Jake was relying on her to be up to the task tomorrow.

'What a pair of old crocks we are, to be sure,' she joked, to cover her embarrassment. 'Between us we could keep a Paget masseur in full time work!' At least she wasn't wearing the silk underwear in which she had luxuriated in London, and there was nothing very seductive about thick cotton men's combinations.

She drew one of the feather pillows under her stomach and folded her arms beneath her head. Max began to massage her shoulder, neck and spine quite vigorously, untightening the tense muscles, then he drew one arm out from under her head and with a surprisingly gentle touch, pulling on each finger separately, turning the wrist this way and that, he worked on her arm until it felt glowing, and yet at the same time pleasantly floppy.

Kneeling above her on the bed he could observe the graceful line of neck and spine, and almost see the tension ease away as her breathing slowed and deepened. As she slipped her hand back under her head the hanging folds of the cotton vest caught and tightened until he could see the shadow of her breast pressing against the fabric. He breathed deeply, struggling for control, reminding himself that they had to share this room, this bed, tonight. He had persuaded her to let him massage her, and it was scarcely the gentlemanly thing to betray the effect she was having on him.

He turned back to the task in hand, working his fingers rhythmically up and down the spine and across the shoulders, but after a few minutes his fingers began to betray him, falling into a wider movement, sliding down her lower ribs, halfway round the front, just above her waist.

Her breathing had speeded up again, but she said nothing. Greatly daring, he moved up once more and began smoothing away the tension to the edge of her rib cage, allowing his fingers to drop marginally down towards those straining breasts.

She gave a sharp exclamation. Convinced he had gone too far he dropped his hands and rocked back on his heels.

The words of apology were never spoken. 'Bloody belt buckle,' she said, rolling over. The ornate metal fastening of the borrowed belt had dug into the flesh exposed below her vest and she unbuckled it impatiently. The trousers, too big for her, bunched in loose folds around her hips. 'Damn. I shall have to take these off before they fall off,' she muttered. And beneath his fascinated gaze she proceeded to do just that, with an enticing wriggle of her slender hips, revealing the other half of the butchered men's combinations which she'd secured with tapes. Lying on the buckle had raised an angry red weal on the pale soft flesh just below the edge of her vest. Before he could stop himself, he leaned across and planted a kiss on it.

There was a swift intake of breath. He looked up in apprehension, to find green eyes smiling dreamily back.

'If this goes any further,' he said, attempting a lightness he didn't feel, 'then I have to tell you, temple terms are off.' His hand ran along the edge of the tape and the loose nether garment slipped down a few inches, leaving his fingers resting on the prominence of her hip bone.

He leaned forward and dipped his tongue into the depression of her navel and she shivered. He felt her fingers in his hair and tried to hold himself back. 'Sylvia, sweetheart,' he said huskily. 'Stop me now or all pledges are off. No further guarantees of good behaviour will be given.' She made no move to stop him. A wordless sound, warm and sensual, swelled deep in her throat. His hands slid around the back of her waist, and down, and down, inside the heavy cotton, until his strong fingers cupped themselves around the ovals of her buttocks.

He moulded them gently, caressed them, the feel of her flesh under his hands sending tiny licks of electricity through his body. As he raised himself to look into her eyes, she brought her head up and kissed him full on the lips. When at last she drew away, his breath was coming in short gasps.

'In the interests of equality,' she breathed, so softly that he had to strain to make out the words, 'I really think you should take those clothes off.'

Fumbling in his haste, her fingers helping and at the same time hindering him, he was soon as naked as she. They both paused a moment, feasting their eyes. 'I've wanted this for so long,' he whispered, reaching out tentatively to cup her breast. Her mouth softened as his lips fastened on hers; he held his body away, not wanting to frighten her. He had waited too long to lose it all by rushing her. Besides, her mouth was warm and soft and giving and he could spend a lifetime there.

They kissed for an age, and she felt lost and bereft when his questing mouth drew away from hers. As her hands moved over his shoulders and his back, exploring, feeling, discovering, his warm lips slid down her cheek to her throat, her naked shoulder, the swell of her bosom, and at last she felt his aroused body pressing against hers, sending shivers up and down every nerve, and causing strange floating feelings in the pit of her stomach, as though a thousand butterflies were swirling there.

After a moment he raised his head again. 'I don't want to hurt you, my darling.... '

'It's only a moment, they say,' she said breathlessly, running her hands over his hips, daring herself to move on. 'And I'd rather it was you than....' Her hands ceased in their caresses as his mouth found her breast. Her head fell back with a gasp.

In his tension and eagerness he misread it. 'Sweetheart, don't ask me to stop now,' he groaned, his hands poised at the cleft of her legs, his fingers hovering at the edge of the soft, moist inner parts where he had never gone before.

Her hands slid brazenly round his hips. 'Don't you dare stop now,' she murmured against his mouth. 'Don't you dare.'

For an age he touched her, caressed her, drew her into his passion until they were both beyond thought and beyond fear, until she had opened herself up to him like a flower unfolding. His tongue darted in and out of her soft mouth and after a moment, found hers responding. She gave a small, smothered cry as he entered her, but after a moment her body began to move to his rhythm, exulting in the feel of their union until it was no longer possible to say that it was his flesh within hers, and hers surrounding his, only that their two bodies moved together, apart, together, as they wound each other up into a crescendo of passion.

31

Early next morning a knock fell on the door but the two entwined figures only moved closer into each other's arms.

Again a knock.

'Go away,' Max muttered into Sylvia's hair. It had been a long night, a wonderful night, with Sylvia a willing and passionate partner; even now he could hardly believe that his dreams had at last become reality. Together they had certainly made up for lost time, but there had not been a great deal of sleep in it.

'What? Sir, it's Lieutenant Jessup.'

'Go away. I'll see you in the morning.'

Outside the door Jessup cleared his throat uncomfortably. 'It *is* morning, sir. Actually, it's gone eight o'clock.'

Max propped himself on his elbow and surveyed the chaos of the room. The spirit stove had burnt itself out at some time during the night, leaving a slight acrid odour behind; fortunately the kettle was on the hearth, or that might well have boiled dry and burnt through. At some stage they must have drawn the quilts over themselves, but on either side of the bed was a tangle of abandoned clothes.

He rolled over to find Sylvia looking up at him from the pillows, eyes wide. 'The idyll is over,' she whispered.

He kissed his fingers and laid them lightly over her mouth. 'No,' he said. 'Only postponed.'

Twenty minutes later they were downstairs, a little less bandbox smart than usual, but otherwise in reasonably good order. While Max sent the landlady's daughter for coffee, Jessup told them he'd found an officer at command HQ who had known both men when they were in service with their first unit, and was willing to speak for them.

Max looked on a shade wearily at the young man's enthusiasm. He'd obviously decided to abandon his former split loyalties and redeem himself for those incomplete notes. He must think he'd already burnt his boats with the colonel, and anyway, Lloyd George carried far more weight.

'I met Captain Vaughan at the battalion mess-dinner. At the château. He's serving a little up the line, since the unit was broken up, but remembers both men well. I took the liberty of telling him what had happened and he was absolutely livid. Should I ask Major Gawston to request his attendance?'

There was a disparaging noise from Sylvia. 'Gawston's more likely to send him straight up to the front than summon him here, for fear he won't toe the army line.' Her eyes lit up and she turned eagerly to Max. 'But if Lieutenant Jessup has the directions then *I* could go and fetch him...I still have the motorcycle...'

'Sylvia, no, I - '

She looked at him with hurt surprise. 'But it's the most sensible way...'

'If you will excuse us a moment, Jessup...' He drew Sylvia out of the restaurant, under the interested gaze of the other officers, and into the deserted office. 'Sweetheart, I don't think you should be hurtling around on motorcycles.'

'Why not? Riding motorcycles is what I do. At least, it's what I've been doing for the last few months.'

He paced across the room, groping for the right words. 'I - we weren't at all careful last night. I don't know if - you could find yourself pregnant.' Then, as if the words were torn from him, 'Will you hate me if I've made you pregnant?'

She smiled. 'Oh, is that all?'

'All?'

'Women have gone through war and famine and ridden great distances on horseback and still had babies. Riding a motorcycle six miles up the line isn't going to make a ha'porth of difference one way or the other. I'm not made of porcelain.' She took his hand. 'Besides, I think we're a bit old for instant parenthood.'

'Age makes no difference.'

'Anyway, you're jumping the gun a bit. You and I - well, we still have a lot of talking to do, I think, before we start worrying about babies. Only not right now.' She briefly considered pointing out that he had no authority over her, except as his clerk, and that only in a voluntary capacity, and that if it had been a man with a motorcycle, he would have been urging him up the line to fetch the witness. But the night had given their relationship a new edge, and she didn't want to fight him. 'What I do know,' she said, crossing to the door, 'is that fetching Captain Vaughan may make all the difference between Jake seeing *his* baby grow up and - and not. So I have to go.'

She sent the waiter to fetch her motorcycle from the stables, tucking her hair into her helmet while Jessup gave her directions. Then with a wave of her hand she hurried down the steps and out into the street

A newly arrived column of Tommies was marching down the main street singing.

Take me back to dear old Blighty, put me on the train for London town,

Take me over there, drop me anywhere,

Birmingham, Leeds or Manchester, I don't care.

She heard her name called and turned to find Max dashing after her. 'Sylvia...'

'What is it?' She saw him wince. 'You shouldn't have run like that.'

'Never mind that.' He took her hands in his. 'Take care, my darling. I couldn't bear to lose you again.'

'Was it so terrible, then?'

'Unbearable.' She looked up into his face and knew he was telling the truth. She stood on tiptoe to plant a chaste kiss on his cheek, conscious of all the onlookers. But then Max's hand was at the back of her head, and he would not let her go, pulling her towards him while his lips found hers in a long and satisfying kiss. Somewhere deep in the pit of her stomach the butterflies were doing pirouettes again.

The group of Tommies marching past whistled appreciatively, but Max showed no sign of letting her go. She was suddenly reluctant to leave him, to leave the comparative safety of the little town, and go out on the road again, towards the fighting and the shells, and away from the shelter of Max's arms.

The kiss came to an end, but she held the moment a little longer, her face pressed into Max's shoulder. She opened her eyes at last to find Max, as pale as she had ever seen him, looking down at her. The Tommies started to sing again.

There's a long, long trail a-winding, into the land of my dreams,

Where the nightingales are singing, and a white moon beams....

Her lip trembled and she thought she was going to cry. Max bent his head again and whispered in her ear. 'At this rate we could polish off every elderly general and colonel in the place.'

She followed his gaze, and there, not more than ten yards away, was a white-haired colonel on the verge of apoplexy at the sight of two figures in trousers embracing.

With a stifled sound halfway between a sob and a laugh, Sylvia pulled down her goggles and leaped onto her motorcycle.

Jessup watched with admiration as she wove past the column of men and disappeared in a cloud of dust. 'She's full of pluck, isn't she, your - er - '

'My wife? Yes.' He saw the look of surprise on the officer's face and, remembering the elderly colonel, said: 'Contrive to get that message across to your superiors, or they'll be charging her with conduct unbecoming her uniform, or some such nonsense.'

He grinned. 'Yes, sir. And shall I tell him you'll be a little late in court this morning? On account of waiting for your clerk and your new witness?'

'If you please. Though I hope she won't be too long: I don't think even I can keep them on a leash for much longer.'

32

When he arrived in the next square, and entered the room where the hearing was to convene, the officers were not there. They'd sent a junior officer with their apologies, citing a late return from the battalion mess-dinner, due to bombing attacks on the road. At a guess, half of them were still sleeping off the previous night's indulgences.

'Will you join me for coffee?' he asked Jessup. 'Or would that be seen as throwing your lot in with us entirely?'

Jessup shook his head. 'I'm past caring.' As they sat in the dining room he stirred his coffee, making patterns in the liquid with the tip of his spoon. 'I hope you won't object, sir, but I went back to the prison first thing this morning to talk to Harrison and Shepherd.'

Max raised an eyebrow, but said nothing.

'I wanted to refresh my mind about the trench collapse. I knew there was something else that Duncan had mentioned, but I couldn't put my finger on it. I wanted Harrison to talk it through with me, as much as he could remember. When they woke him up he was shaking like a leaf; he said he'd been dreaming of the big Irishman again. And then it came back to me. Duncan told me that as they were digging the men out, they'd uncovered a body that had been buried in the wall of the trench earlier that month.'

'In the wall of the trench?' Max set his coffee down untasted.

'Happens quite a lot, sir. The stretcher-bearers are terrific fellows, but if you're under constant shelling, no one can get in and no one can get out. Bodies have to be put in the dug-outs, or buried in the wall of the trench. This was a big Irish Guardsman. They'd buried him some weeks before, when the Guards had our trench, and the body was dislodged in the collapse. His remains were the first thing Harrison saw when they finally unearthed him. It wasn't a pretty sight because the rats had been at him. Harrison says the Irishman has been haunting him ever since.'

'That could be useful. If I can't persuade the panel that the two men were suffering from shell-shock...'

'Oh, they won't let you get away with using that term.'

'Really?'

'In fact we've been ordered not to use it. Even the medics can only say they are suffering from neurasthenia.'

'Is there a difference?'

'Oh, yes. Neurasthenia is an illness - if you're sent back to Blighty with neurasthenia, then the government's under no obligation to pay a pension. But shell-shock is caused by enemy action, which makes it a wound, and with a wound you'd be entitled to a pension.'

He saw the look of astonishment on Max's face. 'It's true, sir, I promise you. If a man's invalided out because he's crippled with rheumatism from working knee-deep in waterlogged trenches, or because his lungs are damaged by pneumonia, then he gets no pension. If he's disabled by German gas, he gets a pension. If you get frostbite in the trenches and have to have your foot amputated and die from the haemorrhage, no pension for your widow. Shot in the foot by a German bullet and pick up pneumonia on your journey and die of it – she gets a pension. All set out in military law.'

They returned to the hearing to find the officers waiting impatiently for them. Soon after, to Max's relief, Sylvia arrived with her witness on the pillion of her motorcycle. While he spoke to the officer, she withdrew to wash the dirt of the road from her face before slipping into her place at the clerk's desk.

Captain Vaughan was a stiff man, but one with a strong sense of duty and justice. He'd brought with him the battalion diary, in which all occurrences from the outbreak of the war to the merging of the shattered remnants of the regiments had been recorded.

'I would like to take you back, Captain Vaughan,' said Max, 'to the occasion last year when one of your sergeants was saved from drowning.'

'Ah yes.' Vaughan riffled through the diary until he came to the relevant entry. 'This followed an attack on the German lines in which we lost more than three-quarters of our number. The barbed wire had not been sufficiently cut by the artillery bombardment and we could not break through. We were repulsed by machine-gun fire from entrenched German positions. Our sergeant was hit in the shoulder, losing blood, and had fallen into a flooded shell hole between the lines. Private Harrison and his officer were returning to our own lines after the attack had been abandoned. Disregarding their own safety, they stayed with the sergeant, under constant enemy fire, until nightfall, when the stretcher bearers were able to come out and relieve them.'

'I understand that Private Harrison was recommended for a medal. But in the event the lieutenant received the Military Cross, while the private received only a commendation. Why was that?'

'The lieutenant in his evidence said he had to keep on at Harrison to keep his end up. Well, not surprisingly.' Vaughan became animated. 'I talked to the sergeant himself, much later, in the field hospital. It was a deep shell-hole, sir, that's why they couldn't climb out once they were in. The lieutenant, who was a tall man, almost six foot, could barely keep his face above the water...'

'And Jacob Harrison is a long way from being a tall man.'

'The Sergeant said the little fellow had his boots wedged in the sloping side of the shell hole and kept coming adrift as the mud shifted. So he had to find new footholds each time.'

'Which led you to conclude that Harrison had shown equal bravery with the lieutenant?'

'More, sir, I would say. The chances of him drowning were much greater, at a shade under five feet, yet he hung on till nightfall when the stretcher party got the sergeant away.'

'Captain Vaughan, you served for just over a year with the two men in your unit.'

'Yes, sir. Until the Battle of Loos. We suffered heavy losses, so we were broken up and amalgamated.'

'I have here the remarks written by their current commanding officer on the condemned men's B122s - their conduct sheets. Before I read them out to the court, I would appreciate your opinion on the two men. Let's start with Tommy Shepherd.'

'Ah, poor Shepherd.' Captain Vaughan shifted uncomfortably. 'In the first year of the war we were pretty desperate for reinforcements and a great many men got into the army as fit who never should have. Thomas Shepherd was one of them. He's not very bright. Willing, but not very bright. That's how he got his black mark, simply from not understanding orders. He only got through by Harrison taking him under his wing. Kindest thing would be to send the fellow behind the lines. Catering corps, or something like that. Or maybe to the horse lines: he's very good with animals.'

'And Harrison?'

'Brave little beggar, sir, as I said. Courage for a man twice his size. Cool and calm under fire. It would take a lot to overset him. Steady, organised kind of man: I understand he was a carpenter and wood-carver in civvy street. He's done well to rise to lance-corporal, but if he'd been a bigger fellow, he would have risen even further up the ranks.'

Max reached behind him for the B122. 'Would you be surprised to find the words 'mentally and physically degenerate' on his records?'

Vaughan's eyes widened. 'I would indeed.'

'Perhaps,' said Max, turning back to the panel, 'one of the officers could explain that?'

The Major shook his head, but Colonel Powell leaped to his feet.

'He's a Bantam, sir. You said yourself, barely five feet tall! We were forced to take them in with the rest of the unit when we were reorganised. When our general inspected us he said it was a disgrace to have so many mentally and physically degenerate men serving in one of our best regiments.'

'And you were unwilling to go against your general?' The colonel twitched his moustache, unwilling to meet Max's eyes. 'Well, let us think about it in more detail, shall we? If your general is right in his beliefs, we shall have to make some changes in our past.'

'I don't know what the devil you are talking about, sir!' barked the colonel.

'To begin with, we shall have to hand the country over to the French,' mused Max, only now he was addressing the court at large – and there were considerably more onlookers than there had been at the start. 'We should never have won the Battle of Trafalgar – Horatio Nelson was such a short man. The sublime poetry of Keats and Pope must be put on the fire – Keats was barely four feet eleven and Pope only four feet six. Put the shackles back on the slaves – William Wilberforce was only as tall as Jacob Harrison. Rip up all the railways and pull down the bridges – Brunel was no taller. And we must take the vote back from half the electorate – Lord Russell, the guiding spirit behind the Reform Bill of 1832 was a tiny fellow.'

There was a surge of laughter, with a smattering of applause.

'Stuff and nonsense, sir!' snapped Colonel Powell.

Max's voice hardened as he turned to confront the officers. 'I should like it put on record, colonel, that a significant number of the brave volunteers from our great cities would, like Brunel and Nelson, Russell and Keats, fail to meet your general's requirements. Many working men - in Glasgow, Cardiff, Leeds, Liverpool, Birmingham, London - weigh no more than eight stone and are often less than five feet tall. They do a good day's work in the docks, the factories, the markets, wherever they are employed. They can do a good day's work here, in all but the heaviest hand-to-hand fighting. They can certainly fire a rifle as well as anyone twice their size.' His voice hardened. 'The War Office has stated categorically that Bantam Battalions have acquitted themselves extremely well in action. If they had been as well-fed in their childhood as you and I - and the general - were, they would perhaps have grown as we did. Poverty is generally to blame for their lack of size. But their hearts are as great, their courage, as we have heard from the captain, is as great. Sometimes greater.

'We have heard, from one who knows him, that Tommy Shepherd should never have been passed as fit. He is a simple soul who lacks the understanding to form part of a fighting force. Those facts are obvious to all, and would be the same were he six foot tall or four foot six. But to suggest that a brave man like Jacob Harrison is morally degenerate is inexcusable.' He picked up the battalion diary and hefted it above his head. 'The record of this brave young man refutes those words loudly and vigorously. His record reveals your general's words about the Bantam soldiers to be an offensive and totally unjustified insult. He showed remarkable ignorance of the contribution that brave men like Jake Harrison have made to the war effort - I trust, gentlemen, that I will not have to report that you did the same.'

33

A ripple of excitement ran around the room as Max sank, exhausted, into his seat. As far as the onlookers were concerned, the hearing was over and done with. All that remained was for the panel to promulgate the new decision and announce the freeing of the two prisoners. The three judges were in no doubt, for Hartley and Smith began to gather up their papers while Major Gawston sighed heavily and stared down at his feet.

Others were less willing to accept the inevitable. As his aide whispered in his ear, Colonel Powell's eyes snapped and he turned on Vaughan before he'd had time to resume his seat.

'Is it not a fact, Captain Vaughan, that you have three times declined to serve on a court-martial?' said the colonel. 'That in fact you have a covert hatred of courts martial? A secret plan to bring them into disrepute?'

Max drew a sharp breath and shot to his feet once more. 'Captain

Vaughan's views on courts martial in general are not relevant to this enquiry,' he said. 'We are here to review the procedures used in this case, and to say whether justice was done.'

'Nevertheless, I should like Captain Vaughan to answer the question.'

'I have served on one court martial. I thought it a travesty of justice and said so.' Vaughan shrugged. 'I don't flatter myself I made any difference: there is no shortage of other junior officers willing to serve in my place.'

'By standing out against the majority decision you interfered with the imposition of the death penalty, did you not?'

'I did. The man was not a coward: he was a civilian who'd signed up in a burst of enthusiasm without any notion of what being a front-line soldier entailed. When he found out, he was not of the calibre to cope with it. It was not a deliberate fault: it is the way God created him.'

'Thank you, Captain Vaughan,' said Max. 'I think we have heard - '

But the Colonel was not willing to let it go. 'And this man you refused to condemn, you did not regard him as a danger to others fighting in the front line?'

'Indeed I did. But he could still do his bit behind the lines, in catering, or horses, or perhaps as a batman to the generals.'

'Oh, hell,' said Max under his breath. He could see which way this was going. In the distance the pounding of guns opened up again after a brief respite.

'Their châteaux are generally twenty or thirty miles behind the lines,' continued Vaughan, who by now had the bit firmly between his teeth. 'A man who serves there has fewer challenges to his bravery than one in the trenches.' He looked straight at Colonel Powell, who everyone knew was closer to the fighting today than he had been for the duration of the war. 'Better for all to remove him from where he is a danger to others. It was not necessary to put an English bullet through his heart to achieve that.'

'Would you agree, Captain Vaughan, that your resentment against the army makes you a less than neutral witness?'

'Resentment, sir?' Vaughan glanced down at his wound and ribbon stripes. 'I think you will find that my military record stands against anyone's.'

'I understand you were refused entry to the officers' course in 1912 - '

Vaughan looked at the panel with narrowed eyes. 'Because I was a grammar school boy, with no rich relatives to buy me a commission? That is so.' He patted his captain's stripes. 'But I can assure you, colonel, that I have gone past any resentment I might have had.' He caught Max's anguished eye. 'Besides, we are not here to discuss my views, but the diary. And that, colonel, is neutral. Everything I have said about Harrison and Shepherd is confirmed in this battalion diary, kept by the junior duty officers. I myself had nothing to do with any of the entries.'

'Thank you, Captain Vaughan, for your time and trouble,' said Max. 'I think we may let you go now. Major Gawston has laid on transport to take you back to your unit.'

'Court will rise,' rapped out a junior officer as Gawston rose once more to his feet. The Major cast an anguished look at his colonel, then back at Vaughan, then down at his notes once more.

Max coughed gently.

But Gawston was not yet ready to pit himself against his senior officer. 'Court will reconvene this afternoon. The prisoners will be brought to court, where Sir Max Bryson will have the opportunity of reviewing their evidence.'

A ripple of disappointment ran around the court, then someone said, 'Still, it will be good to hear what they've got to say for themselves....'

'You've not done yourself any good with the top brass, I fear,' said Max, as he shook Vaughan's hand outside the court. 'I'm sorry to have put you in such an awkward position.'

'Too many of the professional soldiers hate *temporary gentlemen* like me. Powell and his ilk feel it's their duty to make our lives a misery.' Vaughan grinned. 'Especially since I once rather foolishly pointed out that my grammar school, being an ancient foundation, was actually senior to his very minor public school.'

'In that case I'm doubly grateful to you for standing up for the defendants. I only hope we haven't made matters worse for you.'

'What can they do to me that the Hun isn't already doing? No one would place any money on the chances of a junior officer in this show, and I could well be dead tomorrow anyway.' He climbed up into the staff car. 'Like Jacob Harrison, I'd rather it was by a German shell than an English bullet.'

34

Thomas Shepherd was a sad and rather lost figure when they brought him to the witness stand later that afternoon. His army records showed him to be twenty-two years old, but being considerably less than five feet tall, and round-faced, he looked like a very young schoolboy up in front of the headmaster.

'Good afternoon, Tommy,' said Max, taking care not to loom over him. 'Do you remember that when you were in the court before, you swore on the Bible to tell the truth?'

'Yes, sir.' He smiled broadly.

'And will you remember that you are still on oath to tell the truth?'

'I always tell the truth, sir. Promised my mother, I did. Tell the truth, always be polite and don't answer back.' He said it as he had learnt it, by rote, and an ill-concealed ripple of laughter ran around the court.

Max turned away and whispered in Sylvia's ear: 'How many shots in an officer's gun?'

'Pistol or revolver?'

He consulted his notes. 'Revolver.'

'Freddie's revolver took six.'

He turned back to the court. 'Now, Tommy. Do you remember the day when you went to the forward trench and Lieutenant Mackay was hit?'

'Yes, sir.' His eyes grew watery. 'He died, the lieutenant did. I was sad about that. He was a nice kind man. But I couldn't help it. The German enemy, they shot him.'

'I understand that. Did the lieutenant fire when he saw the Germans coming towards your trench?'

'Oh, yes, sir. We all did. Except Jake's rifle didn't go off bang. '

'Yes, we'll talk about Jake in a moment. But coming back to the lieutenant...'

'Yes. Lieutenant Mackay. He didn't have a rifle. He had a revolver.'

'That's right. Now, can you tell me, how many shots did the lieutenant fire from his revolver?'

Shepherd thought hard. 'Five or six. Couldn't rightly tell exact. They was firing all round us. Except Jake.'

'Whose rifle had jammed.'

'That's right, sir.' He gave a big beaming smile.

'How many did you fire, Tommy?'

'Only one, sir.' A gasp of shock ran round the court. Surely the man was condemned out of his own mouth!

'Only one?'

Sylvia rose to her feet, glancing anxiously between Major Gawston and Max. 'I'm not quite clear what to write down,' she said, looking suitably confused. 'Perhaps you could help me, Major? Does Mr Shepherd mean one bullet, or one magazine?'

'I'm not quite clear on that point myself,' said Max, looking her straight in the eye when Gawston stayed silent. 'We shall ask Mr Shepherd. Could you clarify that for us, Tommy?'

'One magazine, of course.' Shepherd turned his broad smile on Sylvia. 'That's five shots, see, lady, 'cos I've got one of the old rifles. I fired five shots, then I was just loading another magazine when Jake said to run.'

'Did you fire any of your second magazine?'

'No. Couldn't.' He shuffled and looked down at his feet. 'I'm a bit slow at reloading drill. Sarge gets cross with me and shouts.'

'No one will shout at you now, Tommy. Can you tell us what happened in the trench after you had fired off the first five shots?'

'I dropped the second magazine. Then the Germans were coming in and we ran.'

'Can you tell us how many shots the Germans fired?'

His eyes widened, tears not far from the surface. 'Lots,' he said simply.

'And throughout the time in the forward trench, you followed the orders you were given?'

'Yes. Jake – Jacob – thass Corporal Harrison, you know? - he said 'retire', so I retired. He jammed his rifle across the trench so I did the same.'

'You always follow orders, do you?'

'Oh, yes, sir.' He nodded vigorously. 'Got into trouble once, because I didn't understand what the captain was saying, see. So after that, Jake said I should watch him and do what he did, and then I wouldn't get into no more trouble. So I did.'

'And Lieutenant Mackay, before he died, had he given you any orders?'

'Yes. He said 'cease-fire'. Then he died.'

'Why do you think he said 'cease-fire'?'

Shepherd shrugged. 'I dunno, sir.'

'Wouldn't you have expected him to order you to carry on firing?'

'He couldn't carry on firing, sir. See, he was dead.'

There was little more to be got from the lad and when Shepherd had been led away from the court, Gawston turned to Max with a frown on his face.

'You see our problem, Sir Max. A conflict of evidence: Shepherd insists Mackay said 'cease-fire', while Harrison says the order was 'retire'.'

Max threw the ball straight back into his court. 'I look to you for clarification, major,' he said, leaning back in his chair and stretching his legs out.

Put on the spot Gawston was forced to talk it through. 'Shepherd had just fired on the advancing Germans and so had Lieutenant Mackay. Perhaps Shepherd couldn't see that they were still advancing, thought they had fallen back, and...'

'And so expected to hear 'ceasefire'? It doesn't make a great deal of sense to me, major.'

'Nor to me, I have to admit. Perhaps we had better have Harrison in.'

35

Jake came in next, between two soldiers with fixed bayonets. When they stepped back a pace he drew himself up smartly, shoulders back, and saluted the panel and the colonel. He had made an effort to turn himself out well and his boots and buttons shone in the afternoon sun.

'At ease,' said Gawston tiredly.

'Now, Corporal Harrison,' said Max, leaning on his table. 'I want to go through some of the evidence you gave to the court-martial and make sure we have properly understood your answers. You will remember that you are still under oath.'

'Yes, sir.' Harrison looked straight ahead, unblinking.

'I should like to take you through the day in question, the day that you were sent forward with Lieutenant Mackay to reconnoitre the forward trenches.'

Sylvia looked up with a frown, her pen poised above the paper.

Why didn't Max start off with the trench blow-in?

'Well, after breakfast the captain said - '

'I'm sorry to interrupt you, but could you take us through from the very first thing in the morning?'

'What? When I got up, sir?'

'Yes. You were sleeping where?'

'In one of the dugouts in the main trench, with four other men.'

'Go on.'

'Well, I didn't exactly wake up because I hadn't really slept. I could hear the rats scrabbling about and - ' His slight figure started to tremble, and the whole court could see the struggle he had to bring himself under control again.

'In your own time,' said Max gently.

Jake drew in a quivering breath. 'Like I said, sir, the rats stopped me sleeping. But I stayed lying down because I was too tired to get up. And it was a bitter cold night outside. At least in the dugout it was a bit warmer. When I sat up I tried to wake the other men, it being my duty to relieve the night watch on time. But I felt unwell.'

'In what way unwell?' demanded the major.

'It's hard to put my finger on it, Major Gawston, sir. Aches and pains all over my body, like I'd got the ague. But it wasn't just that. Couldn't seem to get my hands to do what I wanted them to. They wouldn't stop trembling. And there was a sort of red mist in front of my eyes all the time. And the men were laughing at me because my words wouldn't seem to come out straight.'

'The pain and the red mist,' said Max, 'did they go away when you slept?'

'No sir. Well, see, I *hadn't* slept, not since the trench blew in on top of us.'

'Couldn't you sleep for the pain?'

'That, and him.' He shook again, in every limb.

'With your permission, major, I should like the corporal to be given a seat.'

Gawston nodded, and a chair was brought. Jake collapsed into it as if there wasn't a bone left in his body.

'You were saying, Mr Harrison, that you couldn't sleep, for the pain - and him.'

'Every time I closed my eyes I saw him....'

'Who?'

'The big Irishman.'

Max looked down at him with a compassionate expression on his face. 'Major Gawston, I should like to spare the witness further distress. Lieutenant Jessup has written out what Lieutenant Duncan and the witness have at separate times told him about this incident, and I lay it before the court.'

'Isn't that just hearsay?' said the colonel belligerently.

Max sighed. 'Once you sent Lieutenant Duncan home, Colonel, that was inevitable. Besides, as you have pointed out, this is a review of evidence, and not a trial.'

As the colonel subsided, Gawston took up the paper, read it, looked sharply across at Harrison and then wordlessly passed the paper on.

Max waited while Jake sipped from a glass of water pressed into his hand by Sylvia. 'So when you came back from the Medical Officer and were sent to the Padre, you were very tired through lack of sleep?'

'Yes, sir. Exhausted. I told them I wasn't fit for duty, but no one listened. I did try to do what the Padre asked me, but the words seemed to get muddled, and I got confused, and he dismissed us.'

'Then - '

'If I could say, sir....Major...' He took a deep breath and struggled to get his thoughts into some sort of order. 'When I was - what I mean is, before we got buried in that trench, sir, I hadn't got any problem with making sense. I want you to know that, Major. I never really explained it proper at the court martial, because I was still that confused. But I want to say that I never got muddled or confused before. I was a good corporal, sir, and a good private before that, and I served both my regiments well.' He drew himself up stiffly and put his shoulders back. 'There, sir, that's what I wanted to say.'

'Thank you, Harrison,' said Gawston. 'Your words are noted. Sir Max?'

'Now, I'd like to move on. Together with Tommy Shepherd you'd been sent to the rear, to the Padre's billet, and he'd sent you back again. Almost immediately you were detailed off to a reconnaissance of the forward trenches.' He referred back to the notes of the original court martial. 'You reached the trench without incident, then suddenly you came under attack from the enemy.'

'Yes, sir. They must have been waiting for us. They couldn't have got into the side trench else, without us seeing them.'

'Take us through the events from the moment that you realised your rifle was jammed.'

'I was trying to unjam it, and cursing, sir. Suddenly came to me that with all the coming and going, I'd not carried out my rifle and kit drill. First day, in all my time in the army, that I hadn't checked my rifle. My brain just wasn't right that day, sir, or I never would have forgotten.'

'I'm sure. And after all, you had been sent back to the billets, as Padre's batman, for which you would hardly have needed your rifle.'

'That's it, sir. Exactly. Then out of the corner of my eye I saw Lieutenant Mackay go down. While Tommy - Private Shepherd - was trying to reload, we had no defence at all. I saw the lieutenant come up again on one knee, then he twisted and fell. As he went down, he shouted 'retire'.'

'You are in no doubt of that?'

'What else would he have said, sir? We hadn't a working gun between us. I went across to the lieutenant to try to fetch him out, but I couldn't shift him. He was a big man.'

'What thoughts ran through your mind at that moment?'

'I thought if I could only turn him over, I could get his gun, to cover us. But the firing was coming closer and I couldn't even be sure there'd be a shot left in his revolver anyway. He'd fired a few before he fell, but I didn't know how many. I'd been too busy trying to unjam my rifle to count them.'

'And then you retired?' Max walked across to Sylvia's desk, looked over her shoulder for a few seconds and then walked away, deep in thought.

'Yes. I stood up on the firing step and ducked my head above the parapet for a second. The advance party of Germans were still firing at us from the side trench and I could see more Germans swarming up through the forward trench to join them. There was nothing I could do to help the lieutenant. He was almost certainly dead, and I couldn't shift him anyway.'

'Then what?'

Silence. Jake Harrison turned his head back to where Max was standing, a little behind him. 'Sorry, sir, what did you say?'

Max opened his mouth to repeat the question, then turned, eyebrows raised, as he felt a tug on his sleeve. Sylvia scribbled on a scrap of paper which she pressed into his hand and he looked at it, his expression unchanged.

After a moment he walked slowly to the front of the court and turned to face Jake. 'I said, then what?'

'Well, I said to Tommy, come on, you heard the lieutenant, we got to retire. Then I jammed my rifle across the cross-trench...'

'Why did you do that?'

'Couldn't fire a jammed rifle, sir, could I? But jammed across the cross-trench like that, the first couple of Huns round the corner might just crack their heads on it, and pile up into each other. I thought it was worth a try, to give us time to get back and warn the others.'

'But the Germans didn't come on, did they?'

'No sir. The rest of our men came on down the other communication trench, parallel with ours. Only I hadn't heard them coming. Our fellows went on forward and drove the Germans back. But we weren't to know that. Them Huns might have followed us in real close like, and taken the others by surprise too.'

'Someone has suggested that the Germans might have called out 'cease fire' to confuse the issue. Several of them apparently spoke English.'

Jake rubbed his hand across his face. 'I don't know about that, sir. I wouldn't know a German speaking English from a Scotsman, or a Welshman, or a Yorkshire fellow. They all sound odd to me, even Londoners. I suppose the lieutenant might have known. He spoke German and he might have recognised if they had funny accents. But he's dead.'

'And can't give evidence on your behalf.'

'No, sir.'

'And what about Tommy Shepherd? The court martial pointed out that he discarded a perfectly good rifle.'

'If I could have got to him, I could have taken his rifle and reloaded, maybe got off a shot or two at the enemy. But the lieutenant's body was between us. Tommy was making a bit of a hash of reloading. He's not very quick on drill, see. He's - well, he's a bit slow, sir. But it's not his fault. He's had a tough time. Months ago, to keep him out of trouble, I told him to always do what I did. So when I jammed my rifle across the trench, sir, well, he ran back and jammed his there too. He thought he was only following orders, sir. Like he'd always done.' He looked pleadingly across at the senior officers. 'He didn't know no better, sirs.'

'There you have it gentlemen,' said Max. 'Jacob Harrison knew that the lieutenant was out of shots and out of action, Harrison's own rifle had jammed, so he, not unnaturally, expected to hear the order to retire.' As he spoke he wandered up and down the room. He stopped at the table, half-facing the officers, with his back to Jake. 'He had seen in his glimpse over the parapet that more Germans were coming up to reinforce those already attacking the forward trench and he could have no idea that his own reinforcements were coming up along the parallel trench.'

Without turning, he went on: 'That was how it happened, was it not, corporal?'

Once again Jake did not answer. Max walked in front of him and repeated the question.

'Yessir,' said Jake. 'That's just how it happened.'

Major Gawston sat up in his seat and began to speak, but Max held up his hand. 'Bear with me a moment, gentlemen, if you would.' He turned back to the prisoner. 'Thank you, Corporal Harrison. You and your escort may now dismiss.'

The escort fell in on either side of the prisoner, their bayonets towering above his head and winking evilly in the late afternoon sun filtering through the windows. When they were halfway to door, Max said, in ordinary tones, 'Prisoner and escort, stand still.'

The two soldiers of the escort stopped in their stride, but Jake proceeded for several more paces before realising something was amiss. He turned with a puzzled look on his face.

Max went towards him. 'Did you not hear what I said, Mr Harrison?'

Jake shook his head.

Gawston could contain himself no longer. 'The man's deaf!' he exclaimed.

'Hardly surprising, major.' Max turned back to the panel of judges. 'He had only the previous day been blown up and buried in a trench. No wonder he was unaware that the rest of his unit was advancing to his support - he could not possibly have heard them. We will never know for certain what was said in that trench. Because at least one of the men, probably both, had been deafened by the blast a few days before when the trench was blown in on top of them. I suspect that both Shepherd and Harrison lip-read the lieutenant's orders. And the officer, the only man who could tell us for certain what was said when the three men were under attack, is dead.'

A hubbub of speech broke out all around the court, but Max was not going to lose the advantage again. In the ringing tones which had stood him in such good stead at the Old Bailey, he said: 'All who knew them agree that these two men should never have been on active service that day. But not for the reasons previously advanced to the court martial. I maintain that there is no case to answer. Both men should be invalided out of the army and sent back home without a stain on their characters.'

36

'That must have been the longest minute of Jake's life while Gawston read out his recommendations,' said Sylvia from behind the screen.

'I'm sure it was. And while we may have saved Jake, I don't delude myself that we've changed anything in the long run. The army will go on executing the shell-shocked and inarticulate, up and down the line, *pour encourager les autres*.'

'Pour what?'

' "*To encourage the others*." I think Voltaire said that.'

'But has nobody ever objected before to the way they conduct Courts Martial?'

'A few Members have raised the matter in Parliament. Demanding investigations by the Secretary of State for War.'

'And what does Lord K have to say about it?'

'That the proceedings of a court martial cannot be shown to anyone without the consent of the accused.'

'But if they've already shot him, he never *can* give consent!'

'Quite. And so the Honourable Member is fobbed off with whatever filtered and edited version the Secretary of State for War condescends to give him.'

'If the law is an ass, then army law is a - a demented donkey.' With a final splash Sylvia emerged from behind the screen in her shirtsleeves, stretching and yawning. 'I'm sorry we weren't able to say goodbye to Jake.'

'According to Colonel Powell, letting them talk to anyone else would - '

' – would not be conducive to military discipline!'

'The exact words Jessup quoted. He called by on his way to

Boulogne. He's escorting Jake and Tommy home. They're bundling him back to Blighty too. I told him if he has any problems to look me up in London...which may be sooner than I thought.'

She stopped in mid-stretch as she saw the official letter in Max's hand. 'Problems?'

'Lloyd George is not to go to Russia after all; he's being sent to Ireland. Some sort of rebellion has broken out there.' He sat on the bed. 'You know, Lloyd George always maintained that we should have sent Irish diplomats to solve the Balkan question: he reckons they have the same determination never to forget an insult and never to forgive a slight. They'd have sorted the Balkans out long before it came to war.' He passed his hand wearily across his eyes. 'But rebellion in Ireland - God, what terrible timing. Do they not think we're stretched enough as it is?'

'And while so many of their own men are fighting over here too.' She picked up the envelope and stared down at the Ministerial crest. 'So you are needed back at Munitions?'

'I have to return tomorrow,' he said heavily.

'I see.' She dropped her eyes to the threadbare carpet. This was the moment she'd been dreading. She'd known it would come, known it was unavoidable. She just hadn't expected it to come so soon. 'You'll be able to take the good news to Lily yourself. Give her my love when you see her.'

'You can tell her yourself.' He stood up, a frown furrowing his brow. 'Surely you're coming back with me? I mean, now the new dispatch riders are here...'

'I'm surplus to requirements?' She concentrated on buttoning her cuffs. 'I suppose so. But there's always the canteen. They'll welcome me back with open arms.'

'Won't you find it a bit of a let-down to go back to buttering sandwiches, after dashing hither and yon on your motorcycle?' He kept his voice deliberately light, trying not to show his hurt.

When she didn't answer, he turned away. Like a man in a fever he crossed to the window and laid his forehead against the cold glass. After a moment he spoke over his shoulder. 'I had hoped that....after yesterday....after last night....you might see things differently.' He bit his lip. 'Oh, damnation, I wanted to talk this through with you properly, persuade you to...but we don't have that time any more. Sweetheart, I swore I wouldn't beg, but I'm begging you now. Come back with me.'

'I know you want to do the right thing by me, after last night, but - you shouldn't set too much importance on that. Out here....'

He froze. 'What are you saying?'

'At first, at home, I used to be offended when the sitters made such blatant suggestions.' She made a pretence of sorting out the papers and shuffling them together. 'Then, when I came out to France, I realised that...when the war is on top of you, a lot of people change their ways. It's hard to say no to a pleasant young man when he doesn't expect to see tomorrow.' She shrugged. 'Morals go by the wayside and we all grab at happiness with both hands. Because you never know when your last day will come.'

'I understand that. But you didn't.'

'I might have.' This wasn't going the way she wanted. She couldn't tell the lies she needed to make him turn away from her. 'But perhaps that's all it was last night.'

'You don't believe that. Neither do I. And even if you had...before...what could I say? I've not exactly been a saint in that quarter.'

'You mean Rosie. And then - '

'What do you mean, *and then*? There was no *and then*. There was no one after Rosie.' In his urgency to make the point, he didn't stop to think how she knew.

'Then who were you going to see?'

'When?' By now he was totally bewildered.

'When you walked out. All those long evenings when we returned to London, after I moved into Charles Street?'

'I walked around the houses - along the Embankment - and not just for the exercise.' He ran his hands through his hair. 'I went to my club - even slept there a couple of times. I had to take myself away from you. I was so afraid after that night in the temple, that I would forget myself - and drive you away from me.'

'Oh, Max.'

He came to an abrupt halt in front of her. 'I can't say I've been a saint,' he said softly. 'But I didn't exploit Rosie, you know. It was a mutually satisfactory arrangement which finished when I first met you.'

'I know. She told me.'

'What?'

'I - I went to see her. Before I left England.'

He sank down into the chair, rubbing his forehead. 'I can't pretend to understand why. But if you did talk to her she'll have told you that the only one I ever wanted was you. She was always brutally honest.' His eyes locked with hers. 'But you left anyway.'

'My mind was so scrambled after the explosion. I know how confused Jake must have felt.' It was her turn to pace the floor. There must be other ways, skilful ways, to make him leave without her, but she wasn't experienced enough in deception. He would see through her. She'd have to be honest with him; she owed him that much. 'Max, there were other reasons for leaving, apart from Rosie, and they are the same reasons for not coming back.'

The frown lifted. 'Not my mother and the children? Sylvia, I promised you wouldn't have to take on the children. Mother and Mrs Harmitage...'

'No. Not them. I told you...'

'Then who? My friends? My political associates? I thought we'd gone beyond all that! Lloyd George likes you - he even wanted to offer you a position at the Ministry - and as for Eddie Seymour....' He saw her colour up. 'Eddie?' he exclaimed furiously. 'By God, if he's upset you...!'

'No. I don't want there to be bad feeling between you. He's made no advances to me since I married you.'

'Unlike Hugh Osborne...'

'Oh. So you did hear that.'

'Yes. But you're not telling me that Eddie - '

'Eddie has been the perfect gentleman. But - '

'But?'

He reached out to take her hands but she wrenched them away. 'It's all the fault of that damned picture!' she cried.

'Jameson's picture? You needn't worry about that. You can destroy it if you like - though I do believe I've grown so used to it now that I would miss it.'

'You would - *what?'*

'Miss it.' He smiled wryly. 'I bought it for you, because I could see you were embarrassed to have it exhibited so publicly. I got Eddie to act as middleman, because I didn't want it to look as though I'd given in to blackmail - and I wouldn't have put it past Jameson to double the price once he knew I was interested. It was delivered to Charles Street the day after you left.' It was his turn to colour up. 'You'll think me a pathetic figure, but I have it hung opposite my bed. A consolation in the absence of the original...even though I know she wasn't really the model.'

She flung her arms round his neck and kissed him.

'What did I say?'

'Oh, I don't know.' She dropped her arms and her face grew serious once more. 'It's just that - '

He caught her hands and raised them one by one to his lips. 'No more analysis or rationalisation, I beg you,' he said, pressing a kiss into each palm. 'It's when we think too much about it all that we drive each other away.' He cupped her face in his hands and leaned forward to kiss her lightly on the mouth. 'If ever you doubt me, Sylvia, remember the temple. We were happy there.'

She looked at him with a troubled light in her eyes. 'We were happy here too.'

'But I never told you, then or later, that I love you. I wanted to, so desperately wanted to. But I felt I'd cheated you with that hospital ceremony - and then, afterwards, when I would have told you, you were so scared - '

'Not of you,' she said hastily.

'Of me as a man. As your husband.'

'No.' She shook her head vigorously and her cropped curls trembled. 'Oh, Max, I had problems from before I met you.' She remembered Rosie's words about not making a man feel like a villain. 'Problems that were nothing to do with you.'

'I know. At least, I know now. I saw the files.'

'Of my arrest?'

'And of your prison term. I made some investigations...If the doctor hadn't already died...I swear I would have killed him. Oh, my dear, that such things should have happened....!'

'Don't.' She took a step away from him, her lips quivering. 'One day I may tell you about it. Not now. It's still much too raw. But I am coming to terms with it. I met an Australian doctor who insisted I should talk about it.'

'Did he have a vested interest?' he said savagely. He regretted the words as soon as they were out, but he couldn't call them back.

Her head came up sharply. 'Max, you're jealous!'

'No.'

'Yes. Anyway, you're right. Doctor Delahaye *did* have a vested interest. Though not at all the way you mean.' Her eyes gleamed. 'She's Doctor Annie Delahaye, by the way. Did I mention that?'

'No, you didn't.' He let his breath out on a long slow sigh. 'Sweetheart, don't play games with me. God knows I have enough of that in court.' A pulse was beating in his temple. 'Please. Say that you'll come back with me.'

'Because you're my husband?' She looked across at the bed. 'Because we slept together? No.'

'Because I love you. Because I don't like to think of a life without you.' He slid his arms round her waist and drew her towards him. 'Not that I'm not desperate to sleep with you again. You know I am.'

'Yes.' She gasped as he pulled her into his arms and she felt his aroused body hard against the softness of her belly.

'I want to carry you back to that bed and love you again and again, and know that we'll be together for the rest of our lives. But if that isn't what you want, then we have to say goodbye now and go our separate ways.' He released her hands and slowly stepped away. 'Even though it will break my heart to lose you again.'

'Max.' She caught her breath. 'Last night....'

'Yes?'

'I've never been happier.'

He clenched his hands to stop him reaching out for her again. 'If you come back with me, you can continue with whatever work you choose, take all the freedoms you want. Work at the Ministry, drive ambulances, keep your own name, I don't care. Train as a lawyer, after the last few days' showing!' He tried to laugh, but it failed. 'I love you, don't you understand?' His voice cracked. 'All I ask is that at the end of the day we both come home to the same hearth, to the same bed.'

Her eyes lifted to his, flashing green sparks where the light from the lamp caught them. 'But I might have to work night duties,' she said softly.

'Witch.' She stepped closer to him, but still he held back. 'Be sure you mean it, Sylvia. Truly?'

'With all my heart,' she murmured, and he swept her into his arms. They were both trembling as their mouths met in a long and passionate kiss.

At last he raised his head and his eyes smiled warmly down into hers. 'We shall have some wonderful weekends, sweetheart.' His lips twitched. 'And when you're on night duties, driving your ambulance or hurtling round London on your motorcycle - I shall just have to console myself with the picture.'

An extract from the next book by Glen Davies

To the Ends of the Earth

It was an unusually hot spring day in October when the owner of Lacey's Creek came into town to buy a convict. When the swirling dust had settled she alighted from the carriage, shaking out her crushed skirts. The stocky man on the driving seat looped the reins, jumped down and reached back into the gig to hand her the parasol.

'You ought to have brought Meggie with you,' he grumbled, setting the battered hat on his sandy crop.

'I'm quite capable of putting up my own parasol, Mr Garvey,' she said briskly, suiting the action to the words. 'Besides, this place isn't safe for a young girl, not on Auction Day.'

Garvey looked in disbelief at the youthful face of his employer and started to say something, then thought better of it, but by the twitching of her lips he could tell she was not unaware of the irony of her own words.

Out on the sparkling waters of the Harbour, fifty or more ships of the line rode at anchor, ropes creaking and chains rattling as they waited for a free berth alongside the warehouses that lined Sydney Cove, to load or discharge their cargoes of flax, pine, whale oil, sandalwood, sealskins and livestock onto the quayside. One, the *Perseus*, anchored at the government quay below Fort Macquarie, had brought across the ocean a grimmer cargo of livestock: under the watchful eye of the New South Wales Corps in their tall black hats and bright scarlet coats, gangs of newly arrived convicts, having sweated to unload the hold of the vessel that had brought them halfway across the world, were squatting in chains on the dockside under the pitiless sun.

'Fools that they are,' hissed the woman furiously. 'Do they think they'll get a better price for them by leaving them on the quays in the noon sun?'

'Easy now, missus,' said the foreman in a subdued whisper. 'You lose your temper and we won't be getting' what we wanted, will we?'

He watched her closely, waiting for a reaction as her eyes flew anxiously along the line of convicts, but there was no sharp intake of breath, no start of recognition.

'Hard to tell from this distance,' he said as her shoulders slumped.

She shook her head wearily. 'I don't think he's there,' she said, drawing the veil over her face.

This was the third time in less than a fortnight that they'd dashed in from Lacey's Creek, when the signal station on South Head sent the news to Parramatta that a new convict ship had passed through the Heads and was beating its way up the Harbour to Sydney Cove, and Garvey had run out of comforting words. He could have given her many reasons why the one she was waiting for had not arrived – most of them deadly.